PARSON AUSTEN'S DAUGHTER

In this now celebrated novel about the life of Jane Austen, Helen Ashton bases her story strictly on the Letters and does not alter or add to the known facts, but she fills in the historical background in greater detail than has been usual in most biographies of Jane Austen.

The story moves from Steventon Rectory, where Jane spent her youth, to Bath, where the family moved after Mr Austen's retirement, and to Southampton, where the widowed Mrs Austen lived with her two daughters. Then come the six years at Chawton Cottage, during which Jane Austen's novels were published, and finally her death at Winchester. Gradually a portrait is built up of Jane Austen as she may have appeared to those who knew her: each had his or her own opinion of Parson Austen's daughter, and it is through their eyes that her character is seen.

PARSON AUSTEN'S DAUGHTER

Helen Ashton

COLLINS
8 Grafton Street, London W1
1987

William Collins Sons and Co Ltd
London · Glasgow · Sydney · Auckland
Toronto · Johannesburg

ISBN 0 00 221641 8

First published 1949
This reprint 1987

Copyright Helen Ashton
All rights reserved

Made and Printed in Great Britain
by William Collins Sons and Co Ltd, Glasgow

Author's Note

THIS book could not have been written without the kind permission of Dr. R. W. Chambers to use the mountain of material contained in the notes to his edition of Jane Austen's Letters. From these notes most of my minor characters have emerged and his indices of the doings and movements of the Austen family have been invaluable. My first thanks go to him and to Mr. R. A. Austen-Leigh, who has allowed me to quote many family letters. I have made particular use of his privately printed collection, the *Austen Papers*, which gave me the correspondence of the enchanting Eliza and Aunt Leigh Perrot's indignant account of her trial.

The Oxfordshire County Library has been constantly helpful during the last two years in hunting up for me a long list of books about the clothes, houses, food, ships, customs and public events of the Regency period. They also procured for me the five chief reference books which are needed for any study of Jane Austen ; Edward Austen-Leigh's *Memoir* ; the *Life and Letters of Jane Austen*, by W. and R. A. Austen-Leigh ; *Personal Aspects of Jane Austen*, by M. A. Austen-Leigh ; *Jane Austen's Sailor Brothers*, by J. H. Hubback ; and *Jane Austen, her Homes and Friends*, by Constance Hill. I have to thank Messrs. John Lane for their kind permission to quote, from the last two books, Miss Hill's description of the vanished lodging and the Assembly Rooms at Lyme Regis and Frank Austen's letter to Mary Gibson after Trafalgar.

Among modern books on the subject I have found a constant standby in Miss Elizabeth Jenkins' beautifully arranged and comprehensive *Jane Austen*, now happily once more in print. For the historical background I have returned again and again to Mr. Arthur Bryant's *The Years of*

Endurance and *Years of Victory* and to *England against Napoleon*, by my friend Carola Oman, while the naval part of the story has owed much to her recent *Life of Nelson*. *Country Life* most kindly provided me with photographs and articles by Mr. Christopher Hussey upon Godmersham and Chawton Great House. Mrs. Ragg's booklet, *Jane Austen in Bath*, gave some charming period detail, particularly upon the proprietary chapels. Colonel Lefroy, of Carrigglas Manor, County Longford, gave me details of his ancestor's distinguished career, and Mrs. Jenkyns, of Steeple Court, Botley, a list of Jane Austen's music books, now in her possession, and the Reverend John Firth and his wife most kindly showed me over Number 8 College Street, the house in Winchester, the house in which Jane Austen died.

The drawing of Jane by Cassandra, referred to on page 254, is now in the National Portrait Gallery.

Contents

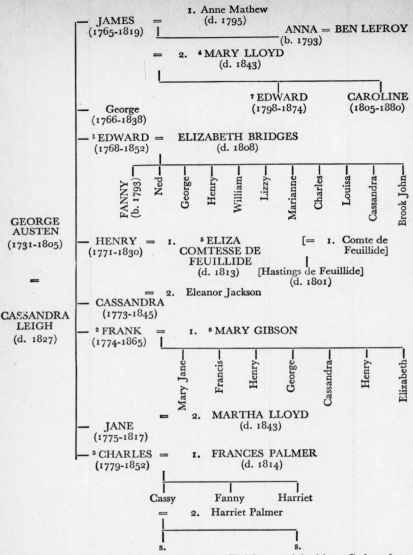

JAMES
(1765-1819)
= 1. Anne Mathew
(d. 1795)

ANNA = BEN LEFROY
(b. 1793)

= 2. **4 MARY LLOYD**
(d. 1843)

7 EDWARD   **CAROLINE**
(1798-1874)   (1805-1880)

George
(1766-1838)

1 EDWARD = **ELIZABETH BRIDGES**
(1768-1852)   (d. 1808)

FANNY (b. 1793) | Ned | George | Henry | William | Lizzy | Marianne | Charles | Louisa | Cassandra | Brook John

GEORGE
AUSTEN
(1731-1805)

=

CASSANDRA
LEIGH
(d. 1827)

HENRY = 1. **5 ELIZA**
(1771-1830)   COMTESSE DE
FEUILLIDE
(d. 1813)

[= 1. Comte de
Feuillide]

[Hastings de Feuillide]
(d. 1801)

= 2. Eleanor Jackson

CASSANDRA
(1773-1845)

2 FRANK = 1. **6 MARY GIBSON**
(1774-1865)

Mary Jane | Francis | Henry | George | Cassandra | Henry | Elizabeth

= 2. **MARTHA LLOYD**
(d. 1843)

JANE
(1775-1817)

3 CHARLES = 1. **FRANCES PALMER**
(1779-1852)   (d. 1814)

Cassy   Fanny   Harriet

= 2. Harriet Palmer

s.   s.

1 Edward Austen changed his name to Knight on inheriting Godmersham
   and Chawton.
2 Admiral of the Fleet Sir Francis Austen, G.C.B.
3 Rear Admiral Charles Austen, C.B.
4 " Mrs. J. A."
5 " Cousin Eliza."
6 " Mrs. F. A."
7 Edward Austen changed his name to Austen-Leigh on inheriting the Leigh fortune.

I

Steventon Parsonage

1775-1790

I

WHEN Cassandra Austen was an old woman, she would sit and remember Steventon. Whether by her own fireside at Chawton Cottage, or in the library of her nephew's fine house at Godmersham in Kent, or in the sunny window at Portsdown Lodge, visiting her brother the Admiral, she would fold her hands on the lap of her black satin gown, under her cashmere shawl, close her eyes, nod her head a little and let her mind run back into the past. The house where she had been born, where her brothers and sister had lived when they were young, had been pulled down by that time ; but in Cassandra Austen's mind it was still standing, exactly as it used to be. She saw it in a clear golden light, an old plain-faced parsonage, huddled down out of the wind, in a grassy valley like the hollow of a man's hand, a valley which had once been a child's universe.

When she thought of that place now, in her old age, there were always children there, running up and down the house, in and out of the garden. They had long grown up and gone away, but in her mind they were still there, calling to one another, " Wait for me, wait for me." She could not convey in words, to the new generation of children sitting and listening round her, the floating airy happiness which sang in her heart when she remembered Steventon. She could only tell them the little useless memories which were nothing to them and everything to her. " My father's rectory would seem a very old-fashioned house to you, my dears. It stood in the fields, a little way off the road, between the village and the church, about ten miles south-

9

west of Basingstoke. You walked through a meadow with elm trees in it and then you came up to the house. It had a latticed porch covered with honeysuckle and two windows on each side ; up above there were five windows in a row and a steep tiled roof with dormers in it. My niece Anna did a very pretty pencil drawing of it once.

" The dining parlour was on the right-hand side as you went in and my father's study was on the left, with a window looking down the strawberry walk. The parlour was a real parsonage room, with a worn carpet and old furniture, not very choice ; there were family pictures on the walls ; we kept the best tea-service in a cupboard in the corner. My mother liked to sit in the parlour of a morning, with the door open, so that she could see and hear whoever came and went, and she would keep the younger children with her while she did her darning and mending. She was never one to trouble about appearances ; ' People must take me as they find me,' was a great saying of hers. She was a small slight woman, very stirring and active, with plenty of sparkle and spirit in her talk. She had grey eyes, a pale face and a fine nose ; the boys used to tease her for being so particular about people's noses. She always said a well-shaped nose was a sign of good breeding and she was very proud that so many of her children had inherited hers.

" My mother was very well connected," Great-Aunt Cassandra would boast, holding up her head and stroking her own long fine nose, unconsciously, as her mother used to do. " She came of a fine family, the Leighs of Stoneleigh Abbey in Warwickshire ; they were called the Loyal Leighs, for their services to King Charles the Martyr. She was no fine lady though, for all her good blood ; she brought up eight children on very small means and she was a good housekeeper, who could turn her hand to anything. She kept all straight indoors and out. She had her dairy and her poultry yard behind the house and always kept Alderney cows. She would go into the kitchen and train her young maids in the ways of a gentleman's house. We baked our own bread and brewed our own beer ; more was done at home in those days than is the custom now.

She never sat down from morning till night ; she must have been a very strong woman, for she lived to be eighty.

" My father was very different, quiet and gentle and none too practical ; he was always wrapped up in his books. He came of good yeoman stock, the Kentish Austens, most of them were clothiers, doctors and attorneys, round about Ashford. My father had no fortune of his own. He was an orphan and had been brought up by his uncle, Francis Austen. This uncle used to say that he had started in life in Queen Anne's day with eight hundred pounds and a bundle of pens ; but he had done very well as an attorney in Sevenoaks, had married two wealthy wives and contrived to amass a very large fortune. He was a kind uncle to my father, for he got him the living of Deane and that was his start in life. My dear father was a very handsome man, tall and upright, with long silky hair which went white quite early and a pair of brilliant hazel eyes, the brightest I ever saw. My sister Jane had eyes something like his, but hers were darker in colour ; none of us had precisely the same, except my brother Henry.

" We children were never allowed to disturb my father when he was at his books. We always had to knock at the study door when we went there for our lessons. He was a wonderful teacher, patient and gentle, he made everything interesting to a child. He took pupils to help make ends meet ; there was little Lord Lymington, I remember, and Master Vanderstegen and a boy called Buller, who afterwards went into the Church ; and Tom Fowle. I liked him best of any," the old woman would say and her eyes would look a long way back into the past whenever she came to that name. Then she would come back to herself and say, gently smiling, " You can imagine that with so many young creatures about the house, my father and mother had very little time to be idle. There were eight of us, for all the Austens have long families. Jemmy came first, then Neddy, who was always my particular favourite, and then Henry, who was so handsome and clever, but not very steady. Those were the three elder boys, who did everything together. Of course there had been poor George, who was not quite like the others ; but he did not live at home, he had fits, we never talked about him. He lived with his foster-mother in a cottage up at Deane, my mother and father used to visit him there. I came after Henry ; then Frank, who was called Fly when he was little, and after him my darling Jane. Last of all came Baby Charles, who was our special little brother. And my father was a dear father to all his children equally, but if he had a favourite, I think Jane was his favourite child."

2

" It was share and share alike for us all, when we lived at Steventon. There was never any money to spare. The big ones had to look after the little ones ; we had to wear out old clothes and shoes in turn. My father was never able to lay by any provision for his family, for the two stipends of Deane and Steventon together did not come to more than a thousand pounds a year. He farmed his own glebe, of course and did it very well, I believe. John Bond, his bailiff, was a very good man with sheep. My mother and father were both good gardeners and did a great deal to improve the Rectory in that way. They planted fruit trees and my father built a high wall with thatch on top of it to shelter us from the east wind. We had a sunny old-fashioned garden, of the sort that children like best, with flowers and fruit and vegetables all mixed up together. It sloped uphill and I remember that at the top there was a terrace of the finest turf. When we were little we loved nothing so much as rolling down that green slope ; but when we grew older we liked best to go exploring in the hedgerows. We had the true Hampshire hedgerows at Steventon ; not narrow lines of quickset, such as you find in other parts of the country, but a winding thicket of ash and hazel, wide enough to hide a footpath or a rough cart track among the trees. We had two of these hedgerows at Steventon. One of them ran along the south side of the garden and then westward it marked the boundary of the glebe. It had only been a rough thicket before my father got the living. He had it cleared out and turned into a prettyish kind of a little wilderness, with seats here and there. It was dry and sheltered and the trees met overhead. He used to take a turn or two in it every day, as he grew older, summer and winter ; it was there he used to think out his sermons. We always called it the Wood Walk.

" The other hedgerow ran up the hill. It was called the Church Walk and the villagers all came up that way to service on Sunday. We used to watch them from the nursery windows, the men in clean white smocks and the women in the long red Sunday cloaks. They would wait in the churchyard till the Rector and his family arrived and all the children used to bob curtseys. We had quite a small church, built of grey stone and flint work, with nothing at all fine about it. It was very old and dreadfully cold in winter. There were hawthorns and elms in the graveyard and a great yew tree almost as old as the church. Inside there was an oak screen across the chancel and a big square pew for the squire's family, but there was nobody to sit in it except the Digweeds. They were two brothers, yeoman farmers, Harry and Hugh, and they lived in the manor house behind the church. It was a fine house, built of flint and dressed stone as the old houses are in High Hampshire. It went back to the times of King Henry the Eighth. It had mullioned windows and great chimney stacks, and a ring of sycamores round it to keep off the wind in winter. My niece Anna made a sketch of that too, when she was a girl. Hugh and Harry Digweed only used one corner of it. They were tenants, but the Lord of the Manor was one of the Kentish cousins, Mr. Thomas Knight. He hardly ever came to Steventon, so that the village people looked up to my father as if he had been the squire. The boys used to go nutting and bird's-nesting in the Church Walk and Jane and I used to take our little baskets and pick wildflowers. We always found the earliest primroses and anemones there in among the roots of the trees, and the finest blue and white violets grew among the graves on

the south side of the church. She and I used to pick them
every year together."

Great-Aunt Cassandra Austen would close her eyes and
smile faintly, as if she could still smell the perfume of those
long-withered violets and feel the warmth of the spring sun
on her hands. It had been so quiet in those days in the
graveyard under the south wall. There had been no sound
except the wind murmuring across the uplands, the distant
tinkle of sheep-bells, the thrilling song of the larks overhead.
The chalk lay so close under the fields of the glebe that
crops grown there had the pale colours of the cotton quilts,
which the village women stitched together out of shreds
and patches ; flax-blue, sainfoin-pink, purple vetch and
clover, biscuit-pale ploughland, the rippling amber-green
of young wheat, the varied yellows of the ripening corn.
The hawthorn hedges were as white as the chalk below
them, the ditches in summer frothed over with the wild
parsley, which the country people called Queen Anne's lace.
It had been rich quiet open country, good for children to
grow up in, good for old folks to remember. Nodding her
head, Cassandra would tell her great-nephews and nieces,
" I hear white violets grow in the churchyard still and they
tell me you can make out the foundations of our house in
the meadow. The grass grows thinner where the walls used
to be. There is nothing left in the meadow nowadays
except the well and the washhouse pump ; they use that
for a drinking trough for the cattle. There is a new rectory
nowadays, a big square yellow house on the other side of
the valley, where it gets the morning sun. It is a very
good house, they tell me, but I liked the old one better,
for all people said it stood too low, and had no view from
the windows and was inclined to be damp. There are some
of my mother's flowers growing wild in the meadow still.
Last time I went there I remember I picked a moss rose
out of the hedge, but that was many years ago. It is not
much more than a dozen miles from Chawton to Steventon,
but I have nothing to take me back there ; not even a
grave. My parents, you know, are in Bath and Jane is in
Winchester." As old age gained upon her, she sometimes

grew confused in her mind and talked of men and women long dead as if they were still above ground, dwelling upon their names with an accent of living love. She had been fifty years old, she used to say, when Steventon Rectory was pulled down.

3

Cassandra Austen was born in 1773, so that she was only in her third year when her sister Jane, a winter child, first blinked her bright eyes at the light, on the sixteenth of December, in the year 1775. That was the year of the great snowfall in High Hampshire. The Reverend Gilbert White, patiently observing the weather, day by day, in his house at Selborne, six miles away, set down in his clear precise handwriting that the first week in January, 1776, had been drowned with vast rains from every quarter. Then upon Candlemas Day came a prodigious mass of snow, which overwhelmed all the works of man. Riding about the parish, he decided that in all his long experience he had never encountered such Siberian weather. Many of the hollow Hampshire lanes were filled above the tops of the hedges, and the wind had driven and heaped up the snow into the most romantic and grotesque shapes ; he observed these with wonder and with pleasure. When he pottered out into his shrubbery to stoop down and peer at the thermometer with his mild old eyes, he noted that the thread of mercury went on falling daily. All creatures were oppressed by the heavy silence. His cocks and hens would not stir out of their roosting places, they were so dazzled and confounded by the glare of the snow. The hares lay sullenly in their forms at the first beginning of the hard weather and would not move until compelled by hunger ; they were conscious, poor creatures, that the drifts and heaps treacherously betrayed their footsteps ; but later they grew desperate for food, came into his garden, scraped away the snow and greedily devoured such plants as they could find. The old naturalist studied their pointed tracks

15

among his cabbages, mixed with the crows' broad-arrows, the dimpled rosettes of his cat's feet, the single track of a roving fox going round the henhouse. His kind heart was much distressed by the pitiable and starving condition of the wild birds and he put out crusts and scraps of fat to help them. On the twenty-first of the month, going out just before sunrise, he saw the silver thread of his thermometer sink exactly to zero, an uncommon degree of cold in those parts. He went indoors again to sit by his fireside and chafe his hands, to hope that the cold would not be fatal to his tortoise Timothy, hibernating in the border under the south wall ; then he began once more to meditate upon his annual puzzle, of where his friends the swallows and house-martins could spend such an inclement winter. He inclined on the whole to think that they hid themselves under roof tiles and in attics. He was too wise to believe the country superstition that they spent the winter at the bottom of his horse pond, snug in the mud, but he could not think that such small creatures could fly overseas.

In the latter half of January the cold was so penetrating that it occasioned ice in warm rooms and under beds. In the daytime the wind was so keen that the strongest could scarcely endure to face it. Over on the Bath Road, from the middle of the month the snow increased so much that it began to stop the road wagons and even the coaches. All the fine folk at Bath, who were going up to attend the State Drawing Room for Queen Charlotte's birthday, were snowed up at Marlborough. The ladies fretted and offered great rewards to labourers if they would shovel out a track to London, but the relentless heaps of snow were too bulky to be removed, and so the date of the eighteenth passed over, leaving all the company in uncomfortable circum-stances at the Castle and other less famous inns. Up in London the Thames was frozen right over and folks were running and sliding on the ice ; but down at Steventon Parson Austen's new daughter was warm in her cradle.

They had a great wood fire in the nursery, but the windows were glazed with frost for days together in spite of it. A child's exploring finger could trace its fortune in

the patterns there. Long pointed crystals formed stars, and
short blunt ones made clumps of swords and cannon, for
boys who wanted to fight with the king's troops, or go to
sea in his ships ; and there were ferns and flowers, as fine
as lace, a bride-veil of ice for a pretty girl. When you
breathed on the window you made a dark hole in the frost,
and through it you could look out into a whirling world of
flakes like feathers. " An old woman is plucking geese
upstairs," the nurse said, laughing. When the snow stopped
the little ones were still kept indoors, but the elder boys ran
out shouting into the white silence. They trampled the
new snow, they shook down great lumps of it off the evergreens in the shrubbery, flung snowballs at the cackling
hens and turkeys and dragged each other about on a home-
made sledge, while their mother watched them from the
window, with the new baby in her arms. Their father left
his sermon, for nobody would be able to get up to the
church ; he came out into the garden and helped them
make a snow man. They stuck an old cocked hat on his
head and called him an admiral. The whole valley was
filled with smooth snow, as if it had been a dish full of
cream ; the fields were rosy in the morning sun. The boys
hoped that it would last for ever, but all too soon for them
the upper sheep-walks were swept bare by the wind and the
holly and the ivy stood forth green again, though they were
scorched on their southern side as if by a bonfire. By the
middle of February a great storm of rain had taken away all
the snow. When Parson Austen went round his glebe with
John Bond things did not promise badly. His wheat looked
cheerful enough and his clamps of turnips were not much
injured. Even his flock of Hampshire Down sheep seemed
none the worse for having been dug out of a drift up at
Deane, but his partridges had been so thinned by the
weather and by poaching that few remained to breed that
year. All that happened in 1776, when old King George
the Third was on the throne. It was the year of the
Declaration of Independence, when the war began in which
we lost our American colonies.

Steventon Parsonage was crammed to the doors in those
early days, and the Reverend George Austen and his wife
had many discussions as to how they should best provide
for their long family. James, the eldest boy, was the one
who took after his father. He was steady and serious and
he loved his books ; the pity was that he was shy and
delicate, but his mother maintained that he would grow
out of that. He was her favourite and she had planned his
future even before he was born, saying " If it is a boy,
George, he shall go into the Church and have the family
livings after you." She thought the world of James and
believed firmly that he would end up as a dean, or even
a bishop ; but his younger brothers said he was a stick and
a milksop, and his father declared that Henry, the third son,
was the more brilliant scholar. " Henry learns everything
quickly, too quickly, perhaps ; he has more taste and much
more natural ability than James."

" Henry has no application," said Mrs. Austen, severely.
" He is idle and mischievous, he would never make a
clergyman." " They had both better try for scholarships
at John's when they are older," Mr. Austen persisted. " I
will coach them myself." At St. John's College, Oxford, at
that date, there were six student scholarships available each
year for anyone who could prove that he was related to
the Founder, Sir Thomas White. The Austens were
Founder's Kin, through their mother's side of the family.
If either of his two clever sons could get in at John's they
would be well provided for. James could take orders and
become a parish priest, as his mother wished. Henry might
stay on at Oxford and perhaps end up as head of a college,
like his clever eccentric uncle, Mrs. Austen's brother, the
Reverend Theophilus Leigh, who had become Master of
Balliol, no less.

Edward, the second boy, was no good at his books,
though he was a dear industrious fellow ; but he had been
born with a silver spoon in his mouth, as the village people

said, he was the luck-child of the family. When he was only a schoolboy, Cousin Thomas Knight and his wife took a fancy to Edward. They were very rich people, who owned a big new house at Godmersham, near Canterbury, and another older one at Chawton, some twelve miles from Steventon. Cousin Thomas Knight had already shown much kindness to the Austens ; it was he who was the squire of Steventon and had presented the Reverend George Austen to the living. The Knights, poor things ! had no children to inherit their great possessions. They looked all round the family, chose out young Edward and made him their heir. They began by asking him to stay with them in the holidays. Parson Austen did not altogether like it at first. He said that Edward must not be forever running off to Kent, to be spoilt and petted by Mrs. Knight. He was a poor man's son, who would have to make his own way in the world and he had better not learn expensive habits ; besides, he was getting behindhand with his Latin grammar. Mrs. Austen, however, was a very sensible woman and knew that there were many more important things in the world than the classics. She used to say to her husband, whenever an invitation came from Kent, " I think you had better oblige your cousins, my dear George, and let the boy go." So Edward was sent to Godmersham whenever he was asked, and the end of it all was that when Edward was fifteen the Knights adopted him.

There was a black and elegant conversation piece in silhouette, cut by Wellings in 1783, to commemorate the occasion. Parson George was on the left of this picture, in a tie-wig, a frilled shirt and knee-breeches, putting the long-haired graceful Edward forward to greet Mrs. Catherine Knight, his new mother. She was depicted seated at a spindle-legged table, playing chess with a female friend, but desisting from the game to smile over her shoulder at Edward in a welcoming manner ; while Cousin Thomas Knight beamed approval, leaning negligently upon a wheel-backed chair. This piece was much admired in the family, it became an heirloom at Godmersham and afterwards at Chawton. The Knights had done quite right to pick out Edward. He was not so clever at his books as James or Henry, but he was an extremely sensible boy, besides being affectionate and having a very kind heart. He loved country sports, rode and shot well, though not so exceedingly well as Frank or Henry, and had inherited his father's taste for farming. He was just the one to become a country gentleman and manage a great estate. It was a fairy tale come true and Edward was the fairy prince.

Francis, the fourth boy, was separated from these three elders by the birth of his sister Cassandra. He was a singularly independent child ; there were all sorts of family legends about his adventurous youth, how he was always called Fly because he was so little and lively and teasing, how he was afraid of no animal about the farm except the big turkey cock and the braying jackass ; how he first went hunting when he was seven years old. He bought a pony for a guinea and a half from a farmer in the village. It was a bright chestnut and he named it Squirrel, though Harry and Ned used to call it Scug to plague him. He hunted the little beast with the Vine for two seasons, jumped everything the pony could get his nose over and then sold him in the end for a guinea more than he had paid the first time. Trust Fly to make a good bargain !

All the boys loved hunting, even James ; when the Vine met on that side of the country they would be up in the dark, scramble through their breakfast by candlelight in the kitchen and be off before daylight on any rough pony or donkey that they could borrow. They all had coats of hunting pink ; Mrs. Austen had cut them from a scarlet broadcloth riding habit which had been in her wardrobe when she married. If they could not get a mount they would follow on foot. When they got home at night they had to groom their own ponies and see them warm and well cared for before they sat down themselves. All the boys rode well, but Fly went better than any, though he was the youngest and smallest of the four. He was the best shot too ; and he was very clever with his fingers, he could mend anything about the house. He put up shelves for his mother, he made her a workbox and a china cupboard ; when there was acting in the barn he used to put up the stage and the scenery. When he went to stay with the Kentish cousins he got the estate carpenter to teach him the use of a lathe and after that he turned all sorts of pretty and useful articles for his mother and sisters. He could not bear to sit with his hands idle. He would make rabbit nets and fishing nets while his father was reading Shakespeare's plays aloud to the family in the evenings. He made his mother a new netting needle whenever she broke the old one and once he even mended her spectacles, very *deedily*, as the country phrase went. They missed Fly dreadfully when he went away at twelve years old, poor lad ! to the Naval Academy at Gosport. His mother and sisters cried to see him drive off in the post-chaise, with his sea-chest and his cot tied up in a mat, looking smaller and more determined than ever ; but Fly was not at all sorry for himself. He had always been wild to go to sea.

5

The two little girls were packed off to school earlier than was the fashion in those days, but Mrs. Austen was glad to have them off her hands until they were old enough to make themselves useful about the house. She never cared for her girls as she did for her boys, she was that kind of woman. Cassy and Jenny always wanted to do everything together. The boys used to tease them about it, crying, " If Cassy were going to have her head cut off, Jane would want to have hers cut off too," and dance round them, jeering, while Jane clung to her sister. So when Cousin Jane Cooper, Mrs. Austen's niece from Bath, went to school, the two little girls were sent with her. Cassandra was ten and Jane was only seven. They were sent first to Oxford, to a Mrs. Cawley, who was sister to the Reverend Doctor Cooper, and herself the widow of a professor. She was dreadfully stern and strict, she made the little girls curtsey whenever they spoke to her and was forever rapping them over the knuckles when they made mistakes in their lessons. They all three hated her from the bottom of their hearts.

Presently she moved to Southampton and there a dreadful thing happened. Cassandra and little Jane both fell sick of a putrid fever. Jane had the fever much worse than her sister ; she lay tossing from side to side, did not know where she was and kept calling out for her mother. Cassy begged Mrs. Cawley to write to Steventon, but she said very sharply, " Do not make such a piece of work about nothing. It is only a little sore throat, such as any child might have ; you must not be always whining and complaining. I am not going to worry Mrs. Austen with any such trifle." Cassandra was quite distracted and could not tell what to do. She crept away and consulted Cousin Jane Cooper. Cousin Jane was older than they were and not nearly so much afraid of the governess. She wrote home to Bath, and her mother and Mrs. Austen came down in a great taking. Poor little Jane was very ill, but she got better in the end. It was Aunt Cooper who caught the fever from her and died of it. She was Mrs. Austen's elder sister and had been a great beauty in her day, the best-looking of that generation. Mrs. Austen was nothing like her, except for the Leigh nose.

Afterwards Parson Austen's two daughters were sent to the Abbey School at Reading. That was a very different place and there they were both very happy. It was a real honest old-fashioned school with no nonsense about it. People sent their daughters there to have them out of the way for a time. There they might scramble themselves into a little education, without any danger of coming back prodigies of learning ; they might be taught to hold up their heads, keep their shoulders back, open and shut a door quietly as a lady should, work a sampler, cipher correctly and be able to make a shirt. The school was kept by two women who both had French names and had married *emigrés*, as the French were called who came over for fear of the rising storm of revolution ; but Madame Latournelle had not a drop of French blood in her veins and could not speak a word of French to the day of her death. She was a homely stout body, plain and motherly, very much of the old school. She must have been getting on for seventy years of age, but she was very active, though she had a cork leg, poor woman ! She was always dressed in the same way, with short ruffled sleeves, a full skirt and a tight bodice, in the fashion of her youth. Her gowns were always grey or brown and over them she had a muslin kerchief, neatly pinned down at the back, with a bow of ribbon at her breast and another on her cap, both cut with notched ends. She always sat in a queer wainscoted parlour, hung round with needlework pictures in black frames, mourning pictures of tombs and floss-silk weeping willows ; this made a great impression on the little girls. Madame Latournelle did not do much of the teaching. She was the one who kept house ; she gave out the clothes for the wash and mended them when they came home again, ordered the dinners, made the tea and nursed the children when they were sick. She gave them all plenty of wholesome food, let them run about the garden a great deal in the summer and in the winter dressed their chilblains with her own hands.

Madame St. Quentin was a much more accomplished woman. She was a good-natured, red-faced Frenchwoman, married to a nobleman from Alsace, who had actually been a secretary at the French Embassy, up in London ; but he had lost his estates and had fallen on evil days. Monsieur St. Quentin, as he now called himself, was glad enough to earn his bread, poor man ! by teaching French to Doctor Valpy's boys at the Reading Grammar School. He taught his wife's pupils too, in his spare time; he was a very good and amusing teacher. The Austen girls both learnt to chatter French very prettily. Then there was a simpering little woman, much like a second-rate milliner, who taught spelling and needlework to the little ones, and a handsome dashing French girl, who afterwards caused a great stir in the town by running away with one of the tradesmen.

Reading Abbey had been a Benedictine house, the third greatest in England, but it had quite fallen into decay after the Reformation. Only the walls of the church, the Chapter house and cloisters remained, great masses of crumbling stonework, with knapped flints shining in them like black glass and ivy hanging down in green curtains over the broken tracery of the windows. The Abbot's Mill, to be sure, was still working. It was down behind the Abbey, on the Kennet river, and there were swans swimming on the millpond, under the trailing willows. The Great Gateway had become part of the school. There was a room in it, over the archway, where the last Abbot of Reading had been tried for his life and there were two great staircases, one in each tower, with gilt balustrades. All that part of the school was very old and the girls rightly thought it most romantic ; but the schoolhouse itself was a comfortable red brick building, with a beautiful old-fashioned garden behind, shut within the Abbey walls. There was a terrace, or sentry-walk, running round two sides of the garden ; the elder girls kept that for themselves and they used to stroll up and down on it, arm in arm, or sit on the battlements and look over into the ruins. It was a very easy-going school. The girls were taught a good deal of French and a little history and arithmetic, the use of the globes and as much science as M. St. Quentin was master of, or thought it necessary for a young lady to know ; but when they had attended their classes for an hour or two in the morning nobody took much trouble to inquire how they spent the rest of the day. The older girls used to gossip together in one turret or another, or hang out of the windows above the gateway to watch Doctor Valpy's boys playing cricket on the public field called the Forbury, which lay just below. The little ones played hide and seek in the shrubbery, kiss in the ring, blind man's buff and battledore and shuttlecock in the garden ; in the very hot weather everybody sat in the shade, telling stories and making cowslip balls and daisy chains. When the bell rang they all trooped in again to supper and nobody so much as said, " Where have you been, mademoiselle ? " Yes, those were happy days.

The young ladies were not allowed out in the town, of

course, by themselves ; though once, when Cousin Edward
Cooper and their own brother Edward came through
Reading by the stage coach, going home for the vacation,
the Austen girls had permission to dine with them at their
inn ; that was a great treat. Sometimes kind Madame
Latournelle would take them to spend their pocket-money
at the little toyshop round the corner ; but the thing which
was looked forward to, year by year, was Reading Great
Fair. It was really a cheese fair, of much antiquity ; the
pupils at the Abbey School used to see the great cheeses
being laid out in rows on straw beforehand, down on the
Forbury, and would hang out of the windows to watch the
caravans come in. The green was lit up every evening
while the Fair was on, and after the children had been
packed off to bed they used to hear the wild beasts in the
travelling circus roaring and howling, and the squeaking
and thumping of fiddles and drums outside the different
booths. Madame Latournelle and Madame St. Quentin
used to take them round the Fair on the first day, but they
had to walk two and two, and hold each other by the hand.
They were not allowed to go inside the marionette-show or
any of the peepshows, or ride on the giddy-go-round, that
would not have been considered suitable for little ladies ;
but they each got sixpence to spend on a fairing. You could
get balls and dolls, little china plates and mugs, big enough
to drink out of, all for a halfpenny and there was gingerbread with gilt dust on it, the best in the kingdom. All
their lives Cassandra and Jane Austen would remember
Reading Great Fair.

Then at the end of the term, at Christmas time or
Eastertide, the dancing master, Monsieur Duval, would
always arrange some entertainment for the parents. He
was an *emigré*, too, of course, and a very good teacher ; all
the girls enjoyed their dancing lessons. For his entertainments the sides of the great schoolroom were fitted up as
arbours. The elder girls dressed them with green boughs
and in each sat a little girl, disguised as a sylph or a
shepherdess. When the company was assembled and
Monsieur Duval gave his signal and began to play, each

would skip out in turn and glide through her steps to the
music of his little fiddle ; or else there would be a stage
fitted up at one end and the young ladies would recite or
perform in turn. The year she went there, little Jane
Austen did best of any. She was the smallest pupil, but
already danced beautifully! all her life she loved dancing.
She was dressed as a sylph, with a gauze skirt of rose pink
and a tiny pair of wings, painted with eyes, to look like a
peacock butterfly. She wore a wreath of moss rosebuds ;
with her round face and her great dark eyes, she looked
enchanting. She had one verse of a song to sing and a
dance to execute and did both to perfection. Then she
pointed her toe, crossed her hands upon her breast and
performed a deep curtsey, turning in a semicircle to include
the whole audience, as she had been taught. She remained
perfectly solemn until her curtsey was accomplished and all
the people began to clap. Then she burst out laughing,
threw up her little arms and ran away and hid behind a
curtain. She cannot have been more than seven then.

6

The girls only stayed two years at the Abbey School, but
when they came home again the Rectory seemed a much
quieter place than it used to be. There were no more
pupils, Edward had gone away to Kent, Frank left after a
few months to go back to the Naval Academy. James was
already up at Oxford and Henry was studying hard to
follow him. He spent the morning with their father, doing
his tasks and themes, while the girls helped Mrs. Austen
about the house or minded Baby Charles. In the afternoon
they had lessons in their turn, sometimes with their father,
sometimes with James, who was a kind and patient teacher.
When he was at home for the vacations he liked to hear
his sisters read lessons and would draw up very fine lists
of books for them to read. Mrs. Austen saw to it that her
girls learnt to cook and to cast up accounts and keep house
cleverly. They spent long mornings in the still-room,

making preserves and syrups, and brewing home-made wine, cowslip and elderberry, damson and dandelion. They made mead, and Cassandra, who was very reliable, had charge of the beehives. They also did a great deal of needlework, for in those days everything was made at home. They had to sew a great many fine seams ; they hemmed all the bed linen, made their own shifts and petticoats and the boys' and their father's shirts. They knitted and darned stockings for the whole family ; when the mending was done they might trim their own hats or make their own cotton gowns for the summer. Cassandra liked this work, but Jane, though she sewed beautifully and could make the smallest stitches of any when she chose, was lively and restless as a child. She hated sitting still so long together and she was naughty about plain work, though she loved to embroider. Once Mrs. Austen had to lock her into her bedroom until she had finished a seam ; but Jane had her revenge about that afterward, writing a charade upon the word *hem-lock* and making fun of her punishment.

Charades and riddles were a great amusement in the Austen family. They used to write them and pass them round in the evenings, after supper, sitting round the candle-lit table. Often Parson Austen or one of the brothers would read aloud to the girls as they stitched. Mr. Austen would usually choose something improving out of Doctor Johnson's works, or a paper from the *Spectator*. James, when he was at home, liked to read the poems of William Cowper. He greatly admired this new poet, who was all the fashion at the University. He gave Jane a volume of Cowper's *Task*, which had just come out ; they were forever quoting something to each other from *The Sofa*, *The Winter Evening*, or the *Winter Walk at Noon*. " *Ye fallen avenues ! once more I mourn Your fate unmerited*," James would spout, while Mr. Austen beat time gently with his churchwarden pipe. James read very well, in a melodious rather melancholy style ; James was all for the dramatic. If he had his choice they would have read Shakespeare every night. He would choose out one of the fine speeches

27

of Cardinal Wolsey, or Henry the Fifth, or one of Hamlet's soliloquies and recite it with much taste and feeling in a truly dramatic manner. Even his mother said grudgingly that it was as good as a play. He had always been wild about acting. When Mr. Austen's pupils at the end of term were called into the parlour to recite the pieces they had learnt by heart, Henry always did better than any, even while he was still quite a little boy, sticking out his arm as if he were in the playhouse and reciting " *My name is Norval, on the Grampian Hills My father feeds his flocks.*" It would not have been thought proper in those days for a gentleman's son to go on the stage, so he would have to confine his eloquence to the pulpit ; but meanwhile, he was forever begging his mother to let the girls off their sewing, just for one night, so that the whole family might read a play together. They did plays by Goldsmith and Sheridan, they did most of the works of Shakespeare ; Henry and Jane read Sebastian and Viola once in *Twelfth Night* and their voices sounded exactly alike, it was quite ridiculous. Then they became ambitious and got a play up for their neighbours in the barn, at Christmas, in the year '87, when Cousin Eliza came to stay and Jane was twelve years old.

7

Cousin Eliza was their most exciting relation ; a French countess, no less, Madame de Feuillide. The girls were fascinated by her ; she had led such a romantic life and had so many adventures. To begin with, she had been born in India and that was not a thing you heard of every day. Her mother, Aunt Philadelphia, Parson Austen's elder sister, had been sent out to Madras to hunt for a husband, since she did not seem able to find one nearer at hand. She had got one in India quite easily, where young ladies were scarce. He was a Doctor Hancock, in the employ of the East India Company, and he made her a very kind husband, only he was twenty years older than she was and his affairs were never very prosperous. Cousin Eliza, who was only Cousin Betsy Hancock to start with, was actually born in Calcutta and she was god-daughter to the great Mr. Warren Hastings, the first Governor-General of Bengal. He actually settled ten thousand pounds upon the child, for a marriage portion ; Doctor Hancock had done him some professional services, and Mrs. Austen had looked after a child of the great man's first marriage, a sickly three-year-old sent home from India. He was Mr. Austen's first pupil and it was not Mrs. Austen's fault that he died young of a putrid sore throat, for she had nursed him as tenderly as if he had been one of her own children.

After Doctor Hancock died Aunt Hancock and Betsy were left badly off, except for Betsy's marriage portion. They came back from India and Aunt Hancock, who was a very foolish, pleasure-loving woman, (at least in Mrs. Austen's eyes), took Betsy abroad for her education. They lived in Brussels and afterwards in Paris and Betsy grew up into the prettiest creature imaginable. Her mother changed her name to Eliza and brought her up to think of nothing but balls, masquerades and the Opera. Eliza used to write the most amusing letters to her particular friend, Cousin Philadelphia Walter, at Tonbridge and Phila used to hand them round the family. In this way the Austen girls heard a great deal of lively gossip about the poor queen whose head was cut off afterwards, Marie Antoinette ; how lovely she had looked in a Turkish disguise at a fancy ball at Versailles, and how she never would wear gloves because she liked to show off her beautiful white arms. Then there was another letter about the fireworks and illuminations for the birth of the little Dauphin, the boy who afterwards died in the Temple prison ; and of course there were pages and pages about the fashions. Ladies in Paris, in 1780, still wore hoops and brocaded skirts and their hair powdered, with three long curls hanging down over the shoulders. Their heads looked as if they had been dipped in a meal tub. Cousin Eliza had her portrait painted like that, in miniature, wearing a white muslin gown and blue ribbons, as a present for Uncle

George Austen, to whom she was always much attached though there was not much love lost between her and Mrs. Austen.

Aunt Hancock married her daughter off in the end to a French nobleman. He was the Comte de Feuillide, an officer, very handsome and amiable and adored Eliza ; but his family were not rich, though they had an estate in Guienne, and Uncle George Austen was not best pleased about the match. He was afraid that his dear Eliza might be persuaded to change her religion, which would have distressed him very much and he feared that the French family might be after the Hastings money. However, he could do nothing to stop the wedding, and at first Eliza was very happy with her French husband. They had a dear little boy, whom she called after her godfather, Hastings. He was born in 1786, the year that the great man fell into disgrace. His trial began the year after, for oppression, bribery and all manner of crimes, in Westminster Hall, to the great indignation of Eliza and her English relations, who did not believe a word of the charges against him.

Eliza had been anxious that her son should be born in England because of his Hastings inheritance and she and her French husband, with her mother, lived in London for some time afterwards. They were people of fashion ; Frank, who by that time was at the Naval Academy, used to call them the First Rates, that being the name for the largest ships of the line. Cousin Eliza's letters now were all about how tiring it was to stand for hours at old Queen Charlotte's drawing-rooms, loaded down with a great hoop and flounces, how sallow and sourfaced the Queen herself was, dark as a mulatto, always frowning and dreadfully mean about money ; how lovely the princesses were, with their golden hair and their pale high-bred faces ; how wild the young princes had grown and how worried the poor King was about their shocking behaviour. Hastings was a delicate baby ; he nearly died in convulsions when he was teething and afterwards he began to have fits, just as poor George Austen had done. Mrs. Austen shook her head and pursed up her lips when she heard of it. Then Aunt

Hancock fell ill and so Eliza stayed behind in England
when her husband returned to France. He was anxious
about the way things were shaping there, and guessed that
the Revolution was fast approaching ; but in England few
people as yet knew or cared about that. Eliza at any rate
seemed gay enough when she came down to Steventon and
they got up the theatricals in the barn.

Henry was the moving spirit. The Austens were a long-
legged family, but Henry was the tallest of them all, six
feet already, and overtopping his father. He was not yet
seventeen, but very handsome and self-possessed, with a
fine voice and a great notion of acting a part. He persuaded
his father to have a proper stage built in the barn ; there
was a row of fifty candles for footlights, with suitable
reflectors behind and a green baize curtain, drawn up in
very handsome festoons. Frank got home from Gosport for
Christmas in time to help with the carpentering and Cousin
Eliza chose the plays. She had seen them both when she
was taking the waters with her French husband at Tun-
bridge Wells, in the previous summer. *Which is the Man ?*
was one and *Bon Ton* the other. Cousin Eliza had a part
in each, Lady Bob Lardoon in one and Miss Tittup in the
other, both sporting parts. She wore a very tight frogged
riding habit and strode about the stage cracking a little
whip. Eliza was not to be trusted with a tragic character.
She had not the features for it and could not keep her
countenance when she had to deliver a sad speech, but she
could perform a comical part with great spirit. She had a
little light skipping figure and she would put her head on
one side, roll her great eyes, shrug her shoulders in the
French manner and pull the most comical faces. She could
make you die of laughing, as Cassy and Jane used to say
when they were at school.

James told her that she spoke too fast and moved about
the stage too quickly, but nobody else found any fault with
her. Henry was very good too. Though he was only
seventeen he looked five years older, with his hair powdered
and dressed in a very *ton-ish* manner, as the fashionable
phrase went. He wore a red coat and a cocked hat and

Eliza and he had some very amusing scenes together. Frank bore a hand with the scenery and brought the house down at the end with a naval hornpipe. Everybody had fine costumes, made up at home ; there were feather headdresses and spangles, wigs, powder and rouge, and the whole affair was voted an immense success.

8

It was repeated the Christmas after, but it was not nearly so good the second time, for Frank by that time had sailed for the East Indies on his first voyage and Eliza had gone back to France. They missed her sadly. The piece was *The Sultan*, with Henry in the chief part. He borrowed all his sisters' necklaces and looked quite seven feet high in his great turban, with his blacked face, as he ranted through his speeches. Their beautiful cousin, Jane Cooper, the one who had been at school at Southampton with Cassy and Jane the time they were so ill, was fetched from Bath to play Roxalana, the heroine, but though she looked very well in her Turkish costume, she was no actress and did not like her part. " My dear Aunt," she protested, " do but look at this speech, and this ; how could I ever recite such words in public ? I should die of shame, I am sure I should." James supported her, maintaining, " My cousin's feelings ought to be respected. It was all very well when we were schoolboys for my father to give a prize to whoever recited the best speech, but now that we are all growing up I think it is improper for the girls to be acting love-scenes. To my mind, the whole play is most unsuitable for us, and I for one would rather not have anything to do with it." James was always a wet blanket. Henry retorted, " Stay out yourself by all means, my dear fellow, but don't expect to govern the rest of us." Mrs. Austen, busy with the housekeeping and the extra bustle of visitors coming and going, did not pay much attention to them, saying, inattentively, " You had better ask your father, children ; he would not like you to act anything improper, I am sure."

" I do not know what Cousin Jane sees wrong with the play," grumbled Henry. " With a few omissions here and there it can be made fit for any audience. Of course if she is going to be *Missish* . . ." Jane Cooper's beautiful eyes filled with tears and Cassandra put an arm round her, while little Jane stared, bewildered. " If we are going to be so very *nice* we had better not act at all," complained Henry, while Cassandra reproached him, " I did not think you would be so unkind. Poor Cousin Jane is quite upset." Parson Austen, dragged from his classical books, had to decide between them. " I do not know the play, my dears, but if there is anything too warm in it, as I fear there is in most of them, it can surely be cut out. I dare say the play is too long as it is. You must not quarrel among yourselves. All this is done for your enjoyment."

So in the end, everything was arranged pleasantly. James did not act after all. He had decided that it would be unbecoming in a young man who was reading for Holy Orders. He wrote them a fine prologue, full of Latin tags and Shakespearean quotations and came out to recite it before the curtain, in the flickering light of the fifty candles ; but all the company were still settling into their places and nobody listened to poor James. *The Sultan* went off admirably and there was a comic afterpiece, Mr. Garrick's *High Life Below Stairs*. It was a silly play, all about servants dressing up to imitate their betters. Henry was very amusing as the valet, but they lacked Eliza for Kitty Clive's famous part of the lady's maid who tries to speak French like a fine lady. However, the players at least enjoyed it.

Jane had a tiny part in this piece. She had just had her thirteenth birthday. She was a thin awkward child, with a sallow skin and long brown curls, very prim and old-fashioned in her ways when in company, though she could be noisy enough when she and Henry or Charles were romping together. Cousin Eliza had made a great pet of her the Christmas before, encouraged her to chatter French and given her a French book to read, *L'Ami de l'Adolescence*, it was called, by one Ardaud Berquin, a bookful of improving tales. Jane's name was written in the first volume and Cassandra's in the second, with the date, 1797 ; it became a family heirloom. Jane was enchanted by Cousin Eliza's pretty ways and used to imitate her walk and talk and her French manner of waving her hands about, pursing up her mouth and shrugging her shoulders. Cousin Phila Walter, who saw her at this stage, put it on record that young Jane Austen was whimsical and affected ; but it was only that the child was trying to copy Madame la Comtesse. She was in a plain phase just then, growing fast ; her nose was too big for her face and her arms and legs were like sticks, but she was wild to act. She crept in to all the rehearsals and knew everybody's part as well as her own. As the country proverb says, *Little pitchers have long ears.* In the end Henry dressed her up in a brown gown with a white apron and mob cap. He gave her some wrinkles and crows' feet at the corner of her eyes! she got a few lines to speak and made a very proper little old woman. The family never knew how much the little sharp-eyed creature had seen and remembered of those two theatrical performances in the barn at Steventon, until years afterwards when she came to write *Mansfield Park.*

9

Charles had followed his brother to the Naval Academy that autumn, 1788, and Henry had gone up to Oxford. Like his elder brother, he had secured a place as " Founder's Kin," and was now the holder of a Fellowship for six years. There was nobody left at home except Parson Austen's two daughters and they got a little room of their own upstairs where they always sat together. Their bedroom opened out of it and they called it the dressing parlour, because that made them feel elegant, but there was nothing very fine about it. They had a common-looking carpet, with a chocolate ground and bunches of flowers upon it and an oval looking-glass which hung between the windows. There was a painted press, with shelves above it for their tattered brown volumes thrown out of their father's library. They had the English Classics mostly, Shakespeare and the older poets, Goldsmith's *History of England*, the improving works of Sterne and Addison and Doctor Johnson. Here and there was something newer, the poems of Cowper or of Crabbe, the parson-poet, who was a particular favourite of Jane's. She used to say in joke, that if only his wife would die she would like to marry Mr. Crabbe when she grew up, though indeed she had never set eyes on him. For amusement they had the novels of Mr. Richardson, Mr. Fielding and Miss Burney. Mr. Austen would not let them read *Pamela*, which he thought unsuitable for their young minds ; but they read *Clarissa Harlowe* and *Sir Charles Grandison* over and over and knew everything that was said or done by Sir Charles and Miss Harriet Byron in the famous cedar parlour. They delighted in Miss Burney's *Evelina* and *Cecilia*. Jane was greatly interested in Miss Burney because she had written and successfully published *Evelina* when she was quite a young girl in her father's house. Jane vowed that some day she would do the same.

The child was always scribbling. Cassandra could not remember the time when Jane did not make up stories and tell them to the others. When there was one which particularly pleased her she would write it down on any bit of paper that she could get hold of. At Steventon, in the dressing room, she filled one copy-book after another with nonsense stories, plays and verses, sitting by the window to get the best of the light, bending over the mahogany folding desk which her father had given her, with one foot tucked under her and a little curl falling forward as she wrote. These early works were always solemnly dedicated to some member of the family, to her father or Cousin Eliza, or one of the boys. There was one called *The Mystery* and another was *Kitty, or the Bower* ; one for a joke was called *The Beautiful Cassandra*. Before she was sixteen she had finished a whole grown-up novel, all in letters, as was then the fashion, called *Lesley Castle*. She dedicated that to Henry, but the funniest of all was *Love and Friendship*. She spelt it like that throughout, because at that age she was still sometimes a little uncertain of her spelling. It was the most delicious nonsense, all about the adventures of two absurd girls called Laura and Sophia and their lovers Edward and Augustus. It made a mock of the romantic novels which the girls got from Miss Martin's library in Basingstoke. Mr. Austen laughed till he cried over it, and said that it must be put away safely.

The longest and most complete thing that Jane wrote was a *History of England, from the reign of Henry the Fourth to the death of Charles the First : by a Partial, Prejudiced and Ignorant Historian*. Cassandra and she had great fun with this ; it was a complete joke, with a lot of amusing nonsense in it about Mary, Queen of Scots, for that bewitching princess was one of their favourite heroines. When it was finished they copied it out very neatly between them, and Cassandra illustrated it with medallions in water-colour, portraits of the principal characters. Cassandra was supposed to be the artistic daughter. She painted very delicately in water-colours, decorating fire screens and so forth ; she did a sketch of Jane sitting under a tree in a bonnet and a round gown, with her face turned away and only her hand and one little foot showing ; faces were so difficult. It was much admired in the family and Mrs. Austen preserved it. There were several of Cassandra's water-colours framed and hung up in the dressing parlour. She had a book called *Gilpin on the Picturesque*, which taught young ladies how to admire and paint a landscape ; a pity that the country round Steventon was so lacking in blasted oaks, dreary heaths, Gothic ruins and rugged mountain crags ! Jane was the musical one, her piano stood in the dressing parlour and she practised most diligently. At one time Mr. Austen paid for a master from Basingstoke to come out and give both the girls music lessons. Later Mr. George Chard, the assistant organist of Winchester Cathedral, added her name to the list of pupils he visited. Jane embroidered beautifully. From time to time they had crazes for making transparencies, pressing flowers, netting purses and making baskets out of filigree paper. All this could be done up there, for Mrs. Austen would never have allowed any litter downstairs in the best parlour, and the girls' friends could come up there to visit them.

In their teens the Austen daughters had two particular friends, Mary and Martha Lloyd, who lived near enough to run in and out easily. Their widowed mother in 1789 had taken a lease of the other parsonage up at Deane, where Mr. and Mrs. Austen had lived when they were first married, before he got the living of Steventon. Deane was only a mile or so away, up the valley, just on the other side of the coaching road from London to Exeter. Though young ladies did not take much exercise in those days, the Lloyd girls and the Austens were all excellent walkers. They thought nothing of jumping over gates and leaping across the puddles in Deane Lane to call upon one another, with a book to lend, a dress pattern to borrow, a scheme to be made for a picnic. The Lloyds were lively stirring girls, with plenty of Welsh humour. Mary was little and dark and active and was the clever one of the two, but she had a very sharp tongue and was inclined to be mean and spiteful. Jane was her favourite ; Cassandra, who was a little afraid of her, preferred Martha, a big noisy blowsy creature, a little stupid, with a gabbling tongue and a soft heart. Mrs. Austen was inclined to turn up her nose at the Lloyds. She said she could not hear that the late Mr. Lloyd had ever been anything particular except a poor little Welsh parson ; but Mrs. Lloyd herself was better connected. She belonged on her mother's side to the family of Lord Craven and there was a queer story about her grandmother, which the Austen girls thought romantic. The Wicked Mrs. Craven, as she was always called in the family, had been a very strange woman, who had beaten and ill-treated her three daughters, starved them and locked them up till the poor creatures were driven to run away from home. Two of them had made marriages which were very much beneath them. Mrs. Austen used to pity poor Mrs. Lloyd, who, at least, had secured a clergyman, for having such low connections. One of her brothers-in-law was a farmer and the other a horse-dealer, she believed.

Mrs. Lloyd, however, seemed not to feel any inferiority. She was a stirring active body, a notable housekeeper, who brought her girls up never to waste a penny. Her chief topic of conversation was the cost of food. If you went to Bath for a holiday she would always ask you, when you came home, what had been the price of salmon in the market, or some such question.

It was the Lloyds who brought Tom Fowle into the Austen story. He was a cousin of the Lloyd girls, related to them through the Craven family. Their elder sister, another Eliza, was married to Tom's brother, the Reverend Fulwar Fowle, a sporting, hunting parson of the old sort, who held the living of Kintbury in Berkshire, to which he had been presented by Lord Craven. Young Tom Fowle had first come to Steventon as a pupil of Mr. Austen. He was a gentle quiet boy, not very clever, but he worked hard and gave his tutor no trouble.

Later on, during the two years when the Lloyds were living at Deane, he used to come and stay with them in his college vacations. Cassandra had always liked him, because he was a gentle boy and did not tease her as her brothers did, but would help her with her lessons. She often needed help because she was not so quick at her books as Jane. Tom was going into the Church, like his brother, and it was hoped that he also might get a Craven living. Cassandra and he had never had eyes for anybody but each other. Up in the dressing parlour at Steventon Martha used to fret lest the men might not admire her when she grew up and Mary sigh that she might not get a husband unless she had a better marriage portion. Young Jane used to laugh at both of them and say, " I mean to be very particular about the man who shall break my heart for me." She was not yet interested in love affairs, she only liked her music and her books. Cassandra never entered into these discussions, she smiled and said nothing, but thought in her heart that there was nobody in the world like Tom. " Cassy is the handsomest of us all," Martha would cry, hugging her with schoolgirl affection. " She will be married before any of us and we shall be her three bridesmaids and dance at her wedding." They were all very merry together, up in the dressing parlour. Mr. Austen in his study, among his books, Mrs. Austen, darning stockings in the dining room, or standing in the kitchen teaching a village girl to make light pastry, would pause for a moment to listen to Mary and Martha, Cassandra and Jane, making merry together overhead and would say between a frown and a smile, " How those girls do laugh, to be sure ! " It was their springtime, their pretty innocent daisy-time, when the morning dew was on the grass and a bird sang in every flowering tree ; the only pity was, that it could not last.

II

Steventon

1791-1795

I

THE last decade of the century was the time when courting and marrying began among the young folks in and about Steventon, when Parson Austen's handsome long-legged dashing sons went out into the world to seek their fortunes and his two pretty daughters began to curl out their hair and think of balls.

Edward, the luck-child, married first. He had no need to wait for better fortune or to trouble his head about how soon he could begin to support a wife and family. He did not go up to the University, but the Knights sent him to make the Grand Tour of Europe. He travelled in South Germany, in France and in Italy and when he came home he was quite ready to settle down. The Knights found him a wife almost immediately, among their neighbours. She was Elizabeth, a daughter of Sir Brook Bridges of Good-nestone House, near Canterbury ; and she was a great beauty, tall, elegant and slender, with tapering fingers, long slanting eyes, a sweet voice and a slow smile. She was as good and well-bred as she was beautiful, Edward and she adored each other, and she had money of her own ; nothing could have been more delightful. Of course the young couple would not come into Godmersham House while the Knights still lived, so they began their married life at a house called Rowling, a mile from Elizabeth's old home at Goodnestone. She could walk across the park to visit her mother and sisters whenever she chose, and all her brothers and sisters-in-law were to go into Kent and stay with her.

Edward had married Elizabeth Bridges in 1791. James, his elder brother, was married a year later, but his match seemed very dull to his sisters. Poor James was fated to be always outshone by his brothers. Parson Austen's eldest son had spent what proved to be the happiest years of his life up at Oxford, as a scholar and a Fellow of St. John's; he did not make much mark there. He shut himself up among his books, and edited a mild undergraduate magazine called *The Loiterer*, in imitation of Addison. His mother fondly said that she believed he had written most of the fine parts himself. James was quite eclipsed by his younger brother Henry, both in scholarship and in society. Henry was an agreeable rattle, while James never had a word to say that could make a young woman look at him twice. Even in the summer after the barn theatricals, when Cousin Eliza came up to Oxford by his special invitation, James was cut out by Henry. Cousin Eliza wandered on the famous lawn of John's, leaning on James's arm, said that she longed to be a Fellow and walk there every day, vowed she was delighted with his rustling black gown and thought his square cap mighty becoming; but her approving eye strayed, far too often, beyond her escort to handsome Henry, strolling beside them, with his lazy smile, his fine figure, his curled and powdered hair. Henry, at seventeen, was as handsome a young man as you would see in a summer's day.

They took her round the colleges and out to see Blenheim, which she declared a charming place, but shabbily furnished, not to be compared with the country seats of the French King and his nobility. She begged both her cousins, very prettily, before she left, to visit her and her French husband in Paris. James did actually go there when he came down from Oxford, in the summer of 1790. He came back more glum than ever, saying that the great capital was a shocking place and that he feared Cousin Eliza and the Comte de Feuillide thought of little but pleasure and dissipation. He also told his father, in private, that the state of France was most alarming. The common people, said James, wagging his head, had been abominably oppressed in times past and now they were ripe to rise up and pull down their rulers. Since they had captured and destroyed the Bastille fortress there would be no holding them. What had chiefly shocked this son of the parsonage was that the property of the clergy had all been confiscated and the Church plate melted down at the Mint : this he could not get over. It seemed to him a most solemn portent.

In 1791 James was ordained and got the curacy of Overton, on the head waters of the Test, a pleasant ride of some six miles through leafy lanes from Steventon. There he received much kindness from a certain General Mathew and his lady, who had rented Laverstoke Manor for a term of years from the Portals, on the General's retirement. They were agreeable people and the General was not un-distinguished. At sometime of his life, in some past war between the French and English, when the Dons for once were on our side, General Mathew had been for a time Military Governor of the enormous province which the Spaniards called New Granada. It stretched from the Atlantic to the Pacific, right at the top of South America, just below the Isthmus of Panama ; a country of immense plains, of rivers pouring from shaggy wooded mountains, of peaks which never lost their snow. The General had been as good as king of that place, once long ago, when he was a much younger man, none of his Hampshire neighbours quite knew why or when. They only knew that nothing infuriated the old man so much as to have you confuse his mighty province with the little sugar island of Grenada, where the blacks had lately risen against the planters. The village people called him the " Old Governor " and that delighted him greatly.

His wife, Lady Jane Mathew, was a haughty high-nosed woman and there was a daughter, Anne, who presently announced her intention of marrying the handsome melancholy new curate. It was quite a good match for James, for the young lady had, or was supposed to have, money and breeding. She was a plain girl, with a brown skin, large dark eyes and a good deal of nose ; elegant, well-dressed and rather sentimental ; she was also rather fretful and sickly. It was hoped that this might improve with marriage. She loved James dearly, indeed she had sought him out ; that was perhaps her charm for a shy and awkward young man who had not the art of recommending himself to more lively young women. The worst thing that could be said about her was that she was five years older than James ; thirty-two to his twenty-seven. About that Jane, at seventeen, was highly indignant, and even the gentle Cassandra thought the whole affair unromantic. Anne's parents did not oppose the match, though James had very little to offer. Spiteful neighbours said that they were glad to find a husband for their dull daughter. General Mathew settled a hundred pounds a year on the bride and the Reverend George Austen did what he could for his eldest son. He gave up his second living of Deane to James and told Mrs. Lloyd that she and her daughters would have to leave Deane parsonage so that the young people might go and live there. There was much lamentation about this among the four girls ; Martha Lloyd in particular hugging them both and crying, " Oh my dearest creatures ! what shall I do without you ? I shall write to you every week, I vow I shall, and you must write to me and never think of the postage. You must visit us constantly. Mamma's new house at Ibthorp will be only twenty miles away." Cassandra kissed and comforted Martha, and Jane made a keepsake for Mary, a minute housewife, out of a scrap of gingham from one of her own gowns. There were fairy needles in it and gossamer thread ; and a pocket no bigger than the nail of her little finger enclosed a strip of paper, rolled up tightly, inscribed with a pair of rhyming verses in minikin letters and the date, *January 1792*.

As soon as the Lloyds were out of the house it was done up for the young couple. It was a pleasant snug red-brick building. It stood just across the way from Deane House, where there was a big jolly family, the Harwoods, always ready for a dance or a frolic. When they had a party they would send down a man with a cartload of stones to fill up the bad places in the lane between Deane House and the posting-station at Deane Gate, where the coaches changed horses at the inn, going up to London from Salisbury and Exeter. Deane Lane was noted for its bad going, it was dusty in summer and muddy in winter. When Mr. Austen was presented to the living of Steventon and he moved down there with his wife, the good lady, who was in delicate health at the time, made the journey in a farm cart, lying on her own feather bed on top of the rectory furniture to avoid the jolting of the ruts. This family legend still made everybody laugh, but Mrs. Austen could never see that there was anything unusual about it. She had been very comfortable, she maintained ; she wondered that nobody else had ever thought of it. When she heard that young Mrs. James Austen meant to keep her carriage she looked down her fine Austen nose and said that Deane Lane would be hard on the horses. There was also a certain difference of opinion between the parents of the young couple about the parsonage house. Mr. Austen, in his gentle way, apologised for not being able to give his son a better one. Mrs. Austen said tartly, " We did very well there ourselves when we were young married folk. The house is not very big, but it is well built and convenient and it has two very good parlours. The garden is sheltered and the Lloyds have done a great deal to improve it. Anne will have plenty of room for her flowers as well as her vegetables ; she can keep her poultry in the orchard and a cow in the paddock. I cannot see that she will have anything to complain about." Lady Jane Mathew, tossing her plumed bonnet, said with cold politeness, " The house is decent and habitable, but Anne has been used to elegant and spacious apartments at Laverstoke House ; it will be a great change for her. I am sure she will make the best of it, but she is bound to feel the change." The old Governor, who doted on his daughter, talked largely of improvements. " A room or two might easily be added. We might throw the passage into one of the parlours and by adding on a bay window make a new drawing-room for Anne. She must have a fit place in which to receive her friends. The dining parlour is mean, very mean and the

44

stairs are narrow, but one must not expect too much. It would be no great matter to widen the stairs. We shall see how much money I can spare them next year." He talked of money difficulties and the likelihood of war with France. His wife said, " My dear, they will not be living here all their lives. There is no sense in spending your money on someone else's house, James will get a better cure presently. Anne is not to be buried at Deane all her days, I hope."

The daughter seemed to have few opinions of her own. She looked on the ground, murmured that she and James would be very happy there, she was sure ; vowed it was all very pretty, would not say whether she preferred blue or green for the hangings and wallpapers. While her mother counted chairs and tables and Mrs. Austen poked in the kitchen cupboards, James and Anne walked round the garden and strayed into the meadow, they were always getting away by themselves. When they came back the General was full of an improved plan for the stables. They were better than the house had led him to expect ; there would be plenty of room for Anne's carriage and James's horses. They must have two horses, one must be able to carry a lady and he had quite decided to keep a few couple of beagles there. James and he could well amuse themselves in the winter by riding out after the long-legged hares of those upland sheepwalks. James brightened at this ; hunting was one of the points which he and his future father-in-law had in common. Mrs. Austen said dubiously, rubbing her long nose, " All this is going to cost a pretty penny. Young people should begin more quietly."

3

The wedding took place at Laverstoke on the 27th of March, 1792 ; and the Reverend James Austen and his bride settled down at Deane Parsonage to a style of living which was rather beyond their income. Young Mrs. Austen was not very house-proud. She left the meals to her cook, the hens and the dairy to the gardener's wife, the vegetables to the

gardener, while she tinkled a tune on her pianoforte, plucked
a few roses for the parlour mantelpiece, walked across to
take tea with the Harwoods or drove over to Laverstoke to
visit her mother. " Mrs. Harwood tells me Anne always
wears white in the mornings," said her mother-in-law dryly.
" Her maids spend their time gadding about the village and
her joints are much too large for such a small family. She
certainly has not been bred to make a good wife for a poor
parson. I do not know how she will ever keep her nursery
in order." For Mrs. James Austen was breeding already.
When her lively sisters-in-law went up to see her, jumping
over gates and leaping across the puddles in Deane Lane,
they would find her lying behind drawn blinds on the sofa,
in very low spirits, sniffing at her smelling bottle and
lamenting that she was neglected and ill-used. " I am so
ill, I can hardly hold up my head. I have not seen a
creature to speak to the whole morning. I am not fit to be
left alone, I am sure." Altogether Cassandra and Jane found
her a poor exchange for the lively Lloyds.

She was forever sending for Doctor Lyford in a hurry.
The old man, in his famous yellow wig, rode over and
scolded her, prescribed tonics and advised more exercise and
fresh air, but Anne would not listen to him. She said he was
unsympathetic, and her mother considered that he did not
understand Anne's constitution. " The poor child has never
been robust, she has so much sensibility. She ought not to
be treated as if she were a strapping farmer's wife, like most
of Doctor Lyford's patients." Mrs. Austen retorted,
" Doctor Lyford has attended me ever since I came into
these parts and I never found him anything but kind and
considerate." To Cassandra she declared, " Anne makes
more fuss about this child than I did about any of my eight.
I have no patience with her." James, however, was patience
itself with his fretful wife.

4

There was another wedding at Steventon that year. Pretty Jane Cooper, who had so blushed to be admired when she performed the part of Roxalana in the barn theatre, had now attached a most eligible lover, a naval captain, Thomas Williams by name. She had met him at Ryde, when she was on a holiday in the Isle of Wight with her ailing father. It had been a short courtship and Cousin Jane's wedding day had already been fixed when old Doctor Cooper died. Her wedding was postponed for a few weeks, but the dashing bridegroom would not, could not wait for long. He knew, as everyone in the services did, that war with France could not very long be delayed and he meant to secure a short term of married life before he got his sailing orders. So, on a cold December morning, 1792, his blushing tearful bride was married to him by her Uncle George in Steventon church. Her brother Edward gave her away and Cassandra was chief bridesmaid, and she held the bride's glove while the ring was put on her finger. It had to be a quiet wedding, with very little white satin and very few lace veils, because of the bride's recent mourning, but there was an uncommonly lively wedding breakfast afterwards at the Rectory, when all the neighbours gathered together to drink the health of the happy couple. The Austen family, to be sure, were not quite at full strength, for Edward was down in Kent with his wife and her first baby, Fanny ; and dear Frank had not yet returned from his first voyage in the China Seas, where he was now a midshipman in the *Minerva*. Young Charles, however, had come up from the Naval Academy for his Christmas leave, a baby-faced boy, with a most engaging grin. He was just in time for the wedding, and with him on the Portsmouth coach arrived a crowd of naval officers in all the glory of blue uniforms, gold epaulettes, laced waistcoats and velvet stocks, to support Captain Williams. Young Charles thoroughly approved of Cousin Jane's choice, for the gallant Captain had already promised to take him to sea in his own ship as soon as he should have finished his two years at Gosport. Mrs. James Austen had stayed at home, tearfully refusing to come and be stared at (" I look dreadfully, I know I do ") but James rode over to help his father perform the service and made one of his long prosy speeches at the breakfast afterwards. Tall Henry was down from Oxford, more than six feet high, just turned twenty-one and handsomer than ever. His family hoped great things of Henry in the way of academic distinction, but on this occasion he alarmed his mother by swearing that if it came to a war with the French, as all these naval men were saying, then he should quit Oxford and go into the Army. " Frank and Charles and Cousin Tom Williams cannot keep all the fun of beating the Frogs for themselves," said Henry, gaily.

Henry seemed to be on very proper relation-like terms with his cousin, Madame la Comtesse de Feuillide. There had been a coolness between them, Eliza declared, but now it was all made up and the pair of them sat together at the wedding breakfast, laughing and whispering all the time over something that nobody else could hear. The ladies of Steventon were all wearing their best for the wedding, the pretty fashions which had already lasted so long, panniered brocaded skirts, lace fichus and petticoats, caps or heavily pomaded curls with rouge and patches, for the older ladies, a drift of scented powder in the hair for the younger ones. Madame la Comtesse outshone everyone in a Paris gown of apple green satin, trimmed with golden gauze and pearls. She quite eclipsed the tearful bride. Mrs. George Austen, with a sniff, told Cassandra that Eliza was ridiculously overdressed for a country wedding.

Cousin Eliza had been at Steventon since August, in what for her were very low spirits. Her mother had died that winter, after a long and painful illness, a cancer of the breast, it was whispered in the family ; and very soon after that her French husband had been obliged to return to Paris. The revolutionaries were in control there now ; they had imprisoned King Louis XVI and his family and proclaimed a Republic ; already they were fighting the Austrian and Prussian armies on their eastern borders. The Comte de

Feuillide had been too long in England, absent from his military duties. " If he had continued here he would have been proscribed as an *emigré*," Eliza explained to everybody ; " then our estates would have been confiscated by that dreadful Revolutionary government, and we should have lost all we have. Can you imagine anything so frightful ? "

The Comte de Feuillide had been away half a year now, and she was beginning to wonder if he would ever be able to get back again. She knew that he was in touch with the *emigré* headquarters, established in Turin and planning to bring the Royal family back again, by force of foreign arms ; it must be very dangerous for him to show his face in Paris. She hoped he was in Guienne, on the family estates, but she had not heard from him for some months. " My poor Jean ! " Cassandra heard her murmur to Henry. " I am quite distracted with anxiety about him. Ever since those terrible massacres in Paris in September, I cannot bear to think what may become of him. One cannot tell where these troubles will end. They say now that the King himself is to be tried for his life, as an enemy of the people. My heart is ready to burst with grief, when I read the terrible things they say in the papers."

Henry filled up her glass and consoled her. " My dear Eliza, whatever you read in the public prints is sure to be exaggerated. Monsieur de Feuillide will come back safe and sound, never fear. He is not such a fool as to let those gentlemen in the red nightcaps get hold of him. Depend upon it, you will get a letter from him one of these days, or he will walk in upon you and astonish you with his escapes and adventures. You must cheer up, Cousin Eliza, you are making me feel quite sad too. You know the bride is the only one who is allowed to cry at a wedding." Eliza touched the corner of a lace handkerchief carefully to her pretty eyes and retorted, " I never was at but one wedding in my life before. That was my own and it appeared a very stupid business to me." She gave Henry one of her large-eyed fascinating looks over her handkerchief. Eliza must flirt with any man in reach, even if it were only a long-legged cousin, ten years younger than herself. She could no more help it than a kitten can keep from playing with a bobbin. Henry burst out laughing at her, while little Hastings ran about among the guests, offering a half-eaten apple or a share of his piece of wedding cake to any guest who pleased his fancy; he was a great pickle and the plaything of the whole family.

The naval officers were all crowding to get near the two charming bridesmaids. Parson Austen's daughters were very much grown since Cousin Eliza had seen them last, and greatly improved in looks. Cassandra at eighteen was a grave beauty, dark-haired and delicately pale, with arched brows and regular features. She was rather silent, but an attentive and sympathetic listener. When she did speak her voice was soft and sweet and for so young a girl she had a great deal of dignity and self-control. Her sister Jane was as yet only a blooming unformed creature of sixteen who some day would be a brown beauty. She was a clear brunette with a rich colour, she had a round merry face, a pretty small mouth and nose, sparkling hazel eyes and brown hair set in close curls round her forehead. She chattered like a starling and made all the young men laugh. Her own secret sorrow was that her cheeks were rather too full, but time might mend this trouble. "They are perfect beauties," declared Cousin Eliza enthusiastically to her aunt. "I am sure they will break hearts by dozens."

"They are both very good girls," said Mrs. George Austen, giving her daughters an inattentive glance. "Cassandra is very sensible, she is quite her father's right hand in her parish. Jane is sadly heedless, I fear. She neglects her music. I often tell her that she will never play or sing really well unless she practises more. She wastes too much time on her scribbling, it is bad for her eyes. She is very short-sighted, you know." Eliza agreed with this, saying with one of her French shrugs, "English young ladies waste too much time on getting accomplishments. Music, drawing and book-learning will never add a lover to any girl's list. Grace, manner and above all beauty are what will count with the men; but beauty they have, dear Aunt Austen, they are two of the prettiest girls in England.

I am sure you will not keep them with you long." Mrs.
Austen only said, " I wish you may not turn their heads
with all these fine compliments. I do not desire either of
them to grow conceited. All I want for them is that they
should amuse themselves for a year or two and then each
find a husband. Cassy would make a good parson's wife,
Jane I daresay would do better with a soldier or a sailor,
but they must take what comes in their way. They are not
fine ladies, to turn up their noses at any good offer and you
must remember they will neither of them have much of a
marriage portion. Do not teach them to think that a girl's
face is her fortune, it is not so these times, whatever it may
have been formerly."

The party was getting lively. Toasts had been drunk to
the happy couple, to the bridesmaids, to Mr. and Mrs.
Austen. One of the young naval officers, with a fine voice,
struck up the old tune, *Come, cheer up, my lads, 'tis to glory
we steer*. It had been sung in the Navy for over twenty
years, but they liked it still and everybody joined in the
proud chorus about the ships and the men that were heart
of oak together. " *We'll fight and we'll conquer again and
again*," they shouted, waving their glasses. One lad, who
had drunk more than he should of the Rector's good wine,
stammered out the wardroom toast for men on their
promotion, " *A bloody war and a sickly season* " ; but he was
shouted down lest the ladies should hear him. Somebody
else had a new song *Britons, Strike Home*, which the company
must hear. Then the hour grew late, Captain Williams and
his bride drove off and the company took their leave. The
December wind, whisking up the withered beech leaves in
the drive behind their departing wheels, seemed like the
great storm of war, blowing up to sweep all that gay
company away.

5

Within a few months they were all scattered. In January,
1793, King Louis XVI had his head cut off and the new

French Republic declared war upon England and marched
into the Low Countries. The war machine creaked round
slowly at first. The Fleet was not manned nor put to sea
for many months, though Captain Williams got off early,
in command of the *Endymion*, leaving his new wife forlorn
in a Ryde lodging. Frank was posted lieutenant in the
Minerva, then with the Home Fleet ; young Charles was
raging to have so many terms still to get through at Gosport.
Henry, like many another young man of spirit, flung away
his books and went into the Army. He became a lieutenant
in the Oxfordshire Militia. There was a great deal of drilling
going on that spring in the Oxford parks, among the lilacs
and hawthorns, and Henry, with his Fellow's gown put by
in a cupboard at John's, was swaggering up and down in a
red coat and cocked hat and Hessian boots, shouting orders
at his ragged recruits. They were rag, tag, and bobtail,
Henry wrote crossly to his family, food for powder, like
Falstaff's recruits. Their ranks were filled by ballot, but you
could buy yourself out if you were a man of substance ; what
were left for Henry and his friends to drill were mostly
pitiful rascals indeed, jailbirds, unemployed men, starved
creatures who had taken the King's shilling to get food and
drink and uniform to cover their backs. There was not much
patriotism among them. You got more of that in the volunteer
regiments which were being raised all over the country,
rigged out in bright many-coloured uniforms of their own
design, lording it about the country towns and breaking the
hearts of the girls like so much crockery.

A small expeditionary force had gone over to Holland as
soon as war was declared, four battalions of the Guards with
the King's second son, the Duke of York, to lead them ; but
the fighting on the Continent was going to be done, people
told each other, by the professional armies of the Austrians
and the Prussians. The English share, the lion's share of the
fighting, would be done at sea. Frank and Charles, with all
the rest of the lively light-hearted young men who had been
at Cousin Jane's wedding, would be in the thick of it. They
would blockade the enemy ports and capture the French
colonies, one by one. Like the drunken sailor in the

Shakespeare play, which Jane and Henry used to read aloud at Steventon, each of these gay young captains hoped to cram his pockets with islands, like so many apples, and bring the ripe playthings home to his sons.

Henry's chance of going overseas was small. His ill-fed, ill-clad recruits were only meant to defend the country in case of invasion, but by August they had been more or less licked into shape and were moved down to the South coast. There were plenty more going the same way. The dusty summer roads were full of marching men, all singing and whistling as they tramped along, to the rollicking new drum and fife tune called *Brighton Camp*, or sometimes *The Girl I Left Behind Me*. It was to Brighton that they were going, to the great city of tents on the Downs behind the little bathing place, which the Prince of Wales and Doctor Russell between them had lately made fashionable. " *I'm lonesome since I left the hill and since I left the valley*," they sang in cheerful chorus, as they plodded southwards, all sure that they were off to beat the French, the wretched little starveling frog-eating Johnny Crapauds, who had made so much trouble in Europe these hundred years. This time they were to be conquered and put in their places for good. Mr. Pitt, for the Government, had promised that the war would be a short one ; Mr. Burke, for the Opposition, had prophesied that it would be both long and dangerous, but said he, it must be undertaken. Few people listened to him ; they all told one another that it would be over and done with by Christmas or quite early in the next year. Nobody could have guessed that it was going to last for twenty tears.

The Austens' nearest neighbour was a Mr. Holder, a pottering pleasant old bachelor who had made his fortune out of sugar estates in Barbadoes and had now come home to nurse his health. He lived at Ashe Park, an old-fashioned red-brick house a little way up the valley. He subscribed to all the parish charities, came to hear Mr. Austen's sermons on those rare occasions when the church was not either too hot or too cold for him and sent down his copy of the *Times* every afternoon when he had finished with it himself. This was a courtesy which was much appreciated at the Parsonage, for London newspapers were not easy to come by in the country at that date. Mr. Austen made it his practice to read the single folded sheet aloud from end to end to his family in the evening, while they did their sewing by candlelight in the parlour. The news, however, was not very interesting to start with, at any rate for lively young girls. It was always many days out of date, often contradictory, all dim and far-off. True, Admiral Hood had snapped up the great French port of Toulon quite early and the Allied armies had advanced briskly through the Low Countries to the frontiers of France ; but there they halted throughout the summer months of 1793, laying unsuccessful siege to one fortress after another. Then, mysteriously, they began to retreat. It seemed that the French generals knew their business better than the Allies.

In Paris the Reign of Terror had begun. The Jacobins, the extreme party, had driven out the moderates and set up their clashing grinding guillotine in the Place Louis Quinze, opposite the Tuileries, which Cousin Eliza said was one of the principal squares of the city. Every day batches of prisoners, aristocrats, enemies of the Republic, were driven there in tumbrils for execution. Up in London Cousin Eliza was infinitely shocked by the tale of these horrors. Many of the victims had been her friends in the old days, scarcely a list was given in the English papers which did not contain some family name which she knew. In October the Queen herself was brought to trial and executed. Eliza wept when she heard that that lovely ill-fated head had fallen. She could remember Marie Antoinette sitting at a banquet at Versailles, fourteen years earlier, in a gown of green lute-string, veiled with transparent silver gauze and bunched with white lilac. There had been ribbons, feathers and diamonds then in the high powdered tower of blonde Austrian hair. " They cut her hair short," whispered Eliza, " before she left the Conciergerie prison, but it had gone quite white already. When the executioner held up her head to the people, the eyes moved, it was the head of an old woman."

Madame la Comtesse was more anxious than ever about

her husband that autumn. She did not know whether he had joined the Royalists in La Vendée, was hiding in Paris, or fighting with the Allied Armies. It appeared later that he had been in the capital all the time, living quietly in a poor lodging, wearing civilian clothes and calling himself Monsieur Feuillide, late captain of dragoons. In midwinter, about the time that Toulon was lost again by the English, he was arrested by the Committee of Public Safety, for a rash, gallant, extremely stupid action. He had tried to bribe one of the secretaries of the Commission to suppress some evidence against an old family friend, the Marquise de Marbœuf. It had been done before and no doubt would be done again, but in his case the official concerned first took his money and then betrayed him to the Committee. Madame de Marbœuf and he were both brought to trial, she for some alleged mismanagement of her estates, which was called an offence against the Republic, he for seducing and suborning witnesses. His landlady and a former mistress testified that he was a *ci-devant*, a noble in disguise. He and Madame de Marbœuf were both condemned to death and went to the guillotine together. The fatal date was February 22nd, 1794.

Cousin Eliza for a time was inconsolable. Certainly the Comte de Feuillide had wasted a great deal of her money and had neglected her for other women, but he had been the husband of her youth, and she shuddered to think of his headless trunk rotting in a quicklime pit in the outskirts of Paris. When she came to Steventon for a visit that summer, 1794, she was black-robed and plaintive. Hastings clung to her and she wept over him, telling him that he was the only comfort she had left, till she set him off too, crying his little heart out. Mrs. Austen said crossly, " Eliza should not upset the boy with these constant scenes." He was a sickly fretful child, nervous and large-headed and he looked paler than ever in his new black clothes. The doctors had hoped that he would outgrow his fits with his teething, but he still had the most alarming attacks from time to time. Poor George Austen up at Deane was just the same. The news about his father's execution which he had picked up from the servants, had particularly affected Hastings. He slept badly and awoke screaming, holding his neck with both hands and sobbing that the bad men were coming to cut off his head, as they had cut off his father's.

Cassandra and Jane petted him, played with him and told him pretty stories, till he grew rosy-faced and plump with good food and fresh air. Their father was kindness itself to the bereaved Eliza, gave her his arm round the garden, picked his finest red roses and strawberries for her, urged her to change her thin kid slippers after a stroll on the midsummer lawn and begged her to put a little shawl round her shoulders when she sat in the shade of the mulberry tree, lest she should catch cold, for the good gentleman had grown into something of a mollycoddle lately. "It is never safe, my dear, to sit out of doors, even in the height of summer. You are a delicate flower, we must not let you fade and wither." Eliza had always had the art of looking as if a puff of wind would blow her away, though actually she was very strong and nothing fatigued her except doing what she did not like. She used to hang upon dear Uncle George's arm, raise her lovely eyes to his benevolent countenance and vow that he reminded her more strongly than ever of his sister, her own dear dead mother, Philadelphia Hancock. Uncle George patted her hand and urged her to regard Steventon as a second home, saying, "Come here whenever you wish it, my child ; " but Mrs. Austen rather markedly failed to second this invitation. Eliza was no favourite of hers. "I am sorry she has lost her husband and her French property into the bargain ; but that is the greater disaster of the two, I fancy," said she. "Eliza never troubled her head much about the Comte de Feuillide of late years. They each went their own way. When she has cried a little longer she will look about her and find another husband, I don't doubt." Cassandra and Jane decided that their mother was really too hard upon Eliza.

Mother and child went back to London in October and the
Steventon household settled down to a dull and quiet war
winter. The news was not particularly good. Certainly the
Terror had come to an end in Paris ; Robespierre and the
rest of the Jacobins had gone to the guillotine in July and
the wave of executions had ended. Admiral Howe had won
a victory against the French fleet, so far out in the Atlantic
that it never got any name but that of the Glorious First of
June. Passengers coming up by the Portsmouth coach to
Popham Lane and Basingstoke related how they had seen
the captured French ships brought into Portsmouth Harbour,
with the wounded still lying about on their decks, all in dirt
and confusion ; while in the British ships, berthed beside
them, the decks were scoured snow-white, the brass shining
and all the crews alert at their stations. Such naval news
always delighted the Austens, who now had two sons in the
Fleet. They had bought themselves a new Navy list and
the girls looked out all the ships concerned in the action.
But Lord Howe, for all his glory, had not managed to
prevent the French grain fleet slipping through his blockade
into Brest. In the Mediterranean the English, having lost
Toulon, were trying to capture a base in Corsica, on land
the Directory's new generals were pushing the Allies out of
the Netherlands. The Duke of York had been badly defeated
in September, at a place called Dunkirk, and all through
that winter his men were driven relentlessly back through
ice and snow, eastward over the Dutch border and across
the Waal river. It was the worst winter for a hundred years,
worse even than the winter of Jane's birth. On her birthday, that December, the snow lay so deep that they could
not see out of the ground floor windows.

All through that bitter weather they were in trouble at
Steventon, family trouble which almost put the war out of
their heads. James's wife had been ailing gently ever since
her baby was born. Poor Anne had always been thin, pale
and silent, but nobody realised that there was anything

particularly wrong with her. She was urged to rouse herself, to take more exercise, to go out into the sun. Then she began to cough, lost weight rapidly, grew flushed and feverish. Doctor Lyford came more often, talked doubtfully of a decline, gave her steel drops and cough syrups and glasses of port, but all to no purpose. The patient improved a little with the summer, drooped again in the autumn, was housebound all winter among the snowdrifts up at Deane. The family told each other hopefully that Anne would revive again with the spring sunshine, but it was no such thing. Instead she died, rather suddenly, in May of the following year, 1795, after only three years of married life. Poor James, who was supposed to have done so well for himself in marrying Miss Anne Mathew, had in fact made a bad bargain. He was left rather a poorer man than before, owing to her feckless extravagant ways, and he had besides a child to maintain. However, the old General fortunately doted on Anna, who was a stout noisy cheerful child, just beginning to get about on her feet. He continued his allowance of a hundred a year to her, instead of her mother. Anna came down to Steventon, to be petted and spoilt by her aunts and grandmother and James came too, whenever he could, to get away from his silent melancholy house at Deane.

7

The expeditionary force was brought home in April, and that spring Holland and Spain both made peace with the French Directory. But those anxious months of summer, the second since the war began, were Cassandra's time for love and happiness, her short blossoming season, which she would remember all her life long.

She was such a steady helpful creature for her years that she was always called upon to be the family nurse. She had been very busy during Anne's illness and after it was over she flagged and looked pale. Her father and mother put their heads together and packed her off on a visit to the

Fowles at Kintbury. Tom Fowle was there, as everybody very well knew. He had taken orders and was acting as curate to his brother the Reverend Fulwar Fowle. A less unworldly pair than the Austens would have thought Tom no match for the beauty of the family and would have kept Cassandra out of his way, for poor Tom had not a penny to bless himself with and must depend on what Lord Craven could do for him in the way of a family living ; but the soft-hearted Austens only saw that the two young people were pining for one another and did not put any obstacles in their way.

So Cassandra spent Whitsuntide, 1795, at Kintbury. It was pleasant country there, just over the Berkshire border. The village was on a low hillside and its red, brown and white thatched houses were grouped about an immense cold grey flint church, with a squat tower like a fortress and a half-circle of vulture-beaks arched above its Norman doorway. From the end of the village street you looked southward to the line of Beacon Hill and the Downs, but the vicarage was huddled below the churchyard on its north side. Its mossy lawns sloped to the water meadows and the silver windings of the Kennet. A less hardy generation would one day pull this house down, because of its cold and sunless position, and build another rectory further up the hill ; but in 1795 the Fulwar Fowles thought themselves comfortable enough there. The living was a good one ; they had a fine house, a gentleman's house, with lofty rooms and great fires, a well-kept walled garden, which produced the best apricots and quinces in the neighbourhood, and a good range of stabling. The Reverend Fulwar Fowle was a hunting parson of the old sort, a rosy-faced broad-shouldered man, fond of his horses and his dinner. He preached short vigorous sermons, played a sound game of whist and was said to be the best cavalry officer in the local militia and the best rider to hounds in all Berkshire. Cassandra was a little frightened of him and Jane complained that he lost his temper too often at the card table and grumbled too loudly when his food was not to his liking ; but Mrs. Fowle managed him very cleverly and pleasantly and did not pay too much attention to his crotchets. Both the Fowles were very fond of Cassandra and the pair of them were really anxious to make up the match. Nobody minded at Kintbury how long the young people sat together in the garden, how often they strayed down past the mill into the water meadows, or how late they lingered by the sliding stream.

When Cassandra was quite an old woman and had nothing left to remember Tom by except a twisted braid of hair in the back of a mourning ring and a water-colour sketch of a slender young man, never very like him, in which dark hair and eyes and black coat had all faded together, what she would best remember was the beauty of the spring at Kintbury. After the hard winter which had killed James's wife, the blossom seemed lovelier than ever before. The old people said that fruit trees never bore so well as after a season of bitter cold. When Tom and Cassandra sat in the little yew arbour, like a sentry box, under the dovecot wall, where the sun shone longest, the ground all about them was strewn with pink and white petals and the lilac bushes, each as tall as a man, swayed their purple plumes in the wind. When they walked by the river the mowing grass was thick with buttercups and daisies and the hedges were set so thick with blackthorn blossom that you could not see the young leaves. There were kingcups and ladies' smocks in the wet places, along the margin of the stream and the swallows, skimming the channels between the banks of water weed, dashed off a spray of crystal drops as they turned on the wing. The cuckoos were calling all day long from one flowering chestnut tree to another. They sang all day as if they could never have done, and in the millwheel a kingfisher had its nest. These halcyons were lucky birds, the country people said. You could have a wish for the first kingfisher you saw in a season, just as you could for the first time you heard the cuckoo's call. Tom and Cassandra caught hands and wished when they saw the glittering blue bird flash away upstream. Then they smiled at each other, for they had only one wish between them.

They spoke of it constantly, as they paced in the water-meadows and she leant on his arm. " I have no right to ask you to marry me, my dear," Tom would confess. " You are too good and beautiful for me, you deserve a better husband. My father was only a poor parson and I have but fifty pounds a year of my own, unless I can get a living from Lord Craven. We may have to wait longer than you think before you can marry and I am afraid we shall never be very rich. I ought not to keep you to your promise." The poor fellow was never very hopeful or happy about his prospects, it was Cassandra who made light of their difficulties, steadily and cheerfully protesting her faith in their future. " I am not afraid of small means and hard work, I am used to it. My mother did not bring us up to be idle, even she says that I contrive very well and am a very good manager. You think I do not know what poverty is, but I assure you I do. I am always up and down Steventon village, my father says I am as good as a curate to him. I know how the farmers live and the labourers. I could be happy on little enough, I should not care for hardship if only we could be together. I would marry you tomorrow on what you have, my dear, and we would trust to time and chance for the rest. Only you must not lose heart and tell me to give you up. It is too late for that, I could not love anybody else but you." With her cheerful talk and her loving looks she brought him to a more hopeful state of mind and before she went home the match was made up between them. Mrs. Fowle kissed and congratulated them both, the vicar clapped his brother on the shoulder and told him that he was a lucky man. " I did not think you would ever pluck up courage to ask her," said the reverend gentleman. " Well, now we will talk to his Lordship when he comes down next week to see his agent. If he thinks there is a wedding in the wind he will do whatever he can." But Cassandra, blushing and turning shy, begged that there might be no talk of that until she had seen her parents.

So the matter was not spoken of directly to their patron when he dined at the vicarage. The seventh Lord Craven was a very fine worldly young man, in the army and not yet twenty-five. He had inherited the estates four years earlier, on the death of his father. His good looks and his wild ways came from his mother, a notorious beauty, one of the mad Berkeleys, who had married again, a month after his father's death, the Margrave of Anspach ; she had long been his mistress. Young Lord Craven had been brought up abroad by his mother and was said to be a wild and dissipated young man. He was also extremely rich. The Craven family owned a great deal of land in Berkshire. Their seat was Ashdown House on the Downs near the White Horse, up above Wantage ; a great lonely place, built in the Dutch taste more than a century earlier by the first Lord Craven, he who had loved and served James the First's daughter, the beautiful and unfortunate Queen of Bohemia. The Cravens also owned Hampstead Marshall, just outside Kintbury, but this had been burnt down and never rebuilt ; only the walled gardens and the park remained. Lord Craven dined at the vicarage, a fine figure of a man in a scarlet uniform and made himself very agreeable, only he and the vicar drank so much good wine that they never appeared at Mrs. Fowle's tea-table at all. His Lordship was very affable and full of promises. " Oh ! Lord, yes, Cousin Fulwar, Tom shall be provided for. That's dead easy. There's Ryton, now, in Shropshire ; that will be vacant as soon as the old parson there dies or retires, and I hear he is on his last legs. You may count on my promise for Ryton, Tom. Meanwhile, there is a little benefice down in Wiltshire, Allington they call it, on the edge of Salisbury Plain. You are very welcome to that if you care about it, but Allington is only big enough to make you comfortable as a bachelor. You are not thinking of marrying, I hope, for that you must wait for Ryton." He laughed loudly, as if he smelt something in the wind ; but pale Tom, looking down, said that he did not mean to marry until he could support a wife, so there they left it.

The Reverend Fulwar Fowle, with a headache next morning after so much port, was inclined to be gloomy. He grumbled that he had expected more from his patron. " Allington sounds a wretched poor place," he grunted.

Mrs. Fowle however said cheerfully, " Lord Craven is a rich man, he thinks that nobody can marry on less than two thousand a year. Tom and Cassy could do very well at Allington for a start and later on I am sure he will find them something better."

So the lovers parted hopefully and Cassandra went back to Steventon. Her father was gravely pleased, saying, " I have always liked Tom Fowle, he is a devout and serious young man. I think he will make Cassy a good husband." Mrs. Austen talked briskly of wedding clothes. " You cannot hope to be married yet awhile, my dear, but you had better buy some muslin and some linen for smocks when you next go into Basingstoke, and make a beginning." Jane hugged and laughed at her sister. " I cannot think what you see in Tom to make you feel so happy. He is a very simple person and you have seen nobody else. I should have looked about me longer before I fixed on Tom." Cassandra murmured, " How can you talk so ? " and her large eyes filled with tears, she never quite knew whether she was being teased or not. Jane kissed and petted her. " Oh ! very well, I give you leave to like him. You have liked many a stupider person. You shall have your own way about Tom and I will promise to love him as a brother. What a fine pair you will be and how I shall laugh at you when you are married ! You are both so soft-hearted that everybody will cheat you and so generous that you will give every penny you have to the poor." Then she cried, quite despairingly, " Oh ! my sweet creature, what shall I do without you ? There is nobody in the world I love as much as I do you. I wish we might neither of us ever get married, but stay at home together all our lives."

8

The engagement was not much talked about outside the family, because the young couple's prospects were still so uncertain, but Cousin Eliza found it all out as soon as she came down with her little boy for her annual visit. That summer, 1795, both Cassandra and Jane noted that she had revived and was beginning to look about her again for amusement. She had laid aside her widow's weeds and sat about the garden in a gown of white India muslin, vowing that it was far too hot for bombazine and crêpe. Black ribbon velvet bows on her slender wrists and a jet cross slung at her neck by a black ribbon, alone reminded her cousins of Monsieur de Feuillide in his nameless grave outside Paris. Eliza was exactly the same as ever, fragile, large-eyed, absurdly sophisticated, full of London gossip. She gave them an account of the final scenes at the trial of her godfather, Warren Hastings, who had been acquitted at last after ten years of legal delays and disappointments. She told them all about the Prince of Wales's wedding. The Royal family had got his debts paid, his Roman Catholic wife, Mrs. Fitzherbert, had left the country, and they had married him to a German princess. " She is a dirty sloven and the old Queen cannot abide her," said Eliza. " She came over here with a wardrobe of the most old-fashioned clothes, panniers, striped petticoats and beaver hats with great plumes in them. They say her ladies cannot get her to wash or change her clothes often enough. The Prince cannot endure her. He could scarcely get through his responses at the wedding, he was so drunk and he spent the night on the floor with his head in the fender. Now he is down at the Pavilion with Lady Jersey, she is his latest favourite and a very elegant pretty witty creature. She is a grandmother, but the Prince always prefers older women."

" I wish you would not tell the girls such stories," said Mrs. Austen crossly. " They are not at all suitable." Eliza shrugged her shoulders and changed the subject amiably to the fashions. " Powder is quite gone out, my dears, and high feathers are only worn at Court. The latest style is to cut the hair quite short, as they do in Paris, *à la guillotine*, they call it over there." Cassandra looked shocked, but Jane listened eagerly. " There is to be a Bill brought into parliament, to forbid the use of flour in the hair, because of the high price of bread ; and that, you know has killed the fashion for powder. Up in London the bucks are having crop-head parties already, with a barber in attendance to cut off their queues after dinner. Some of the younger men look very smart, with short curls like Roman emperors, but the older ones will miss the comfort of a wig. Uncle George is lucky, he has that beautiful long silky white hair. I suppose Henry will not cut off his curls, because he is in the Army." Decidedly Cousin Eliza was not much sobered by her bereavement.

She studied to please them all. With James, the new-made widower, she was all sympathy and regret, gazing up at him with swimming eyes and reminding him that she too knew what it was to lose a beloved partner. James patted her hand, invited her to take a turn with him in the shrubbery and reminded her what consolations lay around her, even in this mortal world. Presently they were to be seen sitting in the shade of the mulberry tree together every morning. Eliza was no great needlewoman, but she made a show of embroidering a scarf for herself, while James read aloud to her and Anna played on a rug at their feet. Then James reminded her of her old taste for music. " You used to play the harp so delicately," sighed James.

Eliza protested that she was quite out of practice, had not touched the harp for years ; besides, there was no instrument at the parsonage. James would take no denial. He drove into Basingstoke, hired one for her and returned with it in his carriage. After that Eliza played to them every evening most obligingly, sitting by the window in the twilight, sweeping her fine arm across the elegant gilt instrument and leaning her pretty head pensively against its carved frame. Her voice was not strong, but it was true and pleasing and she had had lessons from the best masters in Paris when she was a girl, so that she breathed out her songs with much taste and feeling. Mrs. Austen darned stockings and the girls stitched at their tambour frames, while Mr. Austen beat time gently with his hand and James sat back in the shadow, with his dark eyes fixed hungrily upon the charming performer. Eliza turned to him at the end of each melody, begged for his criticism and invited him to choose the next French or Italian air. Would he have

Folâtre, cruelle, or was *Che faro?* still his favourite? It became obvious to his family that, whatever the mind of the widow, the widower was not inconsolable.

Cassandra thought that Eliza's affection for her boy was the most agreeable quality she had. It was pretty to see her nursing and petting him, rocking him to sleep on her lap with old French nursery rhymes. *Il était une bergère* was one, with its soothing refrain of " *ron, ron, ron, petit patapon* " ; and *Sur le Pont d'Avignon* and *Au clair de la lune*. They sounded charming in Eliza's little silver thread of a voice. Cassandra liked to hear her sing them. Hastings' favourite song of all, the one for which he always cried was the lullaby with which his peasant nurse had once sung the unfortunate French Dauphin to sleep at Versailles, " *Malbrouk s'en va-t-en guerre, Mironton, ton, ton, mirontaine*," but Eliza did not like to sing it, for she thought it was an unlucky song. The boy for whom it had been sung had died in misery that June in the Temple prison. " She is a most devoted mother," James pointed out to his family. " She has a kind heart, I am sure, it is a thousand pities she has been in such bad hands. Her mother took no pains to give her good principles when she was young, and she has lived in such a dissipated society since her marriage that it is no wonder she speaks lightly of what should be serious matters. I am not blind to her faults," protested poor James, " but I believe she would respond to better influences if she could only meet with them." " He will have his work cut out," said Jane dryly to Cassandra, "if he tries to make Cousin Eliza take life as seriously as he does."

" I do think she has a very warm heart," protested Cassandra. " We must not judge her too hastily." " You never do that, my dear," said Jane. " You are far too kind-hearted. I never heard you speak ill of anybody in your life, more's the pity." " Do you think she means to marry James ? " whispered Cassandra anxiously. " Not she," said Jane. " Cousin Eliza was never cut out for a parson's wife. She would never visit the old women as you do, or carry round the children's Christmas gifts, or write out her husband's sermons. Can you see her clinking about the village in pattens in wet weather? She has never spent a winter in the country in her life. Besides, James is much too sober for her. She only wants to make a little hole in his heart, I fancy. She does not mean him any real harm, but she must have some amusement in a retired place like Steventon." Cassandra murmured, " I wish you would not talk so," but Jane was unrepentant. " You must not mind me. You know I like to laugh at my neighbours."

Mrs. Austen thought the whole business no laughing matter. She wanted a better wife for her favourite son than a frivolous fashionable widow, all French airs and affectations, with a sickly step-child into the bargain. With simple cunning she invited Mary Lloyd to come over from Ibthorp for a visit and Mary accepted eagerly. She had been dying for James for some time, as Cassandra and Jane very well knew. She arrived all in a flutter, with a couple of new chintz gowns and a very smart bonnet. It was of purple straw, with a very high crown and a wide brim, trimmed with a wreath of China asters and tied under the chin with grass-green ribbons. Mary always liked bright colours. She must have spent her dress allowance for a year on all this simple finery, but it was quite lost on James, who cared nothing for the fashions.

Eliza had been very curious about the visitor before she arrived, " I have not seen Miss Lloyd, have I, since she was a schoolgirl living up at Deane? How old is she now? is she rich? is she handsome? I think I remember that she was very much marked with the smallpox. James says that she is very good-humoured and sensible and accomplished. She does not play or sing, so I suppose she reads great books and talks very learnedly. I shall be quite afraid of her." But when she set eyes on the short and sturdy Mary, laced tightly into her cheap bright dresses, with her fidgety movements, her darting Welsh black eyes, red cheeks, clumsy hands and pitted skin, she lost interest immediately. " Poor Miss Lloyd will never carry the day with your brother," said she, in her outspoken French way. " You must look further afield if you want to find him a second wife." She laid her finger to her cheek and affected to consider the neighbours. " There are the Harwood girls or the young ladies at Manydown Park, where we went to drink tea the other day. They have an odd name, Bigg, or Wither, or Bigg-Wither, *comme c'est effroyable*. There are four or five of them and they are all just grown up, very pretty and pleasing. I cannot tell one from the other. One plays the pianoforte and another on the harp and they all sing. Miss Catherine, I think, is your particular friend, Jane ; how would you like her for a sister-in-law ? But perhaps you do not think James likely to marry again, or not at present."

Cassandra said gently that she believed James was still too unhappy about his wife's death to think of any other woman, but Eliza, with one of her French shrugs, said, " Oh ! my child, that is just the time for a clever girl to catch him." It really did not sound as if she wanted James for herself.

She treated Mary Lloyd with the most exquisite politeness and even offered to dress her hair for her, or advised her how to retrim her gown when they were going up to dine with the Harwoods at Deane House. " You are far too young to wear purple, my dear," she declared. " That is a dowager's colour, in London no young girl would be seen in it. Primrose or French grey, with cherry coloured ribbons, would be far more becoming to your fresh complexion." Mary did not take any of this in good part. She rudely refused the loan of what Eliza declared was the latest London fashion, a clear white muslin gown of absolute simplicity, worn over a satin slip, slit at the hem for ease in walking, cut very low in the neck and very short in the sleeves and tied with a wide sash underneath the arms. None of these country girls had yet seen anything like it. " I should look a figure of fun in a gown like that," complained sturdy Mary, as the three girls leaned their elbows on the window sill of the dressing parlour and looked down on James and Eliza in the garden.

The handsome couple had been pacing the lawn for an hour or so, James in his black clerical clothes, Eliza hanging on his arm in her transparent classical draperies. She was bare-armed and bare-headed and she carried the tail of her gown flung carelessly over her arm, when she turned you saw her exquisite ankles in fine silk stockings and the gleam of a golden garter. " It really is not decent," burst out Mary, as red in the face as a turkey cock. " She has left off her corset and her petticoat, her gown is as narrow as a pillow-slip and she has nothing on under it but a chemise. Her waist is under her shoulders and her neck is as bare as if she were at a dance. You can see right through her gown when she is standing against the light. If she were not so very slender she would look like a bolster tied in the middle. If these are London fashions I am glad I am a country girl."

Jane laughed and said eagerly, " It is simple enough. Four yards of India muslin would do it and leave a bit over for a cap or a neckerchief. I shall take the pattern of it and make myself one for next winter's Assemblies." " I cannot see that she is so very handsome, can you ? " Mary implored her friends, but Jane insisted, " I think she is quite enchanting. I wish I were more like her."

Mary tossed her head and her black eyes flashed jealous sparks. " She would like us to take her for four or five and twenty, but I am sure she is ten years older. She paints her cheeks and I believe she dyes her hair. She must be much older than James. I cannot think what he sees in her. She makes herself very agreeable and talks very cleverly, she has seen a great deal of the world, but she has no principles. She is always making fun of the clergy ; she told me yesterday that in England they have nothing to do but preach other men's sermons, grumble about their meals and watch the weather. I have a very good mind to tell that to James."

" I should hold my tongue, I if were you," Jane advised her dryly. " You will never recommend yourself to James by repeating such trifles." " Then could not you give him a word of warning ? " Mary urged. " He might listen to you, he has a great opinion of your judgment." " Oh ! the advice of a sister can't prevent a man from falling in love if he chooses." Mary's face fell and she said crossly, " I should have thought Madame la Comtesse might have worn black for that husband of hers a little longer, instead of flinging away her weeds and walking about the garden in broad daylight in what is little better than a nightgown. It is most indelicate. She has not been a widow two years yet and already she is absolutely on the catch for a new husband. She cannot be content with the sort of honest flirtation which would suit anybody else, she must needs plague James till he is absolutely wretched. Oh ! I daresay she is your cousin and you do not like me to talk like this about her, but I must speak my mind. I think she is exactly like the Wicked Mrs. Craven."

9

What Mary had not been able to effect, in detaching James from his cousin, came about quite simply in another way. He was cut out by Henry, as usual. That young gentleman came home on leave from Brighton in September, taller than ever and looking uncommonly handsome in the scarlet, white and gold of his regimentals. He had not yet cut off his hair, but wore it in a queue with a couple of greased and powdered curls at each temple. He was doing very well in the army, though he would rather have been in a regular regiment. The Oxfordshire Militia had not behaved well in camp. They had made many complaints about their rations, raided farmyards, stolen eggs and apples, fowls and sucking pigs ; finally had raided the market stalls at Lewes in force. It had ended in something like a mutiny. The regiment had been marched out on to the Downs in a hollow square ; two of the ringleaders had been shot and others flogged, before the eyes of their comrades. It must have been a horrid business for a gay young man to watch, but Henry did not talk of it to his mother and sisters. All his stories were of the gaieties of Brighton, reviews and races on the Downs, the wild doings of the Prince of Wales and his friends and the additions which he was making to the Pavilion.

He looked a good deal older than his twenty-four years

and had a cool mocking air which much became him. He surveyed Eliza's doings with lazy amusement and seemed at first inclined to leave her to his brother, but that Eliza would not permit. There had always been a particular understanding between Henry and Eliza, they struck out lovely sparks of wit and enjoyment whenever they met. Eliza, it seemed, was determined to attach him. There were a few more morning walks in the shrubbery, with Eliza demurely pacing between the two brothers ; then the cooler September mornings won her to riding with Henry. " It would do you far more good than all this idling and poetry reading," scoffed Henry. " I wonder James has never suggested it." James said stiffly that he was afraid Eliza was not strong enough to ride far. He could mount her, of course, Anne's old mare could carry a lady, but he feared he could not spare his own sturdy cob for his brother. Henry, nothing daunted, borrowed a beast from the Digweeds. Eliza rode beautifully, had ridden from a child, Henry vowed that he had never seen a woman with a better seat. They were out every morning together, while James sulked up at Deane.

In the evenings when Eliza sang there were not half so many French or Italian airs. Henry's choice was a gay *bergerette*, or a soldier's song with a marching chorus, in which the rest could join, *Pretty Polly Oliver*, *Over the Hills and Far Away*, *Begone Dull Care*, *Let Us Take the Road*, *The Hour of Attack Approaches*, or *The Girl I Left Behind Me*. The harp was laid aside for these and Eliza made the old Rectory harpsichord buzz like a swarm of bees as she rattled off the merry tunes, looking over her shoulder at Henry where he leant against the wall, waiting to turn over her pages. He sang himself, in a light agreeable baritone, smiling down at his accompanist. *Yes, I'm in love, I know not how*, was Henry's song, " *And Celia has undone me. But on my soul, I can't tell how, The pleasing plague stole on me.*" Mr. Austen always begged for a favourite, twenty years old, a tune of his courting days, the famous air from Mr. Sheridan's musical play *The Duenna*. " *Had I a heart for envy framed, It ne'er could injure you.*"

Henry sang that too very agreeably, whenever it was asked for, besides old airs from the *Beggar's Opera, Come sweet lass,* and *How happy could I be with either.* He was a horrible flirt, his sisters believed, dozens of girls had pined and languished for him in Brighton. He was supposed to be devoting himself to a black-eyed Miss Pearson, up in London, daughter to an officer of the Greenwich Royal Hospital, but he seemed to have forgotten all about her for the time being.

" How long is Cousin Eliza going to stay with us, madam," Cassandra inquired of her mother. " I'm sure I don't know, my dear," Mrs. Austen tartly replied. " She invited herself for her own convenience, not for mine. Your father likes to have her here, I believe. I have given her as many hints as I decently can in my own house, but I don't suppose she will go till it suits her." " I was mistaken in Eliza," James sighed. " I thought she had some feeling for me, but I see that she was only trifling. My eyes are open now, I will not think of her longer." " She has treated James very ill," Cassandra lamented, " I cannot imagine how she could bring herself to make him so wretched." " But how does she do it ? " breathed young Jane, enchanted. " She makes it all look so easy. She turns first one and then the other round her little finger. What French arts does she use ? I must discover." This, this, she seemed to tell herself, was the game which every woman must learn to play. The exquisite polish of Eliza's double flirtation, the wavering balance which she held between the two brothers, quite fascinated their younger sister.

" But you would not wish to torment any man as she has tormented James," pleaded Cassandra, opening her eyes very wide. " Oh ! James's heart is not broken," said Jane coolly, " though I daresay he thinks it is. He will sigh a few sighs and write a few melancholy verses and vow never to look at another woman ; then he will cheer up gradually and when the proper time comes he will marry somebody else. If I were Mary Lloyd I would not despair of him too quickly."

" And will Henry marry Eliza ? " marvelled Cassandra,

who always respected her sister's sharp judgments. " I
should like to see him settled, but not with her."

" He says he will not," disclosed Jane, " but I would not
be too sure about it. I believe they might suit each other
very well, for all she is ten years older than he is ; but it
is she who will decide, not Henry. Oh ! I love to watch
her at it," said Jane, tossing her arms in the air. " She has
so much French address. To captivate Henry, who knows
all her faults, who has made up his mind not to fall in love,
that would be a conquest indeed. She is the most finished
coquette in England, and I must learn to imitate her."

" I am afraid she is a bad example for you to copy," said
grave Cassandra, but Jane only laughed. " The men do all
they can to make us wretched," she vowed, " so why should
we not take our revenge where we can get it ? It is all very
well for you, my dear Cassy, you will have no trouble with
your Tom. He is devoted to you and you want nobody else ;
but I am not going to put up with the first comer. I intend
to break a few hearts on my own account before I settle
down to the stupidity of married bliss, and Cousin Eliza
shall teach me how to do it. I owe it to myself," said Jane,
looking in the mirror. She was then nineteen.

In September after Henry had left them, when the swallows
and house-martens began to gather and twitter on the roofs
and discuss the way to Africa, Eliza also grew restless and
preened her slender wings for flight. " I have been here
ten weeks," she reckoned up with surprise. " I never spent
such a quiet summer before and yet how happy I have been
among you. It must be because you are all so charming.
Shall you miss me when I am gone ? " Mr. Austen assured
her that they would be very quiet without her. She
answered, " Yes, I have been a great disturbance to you all,
have I not ? I daresay you would rather have my room
than my company. I shall sit in my house up in London
and wonder what you are all doing at Steventon." Mrs.
Austen remarked dryly, " I daresay Henry will visit you
from time to time and give you news of us," and Eliza,
smiling gently, agreed, " Yes, I daresay I shall some time
see Henry. Indeed I hope you will any of you call on me

for hospitality if you wish to visit the capital. You never come up yourself, my dear Aunt, I am well aware of that and I daresay the journey would be too much for Uncle George in winter, but if Cassy wishes to buy her wedding clothes, or Jane would like to hear a concert, let them come to me. I hope I shall always have a bed for a friend." Jane looked imploringly at her mother, for there was nothing she would have enjoyed more than a trip to London, but Mrs. Austen said firmly, " I cannot spare either of the girls at present."

So Eliza took her departure, and Jane was left at Steventon to cut her brown curls as short as she dared, in imitation of the new fashion, to make herself a new muslin gown as like Eliza's as she could and to scribble away at a new story. It was all about a certain Lady Susan, a heartless and selfish woman of fashion, who locked up and ill-treated her young dark-eyed daughter and tried to part her from her lover, much like the Wicked Mrs. Craven. Jane had wanted to write about that lady for a long time, but she had not quite known how to treat the central figure. Now she had the model she needed. With innocent cunning she made Lady Susan as much unlike Cousin Eliza as possible in the face, delicately fair, with large grey eyes, soft feline caressing airs and no heart at all. This enchantress flirted with two brothers at once, with the most tantalising grace and united all the females of the family against her. It went faster than anything Jane had yet written, and before Christmas she had got most of it set down. It was all written in the form of letters between the principal characters, as the literary fashion then was, and as each was finished she read it aloud to Cassandra, who listened open-mouthed. No doubt Cousin Eliza would have laughed very much if she had read *Lady Susan*. As it was, Jane could not quite think how to finish it, so she lost interest, put it away in her desk and forgot about it completely. At that time of her life she was always beginning stories which she did not finish ; real life had a way of proving more interesting than her own fancies.

III

Steventon

1795-1796

I

WHEN she was quite an old woman Cassandra would still remember, as if it were yesterday, the day when Tom came to bring her his bad news. It had been a fine October afternoon, and she had gone off by herself up the hedgerow which they called Church Walk. It was too late for blackberries, but she could try for a gleaning of hazel nuts and her mother needed some sloes for a cordial. The thorny bushes were full of them, small, tight and hard, with a bloom on them like black grapes. It did not take her long to fill her small basket and she sat down to rest on a dry sunny bank, at the brow of the hill, under a holly tree whose leaves and berries glittered in the mild sun. It was one of those warm and exquisite days which the country people called St. Luke's little summer. She could see for miles across the pale empty uplands and the distant woods looked clear and sharply blue.

In the hollow below was the brown roof of Steventon Rectory, with its haystacks and farm buildings behind it and its neat square of walled garden to the south, all enclosed in a ring of golden elms. From where she sat she could make out a maid in a coloured gown, taking down washing from the line in the orchard, where the apple trees were red with fruit ; she could see a man in shirt sleeves crossing the yard, leading a horse to the stable, could hear the gentle bleating of the sheep penned in the turnip field of the glebe and see her mother's poultry, bright as coloured flowers, all scattered about on the pale stubble. She watched idly, thinking that it all looked like a pretty toy fit for her niece Anna to play with.

Then she saw a man in black clothes, parson's clothes, coming quickly out of the garden gate and striking up across the field towards her. He moved too lightly for her father, too gracefully for her brother James, it could be nobody else but Tom Fowle. She stood up and waved her hand. He saw her and lifted his arm high above his head ; then he came hurrying up the steep field. She ran a little way to meet him, stumbling on the rough grass, her feet would scarcely carry her. Then she was in his arms and he was holding her up. She forgot her bewilderment in the exquisite delight of seeing him without warning until he led her back to the shelter of the withered hedge and sat down with her under the bright holly tree. Then she, who was so quiet with other men, was all eagerness with him, showering him with her questions as she leant against his shoulder, in the circle of his arm. " How did you come here so suddenly, my darling ? Are you from London or from Kintbury ? and are they all well there ? " Yes, said Tom, they were all well, he had come from there the day before. He had borrowed a saddle horse from his brother and ridden as far as Kingsclere. He had spent a night there, and had walked about on the downs, thinking over something which he had in mind and then he had come on to see Cassandra. She heard him give a great sigh and waited anxiously for him to go on, but he did not seem able to do it ; only his arm tightened round her and he held her more closely to him. " What is the matter ? " said she. " You have something to tell me, I know ; is it bad news ? " He answered slowly, " I do not know whether you will think it good or bad. It is not welcome news to me. It is something about Lord Craven."

Cassandra turned in the circle of his arm so that she could look up into his pale and serious face. " His regiment is ordered abroad," Tom said. " There is to be a great expedition to the West Indies, to Santo Domingo, with General Abercromby in command. It is lying now in the Channel ports. It was to have sailed six weeks ago, but the men were not assembled and the stores were not ready and then the ships were windbound by these equinoctial gales.

Now they are to sail next month and Lord Craven's regiment is to go with them. I saw him when I was in London last week, he is in high spirits of course, full of his preparations, he can talk of nothing but honour and glory. They expect to be gone about two years."

Cassandra felt as if a cold finger had touched her heart, " And I suppose he cannot give you the Shropshire living before he goes," she ventured. He shook his head and the grasp of his arm slackened from about her, he sat staring unhappily at the ground. Cassandra began to tremble a little, " But then, must we wait two years ? " said she. " And what if anything happens to his Lordship ? I think I have heard that the Islands are a very sickly place, are they not ? " Still looking on the ground and avoiding her eyes, Tom said, " There is more in it than that. He has asked me to go with him as chaplain to the regiment."

Cassandra turned cold from head to foot, as if a hand were squeezing her heart. She could not get breath to speak at first and when she did it was only a gasp, " To go . . . so far away . . ." Still looking on the ground, he said, " Yes, it is far ; but I do not know how to refuse. He is the only friend I have who can do anything for me, if I do not take this chance I may offend him. He thinks he is doing me a good turn, the best in his power, he sent for me specially to go to London to talk of it. He has nothing else in his power at present. The chaplain who was to have gone with them has fallen sick suddenly, and he does not know where to lay his hands on another who is young and strong enough. He was good enough to say that I could be of great help and comfort to the men. He pressed me very hard to accept then and there, but of course I could not do that without seeing you. I am to have till next week to decide."

She said, " Oh ! God, what will become of us ? " and then she seized his cold hand in both of hers and urged him passionately, " Don't do it, Tom ; don't go with him ! I cannot bear it if you go to the Islands. I am sure I have heard of our soldiers dying there by thousands. It is a dreadful place. Why must you accept ? What does it

matter, after all, if you offend his lordship? We can do
without his help, you can continue as your brother's curate,
we can live in a cottage together till things mend. Sooner
or later you will get another living, or if you do not I shall
not care at all, so long as we are together. Only do not go
to Santo Domingo, I implore you."

He begged her not to talk so foolishly. "I am very
strong," said poor Tom, "I have never had a day's illness
in my life and I am sensible, I shall not do anything rash,
I will promise you to take care of myself. If it is a sickly
place there will be all the more for me to do for the men.
I shall see the world, like your brothers," he told her with
his sweet serious smile. "I have always envied them. I
never expected to set foot outside the kingdom. Perhaps
some day when I am in Port au Prince Frank or Charles
will come sailing into the bay and we shall meet and talk
of Steventon. Come, my dearest, you must not look so.
You must make a calendar and cross off the weeks, you must
stitch away at your wedding clothes and think of the time
when the war will be over and we shall be together again.
It will not seem very long, I am sure we shall only be away
two years."

2

With such persuasions he almost won Cassandra over, but
down at the Parsonage her family were all against the plan.
Mr. Austen could not take it in at all at first, but when he
did he became greatly distressed, repeating, "Poor Cassy!
it is a dreadful thing for her. I do not know what she will
do. It does not bear thinking of. I cannot imagine why
his Lordship should want Tom to go so far away. It seems
very strange. My dear boy, do you not think your duty
lies at home?" Perfectly content himself with his mild
round of preaching and prayer, teaching, visiting and alms-
giving, he was merely puzzled and distressed when Tom said
anxiously, "The more I consider it, the more I feel that I
have a call to go there. If God has put this work in my way

I have no right to refuse." Brother James, who seemed to feel that this was a reflection in some way upon himself, said crossly, " There is no reason for you to go that I can see. Why cannot you stay and do your duty in whatever parish you can get ? There are plenty of souls to be saved in England, surely, without your running off into foreign parts."

Up in the dressing parlour Jane put her arms round her sister and cried indignantly, " Tom has no right to desert you like this. I would not let him go if I were you. You are too calm, you do not make enough show of your feelings. Why do you not weep and rage and reproach him for being so cruel ? That is what I should do in your place."

" No, you would not," said Cassandra stubbornly. " It is Tom's profession to do good, he must go if he chooses. You did not tell Frank or Charles not to go to sea in wartime, because of the danger. I shall not stand in Tom's way." Her lip quivered, but though the tears stood in her mild eyes, they did not fall.

Down in the parlour, irritably pushing her needle through the Rector's black silk stockings, Mrs. Austen bluntly said what everybody else was thinking. " And if you die in the Islands, or if his Lordship does, for that matter, then what is to become of Cassy ? She will not even be a widow. I have no patience with such nonsense. If Tom is to rush off like this to some island that nobody ever heard of, then there ought not to be any engagement between the pair of you. I am sure her father agrees with me."

Tom said wretchedly, " If Cassandra would rather be free, I shall not hold her to her promise, she knows that well enough." Cassandra gave him a long reproachful look, but he would not meet her eye. He was beginning to lose heart. Mrs. Austen concluded, " Well, you had better not make up your mind until you have heard all sides of the matter. Mr. Holder and General Mathew are both sensible men and they have been in the West Indies. We had better ask for their advice." " They will tell us that the climate is hot, the natives are black and there is a great deal of money to be made out of sugar," said Jane crossly ; Mrs. Austen told her not to be pert. " Cassy and Tom shall walk up to Ashe Park tomorrow morning," she decided, " and in the afternoon James shall bring the General over to dinner. Until then we will talk no more of it."

Next morning Tom and Cassandra obediently walked up to pay a call upon Mr. Holder at Ashe Park. They found their elderly neighbour in his green-panelled library, wrapped up in an Indian dressing gown of a bandana pattern, with a turban on his bald head, supping gruel before a great log fire and complaining that he had but just got over a fit of his tertian ague. " Every autumn, when the cold weather comes in I begin to shiver and shake like an aspen," said poor Mr. Holder, looking very yellow. " That is what you get from a lifetime in the West Indies."

He ordered in a bottle of his best Constantia to warm the young people after their walk. " It is a very nice ladies' wine," said he. " We may hope to get more of it in our cellars, now that we have taken the Cape of Good Hope away from the Dutch ; and Miss Cassandra must taste the ratafia biscuits and dried cherries. Young ladies always like something sweet. If you, Mr. Fowle, prefer a dry wine, you should try a glass of my Xeres. It has been for a roll round Cape Horn, to the East Indies and back. I wish I could drink it myself."

He made them very welcome and when he understood their errand was glad to spin the great tawny green globe, as tall as a man, which stood in the window with its azure celestial companion, on which the constellations were plotted. He laid his bony finger midway along the necklace of islands which ringed in the Caribbean Sea. There, said he, was Santo Domingo, just across the Windward Passage, south east of Cuba. He had never been there himself, it did not lie on the route to Barbadoes, which was far, far down south, off the Windward Islands, out in the Atlantic ; but once, when homeward bound, his ship had been blown northwards out of her course by the tail of a hurricane, and he had seen what looked like three triangles of blue glass, standing up over the rim of Ocean. Those, the master had told him, were the tops of the mountains of Hispaniola.

That was the true name of the island. Christopher Columbus himself had so named it when he discovered it on his first voyage to the New World, but the natives called it Haiti, which in their tongue meant the Island of Woods. The Spaniards had kept hold of the eastern end of the island until this very year 1795, when they had made peace with the French who held the western half and had handed it over to them. " That is why we are sending out this great expedition," Mr. Holder explained. " Ah ! if we could but get Santo Domingo into our own hands it would be a colony well worth having. It is the most fertile of all the West Indian islands. You can grow sugar cane down in the coast, where it is hot and wet and coffee and cocoa and allspice higher up the hills. The forests are full of good timber, mahogany and teak and logwood, if you could but get it out ; and nobody knows what minerals there might not be in the hills. But you cannot go up there," said he, absently spinning his globe. " The centre of the island is nothing but inaccessible mountain peaks, going up to four and five thousand feet. It is all choked with virgin forest, full of thorns and creepers and poisonous snakes. They have the *fer-de-lance* up there, its bite kills in a few hours. Nobody goes up into the mountains except the natives. When the moon is full, you hear them beating their drums all night long and see their fires burning. They practise a black magic which they call Voodoo, it is said that they can raise the dead and make them run to and fro at night on errands. They sacrifice black and white cocks and sometimes human beings. It is certain, quite certain, that they can put a spell on a man which will drive him to his death. I knew a case of it myself, when I was out in Barbadoes. Of course, they are very skilled in poisons."

Mr. Holder continued for some time in this style, but when he saw that he had alarmed Miss Cassandra, who was a favourite of his, he changed his tune. He spun the globe again and talked more cheerfully, telling her about the happy idle black folk down on the plantations, how they loved dancing, singing and cockfighting much better than they loved work, what good servants they made, how pretty their slender impudent girls were when they were young and how well the older women cooked in their own fashion, making turtle soup and pepperpot and broiling fish and chickens with spices over a little hot charcoal fire. Nobody in the world, said he, lived better or had finer houses, than the rich French planters in the Islands. He sighed gently as he looked from the demure parson's daughter in her dove-coloured pelisse and close bonnet, to the pale and harassed young man in his crow-black clerical clothes. They were standing very close together and though he had not been told how it was with them he was sure that Tom was holding Cassandra's little finger tight, behind her dove-grey skirts. " Ah ! I should like to be young again," burst out old Mr. Holder, " and be going out to the islands for the first time to seek my fortune. I would not be such a fool as to come back again to this cold country. I should stay there all my life."

3

Cassandra begged that General Mathew might not be told either what was in the wind, " For he might not like to say all he thinks," she pleaded, " if he knew what Tom was considering." So nothing was said at first when James brought his father-in-law down to dinner next day. The pair of them came in very sharp-set, for they had taken the beagles up on to the downs behind Overton early that morning and had had very good sport. They sat down to three o'clock dinner declaring themselves quite starved.

Mrs. Austen always kept a good table, but on this occasion she had taken particular pains to have plenty, for the General was a good trencherman and James was very greedy. She was sorry there had been no fish to be had in Basingstoke market and they had just finished the stuffed pike from Whitchurch ; but there was a neck of pork roasted, with apple sauce, and a couple of boiled capons from her own poultry yard. The side dishes were eggs-and-bacon and fried rabbits, all set on together, besides a cold saddle of their own mutton on the sideboard. She believed demurely that they would find it very sweet. There were apricot tartlets, syllabubs to please the girls, a great Stilton cheese and the first celery for the gentlemen, with filberts, walnuts and William pears to finish the dessert.

Over this ample meal they lingered, while General Mathew, sitting between Cassandra and her mother, showed himself only too willing to instruct the company about the West Indian campaign. He became very explosive about planters and the slave-trade in general, and the War Office in particular, grumbling and swearing as the army always did about the way Whitehall neglected the troops overseas. " Too little and too late," was the burden of the old gentleman's song. " It would take twenty thousand men to subdue the Islands and what's more, by the end of the campaign, you would not have ten thousand of them left. To my mind, we made a great mistake in going to Santo Domingo at all. We were fetched in to help defend the French planters against their own black slaves, and that's no work for British troops anyway, even if we get a new colony out of it. The Jacobins in Paris sent out agents to promise the slaves their freedom and stir them up against their owners. Now there are six thousand of them up in the hills, under a runaway slave called Toussaint l'Ouverture. They come down and raid the plantations, kill the owners, burn down the houses and go back up again into the forests where we can't follow them. There's the same thing going on in the Windward Islands and in Jamaica, where the maroons are in the cockpit country. White troops are no use for that kind of fighting, we shall never subdue the islands unless we do it with natives. The Creole planters promised to raise us coloured regiments from their own estates and we paid them a good bounty for every man they would put into the field, besides arms and stores and uniforms, but God bless you ! all these fellows want to do is to strut about in scarlet coats and line their own pockets."

He paused, surprised and pleased by the unusual attention with which the Austens were listening to his remarks. " I don't at all like what I hear about the Santo Domingo campaign from a man in Murray's regiment. He has been out at Port au Prince since the very beginning of the war, hanging on with a handful of men by the skin of his teeth, waiting for reinforcements that don't come. Half his men are on the sick list at a time, he tells me. They get sunstroke and fever, they are bitten by insects and snakes, they poison themselves with raw rum ; and in the sickly season from July to September when the rain pours down in torrents and the whole place steams like a laundry, they start dying like flies from Yellow Jack."

That fever, said he, was the great curse of the islands, white men could not stand up to it. " Yellow Jack kills you inside a week," said the General gloomily. " First you get chills and fever and all your bones ache as if they had been broken. Then you turn redder than a turkey cock, as red as my old tunic, even the whites of your eyes are like cherries. Then you grow as yellow as a guinea, your nose bleeds and you have the black vomit and you go out like a snuffed candle. Nothing to be done for it, the doctors told me, except dose the men with salts and give them lemons and limes to suck ; all very little use. I have seen hundreds die of it in my time, down on the Mosquito Coast and even if you recover you're a broken man. I have seen many a tall fellow turned to a walking skeleton, hardly fit to crawl on board the transport that was to take him home." He was grumbling on like this, between gulps and swallows of his port when Cassandra said faintly, " Please . . ."

The company all turned and looked at her. She felt as if she were drowning, her heart beat so fast that she thought she would choke. She saw her father's mild distressed eyes, her mother's pursed lips ; Jane, sitting opposite, started from her chair exclaiming, with her indignant sparkling look, " It is not fair to treat Cassy so." Her mother said, " Jane, sit down," and Brother James muttered sulkily, " I still say he's a fool to go there." The old General, sitting next Cassandra, screwed himself round to face her. His eyes were popping out of his red face and he looked as if he were choking in his tight high stock. " God bless my soul ! what's all this ? " he exclaimed. " There, there, my dear young lady, don't look so. I never meant to frighten you with such horrors, old fool that I am. You were sitting there so mum beside me, as quiet as a mouse, to tell the truth I'd quite forgotten you were listening. Now cheer up, Miss Cassy, drink this glass of your father's good wine and forget my nonsense. None of that has anything to do with you."

He was pushing his own glass at her, Tom, on his other side had turned so pale that she could hardly bear it. She lifted her head and looked at them all proudly. " I have a right to listen," she told General Mathew. " I must hear all that you can tell me. You see, Tom has decided to go out there, as chaplain to Lord Craven's regiment." " Good God ! he mustn't do that," exclaimed the old man. " No, no ; that would never do. It is not a fit place for him." " Tom must do what he thinks right," said Cassandra steadily. " I shall wait for him until he comes again and we will be married when God pleases."

4

That autumn of 1795 was a bad time abroad. England had spent her riches for two years on allies who would not fight ; with the Spaniards, the Dutch and the Prussians all making peace with France there was no friend left on the Continent except the exhausted Austrian army. Certainly the Mediterranean Fleet still had the Bourbon king of the Two Sicilies at their back and that gave them the use of his two great harbours, Naples and Palermo. They were free of the neutral port of Leghorn and they still had a foothold in Corsica. It was a year of blockade. The King's ships tossed night and day off Brest and Toulon for weeks together, without fresh meat or vegetables, never sleeping dry, keeping watch like terriers at a rathole in all weathers ; but the French would not come out and fight them. There was no prize money to be got in this service the Navy complained, only honour and salt beef. General Abercromby's West Indian expedition was still fitting out at Portsmouth amidst incredible confusion and delays, Tom wrote to

Cassandra that he feared they might not get away before the New Year. In the country there was a great deal of discontent and distress. The price of wheat had begun to rise and that was all very well for landowners like Edward and tithe-holders like Parson Austen and his son, but the poor people felt the pinch. The quartern loaf went up to a shilling that November for the first time in living memory. There were bread riots up in London, to frighten nervous people like Eliza, who believed that this was the beginning of a general uprising, such as there had been in France. The old king was actually shot at when he went in his coach to open Parliament, and there were seditious meetings in many places, crying for peace on any terms. The authorities were alarmed and put down these disturbances with great severity. All public meetings were forbidden and there was a general fear of Revolution.

But down in the country all that seemed faint and far off to Parson Austen's younger daughter and her friends, for this was the gay time of the year when the Assemblies were held in Basingstoke. Cassandra did not take much interest in them that year, for with Tom away there was nobody she cared to dance with any more ; but young Jane, whose twentieth birthday fell in that December, was all eagerness, for she had a new beau, another Tom, an Irishman. He was Mr. Thomas Langlois Lefroy, nephew to Mr. Lefroy, the parson up at Ashe and eldest son of a Colonel Anthony Lefroy, who at that time had a very pretty property near Limerick. They were Protestants of the south, a very good family of Huguenot descent. The young man was studying law at Trinity College, Dublin, and had come over to his Uncle and Aunt in Hampshire for the Christmas festivities. Mrs. Lefroy was a good friend to the Austen girls, a pretty, delightful creature, gay and lively, always with many looks of eager love for Jane and she had made several opportunities already for the young couple to meet. Tom Lefroy was a tall pale young man, exceedingly handsome, who held his dark head very high and gave you a sidelong glance out of grey Irish eyes, put in, as the saying was, with a smutty finger. He was not the agreeable rattle which people had expected him to be from his nationality, but a rather silent and forbidding creature ; possibly he was too proud or perhaps he was only shy. Cassandra could not make anything of him herself, but she saw that he was attracted by her sister, though he did not seem to know what to make of her. He listened to her gay talk, followed her about with those bright eyes of his, sat near her whenever he could and paid no attention to anybody else. Cassandra was anxious to see how he would behave at the Assemblies.

These dances took place once a month, during the winter months, on the nearest Thursday possible to the night when the moon was full. People drove in to Basingstoke for them from all round the countryside ; pretty girls and gay young men and their fathers and mothers too, all crammed into carriages, wrapped up in coats and blankets, with their feet in sheepskin rugs against the winter cold. The dancing took place in the big room at the back of the Angel Inn. This was a famous posting house with a great yard where the coaches changed horses, going up and down between London and the West Country, to Salisbury, Exeter and even to Cornwall. Curtis, the landlord, was a very civil obliging man and his wife was a great hand at ball suppers ; she brewed good negus and her white soup was famous all over the county.

The ballroom was upstairs, behind the yard and over the stables and connected with the inn itself by a long passage, a sad place for draughts and catching cold. There were double doors to the ballroom, which could be flung wide open for the arrival of the guests and there was a handsome fireplace at either end, in which a great pile of logs always burnt on Assembly nights. The older ladies liked to arrive in good time so as to secure a cosy place near one of the fires. Oval mirrors above these two fireplaces reflected the crystal chandeliers and the high feathers of the ladies in an endless diminishing perspective. The floor was well waxed with candle-shavings and chalked in patterns, wreaths of evergreen were slung along the cornice ; the musicians sat in one corner with their harp, horns and fiddles, and all round the walls were rout-seats for the ladies, young and old.

There was very little formality or stiffness at these monthly Assemblies. It was like a family party, everybody knew everybody else and all eyes were drawn at once to the face of a girl who had come into the neighbourhood for a visit, to the red coat of a strange officer quartered in the town, or the blue one of a naval officer home on leave. These were always welcome, for gentlemen were somewhat scarce and the ladies were often obliged to sit down for a couple of dances, or partner each other to make up a set. The evening was always opened with one or two minuets, in which the older folk might display themselves, rising and sinking in Court bows and curtseys ; but the young people waited impatiently for the country dances and cotillions to begin. These to them were the business of the evening. All were danced longways, for the square country dance had quite gone out. The most important young ladies present led off the chain in turn and called the figures ; the others ranged themselves down the room, hoping for a long set with a favoured partner. Two dances together were allowed and engaged for, another engagement with the same gentleman later in the evening was permissible ; more than that would be remarked upon with raised eyebrows, pursed lips and critical frowns among the chaperons. These unfortunate ladies, the wives of squires and parsons, doctors and lawyers, had little else but gossip to amuse them as they yawned away the evening behind their fans. The older men withdrew into the card room and sat down to a quiet rubber of whist, but their wives found it a long time till supper was announced and they could go down to eat scalloped oysters and cold chicken and ham, sip orgeat and negus, taste creams and jellies. They had little to do but compare the activity of the young gentlemen, the good looks and pretty behaviour of the young ladies, to count how often they sat out or stood up to dance, and how much or little they talked and smiled together as they waited their turn in the long line of the country dance. That was the time for improving an acquaintance or pursuing a flirtation ; *being particular*, the girls called it among themselves.

The great families of the neighbourhood did not always

trouble to bring a party to these public balls, where the company was somewhat mixed. Lord Portsmouth at Hurstbourne Priors, Lord Bolton at Hackwood, Lord Dorchester and his lady at Kempshott Park, usually preferred to entertain their neighbours once in the winter with a ball in their own noble mansions and spend the summer season in London. Still, there were enough fine folk to be stared at without them. Sir William Heathcote, one of the Members for Hampshire, always came over with his lady all the way from Hursley, on the other side of Winchester, for he thought it important to be gracious to his political supporters. One or both of his elegant daughters might be there, with a brother or two in attendance ; the second son, William, the parson, was sure to come, for he was paying his addresses to Miss Elizabeth Bigg, of Manydown. The other Member, Mr. Chute, the Master of the Vine Hunt, lived close by, a jolly, noisy gentleman who always brought a large party ; he had no sons or daughters of his own, but there was a bachelor brother, a parson, who was a great dancer. It was not considered unbecoming to his cloth for a young clergyman to walk down a country dance, pay a few stately compliments to his partner and ride over next morning through the lanes to inquire how she did, and Mr. Tom Chute was always in great demand.

Then there were Mildmays from Dogmersfield, Jervoises from Herriard, Portals from Laverstoke and also from Freefolk Priors, the Huguenot papermakers who made the notes for the Bank of England. The tribe of Terrys came from Dummer and the Harwoods from Deane House, a lively, noisy crowd of them. Kind Mrs. Harwood often lamented that she could never give the Austen girls a lift in her carriage on Assembly nights, but her sons and daughters were always crammed in so tightly that they could scarcely move. Mr. Austen was not fond of letting his own horses go into Basingstoke at night, these sturdy beasts were too often needed on the farm to be of much use in the carriage ; but Mrs. Lefroy gave the girls a lift whenever she could and the Bramstons, a childless couple at Oakley Hall, were always ready to show a kindness to the

Rector's daughters. Best of all Cassandra and Jane liked to dine and sleep the night at Manydown, with the Bigg-Wither family. Manydown was a grey classic house with a pillared portico, standing among cedar trees in the wide spaces of its own park, just outside Basingstoke. Within were cool elegant saloons adorned by family portraits, marble pillars and chimney-pieces and a great staircase with delicate wrought iron balustrades. Mr. Bigg-Wither was a widower, a peppery, rather alarming old gentleman ; his son Harrison, was a pink-faced schoolboy delicate and stooping, who had a great admiration for Jane. The girls were not handsome, but they were elegant and accomplished. Catherine, who was intelligent and agreeable, was Jane's particular friend, Cassandra preferred Alethea. The eldest daughter, Elizabeth, was just then chiefly preoccupied with her own love affairs. She had two strings to her bow, both parsons, as it happened. John Harwood, the eldest son from Deane House, had courted her since they were boy and girl, but he was only a good, sober, rather stupid young fellow and the Harwoods, though they lived in style, were said to be outrunning the constable. Mr. William Heathcote was the second son of a baronet and Member of Parliament, he had money, came of a very good family and was already Rector of Worting, at the bottom of her father's park. Elizabeth had to admit that he was the better match of the two. She was gravely exercised in her mind as to which of the two she should choose.

5

In that winter of 1795, when the ladies had talked enough of servants, silks and scandal and had run over the war news, they gossiped more than usual about Parson Austen's family. Mr. James had taken to dancing again after a decent interval of mourning and was to be observed dawdling absent-mindedly through the country dances or leaning against the wall, tall and dark, with an air of interesting melancholy, in his white neckcloth, square-toed shoes and black clerical clothes. The livelier young ladies complained that James was always going wrong in the figure, because he was thinking about something else. He would go down two dances with you and never speak of anything but the crops or the weather ; but their mothers told each other hopefully that he would not have come to the Assemblies again if he had not been on the look out for a second wife. " He must need a mother for his little girl. A clergyman should be married, he needs an active sort of young woman who will look after his house and his parish. He is afraid of strangers and is very shy and bookish, a girl would need to try very hard for him. I should not wonder if that Miss Mary Lloyd were not setting her cap at him. She is an old friend of the family and she was at the Rectory for a long visit this summer. I am sure she would have him if she could " ; but another lady, better informed, declared, " He is pining for his cousin, the French Countess ; he is no use to anybody here."

" Miss Cassandra looks very well tonight," a Basingstoke lady said. " I approve that white gown of hers with the green trimmings. She is very handsome, is she not ? " " She is rather too stiff and cold," maintained a jealous young lady. " She is about five times as pretty as any other girl in the room," declared her blunt naval brother, home from sea. " None of the rest of you can hold a candle to her." He gazed at the sweet and lovely Cassandra, gliding about so gracefully in perfect time and his face fell when his sisters told him hastily that she was promised. " To Miss Lloyd's cousin, Mr. Fowle, who has lately taken orders." " A parson ! " exclaimed the young sailor. " What a waste of such a beauty, to pen her up in a country parish. She is the handsomest creature in the world; I never saw such fine eyes, not even among the Spanish ladies. Are you certain she is engaged to him ? " " Of course we are sure," his mother said. " Mrs. Austen told me about it herself. He offered for her this summer and was accepted, only the engagement is not to be talked about yet. There is no money on either side and the young people must wait until Mr. Fowle can get a living." " Aye, we all know how that

91

will end," added another mother of plain daughters. " They
will wait a twelvemonth, or maybe two, and then they will
settle down to a curacy, with what help her father can give
her. Then they will have a child every year, as the clergy
always do and Lord ! how poor they will be. I am quite
sorry for Miss Cassandra, I hoped she might have done better
for herself." " Oh ! she is a sweet girl, very handsome and
good-humoured, I daresay, but her face is her fortune, as
the saying is. Parson Austen has two small livings and no
private means. He has had to take pupils to make ends
meet and farm his own glebe and he has a long family to
put out in the world. There is Mr. James a poor curate,
Mr. Frank only just made lieutenant and the other little
sailor brother no more than a midshipman yet ; and Mr.
Henry is but a militia captain. They have a rich uncle and
aunt in Bath to be sure, who are childless and may leave
something to the girls, and the second boy had the luck to
be adopted by those rich cousins in Kent ; but take it by
and large the Austens are poor as church mice, for all they
hold their heads so high and come of an old family. The
girls may be pretty and taking, but you need more than a
light foot and a quick tongue to catch a husband nowadays.
To my mind Miss Cassandra has done well to take the first
man that offered for her. She might have gone further and
fared worse. She is too quiet for my taste. Miss Jane is
much more attractive to gentlemen."

Then they began to pick Jane to pieces. She was in very
good looks that night, and drew all eyes with her dancing.
Nobody flew so fast down the middle, or swung and spun
so gaily as Parson Austen's younger daughter, in the new
white gown which she had copied from Cousin Eliza's
pattern. Everybody was watching the light-footed graceful
girl ; with her flushed cheeks and her brilliant sparkling
eyes she was the most admired creature in the room. " I
should be ashamed to come to an Assembly in such plain
muslin," sneered a young lady in puce pink with blue
ribbons. " I fancy she must have made it herself ; only
look, it has no trimming at all. Poor thing ! I suppose she
could afford nothing better. The men will all laugh at her."

" The men never know what one has on," sighed a Miss Terry from Dummer. " Miss Jane does not want for partners, she has not sat out a single dance tonight. She has a very pretty taking way with her and makes all the men laugh."

" She runs on in a very foolish way," her mother said sharply. " She gives her opinions too decidedly. She told me to my face the other day that I was talking nonsense when I was only repeating something that I had read in the newspapers, about the Revolution in Paris, I believe it was, or this new expedition to the West Indies. She is very clever, I daresay, and knows about politics, but she should not be in such a hurry to instruct her elders."

" She is always teasing the young men and laughing at them," Miss Terry said enviously. " I should not dare to quiz them to their faces as she does." " They do not like it, my dear, they do not care to be interrupted ; depend upon it, they would rather have a girl listen to them quietly and politely, as I hope you always do." " But they *do* like it," the young lady complained. " Miss Jane is always surrounded by gentlemen, she can pick and choose. She turned up her nose at young Mr. Lyford, the doctor's son, though he followed her all round the ballroom she would not dance with him ; and the other day she said that one of the officers was so dreadfully dull, she had rather sit down two dances than stand up with him." " She had better make the most of her chances while she is young and fresh," declared old Mrs. Terry, awfully nodding her head with its tower of crimson nodding plumes. " She should take her wares to market early, or she may be left an old maid and have to go for a governess ; and you know there's nothing worse than that. I have heard tell of better than Miss Jane that went through the wood and were glad to pick up a crooked stick at the last."

" She has got a new beau this evening, at any rate, who is quite the finest young man in the room," said the daughter wilfully and they all turned to look at Miss Jane's Irish partner. " Bless me ! what a good looking creature he is," exclaimed jolly Mrs. Harwood from Deane. " I wish they may make a match of it. I hear the young gentleman is very well worth catching. His father has a pretty estate near Limerick and he is the eldest son and heir. Miss Jane would be very lucky if she could fix him. I daresay Madam Lefroy has asked him over with that very thing in mind. Miss Jane was always her favourite." "The Irish are all fortune-hunters," declared old Mrs. Terry. "They come over here to make what they can by gaming and are all on the catch for heiresses; Bath is full of them, I assure you. Miss Jane had better mind what she is about. I daresay this great house of his father's that we hear so much about, is little more than a cabin in a bog, if the truth were known."

"Jane is welcome to Mr. Lefroy if she can get him," put in one of the Harwood girls, tossing her head. "He is a very proud ill-tempered disagreeable young man to my mind. He has been walking here and there about the room all evening, looking as if none of us were handsome enough to tempt him. He sat by my aunt for ten minutes and never opened his lips, and when she asked him if he did not think it was a very cold night he seemed quite vexed to be spoken to. She said he never took his eyes off Jane when she was dancing with my brother Earle."

"They have plenty to say to each other," observed Catherine Bigg-Wither. "I watched them as they went down the dance together and they were quite wrapped up in each other. They hardly spoke to anybody else. Then she danced the *Boulangère* with William Heathcote, who had stood up with my sister Elizabeth, but she took good care to stand next to Mr. Lefroy. Now the pair of them are dancing together again. Jane will get herself excessively laughed at about him if she behaves so." "A young lady should not dance with a young gentleman more than twice in one evening," said Miss Terry severely. "It is not at all the thing. I would not do it myself for anything." "You will not get the chance, my dear," remarked Alethea Bigg-Wither. "The Lefroys' Irishman has eyes for nobody but Jane tonight. He keeps staring at her as if he had never seen anything like her." "I should think he is astonished by the way she has done her hair," said little Lucy Lefroy

94

with a schoolgirl giggle. " She has cut half of it off and done the rest in little curls all round her forehead. I never saw anything so *outré* in my life, though to be sure it is not unbecoming. When the dance is over I shall ask her whether it is an Irish fashion. Do you think she will blush ? " And all these slighted young ladies gazed enviously at Jane and her partner. The dance was just coming to an end, and the tall young man and the slender laughing girl were stretching up their arms to make an arch for all the running couples to duck under, before the figure broke up and they all streamed away. " There's a sight to warm your heart," sighed fat good-natured Mrs. Harwood, fanning herself. " It does my old eyes good watch at such a handsome couple. I never saw a brighter pair of eyes than Jane's in all my life."

" She is a little too lively," whispered sour Mrs. Terry, " and not so well brought-up as she should be. She is always scampering about the country, up to her ankles in dirt. When I was driving into Basingstoke the other day she jumped over a stile into Popham Lane, with her hair all blown about and her petticoat inches deep in mud. She was taking a walk all by herself. Her mother should not let her do it. There is a sort of conceited independence about that girl which does not please me. She is as easy with all the young men as if they were her brothers. It will not do ; I am sure it will not do. She will get herself into some trouble one of these days."

And the last word came from Mrs. Mitford, the doctor's wife from Alresford. She had left the neighbourhood, but she was back again on a visit. Everybody in the room knew her, she had lived at Ashe Rectory when she was a child, her father, old Doctor Russell, had been Rector there before Mr. Lefroy. " Are you speaking of Miss Jane Austen ? " she inquired, peering about eagerly. " Pray point her out to me, I have heard a great deal about her already. I have not seen her since she grew up, but the Austen girls were both at the Abbey School at Reading, where my girl Mary now is. So that is Miss Jane ; well, a prettier, sillier, more affected husband-hunting butterfly I never saw in my life."

6

So the dance went on. They moved in to supper and came out again, the chalk dust flew up from the floor, the music went faster and faster. The young men in their coloured coats stamped out the time, ducked down their heads and kicked up their heels ; they swung the girls round till the wind from their muslin skirts made the candles flicker and their sandalled feet almost left the ground. Soon everybody began to sing the words of the country tunes. The ramping tune of *The Morning Dew* was a favourite. " *My father bought at great expense A handsome dappled grey. But when he puts her at a fence She backs and backs away.*" So somebody with a good voice would give out the verse and then everybody would join in the chorus. " *Heigh ho ! the morning dew. Heigh ho ! the rose and rue. Come, follow, follow me, young men For I'll not follow you.*" Then the tune would change and they would get, *Oh ! dear, what can the matter be ?* and *Come, lasses and lads,* and " *A-hunting we will go* " to vary the endless repetitions of *Oranges and Lemons, The Triumph* and *Sir Roger de Coverley.* Somebody would have smuggled in a hunting horn and would begin to sound *Gone Away,* and they would gallop faster and faster till the musicians laid down their instruments and would play no more, for all the clapping and stamping. Everybody would stand up and sing *God Save the King* for silly old Farmer George ; and that would be the end.

Then the girls would be wrapped up in shawls like precious packages, and bundled into the carriages and they would all drive back through the moonlit frosty lanes. At Manydown the young ladies climbed the great staircase, footsore and fatigued, but too happily restless for sleep. They ran in and out of each other's bedrooms, brushed out their curls by the bright wood fires, compared the steps and compliments of their partners, teased each other about these young gentlemen and secretly wondered which of them would ride over next day to inquire how their partners did after the fatigues of the ball. Catherine yawned, Alethea rubbed her eyes, Cassandra sighed for Tom Fowle and wondered where he was. Elizabeth pondered the merits of her two admirers ; and Jane stretched her slender arms and cried, " How soon a ball is past and done with ! I wish it could all come over again."

7

The handsome young Irishman was always in and out of Steventon Parsonage in that December, 1795, when Jane was just twenty-one. He rode over most mornings, a fine figure on a good horse ; sometimes Mrs. Lefroy or her girl Lucy came with him, more often he came alone to borrow a book, to try over some music, to engage Miss Jane for the first two dances at the ball which the Bigg-Withers were giving in January at Manydown. He was free of the girls' dressing parlour and came there to talk or to make music. He had been astonished to find that the Austen girls did not ride and had expected to meet them in the hunting-field. In Ireland, it appeared, everybody rode as a matter of course. " There has never been any money to spare for that in our house," said Jane, who had no false shame about their poverty. " But next time the Vine meet on this side of the country Cassy and I will walk up in our pattens to Deane Gate and see how you take your fences." If he could not ride with Jane he could sing duets with her. He had a very agreeable tenor voice, musical in speech as in singing, as soft as Irish weather ; she had a pretty light untrained soprano and played the pianoforte with delicate precision. *How Sweet in the Woodlands*, they tried, a hunting song which pleased and amused him ; then Jane warbled *Ask if the damask rose be sweet*, a pretty melody from Mr. Handel's admired oratorio, *Susannah*. She had another lament, *How gentle was my Damon's air*, and songs by Arne and Dibdin which suited her voice. They went through a book of canzonets for two voices by Mr. Jackson of Exeter ; then turned to livelier Scotch and Irish

airs. "*I hae laid a herring in saut,*" sang Jane merrily and
The Yellow-haired Laddie and *Robin Adair*. That was
the Irishman's favourite, he was always asking for it, and
Jane would sing it obediently, while he sat and watched her.
Cassandra, stitching away unheeded in the window seat at
a flannel petticoat for one of her old village women, kept
her eyes demurely on her work, but still noted how earnestly
the stranger looked at her sister. "*What's this dull town
to me?*" sang Jane, too gaily for the plaintive words. She
laughed in the young man's serious face, cried out, "That's
too sad a tune for a fine winter's morning," and began to
rattle off the racing jig called *The Irish Washerwoman*, just
to plague him. They read, they talked, they played and
sang, they were always sparring. She rallied him unmerci-
fully about his singing, about a white coat he had, about
the manners and customs of the Irish. Gentle Cassandra
sometimes thought that she teased him more than was
prudent ; she had learnt Eliza's lesson of coquetry too well,
she would frighten him away with her sharp tongue. He
seemed a reluctant lover, unwilling to come, unable to keep
away. Cassandra wondered what held him back. She spoke
of the matter timidly to Jane, but her sister only answered
lightly, " I must fight with what weapons I have."

Mr. Austen in his library never noticed who came or
went, Mrs. Austen was too busy in kitchen and dairy to
trouble herself much about her daughters. She said in
answer to some anxious remark of Cassandra's, " I daresay
the young man does spend a good deal of time here, but it
must be dull for him up at Ashe Parsonage. They have
books and a billiard room, to be sure, but gentlemen cannot
always be indoors. I suppose he finds it more amusing to
come down here and try over music with Jane. So long as
you are there with them I cannot see that it signifies."

Then Mrs. Lefroy grew disturbed. One or two neighbours
spoke to her with nods and winks about the young people,
and one day fat jolly Mrs. Harwood, the most tactless
woman in Hampshire, openly asked Mr. Lefroy whether
she might wish him joy on his engagement to Miss Jane
Austen. He turned very red, drew up his handsome head,

said stiffly, " I can't tell what you would be at, ma'am," and walked out of the room. Mrs. Lefroy said to Mrs. Harwood anxiously, " I beg you will not talk so, madam ; there is no engagement between them, I am sure there is not," and Mrs. Harwood was greatly surprised. " I would not have teased him about it for the world, but you know young people like to be laughed at about their lovers. They have eyes for nobody but each other and I certainly thought the matter was settled by this time. " Mrs. Lefroy insisted, " Pray do not talk of it. The less said about such things the better."

A good deal troubled, she drove down in her pony carriage to Steventon Parsonage next day and by good luck found Jane alone in the dressing parlour, sitting at her tambour frame. She gave Mrs. Lefroy the opening she needed by asking immediately, " Have you not brought my Irish friend with you ? Did he not know you were coming ? "

Mrs. Lefroy sat down in the window seat, untied her bonnet strings, put back her furred driving cloak and sailed straight into battle. " To tell you the truth, my dear, I did not ask him. I fancy he comes here a little too often." It was said in the friendliest way, but it made the girl's colour rise and her eyes sparkle. " He comes to please himself," said she, " I do not press him. I am no husband-hunter."

" No, my dear, I am sure you do not, but people are beginning to laugh at the pair of you. I am sure you are too sensible to be offended with me if I speak plainly. You should be a little more on your guard and not encourage my nephew too far. He is not in a position to make an imprudent match." She watched narrowly, but Jane's needle did not hasten or delay in its passage through the taut silk. The girl stretched her slender hand beneath the frame, pricked her needle through to meet it and said dryly, " If I am his choice, why may he not tell me so ? He is a gentleman, I am a gentleman's daughter ; there is no disgrace in that, surely ? " " He cannot marry simply to please himself," said Mrs. Lefroy ; Jane replied calmly, " Then I am sorry for him." Mrs. Lefroy struggled on, feeling very uncomfortable. " The Lefroys are a very good family, but they are not so rich as people would have you believe. My husband's brother, Colonel Lefroy, has a long family to provide for. Tom is the eldest son and will inherit the property, in due course, but he has his way to make and marriage for him must be at a very uncertain distance, unless he can find a girl with a good portion of her own. His father and mother would not wish him to leave his heart behind in England." She forced an unwilling smile, which faded as the girl looked up at her. " You mean they would not thank him for bringing them back a poor parson's daughter with nothing in her pocket," said Jane.

Mrs. Lefroy murmured, " Do not be vexed with me ; I only want to give you a word of warning." " You should have put a label on your nephew," retorted Jane, " *Do not touch*, for fear he should get damaged among us here in England." She took another stitch and said dryly, "Well, he shall be safe from me. I will not break his heart, I will hand it back to him with a curtsey and tell him I have no use for it. Is that what you want me to say ? "

Mrs. Lefroy replied very sweetly, " I want you to assure me that he has not done any damage to your own heart. That is what matters to me." She got a swift flashing look which she could not interpret. " My heart does not signify, does it ? He may break that if he chooses and nobody will think one penny the worse of him." " I should be very grieved, my dear," said Mrs. Lefroy earnestly.

Jane did not reply until she had taken another two or three careful stitches. Then she said lightly, " Well, I believe I may promise you not to find him too charming. He is certainly the most handsome and agreeable creature that I have yet met, but I daresay there are as good fish in the sea as ever came out of it. He may go back to Ireland for all I care, and marry the greatest heiress his family can find for him. It really does not matter to me." Mrs. Lefroy got no more out of her than that, and went away feeling much troubled. She could not make up her mind whether she had done well or ill in speaking to Jane.

8

Cassandra had had other anxieties that autumn to disturb her quiet mind. General Abercromby's belated West Indian expedition had sailed at last in mid-November. On the high Downs in the Isle of Wight and the hills above Weymouth thousands had gathered to watch the lovely sight of the convoy standing down Channel, with a light breeze and every stitch of canvas set. The ships looked like white towers out at sea ; but a winter gale, springing up in a night, drove half of them ashore on the Chesil Beach beyond Portland Bill. Many soldiers and sailors were drowned in that disaster and for some days Cassandra did not know whether her love had not been among them ; but in the end she heard that General Whyte's command, the ships for Santo Domingo itself, had been safe in Cork Harbour. The convoy was reformed at Falmouth and sailed in February for Barbadoes.

Kind Mrs. Fowle invited her to spend Christmas at Kintbury and see the New Year in with them and she was glad enough to go. She had little heart for the gaieties of her own neighbourhood, where people were dancing through the festive season and giving little thought to the war.

At Kintbury it was quiet and pleasant, though there was not much to do. Mary Lloyd was there as well, on a visit to her elder sister, but the three ladies could not walk in their thin shoes in the water-meadows, where the frost had bleached the grey reeds and stripped the last leaves from the willows, and a bitter wind was making the ripples run the wrong way against the leaden stream. After they had decorated the church with ivy and holly, eaten their Christmas turkey and mince-pies and seen the Rector ride out early to a Boxing Day meet, they were glad to spend their mornings indoors by the fire, while Mrs. Fowle mended the children's clothes, Mary trimmed one of her preposterous bonnets and Cassandra embroidered a trail of leaves round the hem of a muslin gown, which might some day serve for her wedding. " I am afraid it is very dull for you here, my dears," Mrs. Fowle apologised. " You must wish yourselves at Steventon, where there is so much going on." Mary did look a little glum, but Cassandra could say with all her heart, " I am thankful to be away. I had rather sit here with you and talk about dear Tom."

She used to read Jane's letters aloud to them to amuse them. One exquisitely written sheet arrived on her birthday, the ninth of January, wishing her another twenty-three years of happiness and sending her all manner of lively gossip about the doings at home. There had been an exceedingly good ball at the Harwoods, which James had graced with his presence, everyone had spoken of the great improvement which had lately taken place in the widower's dancing. " James used not to care much for balls," complained Mary, with her little plain face all puckered up in lines of jealousy and suspicion. " He used to say that it was not a rational way of spending an evening ; indeed, he was not sure whether a clergyman ought to dance at all." " Jane says a ball is nothing without him this year," reported Cassandra, turning the page. " And Elizabeth and William Heathcote danced together twice. They seemed to be very *particular* ; indeed, it begins to look like a match." " It would please both families," said Mary jealously. " Elizabeth has money and he has family, if his elder brother were to die, Elizabeth would be a baronet's lady." She sounded quite wistful. " And does Jane say how many times *she* danced with this Irish beau of hers ? "

Cassandra turned the letter over, but did not read aloud the sentence which ran, " You scold me so much in the nice long letter I have this moment received from you that I am almost ashamed to tell you how my Irish friend and I behaved. Imagine to yourself everything profligate and shocking in the way of dancing and sitting down together." She reported discreetly, " Jane says he is so excessively laughed at about her at Ashe that he is ashamed of coming down to Steventon any more. He even ran away when she and my mother called there the other day." " I daresay he begins to draw off a little," said Mary eagerly, she never liked to hear of another girl's success.

Mrs. Fowle wanted to hear more, but Cassandra would only say that Mr. Lefroy was a very handsome gentlemanlike young man and had paid a good deal of court to Jane, but that she feared his intentions were not serious. " I hope he will not break my poor Jane's heart for her," said Mrs. Fowle. " Oh ! it is only another of Jane's flirtations," Mary decided. " She has a great many, you know." " I should like to see her well settled," declared Mrs. Fowle. " She has passed her twenty-first birthday, it is time she began to think of making her choice. She should not waste too much time with agreeable idle young men." Cassandra too confessed her anxiety. " But he is to leave the country after next Friday," said she, " as soon as they have had their ball at Ashe Parsonage." " My dear, they cannot surely have a ball in that little parlour. There would not be room to turn round." " Oh ! it was all settled before I came away. Jane and young Mr. Lefroy were talking of it all one morning, walking about and measuring the rooms. It is not a real ball, of course, that is only Jane's nonsense ; they will not have more than ten couples, I believe. You know the two parlours are exactly opposite each other ; they will take up the carpets and lift the doors off their hinges and dance across the passage." " It all sounds very mean and disagreeable, I am glad I was not asked," said Mary crossly. " A crowd in a little room, I should not enjoy it at all. I suppose Mr. Lefroy will be turned out of his study for a week and have nowhere to write a sermon and Mrs. Lefroy will have to play reels and country dances for the company the whole evening. Poor woman ! she will be quite worn out." But Cassandra said, " No ; there are to be a harp and two fiddles hired from Basingstoke and a proper sit-down supper, none of your cold collations on the sideboard. Cousin Edward Cooper and my father's old pupil, Mr. Buller, are to stay at Steventon for the night and they are taking John Lyford and his sister as well as James, so Jane will have no lack of escorts. She has spent all her money on white gloves and silk stockings and has made herself a new gown of rose-pink Persian silk which suits her to distraction. She says she rather hopes to receive an offer from her Irish friend in the course of the evening, but that I think is only some more of her nonsense. She sends you her love, Mary, and offers to make over all her other admirers to you, Mr. Hartley and Charles Powlett and the rest wherever you can find them ; for she intends in future to confine herself entirely to Mr. Lefroy for whom she doesn't care sixpence. I really cannot make Jane out, I never know whether she is serious or not." Mary primmed up her lips, threaded her needle with care and said, " Thank you for nothing. I hope I can find a smart beau for myself when I need one, without chasing Jane's cast-offs. I wish her Irishman may not leave her in the lurch."

They kept going back to her ; the old married woman, the perplexed and loving sister, the jealous friend could not keep from talking about her. She had something in her which drew all eyes and set all tongues wagging. " I wish she were happily settled," Cassandra said. " Sometimes I feel afraid when I think what may become of her."

9

Miss Sukey Lyford, the doctor's daughter from Basingstoke, was quite alarmed when she was told that she and her brother John were to dine and sleep at Steventon Parsonage on the night of Mrs. Lefroy's dance ; however, such a compliment from old patients of her father's was not to be refused. Brother and sister made themselves as smart as they could. Miss Sukey, sturdy as a young tree, wore her blue sprigged muslin, with thread mittens and new roses on her stout black shoes and borrowed her mother's great cameo brooch. John, an oafish youth, lately apprenticed to his father, had a bright green coat and a choking neck-cloth and smelt a little of rhubarb and brimstone, for he had been compounding pills all afternoon in the surgery.

At dinner they were both very shy. Miss Sukey sat beside dear old Mr. Austen, who paid her many compliments ;

John fell to Mrs. Austen, who talked to him about her sciatica as if he had been his father. The beautiful Miss Cassandra was away, but Miss Jane quite eclipsed the doctor's daughter with her rose-pink gown and her witty tongue. The three young men, Cousin Edward Cooper, Mr. Buller and John Lyford, could not take their eyes off her, she was so gay and wild. She quite frightened Sukey.

At the dance it was the same, Miss Jane had all the best partners to choose from. Miss Sukey looked everywhere for the Irishman of whom she had heard so much. He was easily found, tall, handsome, dark, unsmiling; little Sukey thought him quite alarming. She felt she would have sunk if he had asked her to dance, but of course there was no hope of that. Miss Jane and he led off the first country dance and Miss Jane called the figures; the others advanced and retreated, passed back to back, swung round and bowed all down the set. Poor Sukey got Mr. James Austen for her first partner, which was very dreary. Then she had young Mr. Cooper and after him John Harwood and then Mr. Buller; all parsons, and she did so love a red coat! It was quite disappointing; however, Mr. Earle Harwood, who was an officer in the Marines, took her in to supper and though he was supposed to be rather wild was very civil and amusing.

There were not quite enough young men to go round, and after supper the poor child sat out several dances. She did not like that at all. Left by herself in the empty brightly lit parlour, listening to the music in the other room, she felt quite lonely and wished herself at home. Then she saw the faded red damask curtains at the other end of the room stir gently in the draught. Somebody had opened the window, somebody was standing there looking out on the garden, hoary with winter moonshine, on the great yew hedge as high as the house. She heard a murmur of voices, then the curtains parted and out came Miss Jane and her Irish friend.

They walked towards her, not speaking to each other. Miss Sukey fixed her eyes on the floor and wished herself anywhere else. Miss Jane passed her, turned and came back, saying in a gentle voice, " Are you not dancing, child ? "

Miss Sukey shook her head, she blushed very red and tears came into her eyes. " Then if you have no partner," said Miss Jane, " perhaps you will honour Mr. Lefroy. I shall not dance again, I believe I have hurt my foot a little." The stranger bowed and Sukey thought that he looked exceedingly angry, but she could not do anything except rise and put her hand on his arm. They finished the dance together, but he hardly spoke, and she was glad when it was over. Miss Jane had gone to sit by Mrs. Lefroy and she and her Irish friend did not dance together again that evening. Indeed they always seemed at opposite ends of the room.

The Steventon party were the last to leave. They were forced to wait for their carriage, while everybody yawned and only Miss Jane found anything much to say. Mr. James Austen said to the Irishman, " I believe your visit is over," and Mrs. Lefroy said, " Yes, it is scarcely worth the poor fellow's going to bed. He has to get away by the early coach from Deane Gate." Edward Cooper uttered some polite hope of their meeting again and the stranger replied stiffly, " I do not expect to come back at all." There was an akward pause, because his tone had been so unexpectedly harsh and cold. He looked at nobody. Mrs. Lefroy murmured, " You know you are always welcome here " ; but Miss Jane said coolly, " Oh ! he will be much too busy to come back to Hampshire for a very long time. He has a great future before him. When we see him again he will have become a very important and terrifying personage. Very likely he will be Lord Chief Justice of Ireland." She gave him her slender hand, but she did not look at him. The carriage drove up with a roll of wheels and a flash of lamps and they bundled in and went back down the moonlit valley to Steventon. It was very late and they were all tired out, even Miss Jane said nothing all the way home.

10

By the time that Cassandra came home again everybody in the neighbourhood had well talked the matter over, but nobody could decide whether Jane had jilted her Irishman or whether he had disappointed her. Mrs. Harwood sighed, " I am very sorry the match went off, it would have been an excellent thing for the young lady." Mrs. Lefroy, with tears in her eyes, lamented, " I wish my husband had never asked his nephew to come over. I would not have had this happen for worlds. It is a sad business." Her daughters complained, " Jane is as cross as two sticks, she will not talk about him at all, but I daresay she would not have cared for living in Ireland. I believe it is a very strange country." Miss Catherine Bigg-Wither said, " Jane showed her feelings much too plainly," and Alethea declared, " I shall always say he has treated poor Jane abominably ill." Old Mrs. Terry told her daughter, " You see, my dear, Miss Jane did not *fix* him, for all her affected airs. I suppose there was not money enough in the case for such an ambitious young fellow " ; and little Sukey Lyford, quite distressed, feared Miss Jane's heart must be quite broken. Her brother grumbled, " Perhaps she will not be quite so hard to please in future." He was always vexed that he could not get Miss Jane to dance with him at the Assemblies. James Austen persisted, " I am glad it came to nothing. I never could like Tom Lefroy myself," and Mrs. Austen said to Cassandra, " Well, my dear, it seems Jane has had a disappointment, but I tell her she must be sensible and not waste her time moping and sighing. There's no use crying over spilt milk."

Cassandra could not get anything at first out of her sister. Even when they were together up in the dressing parlour, Jane would only tinkle away at the piano and make fun of herself. " Yes, I am crossed in love, or so all my dear friends tell me. I am an object of pity, I must pine and weep and grow thin, if I can ; and another time I must not look so high. I have made a great fool of myself, I have fallen in love with Tom Lefroy and now he will not have me after all." " I thought him very much in love with you before I went away," Cassandra ventured. " Oh ! it was a most promising inclination," Jane agreed dryly. " I never had anybody so warmly attached to me before. Indeed, I believe he might have taken me if I had only been richer, but then you see it turned out that we were all as poor as church mice up at Steventon, so how could my friend offer for me ? He is not to marry to please himself. After all, the handsome young men must have something to live upon as well as the plain. His family have picked out two or three heiresses for him already, each with five or ten or fifteen thousand pounds in her pocket. They are all put by for him in a cupboard over in Ireland, and now that he has amused himself sufficiently here he may go home and take his choice among them."

She began to play and sing with mocking emphasis an air which she used to sing with Tom Lefroy. "*That Damon was in love with me, I once thought and believed ; But now that He is not, I see how much I was deceived.*" She struck a defiant chord and nodded at her sister. "Everyone is laughing at me," said she between her teeth, "and I daresay you are much amused yourself."

A tear dropped on Cassandra's sewing and she murmured, "I wish you would not talk so, you make me very unhappy." Jane jumped up, ran to Cassandra, flung slender arms round her neck and cried out, "Oh ! I am a wretch to plague you so. You have troubles enough of your own. Between your Tom and mine we are a sad pair ; but dry your eyes, your Tom will come back to you and as for mine, I have quite done with him. I shall not break my heart over him, I have had a tumble and now I must pick myself up again and go on. We will not talk about him any longer. The less said about such things the better and what good does talking ever do ? "

IV

Steventon

1796-1801

I

THE year 1796 was a long dragging year for Cassandra. She stitched her wedding clothes and helped her father in the parish, her mother about the house. Jane said to tease her, " You are practising to be a parson's wife," and that of course was true, but she liked to go among the poor people and fancy that she was doing it for Tom. The old folk who had known Miss Cassandra since she was a baby, knew her story too and never missed asking her if she had any news from that foreign country where her heart lay, but more often than not she had to shake her head, for Tom's letters came very slowly. A ship beating up from the islands often took two months to make the passage home, and then there were more delays while the mail coach brought the packets up to Popham Lane or Deane Gate, two miles away. Then the letters, when they reached her, were not the food for which her heart was starving. Tom spoke of his love for her and of their future plans, with many pious references to the scriptures and to that heavenly power which must some day reunite them ; but poor Cassandra wanted to hear what he did in that strange island, whether he got proper food to eat and how much sickness there was among the unhappy troops. There was very little news in the papers of that far-off forgotten war. The headlines were all about the French victories in Italy. The Directory had a new General down there, a young and brilliant Corsican, a man of destiny ; this summer was for most people the first time that they heard his fatal name, Napoleon Bonaparte, though well-informed people recollected that as a young Colonel of artillery he had raised our siege of Toulon.

His army was driving all across the plains of Lombardy like a forest fire, licking up and destroying everything in its path. Mondovi, Lodi, Arcola, the names of his battles rang out like chimes from brown Italian *Campanile*, and in Paris his elegant notorious wife was mobbed and cheered when she drove out in her carriage. She had been a widow of the guillotine, the Vicomtesse de Beauharnais and they said that the general's marriage to her had been the price which he had paid for his Italian command, but the Paris crowd admired her and called her Our Lady of Victories.

Mrs. Austen, that summer, spun her webs like a stout spider with better luck than she had done the year before. Cousin Eliza did not trouble them at the Rectory. She had gone down to Brighton for the sea bathing, but she did not invite either of Parson Austen's daughters to stay with her. Instead she took her old correspondent, the staid Cousin Philadelphia from Tonbridge, as an admiring bewildered companion and chaperon. Jane and Cassandra could well imagine Eliza sauntering along the Steyne in one of her transparent muslin gowns, holding a parasol between her clear skin and the bright dazzle on the water. She would wander in and out of the shops and the libraries or take little Hastings down to the shore, so that jolly old Martha Gunn, the famous bathing woman, who had dipped the Prince of Wales himself, might coax the nervous child into the warm ripples. Presently from among the crowd of dashing officers who came down from the camp, there would be half a dozen to stroll with Eliza up and down the pale crescents and terraces, carry her parasol and her reticule, escort her to the play, or dance with her at night after little Hastings was tucked up in bed.

With Eliza safely out of the way, Mrs. Austen invited Mary Lloyd to try her luck with the melancholy James. He was still full of disappointment and regret, but his mother did not despair of making him see that Mary might suit him as well or better than his frivolous cousin. Mary was neither rich nor handsome, but she was very sensible and good humoured. The whole family had long known and liked her. For James she had the charm of what is familiar and reliable, she would never shock or distress him as Eliza had so often done. Mary was exactly the daughter-in-law that Mrs. Austen wanted for her favourite son. She had been brought up by her thrifty Welsh mother to make a good show on small means and to get sixpenny-worth for every sixpence she laid out. She appeared fond of children and would keep a firm hand on little Anna, who was getting spoilt ; she was a good nurse and would be a real comfort to Mrs. Austen herself in her old age. The good lady was determined to make up the match and she succeeded, James proposed and Mary accepted him. He confessed to her that he had indeed asked Cousin Eliza to marry him during the previous summer, but she had refused him because she could not endure to be married to a clergyman. Mary pretended that she did not mind this, but it rankled in her mind always. To her dying day she never forgave Cousin Eliza for bewitching James.

Martha Lloyd did not visit the Austens that year either. She was at home at Ibthorp, with a lover of her own on her hands, a young officer, " a certain Mr. W." as she coyly called him in her letters to Mary. The girls at Steventon laughed about this and made a nickname of it ; but Mrs. Austen was rather vexed, for Elizabeth Bigg-Wither had married Mr. Heathcote that year, and now it began to look as if the Lloyd girls might get husbands before her own daughters. Rubbing her nose thoughtfully, she took up her quill pen and wrote a letter to Edward's wife in Kent and presently Jane was packed off to spend September at Rowling. Edward and Elizabeth were still living there ; because, although cousin Thomas Knight had died two years earlier and Edward had come into the estates, old Mrs. Knight was to have the use of Godmersham for her life. At Rowling Edward was surrounded by his wife's relations. Her brother and his family inhabited Goodnestone, a charming grey Palladian house among wooded slopes. Her mother, old Lady Bridges, lived at the dower house with three unmarried daughters, Louisa, sickly Marianna and little, laughing Harriet ; then there was another sister, a young widow, Mrs. Cage, and a nursery of grandchildren. There was plenty of coming and going between these three houses. Jane would have gaiety enough down there, races and reviews of volunteers at Canterbury, picnics and dancing at all the country houses round. With any luck she might well meet some pleasant Kentish gentleman who would put that tiresome Irishman out of her head.

So at least her mother hoped, but though Jane's letters were lively enough there was no hint in them of a lover. She talked of nothing but her brothers, how she and Elizabeth were making a new set of shirts for Edward, how Frank had come down to spend his leave and was appointed First Lieutenant to the *Triton*, a new 32-gun frigate just launched, under Captain John Gore. Frank was delighted about that and meanwhile was enjoying any simple amusement which was offered to him. He rode Edward's horses and walked out with him across the hot September stubbles, between them the brothers had killed a prodigious number of partridges. He used to work the big lathe with the estate carpenter and had turned a very nice butter churn for his little cousin Fanny. Everything pleased Fly ; he was a simple good-hearted youth, modest and well-mannered, full of lively stories about wrecks and naval engagements and the strange ports which he had visited in the East Indies. He laughed very much at his sister's ignorance of everything to do with the sea, but was delighted to instruct her. He vowed that he had rather dance with her than with any of the Kentish beauties. Mrs. Austen lost her temper fairly when she heard that and burst out to the shocked Cassandra, " Jane wastes too much time running about with her brothers. That is not the way to get herself a husband." Henry did not come to Steventon that summer at all. His regiment was stationed in Norwich and he was still paying his addresses, or so his family understood, to that same Miss Mary Pearson who was the daughter of an officer of Greenwich Hospital. She was reported to be a most intolerable flirt, a pretty, wicked-looking girl with bright black eyes, which pierced you through and through. She and Henry actually engaged themselves to one another for a short time and Miss Pearson was to have gone back with Jane to Steventon, but she changed her mind. Henry was jilted and when he got his leave he went down to Edward and Elizabeth, who were at Godmersham for October, for the pheasant shooting.

That autumn he took to dangling round his cousin Eliza once more. She had taken a furnished house for the winter in Manchester Street, to be near a doctor in whom she had great faith, who was to cure her little boy's fits. She wrote gaily to her admiring Cousin Phila that she had " quite a levée there each morning and a reasonable quantity of *beaux*, the present hard times considered," and Henry came with the rest to tell her his troubles. He looked pale, thin and lovelorn and talked about exchanging into a regiment which was going out to garrison the Cape of Good Hope ; but his fascinating cousin soon cheered him up again. Nobody could cure a broken heart so well as Eliza. Cousin Phila wrote back to tease her about Henry ; but she only replied gaily, " The preliminaries are so far from settled that I do not believe the parties will ever come together, not, however, that they have quarrelled, but one of them cannot bring her mind to give up dear liberty and dearer flirtation." A few months in London seemed to have convinced Eliza that she was not made for sober matrimony.

2

That autumn in London, 1796, everybody was sick and tired of the war, and the talk in Eliza's drawing-room was all of Lord Malmesbury's mission to Paris, to negotiate peace terms with the Directory. The envoy, however, was coldly received and kept waiting about in the ante-rooms of former Royal palaces by the insolent and careless ministers of the new régime, while news came in of more enemy victories every week. The English fleet had been obliged to quit Corsica, the Spaniards had declared war on us, and General Bonaparte had driven the Austrians back across the River Po, they were retreating fast through the first snows of winter into the Alpine passes. The old Empress of Russia,

Catherine the Great, who had long been a friend to England, had died of an apoplexy and her mad young son Paul, who succeeded her, was known to favour the French. Before Christmas Lord Malmesbury was home again, for the peace negotiations had been broken off in a hurry at only two days' notice. The French had long been preparing a naval expedition against Ireland, and it sailed on Christmas Eve, slipping out from Brest in a thick snow-storm. It actually got into Bantry Bay, but there it was stormbound for a week ; General Hoche lost half his ships and had to give up the attempt. There was another landing made afterwards in February at the little deep harbour of Fishguard, the only place where ships could approach the rockbound Pembroke-shire coast, but that was equally unlucky for the French. They were easily overpowered and the regular troops arrived just in time to stop the Welsh country folk cutting their throats, but it had been an anxious week. Up in London there was an alarming run on the Bank of England, until a proclamation from the Privy Council stopped pay-ment. The country banks all did the same, and there was great uneasiness everywhere.

In that cold anxious time James rode over to Ibthorp to claim his promised bride. The Lloyds' house was right up the Bourne Valley above Whitchurch and the water-cress beds of Saint Mary Bourne, a raspberry-pink brick house with a garden sloping down to the road and the brook. In the summer at Ibthorp the meadows were a sea of grass, with cattle grazing by the stream and bubbling channels of water running here and there under the buttercups, but in the winter the floods came right over the road. The wedding party had to drive through a foot of water to get down to Hurstbourne Tarrant church. It was a queer little flint building, very old, with a witch's hat of a wooden belfry on top of its tower ; the parson's family, the Debaries, were the Lloyds' chief friends, and there, at the end of January, after much hesitation, James was married at last to Mary Lloyd.

While James was on this cold wedding journey his little daughter Anna went to stay at Steventon Parsonage. She was a stout brown-eyed child with chestnut curls all over her head, a long muslin gown and a sash tied up under her armpits. She was devoted to her aunts and loved to sit with them in their dressing parlour in the mornings, when Mrs. Austen and the maids wanted her out of the way. She knew each flower in the chocolate-coloured carpet, each slender leg of the mahogany chairs and tables, and would sit quietly on the floor for an hour at a time, dressing her doll, playing with the scattered beads of an old necklace or teasing her kitten, while up above her head the aunts went on talking together. Aunt Jane's voice was light and clear like water running over stones, Aunt Cassandra's was like the gentle murmur of a brooding dove, and when they burst out laughing together it was like a chime of pretty bells. When Anna wanted to share the joke they said that Aunt Jane was writing a story. She had begun it in October, after she came back from staying with Uncle Edward, and now it was more than half done. It would not amuse Anna, they said ; it was not like one of the fairy stories which she loved to hear, *Goody Two Shoes* or *Red Riding Hood*. It was perhaps a little like *Cinderella*, Aunt Jane confessed. There was a poor girl in it, indeed there were two, who were unkindly treated by a pair of ugly sisters, but each got her fairy prince in the end ; and there was a horrid old woman called Lady de Burgh and a funny clergyman, whose name was Collins. It was to be called *First Impressions*. Anna learnt these names before her aunts realised it, for she was at the age when children pick up words as pigeons pick up peas.

One day when she was downstairs in the parlour she heard her Grandmother Austen talking to her Grandmother Mathew about somebody called Elizabeth. That was the name of Uncle Edward's wife and of Mrs. Fowle, but it was also the name of the girl in Aunt Jane's book and it set Anna off into fits of laughter, pointing her curled pink finger at Grandmother Mathew and calling out, " Lady Catherine, Lady Catherine." " What is that child talking about ? " Lady Mathew demanded crossly. The two aunts looked at each other and Cassandra held up a warning finger, but Anna danced away and began jumping up and down, chanting the hero's name, " Mr. Darcy," over and over. Aunt Jane pounced on Anna, swept her up into her arms and fairly ran with her out of the room, while her grandfather was left polishing his glasses and inquiring mildly, " Pray, who is Mr. Darcy ? We have nobody of that name in this part of the world."

Afterwards Aunt Cassy explained very carefully to Anna that she must not talk about Aunt Jane's story downstairs until it was finished. It was a great secret, a surprise for Grandpapa on his birthday, if it was finished in time. Anna understood perfectly, she nodded her little dark head and pursed up her lips so that no word should escape them. She was very fond of her aunts and she cried when her father came back and she had to go home again. Her grandmothers had promised her that she was to have a new mother. She could faintly remember her own, a slender lady dressed in white who lay upon a sofa, and she expected something of the same sort. She was dreadfully disappointed when it only turned out to be Aunt Mary Lloyd after all.

3

Spring came in slowly that year, 1797, and the frost continued late into February. Jane was kept indoors with a heavy cold and Cassandra walked by herself day after day through the barren fields. A thin piping wind whistled through the bare hedge beside her and sometimes an old hare, disturbed by her approach, would limp away across the frozen stubble. The sky was dark and heavy with unfallen snow. She tried to think about her dear love, who was to come back to her in the spring ; but the dragging weight of her sick longing for him was almost more than she could endure. It quite frightened her to discover that she could no longer remember clearly what he looked like, or how his voice sounded when he spoke to her. Once she stood still in the middle of the open field and pressed her two hands together in anguish ; she said aloud, " Oh ! my darling, where are you ? " as if he could hear her.

At the end of February she dreamt of him suddenly and alarmingly for three nights together ; he was lying sick in a dark hot room, tossing and turning, crying out her name. It was a dreadful dream, she started up crying herself and woke Jane, who kissed and comforted her. Mr. Austen preached patience, her mother complained of her pale looks and would not attend when she repeated that she was sure something had happened to Tom. Then after a few days a bunch of delayed letters came in together. They had been written before Christmas, to be sure, but they sounded cheerful enough. The fighting had died down where Tom was. General Abercromby had gone off with an armed expedition to attack the island of Trinidad, but Lord Craven's regiment had not been ordered to go with him. It seemed almost certain that they would come home again in May and then Tom and Cassandra could get married and live happily ever after. Jane cried and kissed Cassandra, her father, smiling, praised her patience and constancy. Her mother said tartly, " There, you see, you were wrong to be so anxious about Tom. Now you had better hurry and finish your wedding clothes, there is your dress still to be thought of ; nothing has been settled about that." Eliza had offered a length of satin and a visit to the London shops, but Cassandra wanted no finery. She had to be a poor man's wife. She bought a fine India muslin in Basingstoke and sat down to embroider it herself, with wreaths of leaves and flowers. Jane put aside her novel to help her with it. Nobody worked so neatly or with such small stitches as Jane.

The skies changed and grew soft, the wind blew from the west, a fair wind for a ship homeward bound. Lambs bleated under the apple-blossom in the orchard, primroses and violets came out in the hedgerows and Jane and she decked the church with them for Easter. All through that April weather Cassandra went about in a vague dream, light and cheerful, as if she walked on clouds. She had a strange feeling that her dear love was quite close to her, that he was completely happy and that quite soon she would see him. She could almost imagine that she heard his voice. There were no more letters, but she did not expect them. Tom must be at sea already, sailing home through the warm tropic nights, under the enormous stars ; perhaps by this time he had already sighted the Azores. She put the last stitches into her wedding gown and laid it away in lavender, in the bottom drawer of her mahogany chest ; she went up to the church every day to pray by herself for his safe return. When she came back again she was always quiet and contented, until the day came which she would have to remember for the rest of her life.

On that April morning she walked into the cool house out of the spring sunshine and heard them all talking in the parlour with the door open. Her father said, " I was afraid of this " ; her mother, " He should never have gone to that dreadful place " ; and then she heard Jane say, " Oh ! God, how will Cassandra bear it ? " She pushed the door wide open and walked in, but she knew before they spoke, when she saw their three loved faces turned towards her, the news which they could not utter. Even before he went away she had cried out to Tom that if he went to that fever-stricken island he would never come home. She said steadily, " Tell me what has happened," but nobody answered her, only she saw tears on their faces. Then she was sitting in a chair without knowing who had put her into it. Her father was talking to her in his gentle comforting voice, but she could not hear anything that he said, because there was a ringing like bells in her ears. Her mother had come bustling up with a glass of wine and was putting it to her lips, but she could not drink it. Jane, dear Jane, was kneeling at her feet, chafing her hands and looking up into her face. It was Jane's voice which told her at last that Tom was dead.

4

There was little left to add when the letters were read. Tom had died of the yellow fever and had left his poor little thousand pounds to his promised bride ; one of the few times that Cassandra broke down was when she heard that.

Her family and friends told each other that no one could have endured such a severe stroke with more courage than she did, but she knew better. That summer she hardly felt anything at all, she went about wrapped in the black mantle of her grief and scarcely knew what went on about her. She shed few tears after the first agony, she was quite numb ; only sometimes when she woke in the night she found that her pillow had become wet without her knowing it. Most people dared not speak to her about her loss, they watched her anxiously and turned the conversation when it threatened to approach Tom's name. The village folk were wiser and would always lead her on to speak of him, saying aloud what her own heart said to her daily ; " It's the best that are always taken away. He was a sweet young gentleman, you'll go far before you find another like him, but nobody could have kept him back from that dreadful place if he thought it his duty to go there." Then they would tell her of their own losses, and that in some strange way was a comfort to her. She came back from these cottage visits with a heart lightened by weeping, to take up her weary days again.

Jane and she sat upstairs together a great deal that summer. It was a quiet time, for the family loss kept visitors away and Jane got on fast with her novel. James was up at Deane most of the time ; for Mary, now that she had got him, would hardly let him out of her sight. It was 1797, the year of the great mutinies in the fleet, a black and dreadful business which alarmed the whole nation. Back in February, before they got the news of Tom's death, people had hung out flags and lit bonfires for a naval victory over the Spanish fleet off Cape St. Vincent, not before it was needed. While the village children at Steventon were coming up by twos and threes, to get their new pennies from the rector for St. Valentine's Day, Admiral Sir John Jervis had been giving the Dons their Valentines in great style. The enormous Spanish vessels, it was reported, had towered over the English ships, looming like Beachy Head in a fog. Their flagship, the *Santissima Trinidad*, was the largest ship in the world, but though the Dons could build ships they could not make men. So said Captain Nelson, who had broken the Spanish line with Captain Troubridge. The whole Fleet was talking of this Captain Nelson, a thin fair-haired insubordinate little fellow, as brave as a lion, who had lost an eye at the taking of Corsica ; his brother officers had some professional joke among themselves about what they called his patent bridge for boarding first-rates. It seemed that at the Battle of Cape St. Vincent he had captured one enemy ship and then led his men across her decks to board another. He had received the surrender of the enemy commanders himself, his grinning bargeman had taken all the swords of the Spanish officers from him one after another and tucked them under his arm in a bundle with the utmost coolness. Captain Nelson was knighted and made Rear Admiral after this action, and grim old Sir John Jervis became a peer, with the style and title of Lord St. Vincent.

After that, in April, it was a great shock to the nation to hear of mutinies at Spithead and the Nore. The Steventon family, like many other innocent people, were horrified when they heard of what went on in his Majesty's ships, of the press gang, the brutal discipline and punishment, the bad food, wretched pay, harsh treatment and misery. They felt sure that such things could not happen in Frank's or Charles's ships. It was all too dreadful to think about, so they did their best to disbelieve what they read in the papers. However, the mutinies were settled in the end by old Lord Howe, the victor of the First of June, Black Dick as the Fleet called him, after he had been rowed round the ships in Portsmouth Harbour for twelve hours, arguing with the ringleaders. Then in October the Scots Admiral Duncan, fighting among the sandbanks at the mouth of the Texel River, utterly defeated the Dutch Navy, coming out to escort an invasion fleet over to Ireland. There was a great thanksgiving service at St. Paul's that December for these three naval victories, The Glorious First of June, Cape St. Vincent, and Camperdown ; and people told each other that it did not seem after all as if there was anything very wrong with the Fleet.

In this time of naval warfare the Army had nothing to do.
Frank and Charles were both afloat, but Henry, who was
now Captain and Adjutant in the Oxfordshire Militia, could
come up from Norwich to London to court Eliza as often
as he chose. She treated him badly, declared herself so well
pleased with her widowed state that she could not find it
in her heart to change it and said, in her giddy way, that
she preferred independence and the homage of half a dozen
to settling down with one ; however, Henry did not despair
of making her change her mind.

In August she frolicked away to Cheltenham where she
was heard of tasting the waters, strolling under the trees on
the Promenade, dancing twice a week, going to the play
every other night. However, she must have been turning
her future over in her mind all the time, for when she left
Cheltenham she did not go direct to Oxford on her way to
London, but posted over the Cotswolds by Stow and
Kingham. There on a green slope, overlooking the Evenlode
Valley, was a fine Grecian house of white stone, newly hewn
from the Taynton quarries, pointed out to travellers as
Daylesford, the seat of Mr. Warren Hastings, the late
Governor General of Bengal. More than sixty years back,
when he was the starved orphan son of the curate of
Churchill, the boy Warren Hastings had sat one summer
evening, dangling his feet above the Kingham brook, comforting himself with a fairy tale that when he grew up he
would buy back the lost estates of his family and rebuild
their house of Daylesford. He had lived to accomplish his
own dream, but he had gone a long way to do it and had
fished in stranger and deeper waters than the Kingham
brook. His country neighbours whispered to each other that
out there, in Bengal, he had been as near a king as made
no matter. He had made war and peace to suit his own
ends, had sent armies into battle, had put up native princes
and knocked them down again like so many ninepins. He
had shut up old queens in prison, he had taken bribes of
rubies and diamonds by the pocketful and silver and gold
by the cartload, he had fought a duel with one man who
withstood his villainy and had tortured and executed

another who might have borne witness against him. In short, he had been a monster of greed, ambition and cruelty. That was his story as his enemies told it.

His friends had another version, of course, they swore that no man had served his country better than Mr. Warren Hastings, or had been treated worse. He had added to the king's possessions a province as big as England and Scotland put together and had brought it into a state of law and order. Then he had been hounded and pulled down by envious rivals, brought home in disgrace, impeached and sent for trial, all by false witness and jealousy. His enemies had dragged out his trial for seven years in Westminster Hall, it had been a disgraceful puppet-show for the mob, an entertainment for fashionable folk to stare at. He had been acquitted at the end of it, but his private fortune, which had never been as great as slander declared it, had been swallowed up in the costs of his defence.

Nowadays the squire of Daylesford seemed to have outgrown his vivid past. He had mellowed into a pale, quiet, smiling gentleman, getting on for seventy, fragile and dignified, who rode about his grounds on an Arab mare with a flowing mane and tail, which he had brought home with him from the East. He experimented with horse and cattle breeding. He kept a herd of little Indian deer which barked at you, he tried to grow Oriental flowers and fruit, which withered in the inhospitable climate of the Cotswolds. He had laid out his grounds in a very elegant manner and dammed up the Churchill Brook into a leaky pond. His neighbours found him mild, gentle and very pleasant in his manners ; they would go home bewildered after paying him a visit and say to each other that it was hard to believe what a monster the old man had been. His wife was a very agreeable well-bred woman with an astonishing set of diamonds which were looked for at County balls. There had been some scandal about their marriage long, long ago. Mr. Hastings was said to have bribed Marian's German husband heavily to go away and let himself be divorced, but that was all forgotten nowadays. The squire of Daylesford and his lady were a most devoted couple ; they were childless, but an agreeable stepson and his wife lived with them. The house was well worth a visit, if only to see Mr. Hastings' Eastern curios, his tapestry, chain mail and gilded weapons, his porcelain and books, his jewel-bright collection of illuminated Persian manuscripts. He had portraits of himself and his wife by all the famous artists of the day and astonishing Eastern furniture, carved from blackwood, from teak, from elephants' tusks, into luxuriant filigree shapes of beasts and flowers. The old squire was very proud of these curiosities and always delighted to show them to his friends.

He and his wife liked company and he was pleased to see his godchild Eliza. He made her very welcome and told her that she had grown uncommonly like her mother Philadelphia Hancock, when he knew her first. They walked round the grounds and by the lake, came in and dined with some ceremony, then at the appropriate moment Mr. Hastings turned his piercing large blue eyes upon his visitor and inquired mildly what he could do to help her. The great man had long ago discovered that all his visitors wanted him to do something for them. Eliza touched her pretty eyes with her lace handkerchief and explained that little Hastings was a very sickly child. The doctors did not think that he would ever grow to manhood. The de Feuillide estates were in the clutches of the National Convention and she had been told that if she or the boy, who of course were French subjects, went over to Paris they might be restored, but she thought this too rash a venture while the war lasted. She had nothing to live upon except the interest of the ten thousand pounds which Mr. Hastings had so generously settled upon the Hancock family. It was not impossible, said Eliza, looking delightfully pretty, that she might marry again. She had no lack of suitors and her cousin, Henry Austen, had been most steadily attached to her these two years. Her godfather would not wish her to go to a new husband penniless. She had consulted her lawyers, who were of the opinion that the decease of her father, her mother and husband annulled the trust and, in short, she wanted the ten thousand pounds to be vested entirely in herself. Mr. Hastings agreed to this, and smiling wished her as much happiness in a second marriage as he had found in his own.

In September she took Hastings to Lowestoft, for Sir Walter Farquhar, the Prince of Wales' own doctor, had ordered sea air and bathing for the delicate child. Lowestoft was not fashionable like Brighton, there were no Assembly Rooms yet, no card parties, no balls or concerts. It was a place for quiet family holidays. Eliza must console herself by walking on the beach in the keen airs, watching the fishing boats go out and come in, picking up shells and trails of blistered seaweed, reading one dog's-eared novel after another from the small circulating library and waiting her turn with Hastings for one of the new bathing machines, lately invented by a Margate Quaker, with an awning of canvas over the steps, happily calculated to preserve the modesty of the fair sex. When cousin Phila wrote teasingly that Norfolk and Suffolk were neighbouring counties Eliza wrote back, quite crossly for her, that Henry at Norwich with his regiment was twenty-eight miles away, so how could he visit her? However, Henry owned a good horse and a very dashing curricle, so whether he did sometimes drive over to see her or not was nobody's business.

5

That autumn was a sad dull time at Steventon. Mary had been disappointed of her first child and had been quite seriously ill for a short time. Jane had finished her novel, *First Impressions*, and her father had thought so well of it that he offered it to a publisher called Cadell, with a sweetly partial letter in which he compared it to Miss Burney's admired *Evelina*. The old gentleman would gladly have paid for the publication of Jane's story, but the publisher declined to look at her twelve months' work. She would not, however, admit that she was disappointed. She had another and a better notion, she would write a novel in letters, as the fashion then was, using the same two characters, the sisters who were like Cassandra and herself; this time she would call them by two of her favourite names, Elinor and Marianne. Mrs. Austen very much disapproved of so much scribbling. Cassandra grew paler and thinner month by month, caught a bad cold and could not shake it off, and Mrs. Austen fancied that all this ill luck was affecting her own health. She called in Dr. Lyford and that cunning old friend ordered her a course of the Bath waters. The Reverend George could not be tempted to leave home, so Mrs. Austen and the girls went off without him.

Bath was no new place to the Austen family, they had been coming and going to the noble city all their lives. In the previous generation Grandmother Leigh had lived there after she lost her husband. Of her two daughters Cassandra, Mrs. George Austen, had met and married her husband there when he was a young curate at Walcot Church and her sister Jane, the family beauty of that generation, had married the Reverend Edward Cooper, the rector of Whaddon, a neighbouring village. This was that Aunt Cooper, the mother of Jane and Edward, who had caught the fever from the Austen girls at Southampton and had died young. The brother of these two women, James Leigh, had been obliged to add the name of Perrot to his own when he inherited a Perrot estate at North Leigh, near Witney in Oxfordshire. Uncle Leigh Perrot was a very rich man who suffered, as rich men do, from the gout. He spent the summer months at his country house called Scarlets, at Hare Hatch near Maidenhead, but he always went to his town house in Bath for the winter season.

Parson Austen's daughters liked their uncle much better than their aunt. He was a dear generous creature and always most anxious that his nieces should enjoy themselves when they came to stay with him, but his wife was a severe and gloomy woman, with a great notion of speaking her mind. She had not the art of getting on with young people, indeed she was incapable of being very fond of anyone except her husband. This childless couple were devoted to each other, and poor Uncle Leigh Perrot was entirely dominated by his wife. They had a brown, gloomy and forbidding house, No. 1, The Paragon, crowded with heavy mahogany furniture, thick velvet hangings and dim family portraits of gentlemen in scarlet uniforms and ladies in satin, holding garlands or pet lambs. A negro manservant lurked in the narrow hall, shivering as he opened the door to let in visitors. At the back it was lovely, for the little river cliff dropped down sheer below the windows in the true Bath fashion, so that you could see right over the cottages and gardens of Walcot to the Avon and the hills beyond ; but the best rooms looked north-east from Broad Street into the slope of Lansdown Hill. They got no sun at all. The house was right on the pavement and the passing traffic, coming full tilt along the London Road, splashed the windows with mud continually. After the quiet country nights at Steventon it was always difficult at first to endure the noises of the Paragon ; the continual rattle of iron-shod hoofs over the cobbles, the heavy rumble of carts and drays, the bawling street cries and the ceaseless clink of pattens along the high pavement in wet weather.

Number One was not a very gay house for two lively young country girls to stay in. There was plenty of good food and wine and solid comfort, but very little of the right kind of entertainment. The Leigh Perrots were elderly people in poor health, and moved in a small circle of retired service people, of parsons, doctors and attorneys, of well-bred widows with unmarried daughters, who met at each other's houses for tea-drinking, whist and cribbage. Uncle James was fond of his nieces and liked to have an arm from one or other of them when he limped down to the Pump Room to drink his morning glasses at the spring. He gave each of them ten guineas to spend at the milliners and took them to a concert in the fine colonnaded hall at the Upper Rooms ; that was a real pleasure to both the Steventon girls, who loved good music and seldom heard any ; but when it came to dancing they did not get very far. Two pretty girls from Hampshire might adorn themselves in their simple gowns, have their hair cut and dressed by the best hairdresser in Milsom Street with tinsel gauze and feathers and have their finery much admired at home ; but in the great Assemblies they went unnoticed. The season was at its height and the Upper Rooms, at their first visit, were so crowded that it was not possible to get near the dancers. All that they could see as they squeezed through the crowd were the long waving plumes of some of the ladies. Uncle James slipped away to the card room, and his party were left to rest awhile on one of the upper benches, looking down upon the waving and tossing plumes of red and blue, green and yellow, sinking and rising as their wearers curtseyed in the minuet. At the Bath assemblies, there were always formal minuets and cotillions to take up the first hour. The musicians fiddled and sweated away, it was insufferably hot under the twinkling candlelight of the great chandeliers. Aunt Leigh Perrot fanned herself and complained to Mrs. Austen of the heat and the crowd. " The company here is very mixed nowadays," said she. " One never sees anybody one knows, I have quite given up coming. I cannot see a partner for either of the girls tonight." When the minuets were over and the country dancing began Jane tapped her foot to the music and longed to dance, but her aunt, yawning, said that she had a headache and would stay no longer. So they were all carried back along Alfred Street in their sedan chairs, drank warm wine and water, heard their uncle's account of his five rubbers of whist and went to bed. Jane fumed. " That was the most stupid evening I ever spent. I wish I were at home. Do you realise this would have been the night of the first Basingstoke Assembly ? "

6

When they went to the Lower Rooms, in the Orange Grove, beside the Abbey, it was a little better. The rooms were smaller, there was not quite such a crowd and their uncle, a trifle conscience-stricken when he saw his two pretty nieces sitting out dance after dance, applied to Mr. King, the Master of the Ceremonies, who introduced a young gentleman to Jane. They went down their two dances together with great spirit, but after that he was drawn away from

her to sit with his own party at the tea tables and she saw
no more of him. It was all very disappointing. There
seemed to be plenty of young people about the streets of
Bath. Pretty girls were seen everywhere, dashing up and
down Milsom Street with their hats turned up in front,
talking and laughing together at corners of the street,
positively walking or driving alone with handsome Army
officers or Naval men, pale and interesting from recent
wounds, repairing their health at the Spa. Unfortunately
the girls from Steventon knew none of them. They walked
arm in arm up and down Milsom Street all by themselves,
peeping into the bow windows of the shops at sandals of
green and blue kid, at half-boots of nankeen galoshed with
black meant to set off a neat ankle on a Bath pavement,
but useless for the Steventon lanes. They sighed for gloves
of cream and primrose silk, for bonnets trimmed with green
or coquelicot ribbons ; the bright poppy red, highly becoming to a dark-haired beauty, was all the rage that winter.
They bought their Christmas presents, counting the money
carefully out of their long knitted purses. James and their
father got books, Mary and Martha ribbons ; Mrs. Austen
bought good Irish linen for shirts and dress lengths of silk
and Indian muslin to be made up at home.

The girls borrowed a great many books from the circulating library. Romantic novels with a German flavour were
then in vogue, by Mrs. Radcliffe and her followers, *The
Mystery of Udolpho, Clermont, The Orphan of the Rhine, The
Necromancer of the Black Forest*, and *The Midnight Ball* ; there
were dozens of them, all decorated with ruined castles and
abbeys, with monks, nuns and missing heirs, with bandits,
corpses and persecuted heroines, all *horrid*, as the fashionable
phrase was. " Are they *horrid*? Are you sure they are all
horrid? " you would hear the Bath ladies inquiring, as they
turned over one volume after another and the library
assistant would answer wearily, " Oh ! yes, madam, exceedingly *horrid*, I do assure you."

There happened to be a good deal of wet weather during
the six weeks that they spent in Bath in December, 1797.
The rain came driving over with the south-west wind from

the Bristol Channel. It pelted through the classical colon-
nades, it ran in rivers down the steep streets, it dripped from
pediments and wrought-iron balconies, it blackened the
headless stone angels, climbing up and down the Jacob's
Ladder on the west front of the Abbey and splashed into the
hot yellow water of the public bath. The whole valley
steamed with moisture and the Avon ran high between
its banks, swirling under the wide arches of the new Pulteney
Bridge in great brown whirlpools, quite obliterating the
Abbey weir.

Even such desperate walkers as the Austen girls could not
venture out in such a downpour. They used to spend whole
mornings up in the spare bedroom at No. 1, The Paragon.
From the window seat they could overlook the green and
silver floods in the meadows and see right across the shining
wet roofs of the new houses in Bathwick to the pale slopes
where new white villas, like little plaster temples, were
venturing out two by two into the country, all the way
up the hill to the ridiculous towers of Sham Castle. Jane
always made great fun of this edifice. " It makes me die of
laughing," said she, " as we used to say at school. You can
see right through it, there is nothing behind it, it looks as
if it were cut out of a piece of cardboard. It is exactly like
a castle in one of these absurd novels, *Udolpho* or *Wolfenbach*.
Someday I shall write a book myself and make fun of
them all."

When they were tired of reading novels aloud to each
other there was always a dress to alter, a letter to write
to one of the boys at sea, or a hat to trim in imitation of
something seen in Milsom Street. While their fingers were
busy their tongues ran on by the hour. Jane would grumble,
" I think my aunt is really an intolerable woman. She is
so proud and selfish, she has a heart of stone and the devil
of a temper, as the boys would say, she cares for nobody
but herself." " She is very fond of my uncle," Cassandra
would plead. " That is because he is part of herself," Jane
would retort shrewdly. " He considers her in everything
and bears all her tantrums with the patience of an angel,
I pity him with all my heart. Did you hear her at the card-

table last night ? How angry she was because she did not hold as many Kings and Queens as the rest of us ? It must be dreadful to live constantly with such an ill-tempered person." " She suffers with her rheumatism sadly at times," pleaded Cassandra. " She told me that last winter she was not able to leave her sofa for weeks together and often could hardly turn herself in bed." " I don't believe in her illnesses," said Jane crossly. " She eats and drinks too much, she is another of these fine ladies who only have strength enough to do what pleases them. My uncle suffers far more from his gout than she does." She yawned, turned the hat on her hand and looked at it from all sides. " I think it needs another bow perking up at the side to make it quite the crack," said she ; then when she had threaded her needle again returned to Mrs. Leigh Perrot. " I cannot endure the way she gives her opinion on our affairs. She tells my mother how we ought to spend our money, and if my father were here she would tell him how to write his sermons. She says I neglect my piano playing and waste my time scribbling ; it is making my eyes red and I shall frighten all the men away with my sharp tongue and my learned airs. I must take more pains about hunting for a husband, or I shall end up as a schoolmarm." She had been imitating her aunt unconsciously as she talked, puffing out her cheeks, drawing down her eyebrows and the corners of her mouth, putting on a rough ungracious tone. When Cassandra murmured timidly, " For shame, Jane, you should not mimic her," she changed to a broad milkmaid grin and began to hum a country tune. " ' *If all the young men did be ducks on the warter, then all the young maids would get guns and go arter.*' That's what Nanny Littlewarth says," she concluded with a comical air. Cassandra had to laugh, but then sighed, looked down and said under her breath, " I wish my aunt would not always be teasing you about Tom Lefroy."

Jane stitched the bow down more firmly than ever, her lips were set and her eyes sparkled angrily. " She was at me about him again yesterday evening," she burst out, " telling me that my Irishman, as she called him, was not the only man in the world. I must not be too particular, but look about me for somebody who did not need a rich wife, there were as good fish in the sea as ever came out of it and so forth. She reminded me that I was twenty-two and had not much more time to waste. At last I could bear it no longer. I told her Tom Lefroy was nothing to me and no business of hers. She turned as red as a turkey cock and began gobbling ; she could not get a word out. So I rose up, made her a deep curtsey and walked out of the room." Cassandra exclaimed in distress, " Oh ! dear, what will she say ? she will never forgive you," but Jane shrugged her thin shoulders and replied very coolly, " I should not care if she never spoke to me again, but it will be all right, you will see. She is a coward really, nobody ever stands up to her. She will leave me alone after this. I wish I could think she would do the same by you. I have heard her at it already ; she was teasing you yesterday about your Tom."

Cassandra's head sank and she did not answer for a moment ; then she said resolutely, " My aunt did not mean to be unkind. She told me that I must not always be fretting and pining. She is quite right, I must try to hold up my head and look cheerful, for my family's sake as well as my own. It is no more than what I say to myself, every day of my life." She added under her breath, " Tom would not have wanted me to show that I was unhappy."

Jane jumped up, flung the hat into the window seat, put one arm round Cassandra's neck and one cheek close to hers and cried out, " Dearest Cassy, don't mind her. Don't let her make you unhappy." The cheek that she kissed was wet, but Cassandra said after a moment, " I am not unhappy, really, only I cannot put Tom out of my head. I think of him night and day." She fixed her great eyes on Jane and said, " I must tell you something that happened to me yesterday. I was in the Pump Room with my uncle when up came a surgeon called Nicholls, the man who attended Admiral Nelson when he came here last summer, after losing his right arm in the action at Teneriffe. Mr. Nicholls told my uncle that the case was beyond him. It had been bungled in some way by the Fleet surgeon, who had taken up the great nerves of the arm with their ligatures. Poor Admiral Nelson was in dreadful pain and Mr. Nicholls sent him straight up to London for treatment. I was listening to all this very carefully, because you know I am always interested in anything to do with nursing, and when he saw that Mr. Nicholls turned round to me and told me a very strange thing. He said that when a limb was been taken off, for weeks afterwards the patient goes on feeling as if it were still there. He has observed it time and again." The two sisters looked at each other and Cassandra said, with her lips trembling, " That is how it is with me."

Downstairs her elders were shaking their heads over her. " Cassandra is not near so handsome as she used to be," her aunt declared. " She is grown shockingly thin and has lost all her colour. She used to have just the kind of beauty to attract the men, but now her bloom is quite gone." " Aye, poor thing ! she looks very bad sometimes," her uncle lamented. " I used to think that she would marry sooner and better than Jane," Mrs. Leigh Perrot continued, " but now I fear she may go into a decline or end up as an old maid. I was telling her yesterday that she must pluck up her courage and try to look more cheerful, and she burst out crying and ran away from the room." " I am sorry you spoke to her about that," said her husband, with unusual severity. " I did not mean to vex her," admitted Mrs. Leigh Perrot, looking for once ashamed of herself. " But young people must not be nonsensical, they must learn to take advice from their elders. I fancy you have bred up your girls to be a little too independent, Sister. Jane quite flared up yesterday when I spoke to her plainly about that Irishman of hers, she answered me very sharply and flounced out of the room. It was not at all pretty behaviour." Mrs. Austen said doubtfully, " Jane has always been a difficult girl to manage. When she is in one of her moods I think it is better to leave her alone. She has taken this business of Mr. Lefroy harder than I expected." " I cannot understand a fine young man treating a pretty girl so ill," lamented Uncle Leigh Perrot. " I do not know where he could find a better wife." " Oh ! if she had had a thousand or fifteen hundred pounds

I daresay he would have taken her," pronounced Mrs. Leigh Perrot, who never spared anyone's feelings. " But as you and George have not been able to provide properly for either of the girls, Sister, I do not see how you can expect to marry them off." " Well," concluded her husband, " I am truly sorry that neither of them have found anybody here to put these disappointments out of their heads, for I swear I think they are two of the finest girls in Bath."

Mrs. Austen took her daughters back to Steventon in time for Christmas, where there was always a great deal for them to do at that season. They had to visit all the cottages with soup and jelly for sick folk, toys for the children and clothing for the old women. They had to decorate the church with holly and evergreens, and Mr. Austen had to prepare his Christmas sermon, preaching for the fifth wartime winter in succession on peace and good will, with what heart he might. And on the last day of the year Captain Henry Austen, of the Oxfordshire Militia, was quietly married to Madame la Comtesse de Feuillide in the black pillared church of St. Marylebone, the parish in which she was then living. None of his family were there. Mrs. Austen had said tartly, " It is far too long a journey for old folks like your father and myself to take in midwinter, all to be at a wedding we don't approve " ; and on that New Year's Eve, as they all said good night to each other, the old lady burst out with some- thing like an angry sob, " I shall not wish you a happy New Year, girls, for I see very little hope of that. I shall only wish us all a better year than the last one, for I don't remember ever having so many disappointments in one twelve month in my whole life."

7

It was after this visit to Bath, in the year 1798, that Jane began to write her next novel. This time she took for her heroine a humble simple girl just seventeen, as fresh as a daisy, as soft and helpless as a kitten with eyes hardly yet open, as innocent and awkwardly inquiring as a young colt and sent the sweet fool to Bath with a head full of Gothic romances and a heart ready to be broken by the first comer. She was called Susan at first and afterwards Catherine and the story in the end became *Northanger Abbey*.

That was the year of the great invasion scare. There were several others afterwards, but this was the first one and there was good reason for it. The Directory favoured the attempt and had sent their terrible new young general, Citizen Bonaparte, to the Channel coast. He had been in Boulogne that winter, making his preparations and it was supposed that in the long dark nights of early spring, when there was no moon, he would try to bring over his landing force in small boats. The volunteers, grown a little indifferent after five years of war, had been told to go back to their drilling ; they practised their exercises on Sunday mornings after church on the village greens, while up in London the King reviewed eight thousand of the best of them in Hyde Park. Beacons and semaphores were set up on the Downs to pass the alarm of any landing, and people living near the coast were instructed to pack bundles of food and clothing and be ready to fly inland by fields and footpaths as soon as they heard the church bells rung backwards, leaving the roads clear for the troops. Parson Austen and his churchwardens were to prepare to take in these refugees and care for the sick and wounded ; the Hampshire magistrates were to see all cattle and horses killed or driven away, all corn and hay set alight, bridges broken down, roads blocked and food destroyed or carried away, to keep it from the French.

Edward at Goodnestone was busy with the same precautions, for Kent was considered the most likely place for a landing. Flat-bottomed boats and barges had been seen lying in the invasion ports and it was even said that firing had been heard across the Channel at Dover. Henry and Eliza at Ipswich were in the thick of the East Coast defence preparations, but the wedded pair were judged very happy from their letters. Eliza wrote gaily to Cousin Phila that the inhabitants of Ipswich were much more fashionable than she had expected and vied with each other to show hospitality to the military. They had all hastened to call upon the

Adjutant's bride, were dazzled by her French title and competed to secure her for their elegant entertainments. Henry's brother officers and their wives were equally attentive. She was spending her time dining, dancing and playing cards ; the handsome pair were constantly to be seen driving about the Suffolk lanes in a new fifty-guinea curricle, Henry in his scarlet driving cloak, she herself in her furred wedding pelisse, with a great sable muff which came right up to her elbows and a killing bonnet. Pretty Eliza vowed that she had quite given up what she called *trade* since her marriage ; she could still however discern that a certain Captain Tilson, Henry's chief crony, was remarkably handsome and that a couple of the lieutenants might be flirted with very satisfactorily. As for the Colonel, Lord Charles Spencer, she was entirely in love with him. He was a most charming creature, so mild, so well-bred, so good ; alas ! that he was married as well as herself ! Henry, she reported, bid fair to make an excellent husband, delightfully devoted and tender ; he let her have her own way in everything and spoilt her dreadfully but that, she felt sure, was the best way to manage her. She was thoroughly enjoying her campaigning and vowed that she meant to be drilled and to bespeak her regimentals without delay, so as to be ready to take the field in a new frogged military riding habit if indeed the French came.

Most people really seemed to believe that they might. People watched the moon and whenever the wind dropped talked nervously of *raft-weather*. The newspapers brought out prints of the means by which the assault troops were to be ferried over, rafts worked by paddle-wheels, bristling with cannon, and surmounted by towers full of soldiers, with a windmill or two on top. The public found the machines alarming, but the Navy roared with laughter at such crazy contrivances and only wished they might watch seasick Frenchmen trying to work them across in a heavy sea. They knew well enough that the scheme could never be put through while the King's ships were watching Brest Harbour and the Texel like terriers at a couple of rabbit holes. General Bonaparte knew that himself ; it was told afterwards that once the long dark April nights were over he had given up the invasion plan for that year. " The pear is not yet ripe," he had told his masters and while the betrayed Irish were rising in rebellion all over the south, expecting his landing, he had massed his real forces at Toulon and slipped away for Egypt. That strange mind of his was simmering with plans for the conquest of the Middle East and a triumphal march to India.

Frank Austen would have known that before any of the home people. He had been first lieutenant in *H.M.S. London* since February, blockading those few Spanish ships which had escaped from the battle of Cape St. Vincent in the white-walled harbour of Cadiz. When Admiral Nelson came out in his flagship, the *Vanguard*, with his stump healed and his health restored, and sailed by them to Gibraltar, the whole ship's company could guess that he had orders to go into the Mediterranean in search of the French. Unfortunately an untimely May storm dismasted the *Vanguard* and dispersed the squadron. The French slipped through his fingers in the most heart-breaking fashion, all for lack of frigates to watch their movements. They captured Malta and disappeared to the eastward. The little Admiral chased them to Alexandria, got there before them, found the great harbour empty and came back to Syracuse. He had had the worst luck in the world in this affair and was sharply blamed at home. However, he got much help at this time from the King and Queen of the Two Sicilies. They were a poor pair of allies, he a vicious tyrant, she a domineering intriguing Austrian princess, sister to Marie Antoinette and always in terror of a Jacobin revolt among her subjects ; but while they were in a good humour the Fleet could use their three great harbours, Naples, Palermo and Syracuse.

Our Ambassador, Sir William Hamilton, was luckily a most skilful diplomat. He had married a low-born beauty, his former mistress, the loveliest and most admired creature of her time. Lady Hamilton had obtained great influence over the Queen of Naples and persuaded her to have the English ships quickly supplied with everything they needed.

General Bonaparte had won a battle against the Turks in sight of the Pyramids, and taken the great city of Cairo and was marching upon Syria by way of Acre ; but before he got there Admiral Nelson led his squadron into the shoals of Aboukir Bay and there destroyed and burnt all but two vessels of the French fleet. General Bonaparte failed to take Acre and plague broke out in his Army, so he poisoned his sick at Jaffa, it was whispered, and then fell back upon Egypt.

8

When the church bells were rung, bonfires lit and flags hung out for this victory, the Battle of the Nile, the Austens were at Godmersham to share the village rejoicings, for Edward and Elizabeth had just moved into that great house. Old Mrs. Knight had endured three years of widowhood there, sitting by herself in the echoing marble halls and panelled saloons, walking in the green spaces of the park, a solitary sable figure in her crape veils and weeds, kneeling in church on Sundays opposite the monument which she had erected to her husband, a marble sarcophagus with a broken column on top and a fine inscription about his lineage, public activities and private virtues. Now she could endure it no longer. There was a formal exchange of letters between herself and Edward, all mutual compliment, gratitude and affection ; the family thought that Edward's letter to his adopted mother, in particular, was very handsome, the prettiest letter you ever saw in your life. It did Edward's head and heart alike great credit and was preserved by old Mrs. Knight among the family papers. She had the highest opinion of her adopted son and was thankful to hand over the responsibilities of the great estate to him ; she felt that a man's hand was needed. She departed gracefully to a snug house called White Friars, in Canterbury, where her hours would be marked by the chiming of bells and the slow progress across her lawn of the shadow thrown by the cathedral towers. Canterbury was only eight miles from

Godmersham, it would become the family house of call.
When Edward went in to sit on the bench at petty sessions,
when Elizabeth had a visitor to see the Cathedral, or took
her increasing tribe of handsome and well-mannered children
round the Canterbury shops, they would all end up at
Grandmother Knight's house, while she in her turn drove
out weekly to visit them at dear Godmersham.

It was a lovely house, long and low, with spreading wings
of a warm red brick dressed with white stone. It lay in an
open green valley among terraced gardens, beyond were
wide spaces of parkland, coverts and copses, farms and
barns. An avenue of lime trees led from the garden to the
ancient church and the Stour wound through the meadows,
artfully delayed into the semblance of a lake. Beyond the
river the valley was ringed about with chalk downs and
hanging woods, just beginning to mellow from green to gold
in the fine Michaelmas weather of 1798 when Edward's
parents and his two sisters arrived.

They drove up to the north front, alighted at a classical
porch, between obelisks bearing lamps and entered the great
central hall, flagged with black and white marble. Its six
tall mahogany doorways were framed in Grecian mouldings,
its garlanded frieze, enriched by masks and cherubs, was
pierced by three bullseye windows. A shimmering dazzle
of white cross-lights and reflections filled the echoing space.
In summer the hall would have been as cool and empty as
a well ; but on that autumn day the great fireplace, adorned
by a plaster relief in the antique taste of warriors sacrificing
at an altar, was heaped with crackling logs out of Edward's
woods, a great fire as warm as his welcome.

Edward at thirty was already growing stately and urbane,
but he was as affectionate as ever, he was not a man to
forget his own family. He had been watching for the sound
of the carriage and came out at once himself to greet them
and lead them all into the great drawing-room. It was most
richly decorated with masks, shells and great springing
acanthus leaves, with loops and swags of plaster foliage, with
baskets of fruit and groups of musical instruments in carved
panels. It had a marble chimney piece, a host of gilt,

lacquered and embroidered chairs and was hung with family portraits ; but still the most precious object in it was Edward's wife, sitting in a silken chair on a needlework carpet in the shelter of a Coromandel screen, looking like a glowing and bountiful antique goddess of plenty. She rose to kiss them all in turn, murmuring, " Dear Jane . . . dearest Cassandra . . .'' and laying her soft cheek to theirs. She seemed to grow more beautiful and more loving, year by year.

It was a most delightful visit, Edward, now happily master of his inheritance, found some pleasant entertainment for them all in turn. His father and he walked about the estate, discussing the condition of the farms and planning improvements. The Rector of Steventon, who had farmed his glebe for so many seasons, had his own stout Hampshire opinions about pigs and sheep, the rotation of crops and the planting of trees, and Edward deferred to his father very pleasantly. Mrs. Austen spent much of her time with Elizabeth ; they walked about the flower garden and the house, discussing new flowers and furniture, and Mrs. Austen enjoyed a daily grandmotherly chat with Sackree, the nurse, about the health and behaviour of the four children. Cassandra and Jane used to wander about the park and by the river, or sit in the Ionic or Doric temples, from which you could look down upon the house. On wet days they had the run of Edward's library, his books, his collections of coins and cameos, his portfolios of engravings. On Sundays they all walked down the lime avenue to church and sat in the family pew. Elizabeth took them out with her in the carriage to return the calls of a new set of neighbours, the Finch-Hattons at Eastwell, the Tokes at Godinton, the Faggs at Mystole, the Wildmans, who had just bought Chilham Castle. Then there were the Knatchbulls at Merstham Hatch (old Mrs. Knight had been a Knatchbull), and Elizabeth's elder sister Sophia, married these seven years to Mr. Deedes at Sandling and already bringing up a long family. They went into Canterbury several times to visit Mrs. Knight and they drove all the way to Goodnestone to spend a night or two with Elizabeth's mother and sisters.

The Austen girls ate roast partridges and drank French wine, took tea, listened to music, turned over engravings after dinner in a dozen elegant drawing-rooms, they strolled in other people's rose gardens, peach-houses and vineries. Everybody, it seemed, was rich in Kent.

9

When Jane went home to Steventon with her parents she missed the elegance of Godmersham sadly. Cassandra had been left behind for a few more weeks of festivity and to attend the Ashford Assemblies. Jane wrote faithfully twice a week, relating all the small happenings of Steventon, giving messages about pigs and maidservants, about a new circulating library, about dressmaking and Christmas charities and Mrs. Austen's imaginary ailments. The old lady declared that she had an asthma or a dropsy, she was not sure which, besides water in her chest and a liver disorder. Dr. Lyford wanted her to look yellow and throw out a rash, but she would do neither, so he had prescribed twelve drops of laudanum as a composer and Jane was to have the dignity of dropping it out. Reading between the lines, Cassandra feared that Jane was having rather a solitary dull time with her two elderly parents. She had made herself some caps, though it seemed a pity to tuck all those bright brown curls out of sight. She had been trying to play the serious parson's daughter and had visited some of Cassandra's old women ; she wrote of walking alone to Deane in a hard black frost, a thing which she had never had to do before, but there was no company of her own age at Steventon in this, her twenty-third year. " People get so horridly poor and economical in this part of the world," wrote Jane, " I have no patience with them. Kent is the only place for happiness."

Mrs. Lefroy had paid a morning call upon the Austens to hear about Godmersham. Jane had been too proud to ask after her Irish friend, but an innocent inquiry from Mr. Austen established that he had been called to the Bar and had sat down in Dublin to wait for a practice. He was not married yet, but that could only be a matter of time. Mrs. Lefroy also brought a letter from a certain Mr. Blackall, a Fellow of Exeter College, Oxford, who had stayed at Ashe Parsonage that summer and had paid Jane some ponderous attentions. He wrote that he would have liked to pursue his acquaintance with the Austens and even hinted with ineffable condescension at something closer, but his circumstances would not permit of his paying his addresses to Jane. She wrote dryly, " It will therefore be most probable that our indifference will soon be mutual, unless his regard, which appears to spring from knowing nothing of me at first, is best supported by never seeing me. There is less love and more sense in it than has sometimes appeared before, and I am very well satisfied. It will all go on exceedingly well and decline away in a very reasonable manner." Mr. Blackall had not touched her heart in the least, she had thought him tiresome and absurd, but would later be indebted to him for some features of Mr. Collins.

James's Mary was now very near her lying-in and Jane reported that she was heartily tired of her child and longed to be rid of it. She could not endure little Anna stamping and shouting about the house, so James took his daughter down to Steventon ; but his wife remained very fretful and nervous and whenever he went down to visit his own family would cry out on his return, " Why have you been so long away? You went out at seven and now it is almost midday. You told me you were only going to ride round your own fields and now you have been all the way down to Steventon. I think you might consider me a little more than you do. You have no notion how ill I feel." She had one of the Ibthorp friends, a Miss Debary, to nurse her while she was abed, a tiresome fussy woman who encouraged her to fidget about herself. She sat beside Mary's sofa, knitting herself a gown in worsteds and alarming Mary with stories of deaths in childbed among the neighbours.

It was a great relief to the whole family when on November 17th, 1798, Mary produced a fine healthy boy. Luckily he had not taken after his plain little mother, he was a true Austen with large dark eyes and he was to be called

Edward after his uncle. Jane wrote the news to Cassandra at Godmersham, where they all drank little Edward's health. She added, " Mary does not manage matters in such a way as to make me want to lay in myself. She is not tidy enough in her appearance ; she has no dressing gown to sit up in, and her curtains are all too thin. Elizabeth was really a pretty object with her nice clean cap put on so tidily and her dress so uniformly white and orderly." This caused great laughter at Godmersham.

The winter festivities had been not quite so gay as usual. They could not compare with Kent, where Elizabeth's little sister, Harriet Bridges, was now going to dances and being much admired and the Ashford Assembly had been graced by the presence of Prince William of Gloucester. However, Jane wrote in her sprightly fashion about her dresses and her partners. For the December Assemblies at Basingstoke she had robbed Cassandra's old black velvet bonnet of its frill and had confected a black lace cap with a most dashing air. It had silver ribbon wound twice about it and a coquelicot feather sticking up in front in the latest Bath fashion. Black was an odd colour for a girl to wear at a ball when all the rest were in milky blues, blush pinks and primrose yellows, Jane must have been a black swan among her fellows, but she reported that her black headdress had been openly admired by dear Mrs. Lefroy and secretly, she imagined, by everyone else in the room. In fact, Parson Austen's daughter flattered herself that she must have looked like the Prince of Wales's new mistress, Lady Conyngham. She had danced every dance without fatigue and Catherine and she had actually teased that stiff parson, Mr. Calland, into taking part, though he said it was against his principles. Altogether she had enjoyed herself far more among her old friends in the small familiar ballroom above the stable yard behind the Crown, than ever she had done at the grand Bath or Ashford Assemblies.

Her pleasantest pieces of news were about her Naval brothers. Charles had been home on leave and had escorted her to the local dances. He had grown into a tall handsome young fellow, had given up powder and wore his hair cropped, showing his long well-shaped Austen head. He was in high spirits, for he had just had a step in his profession. Charles had made one lucky voyage under Captain Williams, the husband of pretty cousin Jane, in his frigate the *Unicorn*, when she captured *La Tribune* after a chase of two hundred and ten miles and then had been promoted to second lieutenant in the *Scorpion* ; but now he was going to the *Tamar* frigate, a new and much finer ship. And Frank, dear Frank, was made ! He had been raised to the rank of Commander and appointed to the command of the *Petrel* sloop, then with the Mediterranean squadron. Jane wrote gleefully that Cassandra must spend her father's Christmas present on a new muslin gown, to celebrate Frank's promotion. " If you don't I shall never forgive you."

At the New Year there had been a famous ball, given by Lady Dorchester at Kempshott and she had been able to cut a dash in a new piece of finery, a Mameluke cap ; it had been lent her by Mary, who had had a present of it, but lacked the courage, or the features, to wear it. Egyptian fashions had been all the rage in Paris that year, since General Bonaparte's campaign began. Madame Bonaparte and her friends were all wrapping themselves up in fine Cashmere shawls, they copied the Arab burnous and the Turkish slippers and trousers ; the turban and the fez were the latest thing in evening head-dresses, scarabs were mounted as brooches and Sphinx heads appeared upon porcelain and furniture. English ladies, since dear Lord Nelson's noble victory in Aboukir Bay, were retaliating with sea blue cloaks and scarves, patterned with gold anchors *alla* Nelson. Lady Hamilton had worn one at a ball in Naples in honour of the returning hero and the fashion had caught on at home like wildfire. It was the mode to transfix the folds with a great gilt brooch shaped like a curved Turkish dagger, just above the heart. The colours most in favour that winter in Paris were Desert Sand and Egyptian Earth, a watery blue which the modistes had christened Eau-de-Nil and a bright green called Crocodile. Jane luckily had a pair of bright green morocco shoes ; she had worn them at Kempshott with her white muslin gown and had stuck Mary's crimson fez sideways on her chestnut curls. Cassandra wished she could have seen her sister in this disguise ; the girl must have looked enchantingly bold and strange, like a young Eastern warrior, like Viola disguised as Cesario, in the *Twelfth Night* scenes which Henry and she used to read aloud together.

Kempshott had evidently been the highest peak of the Christmas festivities. Jane had not grudged the inflamed eyes which she had next day, partly from the cold of the wintry drive, partly from the dust which flew up from the chalked floor ; that was an old trouble of hers. Perhaps her mother was right when she prophesied that Jane would ruin her swimming brown short-sighted eyes before she was an old woman, with so much reading and writing.

She and Charles had attended the New Year's Assembly at the Crown, but it had evidently been a little flat after the glories of Lady Dorchester's ball. James and his wife had been in the party and Mary, secure in her new maternal dignity, had been less fidgetty than usual. There had been the usual civil, kind and noisy crowd of country neighbours and the room had been rather too full, but there had not been quite enough men to go round. Jane had spent the evening chiefly with the Manydown party, but had not thought that she was very much in request. She had fancied that people were rather apt not to ask her till they could not help it. " One's consequence, you know," she wrote in her pretty steady hand, " varies so much at times without any particular reason." It did not sound like her, she usually had so much confidence in herself. However, she could be witty immediately afterwards at the expense of a very good-looking young officer who had wished to be introduced to her, but somehow or other had not quite contrived to bring it about ; and she boasted that she had sat down for two dances rather than stand up with Lord Bolton's eldest son, who danced too ill to be endured.

The next Thursday Assembly had been duller still. Charles's leave was over, he had gone off to his ship and there had only been eight dancing couples and but twenty people altogether in the half-empty room. Several families had been kept away by the sudden serious illness of old Mr. Bigg-Wither, who had caused great anxiety among his friends and relations. His misfortune had been a fine subject for conversation at the ball, which had been chiefly composed of vulgar Jervoises and noisy Terrys. Jane sent an odd list of partners, but said that she had spent a pleasant evening, though with no particular reason for it. " But I do not think it worth while to wait for enjoyment until there is some real opportunity." Reading these letters through and through at Godmersham, after the children had gone to bed, while Edward snored gently in his armchair after a day in the woods and Elizabeth turned over the pages of *La Belle Assemblée*, Cassandra felt obscurely worried about her sister. She did not think that Jane sounded very happy.

10

Cassandra had never been away from Jane and Steventon for so many months before. She returned in March, 1799, and was greeted with all the warm affection which the Austens had for each other. Her father had a more fragile air than she liked, but her mother was in excellent spirits and Jane seemed composed and cheerful. There was plenty of family news to talk over. Frank was on the Toulon blockade, Henry had gone over to Ireland with Colonel Spencer, Eliza had taken her little boy to Dorking for the summer. Cousin Edward Cooper had been given a cure of souls worth a hundred and forty pounds a year, but it was a long way off at Hamstall Ridgway, in Staffordshire, " So we should not see much more of him and his family," said Jane, " until some twenty years hence, when several fat plain girls will be introduced to us as our Hamstall cousins." Poor pretty cousin Jane had been killed in a carriage accident that winter and her husband Sir Thomas Williams was now a sorrowing widower. Charles had run into him at Deal, in the Three Tuns, which the Fleet always called " The Worst Inn in the World." That had been a piece of luck for dear Charles, who after offering condolences, had said with his own sweet disarming smile that he wished with all his heart he might serve again under his old Commander. Sir Thomas very handsomely said that nothing would please him better. He had pulled a string or two at the Admiralty and now Charles was with him in the sloop *Endymion*. Dear Charles was always very adroit at getting his own way. There was one other piece of news which Cassandra had not found in her sister's letters. That month at Abergavenny Mr. Thomas Langlois Lefroy, eldest son of Colonel Anthony Lefroy, of Limerick, had married Mary, only daughter and heiress of Jeffrey Paul, Esquire of Silver Springs, County Wexford. " I wonder Jane did not tell you of it," said Mrs. Austen, glancing at her younger daughter, but Jane only shrugged her shoulders and said calmly, " He may marry whoever he chooses, it is nothing to me."

Martha Lloyd arrived just afterwards for a visit and the three young women re-lived their schoolgirl days, running up to Deane to see Mary and Baby Edward, reading and sewing in their dressing parlour and talking about their love affairs, but not in the light-hearted fashion of the old days ; that was gone for ever. Poor fat Martha, with her soft heart and her foolish head, was very woebegone these days, for the handsome careless soldier, who used to be nicknamed " Mr. W.," had left her in the lurch and married a girl with a better fortune. She talked about it continually, reducing herself to tears whenever she did so. " Yes, I know he was a great flirt, and Mary told me he did not mean anything serious. He was for ever being *particular* with one girl and another, but he never seemed to like any girl so well as he did me. Everybody thought it would have been a match. I believe his friends set him against me, I can tell you I have not been at all well treated. Oh ! it has been the ruin of my life, I shall never love anyone else so well. I cried for days together when I heard that he was gone away. I shall die of a broken heart, I know I shall," wept poor Martha, " and then perhaps he will be sorry that he treated me so cruelly."

Cassandra dried her tears and Jane tried to put some spirit into her. " He is not worth crying over, my dear girl, I am sure he was not half good enough for you. You must put him out of your mind altogether." " Oh ! I cannot, I cannot," Martha sobbed, her tears flowing afresh at the very thought. " You do not know what you are saying." " Do I not ? " said Jane, between her teeth, " I have been disappointed myself, remember." She stood by the fireplace, with her arm on the chimney-piece, tapping her foot impatiently on the floor, while Martha sobbed, " Oh ! I am so sorry for you, I don't know how you can bear to think of Mr. Lefroy married to somebody else. I am sure she is a hateful girl and I hope she will plague his life out of him." " Oh ! I have laughed myself out of being distractedly in love with my Irish friend," vowed Jane. " I daresay he has married a very good sort of girl and I wish them very happy ; and in any case you know, even if he does not like her very well, he will always have several thousand pounds to console him." Her tone was light and dry.

Martha dabbed her swollen eyes. " I do not know how you can talk so," she exclaimed, " I shall always say that he behaved very badly to you." " I beg you will not say it to everyone you meet," Jane told her sharply, turning round upon her. Martha shrank away and stammered, " No, no, I will not be talking, I promise I will not ; but I had rather have you well married than be married myself. I could do very well single, if I had only enough money to live upon comfortably and had pleasant company and a Ball now and then ; but I am afraid to grow old and be poor and be laughed at. I would marry any man who offered for me, rather than die an old maid."

Cassandra looked sad, but Jane said angrily, " I would rather teach in a school (and I can think of nothing worse) than marry a man I did not like." " Oh ! I should not care to marry a disagreeable man, any more than you would," Martha defended herself feebly, " but I do think I could like any pleasant well-bred man with a sufficient income well enough to marry him. I feel sure I could." Jane flung her arms in the air, said, " Oh God ! " and turned away. Cassandra urged Martha gently, " Do not let us talk about " Mr. W." any longer. I am sure you will find somebody much better one of these days." " You are always both of you so good to me," sobbed Martha, flinging her arms round Cassandra and kissing her. " There is nobody I love as well as you two. I wish I could marry one of your brothers and then we should always be really sisters. Mary has had all the luck."

11

In May of that year, 1799, the Godmersham family made up a delightful scheme. Edward had now reached the age when it was proper for him to suffer from the gout and he had spent half the winter taking James's Powder and sitting with his right foot in a wide shoe, or wrapped up in flannel. Dr. Scudamore prescribed a course of the Bath waters, so Edward and Elizabeth arranged to visit the Spa for six weeks. They left the three younger children, George, Henry and William, at home with Nurse Sackree, but took little Fanny and Neddie with them, and generous Edward invited his mother and Jane to come too ; he said it was Jane's turn for a frolic.

He picked them up at Steventon in his great travelling carriage and they all drove off to Devizes. The whole party, including gouty Edward and the children, supped off lobster, asparagus and cheese-cakes at the Bear Inn, and next day jolted on over the pale hills, by Melksham and Box and down the winding valley into Bath. It rained for most of the way and all the umbrellas were up in the streets as they drove past the dark house in the Paragon, but when they reached Queen Square the thunder clouds parted and the delightful city was all in flower to greet them.

Edward had taken two whole floors of No. 13, Queen Square, he and his wife had the first floor and Jane and her mother were up above. The lodgings were kept by a decent widow in mourning, with a black kitten to match, a plaything for the children. Jane flung open the window to smell the rain-washed air and the wet lilacs, tossing their plumes

148

in the square garden. She had a charming perspective view of the roofs and chimneys of Brock Street up above her, white against the purple sky. Three poplars in the last garden in Queen's Parade were thrashing about in the May wind, with a green brilliant fleece of leaves rippling up their branches. Jane sat down by the window, unfolded her mahogany writing desk and dashed it all off to Cassandra, while the elder ladies directed the maid about the unpacking and Edward sallied out to taste a cheese at Fortt's.

Aunt Leigh Perrot urged Edward to consult their own Doctor Mapleton, who always treated Uncle James with so much attention and skill ; nobody in Bath wrote so many prescriptions as he. Edward, however, always preferred to make his own arrangements. He picked another doctor out of the crowd of periwigged gilt-caned old gentlemen inhabiting the Circus, which irreverent people nicknamed the Pillbox, and presently was deeply engaged in the business of his cure. He was to be physicked and drink the waters three times a day, besides taking no wine, which he minded most of all.

Every other evening he was carried in a sedan chair through the courtyard of the White Horse Inn to the bath, where he donned yellow canvas coat and trousers and waded about up to his neck in the steaming turbid water for a couple of hours, pushing before him his floating lacquer tray with his snuff box and handkerchief upon it. Then his chairmen would carry him home wrapped in flannel, right upstairs into his bedroom, where he could roll straight from his sedan into bed and sweat out his aches and pains. Uncle Leigh Perrot and he often went into the warm bath together for company, while old Mrs. Austen, indulging more mildly in the cure, used to walk down with her son and brother to the Pump Room for their daily glasses from the hot spring. The children at first were wild to taste it, for they thought it must be something quite delicious, but Ned wrinkled his nose over the draught and pert Miss Fanny vowed that it tasted like the water eggs were boiled in.

They loved seeing the sights of Bath with their pretty Aunt. She took them all round the Abbey and held them

up to watch the sick people wading about in their yellow
bathing gowns in the public bath, right in the middle of
the street ; how funny they looked ! Aunt Jane said that
this bath had been made by the Romans and that very
likely if you were to dig underneath the houses you would
find more of their baths and temples buried in the earth.
She was full of charming stories about the Romans and the
Benedictine monks of the Abbey ; she knew all about how
the queen of James the First had been frightened by a ball
of fire coming up through the water while she was bathing,
how Beau Nash had torn off the Duchess of Queensborough's
lace apron at a dance, and how he had taken all her winnings
at the card table from the great Duchess of Marlborough,
to help found the Mineral Water Hospital. Then there was
the story of how Doctor Oliver, whose picture was stamped
on the biscuits they liked so much, had left the secret recipe
to his coachman, because he had nothing else to give him,
and the coachman had made his fortune out of them. She
read them funny bits out of Mr. Sheridan's play, *The Rivals*,
about how the fine gentlemen used to go out before breakfast
and fight duels in the King's Meads. Their governess at
Godmersham did not make history nearly so interesting as
Aunt Jane did.

Cassandra at Steventon got long letters from Jane, with
dear little messages from Ned and Fanny to Grandpapa and
Aunt Cass, to Uncle and Aunt James, to the black-and-white
turkeys in the Steventon poultry yard and the chaffinch on
her nest in the hedge, for they were still at the age when
animals and people are one family. Jane chiefly sent news
about shopping. Elizabeth and she had been up and down
Milsom Street, hunting presents. Jane had bought stockings
for Mary and shoes for Martha, she chose for herself a
lace cloak, almost too handsome to be worn, she drew a
little picture of its pattern in the margin ; and she had
found just the right black lace veil for Cassandra and herself
to give to Mary. Elizabeth had given Jane a very pretty
hat in the French taste trimmed with narrow ruched purple
ribbons. Bunches of artificial fruit were all the rage that
summer, and Elizabeth had bought a cluster of very life-

like strawberries at Perivale's, the drapers in Milsom Street, but their fruit was very dear and it was not much cheaper in the little shops under the Stall Street colonnade, or down in Walcot, where their rich mean Aunt liked to go bargain-hunting. You could buy four or five pretty sprigs of flowers for the price of one Orleans Plum. Jane had felt obliged to be thrifty, but had consoled herself with the flippant reflection that it did seem more natural somehow for flowers to grow out of the head than fruit. And Edward in his lordly way had gone out and bought a pair of black carriage horses so perfectly matched that he had been obliged to give sixty guineas for them.

Her letters were sprightly enough, but when you looked into them actually they were having rather a quiet time. Edward was much taken up with his cure and did not care for going out in the evenings so that they only went to one concert and not at all to the theatre. Once he met a Kentish neighbour, Mr. Evelyn of St. Clere, near Wrotham, who invited them to his house on Queen's Parade, but Elizabeth did not feel equal to the occasion. " We were to have dashed away at a very extraordinary rate by dining out," Jane wrote in what might have been quiet exasperation, " but it so happened that we did not go." They had a tea drinking in the Paragon and Doctor Mapleton's three amiable daughters, Marianne, Jane and Christina, took their old acquaintance Miss Austen for a sweet walk, on a golden evening, to the little village of Charlcombe in its narrow little green valley, and back to tea afterwards at their house in Belmont. Otherwise the diversions of the party were chiefly such as would amuse the children. They were rowed over the river to that sweet retreat Spring Gardens, to an *al fresco* breakfast under the chestnut and lime trees. They strolled in the green Barton Fields on Sunday, when the May sunshine was bright on the white pillared curve of the Royal Crescent. They watched a Lady Willoughby presenting colours to a corps of yeomanry, with plenty of drum-and-fife music, scarlet and blue uniforms, fine gentlemen on horseback and coachloads full of ladies in muslin gowns. They refreshed themselves at Sally Lunn's bunshop and at Mr. Gill's, the pastrycook's, with a jelly, a tart, or a small basin of vermicelli ; they went to an opening entertainment at the new Sydney Gardens, where there was music and a fine display of fireworks.

Had there been nothing more worth while for Jane than this ? Cassandra asked herself, turning the letters over to read them again. Had there been no handsome captain at the review, to peep under the bent brim of the new hat with the ruched violet ribbons and tell her how the shade of it became her clear pale skin, her brilliant eyes and nut brown hair ? Had there been no witty and well-spoken parson or lawyer, to turn over books and prints with her in the Milsom Street library ? Had there been no dashing sea-officer on leave to lead her out at the Assembly Rooms and press her for another pair of dances, because in such a public place where nobody knew them it could not matter how often they danced together ? Had there been nobody but her uncle or her brother to arm her about under the moonlit trees, at the Sydney Gardens, where the twinkling lights were like coloured fruit upon the bushes, to hear the distant music drift across the dark canal and watch the rockets curve above their own reflections in the glassy water ? Well, it did not appear, when Jane came home again and all was told, that she had done anything very much at Bath except wait upon her elders and relieve them of the care of the children. " I should not think it had been worth her going," Mary said, in her own fretful self-centred fashion. " I own I was vexed myself that Edward and Elizabeth did not invite me to go with them, instead of Jane. Indeed I thought it quite on the north side of civil, James and the children could have done very well without me for a week or two. I daresay Cassy would have gone up to Deane and looked after them for me. I really needed a holiday, but of course I could not mention it if Edward and Elizabeth did not think of it for themselves. But now I am very glad I did not go. I do not believe I should have enjoyed it at all."

12

Ever since the beginning of that year, 1799, Frank had been knocking about the Gulf of Lyons in the *Petrel*. His family could fancy him lying off the shining lagoons at the mouth of the Rhone, running down to Barcelona and back round the low red coasts of Majorca and Minorca, smelling the aromatic offshore breeze from the Corsican mountains, coming back to take a look in at Toulon or Villefranche, to see if the French would put their noses out this time. The Fleet cruised and cruised and one day was so like another that they were hardly distinguishable. Frank and his fellows grew sick and tired of silvery olive groves and twisted pines, of frowning limestone headlands and little white and yellow ports, all exactly alike, set down between sea and mountain. They were at sea sometimes for weeks together, in white and black squalls, in great gales and lumping seas, in sea fogs thick as buttermilk, in oily dazzling calms, in nights of glittering moonlight and innumerable stars. They got spongy gums and aching muscles after weeks of salt beef, when the limes and lemons had run out, the biscuit was getting bad and the water green and slimy in the casks. There was little glory or prize money to be got that year, Frank wrote, on the Mediterranean station. Most of the time they were hunting privateers, taking prizes of small Spanish coasters and the like ; usually they were simply watching and waiting to see whether the French would come out and fight.

Once he did have a chance of something better. Admiral Brieux had slipped out of Brest, dodged the blockade, passed the Straits and vanished into the Mediterranean. He might be making for Toulon, or worse for Egypt, to fetch Boney home. Lord St. Vincent sent urgent dispatches to Lord Nelson in Sicily, warning him of his danger and Frank got orders to carry them. The *Petrel* sloop was little, but she was fast. He crowded on all sail, made a quick scurry through the dangerous windy strait between Sardinia and the high peaks of Corsica and ran down across the

Tyrrhenian Sea till he sighted, over the horizon's rim, the great amphitheatre of mountains behind Palermo. That was in May, while his family were amusing themselves at Bath.

Lord Nelson had been in Palermo since the January of that year, 1799, when he had rescued our shabby allies, the King and Queen of the Two Sicilies, with their family, their treasure and many of their courtiers, from an insurrection in Naples and had carried them all over in the *Vanguard* to their second capital, Palermo. With Naples a lost harbour to him and the French in Malta, Lord Nelson had to make his headquarters in Sicily. He was living in a palace on the waterfront at Palermo with old Sir William Hamilton, our Ambassador to the King of Naples and his admired lady. There was a good deal of gossip beginning to blow up at this time both in the Fleet and at home, about the little Admiral. It was freely said that he was not in his usual state of health, that the head wound which he had received at the Battle of the Nile still troubled him greatly, that he was nervous, irresolute, irritable, at times almost distracted. The beautiful Lady Hamilton had altogether too much influence over him. She was playing at politics with the Queen and fancying herself a great heroine, and these two women were ordering the Admiral and his ships here and there to please themselves. Spiteful people already hinted that Lady Hamilton was the Admiral's mistress. Old Lord St. Vincent had always given Lord Nelson plenty of rope, but he had gone home, and Admiral Keith, his successor, was much displeased by the whole situation. Certainly that summer the King and Queen were restored to their palace in Naples, and the wretched revolutionaries were sought out and punished with great severity, so that the Fleet could use Naples Harbour again ; but Lord Nelson seemed unable to recover Malta, and at the end of the summer the worst thing possible happened. General Bonaparte left his deserted French Army to rot in the desert, slipped through Lord Nelson's fingers, landed in Provence and got safe home to Paris. There he and his friends turned out the Directory by an armed *coup-d'état*.

France was to be ruled in future in the antique manner by
three Consuls, of whom General Bonaparte was to be chief.
Nobody supposed that the other two would count for anything much.

13

That August, 1799, was the time that the queer thing
happened to Aunt Leigh Perrot. It was breath-taking,
incredible, as if the pavement of Bath had opened under
her flat respectable feet and a black hole, with steam rising
from it, had gaped to swallow up the proud disagreeable
woman. She was accused of having stolen a piece of lace
from a shop and the magistrates had positively committed
her to Ilchester Jail, to stand her trial at the spring assizes.
The Austens' neighbours were all talking about it, putting
their heads together and changing the subject hastily if any
of the family came in ; no doubt the same thing was going
on over half the tea tables in Bath. Nodding and winking
and lifting up their hands her enemies, for she had many,
hinted that at her time of life it was not unknown for rich
well-fed imperious old ladies to do odd things. " If a poor
man's wife helps herself to somebody else's belongings she
is hung or transported for a term of years ; but Mrs. Leigh
Perrot has a rich husband who can pay through the nose
to get her let off. For my part I wish she might be sent to
Botany Bay, I cannot abide the woman."

" No, no, it is no such thing, you do not properly understand the matter. Mrs. Leigh Perrot has been shamefully
used. It was all a mistake. She was walking down by the
Cross Bath with her husband, as they do every day, so that
he may drink his glass of water at the Pump. She left him
and went into one of the little shops under the Colonnade
in Stall Street where she bought a piece of black lace for a
cloak. The shop was Miss Gregory's, she often has great
bargains in laces and ribbons, and you know Mrs. Leigh
Perrot loves a bargain, for all she is so well-off. The shop
was kept before by people named Smith, but they went

bankrupt. This Miss Gregory is Mrs. Smith's sister ; there is another odd fish, I think called Gye, at the back of them and they are all nothing but common swindlers. Mrs. Leigh Perrot was walking back with her husband from the Pump an hour after when the shopwoman ran out and asked her whether she had a card of white lace with the black. Mrs. Leigh Perrot opened the parcel in her hand and there the white and the black edgings were together. She thought it was all a mistake until two days later a constable came with a warrant for her arrest." " Poor Mr. Leigh Perrot got up out of his bed, sick as he was with a fit of the gout, all in a sweat from the Hot Bath and unable to move but with two sticks. He went with his wife before the Mayor, and there were these wretches, Miss Gregory and her partner, both swearing that they had seen her help herself to the lace. What do you think of that ? Oh ! it is a most shocking affair, I never heard of anything like it in my life." " Have you not, indeed ? I knew of a case very like it, last year, where a gentleman was served the same trick. Indeed I am told that these black-hearted villains here have made several similar attempts before now in this very city, only it never came out. The wretches must have marked down our poor friend as somebody timid enough to be scared and rich enough to pay handsomely, rather than go through a public trial, for that, you know, must be a terrible business for a delicate female." " They did not know this lady very well if they thought she would be easy to frighten." " No, indeed ; she is determined to carry it all through with a high hand. She swears she is innocent and thinks she has only to stick to that ; she never dreams that the verdict might go against her. Poor Mr. Leigh Perrot is not so confident. My husband tells me that he has arranged to sell all his property and go with his wife to the ends of the earth, if she is to be transported."

" Oh ! heavens, it surely could not come to that ? " " We must hope not, indeed, but you know these villains would swear black was white if need be, and it seems there is only her own and her husband's word against theirs." " Well, I pity poor Mr. Leigh Perrot with all my heart and his wife too. For all she is so proud and disagreeable one would not wish her to lie in the common prison." "The case is not so desperate as that. She is lodged in the jailor's house and her husband is with her, but there she must stay till Easter, when the judge comes down for the Taunton Assizes. I wish it may not be the death of her and him too." That was how they were talking in Bath, returning again and again with a shocked fascination to the details of the disaster, eyeing each other and thinking with secret discomfort, "Why, it might have happened to any one of us. It might even have happened to me."

At Steventon they were all distressed and shocked beyond measure. Mr. Austen could not take it in at all. "Your poor sister could never have done such a thing. These people must have been deceived in some way or another, they could never have formed such an atrocious scheme. It is all a dreadful mistake. One does not know what to think." "One knows exactly what to think," pronounced his wife. "It is the most wicked abominable plot. Nobody who knows her character could be deceived by it for one moment. The jailor's house is no fit place for my brother and his wife to spend the winter in. These Scaddings are very good people and do the best they can, but she says they do not know what comfort is. My poor brother and sister have but the one room to sit in by themselves with a smoky fire in it, and dogs and cats and dirty squalling brats run in and out all day long ; it is as noisy as Bedlam. They are forced to sit down at the same table with the whole family. Scadding is a swearing vulgar man and the children are very ill behaved, they put bits of greasy toast on my brother's knees and spill the table beer over him. He bears it all like an angel, the poor woman says in her letter, but really it is more than flesh and blood can stand. Did I read you the piece where she said that the other day Mrs. Scadding actually licked her own knife to clean it from fried onions and then helped the butter with it ? "

Jane laughed out loud and Cassandra could not keep a straight face. Even Mrs. Austen was obliged to smile too. "But it is no laughing matter, my dears," she lamented.

" Do but consider what comfort and elegance they live in
when they are at Scarlets, or in the Paragon. They are not
young people any longer and my poor brother suffers so
with the gout. It is very hard for them with so much unpleasantness ; I declare my heart bleeds for them. I wish
I might go there and do what I could for them, but how can
I leave home ? Besides my own health would never stand
it." On this Cassandra, all anxiety, and Jane, all generous
indignation, eagerly offered to go instead of her. Mrs.
Austen rubbed her nose and looked doubtful. " Cassandra
is the better nurse, though Jane could be more easily spared ;
but you do not get on so well with your aunt as Cassy does,
my dear." " I am sure I could put up with all her odd
ways, I should not let her provoke me if I thought I could
be of help to her. I could keep the children in order, and you
know I always make my uncle laugh with my nonsense,"
said Jane eagerly.

" I am not sure that it would be fit for either of them to
go," their father objected anxiously, " To be living in such
a situation for four or five months, they might see and hear
very dreadful things. I am not happy at the thought."
Cassandra hung over him and tried to soothe him ; Jane
said, with some impatience, " We are not hot-house plants,
we shall come to no harm." She got her way and the offer
was made, but their aunt stoutly refused it, writing firmly,
" I could not suffer such elegant females to be lodged in
this vile place," which made Jane quite angry. The trial
took place at the very end of March in the tremendous dark
Hall of Taunton Castle, before Mr. Justice Lawrence. James
was to have gone over with Mary to attend it, for he
always paid great attention to his rich aunt, but the poor
fellow broke his leg out riding a few days earlier and could
not bear the journey. However Mrs. Leigh Perrot was
supported by many other relatives and friends, all wishing
to show how heartily they believed in her innocence. The
old lady spoke up very stoutly for herself and had brought
three-and-twenty witnesses to testify against her accusers,
but the learned judge did not trouble to hear them all and
very properly summed up entirely in the prisoner's favour.

The jury were only out some seven minutes and Mrs. Leigh Perrot was triumphantly acquitted.

14

She returned in triumph to Bath and all her acquaintances flocked about her, kissing and crying, to hear her story. It was a most gratifying reception. She told it very well with a good deal of dry humour, but was highly indignant with the judge for being so easy with the shop people. " They should have been set in the pillory at least, my dears, indeed they richly deserved the gallows. My counsel did not manage the case at all well. I could have asked those villains many more inconvenient questions than he did. I would have made them squeak pretty loud. Imagine, these wretches have now got off scot free, they're not to have any punishment at all for what they made us suffer. I own I think our boasted laws are strangely defective, it is we who are the sufferers in the end. My poor good man has been put to a very frightful expense over the collecting of witnesses, their two days' house and eating at Taunton alone amount to ninety-three pounds. Altogether he spent nearer two thousand pounds than one and will never see a penny of it again. It is fortunate that we have no children. However," she would conclude with great spirit, tossing her turbaned head, " All's well that ends well. The man is fled, the shop is ruined, and my character is cleared. Lace, I am glad to say, is *not* necessary to my happiness." Her nieces took this up, and for some time afterwards, when any little thing went wrong, Jane and Cassandra were accustomed to say to each other, smiling, " Lace is *not* necessary to our happiness."

March of that year, 1800, the month of the trial, was also the month when Frank earned his first sprig of laurel. Cruising by the yellow barren Provençal shore, six miles off Marseilles, he had a running fight of three hours with a French vessel, *La Ligurienne* and captured her without losing a single man. This prize of his was a fine vessel not two years built ; she carried fourteen long six-pounders and two thirty-six pounder carronades, all brass, and one hundred men on board of her, to his own eighty-nine. It had been a neat little affair, it would mean promotion for Frank and good prize money at last for himself and his crew. That spring also General Bonaparte, the first Consul, crossed the Alps, like young Hannibal before him, and fell upon the Austrian army. He defeated them heavily at Marengo before the end of the summer and drove them finally out of Italy ; but he lost Malta in September and with it the command of the Mediterranean. It was Admiral Lord Keith who actually took the yellow island. Lord Nelson had asked to be relieved of his command thirteen months earlier, on grounds of ill-health, but it was freely said that he and Lord Keith would never pull together. There had been an odd business off Malta, when the little Admiral had ignored a signal of recall in the heat of battle ; but the Commander-in-Chief had passed it over, because it had ended in the capture of a French prize, though it was said in the Fleet that Lord Nelson could have been broke for it. The trouble between the two men had come to a head finally when Lord Nelson took two ships off the Malta blockade to convoy the Queen of Naples to Leghorn, on her way to Vienna. Old Keith declared roundly that Lady Hamilton had had command of the Fleet long enough, Sir William found himself superseded and the Hamiltons and Lord Nelson returned to England together with rumour roaring behind them.

Captain Frank Austen, after the fall of Malta, got a spell of service in the Eastern Mediterranean. He was heard of by his family off the Egyptian coast, where a Pasha had presented him with a sabre and an embroidered pelisse, for the rescue of a Turkish ship. Jane said that as he had no wife yet she hoped he would bring the garment home for one of his sisters. Old General Abercromby, whose name Cassandra remembered only too well as the commander of the ill-fated expedition to Santo Domingo, had landed in Egypt and was making his dispositions to round up and capture the remains of Bonaparte's lost army there, a campaign which was to be the death of the tough old Scots commander. And in October Frank, putting in at the lovely little Venetian harbour of Rhodes, was met by an agreeable Captain Inglis, who had the best of news for him. " I am to collar you and turn you out of the *Petrel*, Austen, you are made Post Captain and may go home to England on leave."

15

His family had known it months earlier, such were the delays in news and letters from the Mediterranean. They were all delighted that dear Frank was coming home after his long absence, the more so as his father was beginning to feel his years. Mr. Austen would be seventy that year and he was growing fragile and fidgety. He did not go about the glebe as he used to ; he had his long walk and his short walk round the garden, pottered in and out, sat amongst his books and was easily upset by cold and bad weather. His wife and his elder daughter-in-law had begun to put their heads together and consider whether he ought to retire. Mary Austen was a great one for plots and plans and for turning people round her little finger. In her quiet hard secretive mind she had worked everything out to suit herself. James was thirty-five and she had been married to him for three years. She was sick and tired of scraping and pinching up at Deane on the curate's stipend. She considered that her dear James, with his scholarly mind and his eloquent preaching, was worthy of better things than the cure of Steventon, but it might at least be a stepping stone. She coveted the comfortable big Parsonage, the gardens and the glebe, she envied the way the villagers looked up to old Mr. Austen as if he were the Squire. Her precious boy, her only child Edward, ought to have a proper provision made for him and her stepdaughter too, though that came second with Mary.

She had always been able to pull the wool over old Mrs. Austen's eyes and set about it very cleverly. She would say with a frown, as she watched the rector toddling down the drive to visit some sick parishioner, " I do not think the dear old gentleman ought to be out in this East wind. People should have more consideration, they should not send for him so often as they do. James would go instead of him, you know, with all the pleasure in life." Mrs. Austen, darning her husband's black silk stockings, would reply placidly, " The old people like to see my husband, they are used to having him go when they are sick." But Mary was not to be put off so easily. She kept on suggesting to her mother-in-law that the time had come for Mr. Austen to retire, " I do believe he should live in some warmer climate. Our winters up here are so very cold and I am sure he feels it. Do you not think he ought to be relieved of his duty ? Can he get through with it without the most injurious fatigue ? Would it not be better for him to settle in some pleasant place like Bath, while he still has the power to enjoy it ? "

Mrs. Austen confessed, " I should like Bath very well myself, it always suits me " ; and began to turn the matter over in her mind, while Mary pressed her eagerly. " Oh ! If you were to fix on Bath, I am sure it would be the very thing for you all. The dear old gentleman would never be dull there. He would have the book-shops and the library to amuse him and could go to church in the Abbey on Sundays. You would have your brother and his wife to visit and a whole circle of old friends ; you need never miss your game of whist or your pool of commerce. You would have good Doctor Mapleton at hand in case of illness. You know you have your own health to consider as well as his. It is quite melancholy to think of you both wearing out your lives in a place like Steventon, where you live so very retired and seem shut out from all the world except your own family." " Steventon is dull in the winter, to be sure," admitted Mrs. Austen, " I have lived here close on forty years and I own I should like a change. I have not been at all in good health lately, I think I owe it to myself to move, but what about the girls ? I do not think either of them would want to live in a town. Cassy is so fond of a country life and Jane dislikes Bath, she says it does not

agree with her." " Oh ! that does not signify at all,"
exclaimed Mary, with her plain pock-marked face reddening
with excitement. " They must allow you to know what is
best for them. Do but consider for a moment, how are
they ever to get husbands in a retired village like Steventon ?
Jane will be twenty-four this December, and Cassy is rising
thirty, if we do not take some trouble about the matter they
will both die old maids. A larger society would improve
Cassy's chances ; she is very handsome, but her spirits are
too low, she wants animation. If she could but meet some
older gentleman, a widower, you know, with children who
needed a mother," Mary improvised, " what a wife she
would make him ! Then dear Jane is growing very sharp
and disagreeable in some of the things she says. She makes
fun of all the young men hereabouts, calls them puppies and
says they are not handsome or clever enough to tempt her.
She needs to be more from home. She is quite right, there
is a great dearth of eligible young men in these parts. Last
winter there were never enough partners to go round at
the Assemblies. Jane did not get her share, it was observed ;
people said to me that they were sorry to see her passed
over, and this year I dare say it will be worse. Oh ! the
girls are thrown away in our little society here, you must
take them to Bath ; it is the finest place in the kingdom to
get husbands. And it really is time," said Mary, letting her
polite mask slip aside for a moment, " for dear Mr. Austen
to retire and make way for a younger man."

16

Mary was able to work away like this at her mother-in-law
behind the girls' backs as she dared not have done to their
faces, because it so happened in the Autumn of 1800, that
both Parson Austen's daughters were away from home at
the same time, a thing which happened very seldom.
Cassandra had gone first in October down to Kent, to attend
the Faversham Balls and Jane went later to Ibthorp, to stay
with Mrs. Lloyd and Martha. Mary may have had a finger

in that pie, at least it fell out very conveniently for her purposes.

Cassandra, away at Godmersham, found Jane's letters getting very tart, though she sent little bits of home news as faithfully as ever. Her father was making a new plantation by the side of the Elm Walk, and there had been long amiable indeterminate discussions with everybody as to whether it should be a little orchard of plums, pears and apples, or a nursery of young larches, acacia and mountain ash. Two of the great elms in the drive had come crashing down in an autumn gale and James Digweed, twisting himself about and making faces, had supposed they must have fallen for grief at Miss Cassandra's long absence. James was the third son of Farmer Hugh Digweed up at Steventon Manor, a very dull oaf; he had lately taken orders and it was a family joke that he was supposed to be Cassandra's admirer, much to the regret of little Miss Sukey Lyford, who was pining for him. Jane could tease her sister about James Digweed with perfect ease, but both of them knew without speech that Cassandra would never look at him or any man after Tom Fowle. Mr. Heathcote, that sporting parson, had broken his leg out hunting; Earle Harwood, the officer in the Marines, had contrived to shoot himself in the foot, much to the alarm of his family. Jane had been up with the James Austens to dine with dear old Mr. Holder; Mary had thought it a dull evening, but Jane had quite enjoyed sitting over a good fire in a handsome room, laughing at the old gentleman's infamous puns. Charles had ridden up from Gosport for a dance, looking very gay and handsome.

About the first Basingstoke Assembly she wrote quite crossly for her. She had worn her old muslin gown, with a bit of the same stuff twisted round her head and one little comb. Chairs, supper and partners had all been short; there had been very few beauties in the room and such as there were not very handsome. Mrs. Blount, the chief of them, had appeared exactly as before, with the same broad face, diamond bandeau, white shoes, pink husband and fat neck. There had been several stout girls with short noses who puzzled Jane, but all turned out to be the Misses Atkinson. Sir Thomas Champneys had brought a daughter, a queer animal with a white neck ; and there had been a tribe of the Misses Debary all in black, mourning statues for the death of a rich uncle.

Jane could not endure these girls, whom she always called the endless Debaries. They were the daughters of the rector of Hurstbourne Tarrant, good dull chattering creatures, and she always had more than enough of them when she went to stay with Martha Lloyd and her mother. This she did in mid-November and was soon confessing in a letter to Cassandra that she always found the road from Ibthorp to Hurstbourne Tarrant much dirtier and more impracticable for walking than the Debaries did from their end of it. Three of them had put on cloaks and pattens and come clinking up through the floods to visit her on the morning after she arrived, but she had been lazy and had not yet returned the civility. They had been tumbling over each other to tell Jane and Martha about the lady who was to marry Charles's captain, Sir Thomas Williams. She was a certain Miss Wapshire of Salisbury, a distinguished beauty, gushed the Debaries, about seven or eight and twenty and so less dazzling than she used to be, but always remarkable for the propriety of her behaviour. She sounded as if she might be a suitable successor to poor pretty Cousin Jane, already two years in her grave ; her Steventon cousins could heartily wish Sir Thomas happy in his second choice. The match was considered certain and near at hand.

Otherwise there was not much news to be had from Ibthorp ; even such desperate walkers as Martha and Jane had been kept indoors for days together. The floods were out, the ways all floated in the valley and the wind so strong that there was no pleasure in climbing the high downs. Martha's little Welsh mother was growing bent and very frail and there was a tiresome poor relation, Mrs. Stent, who was very dull. However, when Jane and Martha were together, they always had plenty to talk about and Jane intended to carry dear Martha back to Steventon for Christmas.

Cassandra was not there when the two of them arrived, all that she knew was what Martha told her afterwards, " Oh ! my dear, it was the most shocking thing. I am sure I shall never forget it. We had had such a long cold journey, you know ; it rained all the day down the valley to Hurstbourne Priors, and then the coach was late, and then we had to change again and when we got to Steventon in the post-chaise we were both so tired and frozen that we could hardly speak, at least I know I was. Mrs. Austen was sitting by the parlour fire and my sister Mary was with her. They both looked very queerly as if they had been talking over something important. We had hardly sat down to warm ourselves and I was beginning to give my sister Mary all the news from home, as one does, you know, when I heard Mrs. Austen say without any warning, ' Well, girls, it is all settled. Your father and I have decided to leave Steventon and go to Bath.' I can tell you I was all in a pother. I could not tell what to say, I was so taken aback. ' Oh ! my dear Mrs. Austen,' I believe I said, ' what will you all do in Bath ? You will be quite lost in that great place and how will all the poor folk here get on without you ? ' "

" Then I heard a strange noise beside me, I looked round and there was dear Jane tumbled down upon the floor in a fainting fit. I never knew her do such a thing before. I suppose it was the surprise of having the news blurted out so very suddenly. I screamed very loud and Mary jumped up and ran to her. Mary always knows what to do when anyone is ill, she does not get flustered as I do. We rubbed Jane's hands and when she could look up we made her drink a glass of hot wine, but we had quite a piece of work to revive her. Old Mrs. Austen was very much put about, she said she had never thought Jane would make such a silly fuss. Jane laughed at herself afterwards, you know the way she does, and said she could not imagine what had come over her ; but she looked very badly all that evening, as white as a sheet and did not seem like herself for two or three days afterwards. Then she cheered up and said she thought a change would do you all good, she talked about concerts in Bath and so on, but it had been a blow, I am sure it had been a great blow." And honest Martha, opening her eyes very wide and looking quite perplexed, said then and afterwards, " It was the only time I ever saw Jane overpowered."

V
Bath
1801-1805

GOING away from Steventon was like the game they used to play when they were children of rolling down the grass slope at the top of the garden. You went slowly at first, then faster and faster and in the end you could not stop yourself, you tumbled headlong all the way to the bottom. At first there seemed plenty of time for everything. Cassandra was urged not to hurry home, the move was going on very nicely without her. James did not want his father's library and would not farm the glebe, but dear Mr. Holder would take that over. The fields lay conveniently next to his own property and he would be glad to employ John Bond, the bailiff, who was exceedingly well satisfied because now he need not change his work or his cottage. James was going to put in a curate up at Deane, but the curacy had been declined both by young Mr. Peter Debary, brother of all those endless girls, who wished to be nearer London, and also by James Digweed. Jane told her sister teasingly that he evidently did not want Deane parsonage unless she would consent to be one of the fixtures. James was to have the black horse and the brown mare, Mary would take over Mrs. Austen's poultry and Cassandra's bees, the furniture was after all to be sold, they could buy as good or better in Bath.

By the time that Cassandra came home the farewell visits had already begun. Carriages drove up to the door almost daily from every manor and parsonage in the neighbourhood. Flocks of ladies young and old, in their best bonnets all plumed with cocks' tails and guinea-fowl feathers, came to cluck over and lament the Austens' departure ; the Heathcotes, the Harwoods, the Bigg-Withers, the Blatchfords, the Terrys, the Bramsons and the Chutes. Everybody said the same things, how sad it was to lose them, but how delightful the winters would be in Bath and then how pleasant to spend the warmer months by the sea or in Wales !

Mrs. Lefroy came down several times with a basket for roots and cuttings, she was a great gardener and some of the choicest geraniums had been put aside for her. She, dear soul, was going to miss them more than anybody. She would have liked the curacy of Deane for young Mr. Rice, who had just married her daughter Lucy, it would be quite delightful to have the young people so close. Jane said, " Lucy must be prepared to have Mary interfere in all her household concerns and abuse her for extravagance." That was Mary's way, she had grown very sharp after money since she married James. She was not above trying to beat down the price of everything, and it was quite irritating to watch her going round the house and garden with a sharp eye for dilapidation, planning what improvements she would make when she and James came to live there. Several family breezes blew up about what was to be taken and what was to be left behind, and the girls began to feel that they would be glad when all the hustle was over and done with.

May, 1801, was the date fixed for their departure. The Rector had wanted to celebrate his last Easter Festival before he went and visit every cottage in the parish to say good-bye. Jane and her mother left first, for Mrs. Leigh Perrot had invited them to come to the Paragon and begin house-hunting from there, while Cassandra took her father for a visit to Ibthorp. On a bright morning, when the cuckoos were flying and calling across the upland fields and the wind was shaking the lilac bushes, the post-chaise came rattling up to the door. Mrs. Austen was bundled into it with all her shawls and bandboxes, Mr. Austen pottered out of his study to say good-bye, only Jane was not ready. It was unlike her, she was always so punctual. " Run upstairs and tell her to hurry," urged Mr. Austen, in great distress. " Say her mother is waiting. You should not keep the horses too long in this wind."

Cassandra ran upstairs and there, in the dressing parlour stood Jane. She was ready dressed for the journey in the new brown cambric gown which Cassandra had bought for her in Canterbury, with her brown spencer on and her straw bonnet tied under her chin ; she even had her short gloves buttoned and her little mahogany writing desk in her arms. She stood perfectly still, looking at Cassandra and opened her lips to speak, but no sound came out of them. " They are waiting," said Cassandra, going up to her sister and taking the little square box from her. " It is time to go."

Jane looked all round the room, their own room, at the painted press with the book-shelves above it, at the round gilt mirror, at the old faded carpet, with its bunches of prim flowers upon a chocolate ground, from which all the colours had quite faded away. " I did not know I should feel it as I do," said Jane faintly. " It is like being torn up by the roots. You and I have been so happy in this room." Cassandra put her arms round her younger sister and said, " Oh ! my dear, we shall be happy in Bath." " I daresay we may," said Jane, " but we shall never be two young girls together any more at Steventon. All that is over."

Cassandra had no words. She felt the straining clasp of two slender arms and caught a sigh like a flame going out, or like something dying. Then Jane pushed her off and walked out of the room with a firm step. Left behind, Cassandra heard the slam of the post-chaise door, the clatter of hoofs and wheels which followed it, the post boy's horn at the gate. Jane was gone and soon she would have to go too. Parson Austen's daughters had finished with Steventon.

2

That spring, 1801, when Frank came home from the Mediterranean, was one of the most dangerous moments of the war. The First Consul, like young Hannibal before him, had crossed the Alps and in mid-winter had wiped out the Austrian army among the snows of Hohenlinden. In February they had made peace with him. His Egyptian army had long been written off, but the war in Europe was over for the moment and he had come back to Boulogne to look over his invasion barges. Poor Frank, who was longing for a ship, was vexed to be spending the next six months or so on the East Coast raising and drilling the Fencibles. " It is a new government plan, a body of fishermen and long-shoremen, half of them smugglers, I fancy, who should be with the Fleet. They are to patrol up and down and light bonfires if they see any suspicious craft inshore ; it is all nonsense. Boney will never get over." He did not wish his mother and sisters to think he was in any particular danger.

Where he wanted to have gone was to the Baltic where the Danes, Swedes and Russians had banded themselves together in a league of armed neutrality against us. A squadron had been sent to give the Danes a lesson. Old Admiral Hyde Parker, a slow dull fellow, was in command, but he had Lord Nelson under him and Frank would have given an eye or an arm himself to have been present at the Battle of Copenhagen. It had been the strangest affair, another Aboukir, the little Admiral slipping in by the back door through the sands round the anchored enemy fleet to perform another of his insubordinate miracles.

At Bath old Mr. Nelson, the hero's father, a familiar figure to everyone with his great hawk nose, his long hair, his air of mild and gentle surprise, found his hand shaken violently by total strangers as he wandered out from his Pierrepoint Street lodging to totter up and down in the sun on the South Parade. The Admiral's thin, peevish, frowning wife found herself the centre of much attention and civility at card parties in the Circus and the Crescent. People would have congratulated her on her husband's victory if it had not been generally known that they had parted for ever. The name of Nelson stopped the show at the theatre, ballads upon the Baltic action were hawked about the streets, and the Admiral was voted the Freedom of the City. Bath society was pretty well divided that year between those who considered that the Admiral had treated his wife very badly and those who wondered how he could have endured so tiresome a woman for so long. He was seen everywhere in

London that summer with the Hamiltons, but it was not yet known that Lady Hamilton had secretly borne him a daughter.

Jane sent word of their house-hunting to Ibthorp, together with whatever scraps of news might make Cassandra laugh about their entertainment in the Paragon. Her aunt had made their visit an excuse for tea-drinking, whist and cribbage, little parties full of *card playing old toughs*. The only man for Jane to set her black cap at unfortunately already had a wife and ten children. Her aunt had a bad cold and was deafer than ever. She had been a walk with Dr. Mapleton's daughters, but poor Marianne, their favourite, had lately died of a decline. A Mrs. Chamberlayne, as desperate a walker as herself, had taken Jane out to Weston at a great rate under a hot May sun, stopping for nothing and posting across the churchyard at Weston as if she were afraid of being buried alive. Another afternoon they had tramped to Widcombe and Lyncombe and had seen the lovely yellow house where Fielding wrote his novels ; how Tom Lefroy and she used to laugh together over *Tom Jones* !

Her uncle had thought it proper to take her to a ball at the Assembly Rooms, where she had worn a very pretty yellow and white cloud just sent home by Mrs. Mussell, her aunt's dressmaker, but the great room had been practically empty, only four couples performing in the minuets before the tea interval, surrounded by a hundred spectators. The breaking up of private parties after tea sent some scores more to the ball and though it was shockingly and inhumanly thin for Bath there had been people enough, Jane supposed, to have made five or six Basingstoke assemblies. She herself, however, had got no partner. She had been obliged to while away her evening watching other light-footed young women going down the dance, seeing an acquaintance running round the room after a drunken husband and picking out the heroine of a recent scandal. " I flatter myself that I have a very good eye for an adulteress, for though repeatedly assured that another in the same party was she, I fixed upon the right one from the first. She is not so pretty as I expected, her face has the same defect of baldness as her sister's and her features are not so handsome," wrote Jane, dipping her pen in gall. " She looked rather quietly and contentedly silly than anything else." The best amusement Jane had had was a drive in a phaeton over Kingsdown with a certain dashing Mr. Evelyn, Edward's neighbour in Kent. And dear Charles, now a commander and serving in the *Endymion* under Sir Thomas Williams, had got thirty pounds prize money after the capture of a French privateer and had sent each of his sisters a topaz cross of five stones on a gold chain. Sweet Charles ! he must be well scolded when he came on leave, the generous fellow would always have pockets to let if he spent all his prize money on his sisters.

Uncle Leigh Perrot was delighted that his nieces were coming to live in Bath and tried to settle them just opposite in Axford Buildings, but the girls had no wish to be always under their aunt's eye, or to be forever counted upon to make up a table at her dull card parties. Mrs. Austen hankered dreadfully after leafy Queen Square, where dear Edward had once given them such an enjoyable holiday, but Mrs. Leigh Perrot put her foot down on that. " Sister, you could not possibly afford the rent of a Queen Square house. The bottom house in Gay Street, on the left-hand side going up, would suit you better, or the corner house in Chapel Row, which was advertised last week, though to be sure it is rather small and looks east. Charles Street has better houses, but there you are getting rather down hill and the coaches on the Bristol Road will trouble you."

Uncle James and his pretty niece amused themselves by walking all over a house in Green Park Buildings. Two terraces here with high pavements enclosed a triangle of garden, a sheltered sunny corner with some good trees in it, a haunt of dogs and nursemaids. The rushing Avon went by the end of the street and on the other side rose the noble wooded precipice called Beechen Cliff. Uncle and niece reported a good dining-room with a parlour behind and a drawing-room on the first floor, the back half of which might make a bedroom at a pinch. Jane had planned just how they might all fit into it and had run all the way up to the attic to poke her head out of the window and see whether she could get a view of Sham Castle. She told her uncle that she liked the notion of living on the western edge of the city. In summer Cassandra and she would enjoy climbing the hills and looking down on the steaming town. " I am like the starling in the fable," said she to Uncle James, " I don't like to feel that I can't get out," and for a moment there was a wild gleam in her eye which quite astonished the old gentleman.

However, Aunt Leigh Perrot would not hear of their going to live in Green Park Buildings. " No, no, my dear, it is much too near the river ; the water would come into the cellars every winter." Jane said rather crossly that the landlord at Number Twelve had raised the floor to prevent just such an accident, but her aunt replied crushingly, " Water may be kept out of sight, but it cannot be sent away. You do not know the Avon floods as well as I do. The lower part of the town is a most unhealthy situation, Dr. Mapleton tells me there is a great deal of sickness there, putrid sore throats and so forth, he could not recommend it."

Green Park Buildings evidently would not do. The King Street houses were altogether too small ; Trim Street was picturesque enough with its overhead arch and General Wade's fine house with the military trophies above the windows, but it was dark and narrow and not considered quite respectable, they must at all costs endeavour to keep out of Trim Street. Westgate Buildings, though handsome in themselves, were very gloomy and Aunt Leigh Perrot evidently thought that her carriage could not well be seen waiting in such an ungenteel neighbourhood.

It was Mr. Austen who finally decided the matter, saying gently, " I fancy it would be pleasant to live in one of those new houses across the river." His fancy, it seemed, had been caught by an advertisement in the *Bath Chronicle* of a house to be let for three years, No. 4, Sydney Place. This was in the Bathwick Estate, a new development visible from the back of the Paragon. You crossed the Avon by Robert Adam's Pulteney Bridge, with its shops and houses overhanging the water like so many bird-cages and then walked all the way down the wide airy promenade called Great

Pulteney Street. It was planted with trees for its whole length and had something of a foreign air. Minor streets started out ambitiously on either side into the meadows, but few had got further than six or eight houses. The vista was closed by an Italian villa like a painted act-drop and by the green trees of Sydney Gardens.

There, almost on the corner, was No. 4, in a terrace standing sideways to the villa on the north, a creditable comfortable house not ten years old and built of clean dove-coloured stone. The Austen family poked all over it and liked it better than anything they had yet seen. It was tall and narrow, it needed painting and there seemed to be a great many stairs, but the offices were good and there was a particularly handsome double drawing-room on the first floor. From the back windows you could look across the meadows, could see the long brown curve of the Paragon and the Vineyard, make out Aunt Leigh Perrot's windows and all the terraces and crescents going up Landsdown like a giant's staircase. Mrs. Austen flung open the folding doors and paced out the drawing-room from one end to the other, announcing with satisfaction, " It would make a very good room for a party." Mr. Austen said nervously, " I hope you do not think of giving many, my dear. I am not fond of dinner visiting ; late hours no longer agree with me, I am sorry to say. My health will not stand them." His wife reassured him, " Oh ! we shall give no dinners in general, my love, we shall not be able to afford that ; but we can have an occasional tiny card party. I own I could not do without my game of whist. It will be my chief pleasure in Bath. Here I can always be sure of making up two tables without any difficulty."

Jane said rather crossly under her breath to Cassandra, " I hate tiny parties, they force one into constant exertion. If they were larger they would be less intolerable." The sisters peeped out from one of the three tall windows, which had been lifted to let in the morning sun. There was a narrow iron balcony outside with a sideways perspective up the brown front of the villa ; they could overlook the leafy Gardens, the canal with its Chinese bridge and the classical temple which sheltered the band on gala nights. " It will be pleasant to sit out here on summer evenings," said Cassandra in her soft hopeful voice. " We can listen to the music and watch the fireworks, the transparencies and the illuminations, without being jostled in the crowd. All that, you know, will be quite enjoyable and on summer mornings we can rest in the shade of the trees." Jane swung her sister's hand to and fro and laughed, teasing her. " You will be telling me next that it will be pleasant to go into the Labyrinth, as we used to do when we were children."

Their idle talk caught their mother's ear and she said sharply, turning round, " I hope all these fireworks and festivities will not disturb us too much. I own that is the one thing I have against the house, it is a little too near the Gardens." A shadow crossed Jane's face and she turned from the balcony. " It will not signify," said she in a tone of controlled impatience. " We need not let such trifles affect us, we can shut the windows and pull down the blinds." " To be sure we can," said Mrs. Austen, quite satisfied. " I was only thinking of your father. Well, my dears, I really think we must have it. After all, it is but for three years and if we do not care for the house in the end we can look about us for something better. We can tell the workpeople to begin the painting as soon as the lawyers have done with their matters. The house will not be vacant until midsummer, but it is not at all the thing to stay in Bath in the hot weather. Why should we not make a little tour in Devonshire and then come back and settle into our new house in the autumn ? "

3

Jane and Cassandra hardly ever spoke afterwards about that lost, that unlucky bygone summer. When Cassandra was quite an old woman she once told her niece Caroline, in a moment of distress and emotion, that her Aunt Jane had met and loved a nameless stranger that year in Devonshire. " He was one of the most charming people I ever met,"

Aunt Cassy said. " He was the only man I ever knew who could have been worthy of Jane " ; but when young Caroline pressed her for the whole of the story the old lady took fright, closed her lips firmly, shook her head and refused even the young man's name. She had promised Jane, she said, that she would never speak of him to anyone.

It had not happened at Lyme Regis, though some people imagined that it must have done after they had read *Persuasion*. They did not go to Lyme that year at all, only to Teignmouth and Starcross on the green shores of the estuary and then by way of Exeter to Sidmouth. It was there that Mr. Austen fell ill. The breathless heat of the Devon summer had tired the old man and he exerted himself too much travelling from place to place in hired carriages on bad roads, besides walking round Exeter and looking at the cathedral. After they got to Sidmouth, one hot night, he had a feverish attack which much alarmed his wife and daughters. He complained of giddiness in his head, his face was flushed and his hand burning hot, he trembled very much and seemed unable to speak. Fortunately there was an excellent doctor close by who came at midnight and bled the old gentleman, which revived him, though he was still very weak. The doctor told the anxious family that there was no immediate danger, but prescribed rest and complete quiet.

They remained at Sidmouth for two weeks, until Mr. Austen was fit for travel. It was a pretty innocent fishing village, struggling to turn itself into a watering place, with one or two bathing-machines and a tiny circulating library. The doctor, who was a very pleasant gentlemanlike man, without many patients, came to visit Mr. Austen every day and his wife invited the girls to take tea with her in a neat white villa close to the shore. The doctor's brother was staying with him and it was he who had so much pleased Jane. Caroline would tease her aunt in vain thirty years later to tell her what he had looked like, but the old lady would not or could not remember. Caroline imagined him dark, pale and eager, handsome, quick-moving and tall, with a witty tongue, a fond heart and every charm which could engage a woman's love, a being to remember for a lifetime. Jane and he seemed made for each other.

He came to see her every day ; they sat together on the shingle beach throwing stones into the water, or wandered up the dark red cliffs and over the flat-topped hills. Cassandra sometimes wondered that her mother did not remark how very long they were gone, but Mrs. Austen was so anxious about her husband that she would scarcely leave his room, except when Cassandra took her place for a meal or a turn in the garden. The old lady had no time to wonder where her younger daughter was and Cassandra held her breath, for fear of disturbing the short enchantment. Sitting by her father, she allowed herself to remember that other summer, six years ago, when she too knew what it was to love and to be loved. She never guessed that her sister might have the same ill-fortune as herself.

The days slipped by almost too quickly. Mr. Austen got up, he came down and sat in the garden, the doctor advised them that he would take no harm from the journey to Bath. When all was ready and the post-chaise at the door, Cassandra went into the parlour and saw her sister standing by the open window with the dark stranger in earnest talk. He had her hand in his. Cassandra could not see their faces against the light, but she heard him say, " You will hear from me. I shall come to you wherever you are. I promise it will not be long." Her coming disturbed the pair of them. They turned round hastily and moved away from each other ; then the young man stammered a farewell to both sisters, flung himself over the low sill of the open window into the garden and disappeared. When Cassandra dared to face her sister she surprised a look of exquisite bewilderment and felicity, but there was only time for a single clinging embrace, then they were called and must hurry away. The strange dreamlike moment was gone for ever.

Mrs. Austen never understood the matter from first to last. She was too much occupied with her husband's convalescence and her own fatigues. Cassandra was kept busy with all the petty difficulties and annoyances of finding servants, arranging furniture and moving into a strange house. Jane went about silent, disarmed and gentle ; only as the warm autumn days succeeded each other and the smell of burning leaves began to hang about Sydney Place, she grew a little pale and strained, as she watched the post for a letter which never came. The city was in a cheerful bustle, as always at that time of year, with clean curtains going up in all the windows, dead leaves being swept up in all the gardens and fresh visitors arriving daily for the winter season. There seemed more uniforms than ever in the streets, soon peace, it was said, would bring all the naval officers on shore, like gulls at low tide, and Frank and Charles would come with the rest. It was just then when everything seemed most hopeful that Mrs. Austen got the letter with the fatal news in it.

Cassandra was always thankful that she had been alone with her mother when it came. " Why, here's a letter from Sidmouth," said Mrs. Austen, putting on her spectacles, and breaking the black wafer, " from that doctor who attended your father in the summer. Well, this is very civil of him, a very pretty letter, to be sure. He hopes your father has quite recovered and begs we will send news of him. I must write and tell him what Dr. Bowen thinks of his patient." Dr. Bowen was their new doctor in Sydney Place. The old lady had quite taken him to her heart and thought him almost the equal of dear Dr. Lyford.

She went skimming through the letter in an irritating way she had, nodding her big mob cap over it and only dropping out a word or two here and there to her anxious listener. " Begs to wish us the compliments of the season . . . hopes we may be persuaded to visit Sidmouth next year . . . is convinced it was fatigue and not the relaxing situation of the place which overpowered my husband. Ah ! he needs all the patients he can get, poor man, he has his living to earn, but I do not think we should go to Sidmouth again, do you, Cassy ? I do not believe it suited your father or myself . . . Regrets not having written earlier . . . quite anxious to know how dear Mr. Austen did, but has been much disturbed by a recent bereavement in the family. Now what is all this ? He crosses his words so much that

one cannot read them . . . thinks we shall be sorry to learn
of the sudden death of his brother, but I did not recollect
he had a brother. Stay, was there not some pleasant polite
young gentleman who was so obliging as to take you and
Jane out walking once or twice ? "

" I'm afraid it must be the same," said Cassandra,
trembling in every limb. " Why, you look quite pale, my
dear," said Mrs. Austen, peering up over her round silver
spectacles. " This has been a shock to you ; Jane will be
sorry too. I fancy she saw more of him than you did. I
confess I hardly recollect the young gentleman myself. Well,
I'm sure I am very sorry to hear it. I wonder what the
matter was. There is nothing about it here, an accident or
some sudden illness, I suppose. I will write and send a civil
message when I have the time, but there is no great hurry,
the acquaintance was very trifling." " I think," said
Cassandra, rising and putting aside her work, " that if you
can spare me I should like to run up and tell Jane." She
went up in a silent agony to the room where Jane sat
reading and began haltingly, " There is a letter come from
Sidmouth for our mother." Jane cried out despairingly,
" Why does he not write to me ? will he never come ? have
I nothing after all to wait for ? " Cassandra had to speak
out then and watch her sister's young eager look wither
into the face of an old woman as she did it. " Oh ! my dear,
I do not know how to tell you. When Tom died you were
the only one who could comfort me, but now it has all
happened over again and I do not know how to help you.
You will not see him again, he cannot come to you. Oh !
my dear, he is dead . . . he is dead . . ."

4

In the following March, 1802, peace was signed with France.
When the laurelled mail-coach came down from London,
placarded with the news, bells were rung, bonfires lit on
the hills, fireworks went up in the Sydney Gardens, simple
people put candles in their windows and went cheering

about the streets because they thought the ten years' war was happily over. Up in London people called it the Experimental Peace and clever Mr. Sheridan said, " It is a peace that all men are glad of, but no man is proud of." Nobody liked its terms and old gentlemen in the Pump Room grumbled that we were giving away our conquests with both hands. Malta, Minorca, the Cape of Good Hope, all were tossed back, and Cassandra suffered a pang when she read that Santo Domingo had been returned to the French, her lover seemed to have died there in vain. The French Republic was recognised and General Bonaparte was made First Consul for life, from this time he styled himself in royal fashion, Napoleon. The mob applauded peace, but knowledgeable people told each other that it could not last ; Napoleon intended to make himself supreme in France and then to conquer Europe. Meanwhile the Fleet returned to port, ships' crews were paid off, the militia and the fencibles disbanded and the army reduced to a mere forty thousand men.

The packet boat began to run again between Calais and Dover and fashionable folk were all going over to visit Paris ; Eliza vowed that she would never be happy until she had been herself. The family had worn black all that winter for her poor little Hastings, who had died in his fourteenth year after long illness. Henry, too, had alarmed her by a period of ill-health, a cough, a pain in the side and every symptom which threatened a galloping consumption. However, he had recovered and had now quitted the army. The handsome pair were living quite in style in Upper Berkeley Street, in a furnished lodging. They sometimes talked of resigning the world and retiring into Wales ; but they both actually preferred London. Henry and his friend, that remarkably handsome Captain Tilson, together with a Captain Maunde, had a plan for setting up together as bankers and army agents. Old Mrs. Austen was disappointed by this end to her many plans for the cleverest of all her sons. She had always hoped that Henry would end by taking Orders like his father and eldest brother ; but Eliza could not picture herself as mistress of a vicarage.

She of course was wild to go to Paris. " Dear Henry, you positively must take me over," she pleaded, rolling her eyes. " I have not been in Paris since before the Revolution, it is an age. I hear the First Consul is the handsomest man possible, he has a head like an antique statue, it is a sight to see him reviewing his troops on a white charger in the *Champ de Mars*. He has proclaimed an amnesty for the *ancien régime*, and we are all to be very welcome if we will but attend Madame Josephine's receptions and make our curtsey to the poor lady." Henry drawled lazily, " You would find the General a very vulgar fellow, my dear, a fat little Corsican with shocking manners. They tell me his wife is much the better worth seeing of the two."

Eliza retorted immediately, " She has bad teeth, she dare not open her mouth when she smiles. Her husband, the Comte de Beauharnais, was only of the *petite noblesse* after all and she was nothing but a planter's daughter from Martinique, for all her airs and graces ; but I confess I should like to attend a reception at the Tuileries, if only to see the latest fashions. I hear the dressmakers have brought in a completely new line, everything is in the classic taste, long shawls are quite out and cameos are all the rage. The Opera is open again and the restaurants are as good as ever. Some of my old friends are positively getting back part of their estates ; with a little bribery and a little civility here and there in the right places I might regain some of my de Feuillide property. Do you not think it would be worth trying ? " She put her head on one side and cajoled her husband in her old fascinating way, but he was firm that they had better wait a few months until they saw how the land lay.

5

The first summer of the short-lived peace, the Austens went back again to Devonshire, but not to Sidmouth, for Mrs. Austen had taken a dislike to that place. They went instead to enjoy the red cliffs and white sands at Dawlish. It suited the old folk very well, but Jane found the steaming heat of the Devon summer almost as trying as Bath. She confessed to being plagued by nervous headaches and did not sleep well. Often in the breathless small hours Cassandra would wake and see her sister wrapped in an Indian shawl by the window, silently watching the moonlit sea. When they returned to Bath Uncle Leigh Perrot said crossly that Jane did not look any the better for her holiday.

In November of that year, 1802, Mary invited her sisters-in-law to come over to Steventon. The girls had looked forward to this, but actually the visit proved a disappointment, for James and his wife had begun to improve the place and the garden was all dirt and confusion, with planks and heaps of gravel everywhere. They had felled several of the larger trees near the house and Jane's first cry was, " Oh ! you have cut down the great walnut " ; but Mary only replied, " Yes, we think it has opened up the prospect amazingly. James would always be planting and improving if he had the money for it, there is nothing he likes so well, but it would have been ridiculous to have attempted anything much in our absurd half-acre at Deane, especially as we knew we should not be there for ever. Indeed I am sorry we put in so many fruit trees as we did ; only last year we planted an apricot against the stable wall, a rare Moor Park, and it quite went to my heart to leave it behind for the curate."

Jane observed dryly, " You have certainly been very busy, Mary, you have quite changed the old place. I hardly recognised my mother's garden." " I think we shall give it the air of a gentleman's residence in time," said Mary, unconscious of any disapproval, " but we have five years' work before us. I wish we could remove the farmyard, it is a terrible nuisance to have it so close, but luckily the barns and sheds are behind the house and you do not see them from the road. The Rectory has always been a solid roomy mansion and looks as if a respectable county family had lived in it from generation to generation. A traveller by the road might very well take it for the squire's house." She preened herself discreetly, glanced about the blighted November garden and pointed out the spot where she intended her greenhouse. " I cannot," said she, " live without a greenhouse."

Decidedly Steventon was a very different place under Mary's rule. Mrs. Austen had been a practical housekeeper and there had been no waste in her day, but she had never stinted parlour or kitchen of good food. They had lived exceedingly well at the Parsonage, eaten their own beef and mutton, killed their own pigs, had their well-filled poultry-yard and dairy. Each season had provided its own dishes. They had eaten fat carp and eels in Lent, Simnel cakes on Mothering Sunday, Hot Cross buns on Good Friday and coloured eggs at Easter. On Whit Sunday they had a dish of Test trout and a green gooseberry tart ; there were always fat ducklings and peas on the King's birthday in June, stubble geese at Michaelmas, partridges, hares and pheasants when the shooting began. At Christmas there was very good cheer, stuffed capons and turkeys, plum-puddings seven times boiled, frumenty and mince pies. It had not been all for themselves. All the men and women in the parish who were over sixty-five came up for their Christmas dinner. They got a great sirloin and plum pudding, as much beer as they chose to drink, a bowl of punch to drink the king's health and a shilling to take home.

They brewed their own beer at the rectory, a barrel at a time and very good it was ; they baked their own bread daily. Nobody even counted the eggs in the larder, the bowls of cream and slabs of butter in the dairy, the curd-cheeses laid out on nettle leaves, the pots of jam on the shelves or the little cakes in the cupboard. The young ladies made elder flower and cowslip wine, rose leaf salve, candied violets, quince and damson cheese and blackcurrant cordial. Cassandra brought in dripping combs of honey from her long row of hives at the end of the orchard and brewed mead, very sweet, strong and heady. When they killed one of their own pigs there were always presents of legs and shoulders, spare ribs and brawn for their friends. The girls carried bowls of broth and slices of chicken to sick folk, there were apples and cakes and often a bit of bread-

and-cheese for any village child who came up to the kitchen door on an errand. Old Mrs. Austen had always been generous in these little matters and her husband liked to quote the text, " *Thou shalt not muzzle the ox that treadeth out the corn.*"

Young Mrs. James Austen, however, was a pinching, scraping, cheese-paring woman. She had turned off the old servants to save their keep, she kept cheap young girls from the village who did not know their work and then scolded them all day long. They complained that her meals were heat-ups and scraps, she gave dripping for butter, she sold her eggs and poultry, the servants must pay for their own tea. James always had a bit of something special for himself, a creamed sweetbread, scalloped oysters or a delicious fricassee of chicken and asparagus in a silver porringer, because he was a greedy man and Mary liked to spoil him, but everyone else in the house went short to make up for it. She locked up her stores and doled them out weekly, she cut down the Christmas dinners and gifts and said that feasting was wrong in war-time. Old Mrs. Austen's parish soup had been as thick as porridge, with carrots and turnips and even scraps of meat floating in it, but Mrs. J. A's. charity broth was as thin as dishwater. There was great distress among the poor at that time, even though the war was over, bread still cost four times what it used to do and there had been six bad harvests running. The children begged for halfpence and who could blame them ? But they got short shrift at the Rectory door. James confessed that with the rise in the price of corn his tithes brought in much more than they used to do, but Mary cried out that all the new taxes pressed very hard on the clergy.

Decidedly the Rectory was not like their own home any more. However, James seemed gravely pleased to see his sisters and the children, tall Anna and little stumbling Edward, could hardly be separated from their pretty aunts. They all went to hear James preach on Sunday, they celebrated Edward's fourth birthday and enjoyed visits from all their old friends. Madame Lefroy was as lively and loving as ever and talked of a visit to Dublin ; now that the rebellion was over and the country united to England all was said to be peace and gaiety there, and her husband wished to visit his relatives. She reported, after a moment's hesitation, that Tom Lefroy was living in Leeson Street, Dublin, and doing very well at the Irish Bar. He was happy with his wife, and they had begun to raise a family. Jane said lightly, " I was always sure he meant to get on in the world. Pray tell him when you write that I wish him very well." Madam Lefroy said anxiously to Cassandra, when she got her alone, " I hope Jane has quite got over that business about Tom." Cassandra assured her gently that it was all long forgotten, but Madam Lefroy persisted, " She does not look as well or as happy as I should like."

6

The Bigg-Wither family were particularly attentive and insisted that Cassandra and Jane must spend a week of their stay at Manydown. Handsome Elizabeth, who had secured the Member's second son, the Reverend William Heathcote, had lately become a widow after only five years of marriage, poor thing ! Fortunately she had the comfort of her infant son William, a lively, healthy boy who must in due course inherit the baronetcy and the great house at Hursley. Catherine and Alethea remained at home unmarried, with their old father and their sickly brother, Harrison ; Harris was his nickname in the family. The death of an elder brother had made him the heir to the Manydown estate, and there was nothing his family wished so much as to see him happily married. He had not lost his trick of sitting in a corner and fixing his eyes on Jane. Cassandra soon fancied that she detected the scent of a feminine plot, for Mary kept praising Harris. " He is so much improved in health and manner, and he is always so polite and attentive. It is a thousand pities he is not married, his old father cannot last much longer and then Manydown will need a mistress. Such a beautiful house, so excessively handsome and convenient ! In the old days there was nothing like the Manydown balls, but nowadays everything there is dull and quiet. They need someone to liven them up." Catherine and Alethea hugged and kissed Jane, vowed she did not look a day older since they parted and declared that they missed her continually. " We have all been as dull as ditch-water since you and Cassy left Hampshire. The Assemblies are nothing without you." Mr. Bigg-Wither patted Jane's hand with an old man's privilege and hoped she had not left her heart behind in Bath. " We wish we had you back here," said he. It was the nearest anybody came to giving the scheme away, but Cassandra did not think Jane missed it. She seemed unwilling to go to Manydown, hung back and feared Mary might be offended if they left her, but Mary herself insisted on their going. " I would not have you miss this chance for worlds."

At Manydown Harris was Jane's shadow. Heavy, plain and silent, he was always at her elbow. He followed her about through the great rooms, watched her as she ran up and down the fine staircase, took her out and about the gardens, walked with her and his sisters through the frozen spaces of the park, mutely inviting her to consider all he had to offer. Cassandra fancied that his sisters manœuvred to leave him alone with Jane, but she was too quick for him. She would always keep Cassandra or Alethea at her side and though she talked to Harris in her invariable pleasant friendly way, the scheme did not prosper. The week slipped by very quickly and poor Harris became visibly disturbed.

On the last afternoon he insisted that Jane and he should drive down together to say good-bye to Elizabeth at Worting Parsonage. Jane protested, " It is less than two miles across the park ; why should we not go on foot ? Your sisters, I am sure, would enjoy the walk ? " But the girls, on a look from their brother, declared it too wet underfoot for such an expedition and Cassandra had a cold and must not venture. It ended in the two of them setting out together in the phaeton, Harris in his great driving coat with its five capes, Jane wrapped from view in a couple of sheepskin rugs, with a borrowed bearskin tippet of Alethea's round her shoulders, coming well up to her chin.

They were not back until after dark ; but when they walked into the green panelled library, where the three girls were yawning over a roaring fire, it was seen at once that the drive had been memorable. Jane looked pale and chilled, but Harris for once was excellently well pleased with himself. He had a colour in his cheeks which was not all due to the nipping north-easter and he strode up to the hearth with a confident air and spoke out plainly to Cassandra. " Your sister has made me the happiest of men. We are to be married as soon as your parents will permit of it."

Catherine and Alethea both jumped up and fluttered round them, kissing and exclaiming, " Dear Harris, dear, dearest Jane ; now we shall have you with us always, you will be our own sister ! How delightful this is ! How pleased our father will be ! " Jane looked pale and chilled, she said not a word, only smiled faintly. When Cassandra at last got a chance at her she kissed lips which did not move and a cheek soft and cold as snow. " Let her come to the fire," commanded Harris, his own man for once. " You will smother her among you." He took his promised bride by the hand, led her to the best chair, knelt to make up the fire for her himself, then tugged at the bell rope and sent for a glass of mulled claret. " Your hand is like ice, my poor girl," he fretted, chafing her fingers between his own. Cassandra realised with a flash of jealous vexation, " He is not afraid of her any more. He might have been married to her for years already." Jane listened, dazed, resigned her hands to him obediently, drank the wine when it came, but hardly said a word to anyone.

Dinner was a solemn meal, in the white-panelled, candlelit dining parlour under the stare of the family portraits. Old Mr. Bigg-Wither had Jane at his right hand. After the cloth was drawn and the servants were gone he solemnly kissed her hand ; the glasses were filled with his best wine and they all drank a health to Jane and Harris. He could not take his eyes off her. " Is she not lovely tonight ? " he kept saying to Cassandra. " So graceful, so elegant, with such a pretty, delicate colour and such a proud air ? Do but look at the turn of her head and the curve of her cheek, as she speaks to my father. I declare I will have some of my mother's diamonds reset for her, as an ornament for the head. Will they not look lovely in that dark brown hair ? Oh ! she is an angel and I am the luckiest fellow alive. I do not deserve her ; I cannot believe in my own good fortune. I never thought she would have me." Cassandra began to suspect that the timid young man must be a little the worse for his father's good wine from Portugal.

After dinner in the library, over the teacups, Jane drooped and was markedly silent. Harris asked her to sing for them, but she said that she had no voice ; a little later she confessed to the headache, and asked to go to bed early. Her future sisters-in-law looked at each other knowingly, nodded their heads and said, " She must be tired to death." They insisted on going upstairs with her, while Harris watched them from below ; took her to her room, offered a composing posset and would not leave her until she was safe among the chintz curtains of the fourposter bed. Catherine took the empty silver porringer, Alethea blew out the candle and they tiptoed away. They were kindness itself, but between them they prevented Cassandra from being alone with her sister. She withdrew to her own room, all anxiety and shed a few tears herself before she fell asleep, praying with all her heart for her sister's happiness.

7

In the morning the servant came as usual, opened the shutters and lit the wood fire on the hearth, but scarcely woke the overtired Cassandra, who was still dozing when all of a sudden Jane was at her bedside, wringing her hands and weeping, " I cannot . . . cannot do it. Cassy, you must take me home."

She was quite beside herself, walking up and down the room in the utmost confusion of feeling, already dressed for a journey. Cassandra drew her to a chair by the hearth,

knelt at her feet and caught her restless hands, imploring,
" You cannot mean it, you are not yourself." " I mean it
as much as I ever meant anything in my life," insisted Jane,
" I cannot, indeed I cannot marry him, it is out of my power.
Oh ! do not turn against me, do not let them plague me
into it. If you do not help me I cannot tell what I shall
do." Cassandra embraced her and found her trembling
from head to foot. " Of course I will help you," she
promised. " You are my dearest sister and you know I
only want you to do what will make you happy, but will
you not give yourself a little more time before you decide ?
When you have turned it over in your mind perhaps you
will think differently."

" I have been turning it over in my mind all night long,"
said Jane bitterly. " I have been walking up and down
thinking about the matter. Harris is kind and good and
he loves me dearly. He would make me an excellent
husband, I don't doubt ; I should never get a better and
I am twenty-eight this month and should be thinking of an
establishment. Mary would say he is my last chance. He
is rich and generous and his family would welcome me. I
should be close to dear Steventon with all my old friends
about me. He has even promised that if you are ever left
alone in the world you shall make your home with us. It
was his own offer and he made it most delicately and
generously, he did not remind me that you and I shall have
very little to live upon when our parents are dead. He is
kindness itself, he will not let me remind him that I am six
years older than he is and have no fortune. He says he
wants nobody but me. Yesterday evening I believed that I
could do it, but in the night I knew it was not possible. As
soon as it was light I sat down and wrote him a letter to
say so and then I packed my box. When the maid came I
gave her the letter and desired that she should take it to
him. By this time he will have read it, he will know that
I have changed my mind. He will come wishing to see me
presently," said she, looking wild and staring. " You must
tell him to go away, Cassy, you must make him understand
that I am quite decided. You must make them all leave

me alone. Say I will not see any of them, say I only want to go home."

From that nothing would move her. She seemed quite frantic with misery. Cassandra could only comfort her and promise not to let anybody in. " I will lock the door when I go out and tell the maid you must not be disturbed. I will say you are laid down upon the bed ; indeed I wish you would do so now and not tire yourself with walking and talking. Do not cry so, you will wear yourself out." She persuaded Jane to lie down while she dressed herself and went down to encounter the family.

Harrison Bigg-Wither was walking up and down in the gallery, evidently waiting for her. He broke out as soon as he saw her, " Dear Miss Cassandra, what is to do now ? Can you explain what I have done to vex her ? She cannot be sure of her own feelings. Last night we were so happy, she told me she would marry me this side of Christmas. Am I not to see her ? May I not try and persuade her to change her mind ? Will you speak to her yourself ? Or shall my sisters try what they can do ? Would it be better to go after her to Bath and see if her parents will support me ? " He was really dreadfully tiresome, refusing to hear reason, walking after Cassandra along the gallery and down the great staircase, careless of who heard him. She saw a housemaid shaking out a pillow behind an open door, a footman stepping back with a brushed coat on his arm ; both she was certain, must be all ears. She pitied Harris, but could only try to quiet him, urging, " I can hear no more of this ; I wish you will not speak of it any longer. Her mind is quite made up, you will not change her. Indeed, indeed, you must leave her in peace ; there is nothing more to be said."

She left him gazing helplessly after her, descended to the morning room and there found his sisters all distress and natural indignation. Harris had told them the whole already ; Cassandra wished the spoilt, motherless young man had not this habit of turning to his sisters in every difficulty. Alethea lamented, " I was never more disappointed in my life. Dear Jane, there is nobody we would rather have had for a sister. Poor Harris is broken-hearted. He has always adored her, you know, it has been his hope for years that she might one day come to think of him, but he never dared to ask her until now. They have so many tastes in common, I am sure they would have been exceeding happy together. We always said she would be just the wife he needed, so lively and gay as she used to be, though to be sure she is a good deal changed since you all went off to Bath. We had thought that she would have shaken him out of his doleful dumps, taken him about and made friends for him everywhere. Now I suppose he will shut himself up again in the library and be as dull as ever. Oh, it is the greatest pity, I cannot get over it." Cassandra protested, " But if she cannot love your brother you would not wish her to marry him, surely ? "

Alethea looked glum ; Catherine, the elder sister, already a little faded and querulous, struck in, " I fancy we women talk altogether too much about loving and being in love. There is such a thing as being too romantic. Jane liked my brother well enough last night to accept him ; what has he done this morning that she should change her mind ? It is not very pretty of her to blow hot and cold like this. Harris has everything to recommend him, surely ? His situation, his character, his fortune and our old friendship. He has paid Jane a very high compliment. I do not known what better establishment she should wish for at her time of life ? She and I are just of an age, you know ; and all I can say is, that if any man made me such a respectable offer as Harris has done, I would accept it gratefully. I only hope Jane will not live to be sorry for this morning's work." Plainly Catherine was greatly offended. Cassandra pleaded, " Dear Cathy, you must not let this come between us. We have all been friends together for so long " ; but Catherine, drawing up her head, said coldly, " I do not see that anything can ever be quite the same after this. It is no very pleasant thing for my poor brother to be jilted."

Mr. Bigg-Wither, too, was gravely disappointed. At breakfast he buried himself in his newspaper and would not talk of anything but crops and the weather. Only when

Harris began to beg and tease Cassandra again to put off their departure, did the old gentleman bang down his Minton cup and say loudly, " Let her go, let her go ; we all know the girl is as obstinate as the devil. She has treated you ill, but it does not become you to be whining after her. There is nothing more to be said. I wash my hands of the whole business, let me hear no more of it." And he got up and stumped out of the room, leaving his daughters trembling.

The chariot had been ordered for eleven and came to the door punctually, but neither of the gentlemen were to be seen. Jane came down looking pale and determined. She offered a cheek to Catherine, who was stiffly polite, and to Alethea, who was openly crying. The butler opened the double doors and let in the cold morning wind, the horses tossed their chestnut manes and stamped and fretted on the gravel. Jane and Cassandra were half-way down the steps when Harris came round the corner of the house. He started at sight of them, then took his courage in both hands and met them at the foot of the steps. He looked full at Jane and said earnestly, " Will you not change your mind ? " Then as she did not answer he stared, licked his lips and begged her, " Let me send the chariot back to the stables ; let me tell my sisters that you will stop another day."

The footman held the carriage door open, keeping his eyes on the ground, the coachman gazed woodenly between his horses' ears. Cassandra felt Jane's arm tremble in hers, but she answered in her low, breathless voice, " Don't, don't . . . I beg you will not trouble me. My mind is made up, I shall not change it. You had better let me go." Harris stared all round him, dropped her hand and turned away. Jane sprang into the chariot, her sister followed ; the door was shut smartly, the coachman gathered up the reins and they drove away. Cassandra looked back at the tall pillared front of Manydown, white in the winter sun, at the leafless trees and bleached grass of the park and a sharp sigh escaped her. She had been happy so often at Manydown in her youth and she wondered whether she would ever stay there again. Jane sat huddled in her corner with her hand pressed to her lips. She was not crying, but she did not turn her head to look back at the house of which she might have been mistress. She had put all that behind her and now sat staring into what seemed an empty future. The sisters hardly spoke at all on the way home.

8

When they got back to Steventon Mary was exceedingly put about, but chiefly on her husband's account. "It is Thursday already and if poor James is to take you to Bath he cannot be back in time to preach on Sunday." Cassandra protested, "We may perfectly well post from Deane Gate," but Mary in her usual whining style declared, "It would not be at all proper for you to go so far alone. It is very inconsiderate of Jane not to wait until Monday. James would be very glad to go with you then, stay a day or two with his parents and see his aunt and uncle." She was always very anxious that James, who hoped to become his aunt's heir, should keep himself in her eye. When Cassandra murmured, "Jane is afraid that Harris or his sisters will come here and press her again to marry him," Mary exclaimed, "And a very good thing too! She ought to consider how much her family might benefit by the marriage. Such an opportunity is not likely to occur again at her age. She ought to wait a little, she ought to consider where she could find such another husband. What can she possibly have against him?" Cassandra sighed; there was nothing at all against Harris, except that he was not that other man. She could only repeat, "He will never succeed with her, she does not love him." "Oh! Love and dove and all that nonsense," snapped Mary. "I have no patience with her. Well, if Jane has made up her mind I suppose there is nothing more to be said. I will order the horses and we will have a little something to eat while we are waiting. I'm afraid there is not much in the house except some cold meat. I suppose you can make do with that. I certainly did not expect you back so soon. I will tell James that he must make ready

to go to Bath with you and I will see about packing his
bag."

Old Mr. Austen and his wife were very kind about it all.
Mrs. Austen could not but wish that her daughter might
have been the mistress of Manydown, but she said in her
own blunt way, " Jane is twenty-eight ! she is old enough to
know whether she can endure Harris as a husband or not.
For my part, I always thought him a very dull dog," and
Mr. Austen said innocently that his girls should marry for
love and not for money. In the Paragon James and his aunt
thought these sentiments altogether too unworldly. " If she
had been my daughter I would not have allowed her to get
these high-flown notions into her head. It was her duty to
her family to take him," said Mrs. Leigh Perrot ; while her
husband shook his head over Jane's bad luck. He would
have liked to see his favourite niece married to one of the
richest young men in Hampshire. " But it does not signify
talking," he admitted, " for when my little Jane makes up
her mind all the King's horses and all the King's men can't
change it." So in the end the family left Jane to herself ;
and all that winter she went about the house in Sydney
Gardens, scarcely seeming to know where she was or what
she did. Cassandra used to sit and watch her, but could not
tell what to do to help her.

In many of the Bath gardens there were old mulberry trees
with propped branches and split trunks held together with
chains. The story was that Mary of Modena, James II's
Italian queen, who set up the fountain in the middle of the
Cross Bath, had given these trees to the Mayor and
Councillors of the city in gratitude for her cure. The trees
had been sent for all the way to Modena and boxes of silk
worms had come with them, for the queen had hoped that
the climate of Bath might prove warm enough for the
establishment of a silk industry. The silk worms all died
quickly, but the mulberry trees did not. Several of them
still survived up and down the town and one such grew
behind a house half-way up Sion Hill, overshadowing the
whole garden between its high stone walls.

Cassandra watched it that year on a still autumn morning.

There had been a sharp frost in the night, the first of the year, and as soon as the sun touched it the tree began to shed its broad leaves. Steadily and without ceasing they pattered down until the blackened city grass beneath was covered by the golden shower. It looked as if the sun were shining underneath the branches, where it never did even at midsummer. When Cassandra walked into her friend's room the mulberry had been a leafy tree, when she went away after paying her visit its branches were already completely bare. As she walked down the steep hill on the raised pavement she thought with sad resignation that her own youth had dropped from her like that ; in a morning, in a single hour, the frost had numbed her whole being. They had told her that her heart would bud and blossom again, but it had never done so ; when she lost her lover the chill had been mortal. All that was past and gone for her, she had made peace with life and had finished fretting ; but must it be so with her sister ? Cassandra wondered and puzzled continually about what was to become of Jane.

9

In two years the Austen family had slipped quietly into a circle of friends. There were always plenty of clergy in Bath, both active and retired, besides the doctors and their wives who lived in the Circus, attorneys and half-pay officers occupying the new terraces and crescents on the Landsdown slopes and a good many poor widows and old maids, lodging in the first or second floors of houses in the lower part of the town. All these decent people had settled in Bath because they could live cheaper and more agreeably there than in London or the country. The gentlemen spent the greater part of their time in the coffee-houses or at the Club, the ladies occupied their mornings with household cares, shopping and visits. Their evenings were mostly spent in tea-drinking, seasoned with a rubber of whist or a pool of commerce, avidly played for tiny stakes and garnished with a little quiet gossip. None of these people troubled themselves much about the visitors to the Spa; they were wrapped up in their own affairs and had little money to spare for public entertainments.

Mr. Austen was perfectly happy in Sydney Place and did not seem to miss the daily work of his parish. He toddled down Great Pulteney Street every morning to the Pump Room with a handsome daughter in attendance, drank his glasses of yellow water and discussed the news with half a dozen retired parsons like himself, with long white hair down to their shoulders, great neckcloths and black clothing; old Mr. Nelson, who had died a year earlier, had been just such another. Mr. Austen would choose the fish for dinner at the market or lean upon the balustrade and watch the swans stemming the green current above the Abbey weir. Sometimes he would get as far as Milsom Street, where he would sit down contentedly at the library and turn over the latest prints while his daughters changed their books. If the pavements tired the old gentleman they could always bundle him into a sedan chair and walk beside it, talking to him through the window, while two stout Irish chairmen trotted him easily home.

On Sundays there were almost too many church services to choose from. Mrs. Austen thought the great soaring Abbey rather too cold for him and preferred St. Swithin's, Walcot, where he and she had been married. It had been rebuilt since Mr. Austen was a curate there in the '60's and now was a handsome modern basilica with three storeys of windows, more like a house than a church. It overhung Walcot parish like a three-decker. The interior was adorned with wide galleries, Ionic pillars and a greater profusion of draped marble urns, obelisks and weeping cherubs than any other church in Bath. The old couple could go arm in arm very happily to St. Swithin's on Sundays and were welcome to dine in the Paragon on the way home. Then there was quite a choice among the new proprietary chapels, where the lower orders were not admitted and for the price of a sitting you could be sure of a cushioned pew among your friends, a warm fire, a sound Anglican service and a sermon by your favourite preacher. The Octagon Chapel in Milsom

Street was delightfully warm, with four great roaring fire
one in each corner; it was famous for its music and a
fashionable congregation flocked to enjoy the anthems and
oratorios which echoed under the delicate rococo plaster
roof. Dr. Gardiner, the rector, was a friend of the Leigh
Perrots and was often to be met making up a rubber in
their house. Then there was Margaret Chapel in Brock
Street, much frequented by the doctors' families from the
Circus. In summer the Austens sometimes found it a
pleasant walk to cross the river and climb the green slopes
to the tall and slender Lansdown Chapel, though the hill
was a little too much for Mr. Austen; and in winter the
inhabitants of the Bathwick Estate had their own cosy little
Laura Chapel in the meadow at the back of Henrietta
Street. All this pleased Mr. Austen greatly and few days
passed that he did not say happily, " Ah! my dears, we
did a very sensible thing, to be sure, when we left Steventon
and came to Bath."

Mrs. Austen handed over the housekeeping finally to
Cassandra, played cards three or four times a week and began
to indulge in a number of minor ailments for which Dr.
Bowen prescribed most sympathetically; only her daughters
did not find very much to amuse them in the city. Fashion
had changed entirely during the ten years of the war and
Bath was no longer a place for pretty girls to get husbands.
The balls at the Upper and Lower Rooms had dwindled
sadly! they were only attended by the tradespeople and the
visitors. They had been replaced by the elegant stupidity
of private parties. People met in a quiet economical way
for a game of cards and some light refreshment, they drank
orgeat and negus and nibbled rout cakes, but nobody gave
dinners any more. It was a society of elderly people. Few
young men came there except for a short visit and there were
too many elegant pretty-behaved young women with little
to do but wait upon their elders, frequent the concerts and
libraries, indulge fancies for this or that religious service and
strike up small friendships among themselves. These young
ladies all voted Miss Cassandra very pleasant and sensible,
but they did not greatly take to Miss Jane, who got the name

for being something of a blue-stocking. She read a great deal, did not talk much in company, had a peculiarly observant eye and sometimes came out with a cutting remark. On the whole people were a little afraid of her. She could not or would not play whist, so she was left out of evening parties, or if she came was given a book of engravings to turn over in a corner, while her elders gathered round the table and only talked of court cards and trumps.

It was about this time that a dowager of his acquaintance startled Mr. Leigh Perrot by remarking querulously as the deal went round, " Did you not tell us that your younger niece was very pretty and lively ? Or am I mistaken in the lady ? " Jane's uncle answered with surprise, " Why, so she is," then was provoked by his partner's raised eyebrows and dubious shake of the head to reconsider the matter. He realised when he came to think it over that Jane was gay no longer. She who had once brightened his dark house when she entered it, with her quick tongue, her teasing smile and the lively sparkle of her brilliant brown eyes, had changed without his noticing it into a slender, elegant silent young woman, who could sit in a corner all evening and be no more remarked than a poker or a fire-screen.

He went blustering round the family about it all, but got little satisfaction. His wife said, " I think Jane is prettier-behaved than she used to be. She does not give her opinion unasked quite so often and is grown quite civil and obliging. Of course she never troubles to put herself out, or entertain people she does not like. I do not see anything in particular the matter with Jane. She is growing older, that is all. She is settling down and quite time, too." Her mother said vaguely, " Jane does very well, I think. She does not care for card parties and of course she is not young enough to go running about to balls. Besides it is not the thing to be seen at the Assemblies any more. Perhaps, brother, you would take her with you in Passion Week when you go to hear *The Messiah* at the Octagon Chapel. Jane would enjoy that. She likes good music and you will have a ticket to spare, for my sister is getting so deaf that an oratorio is no pleasure to her." Cassandra said, with rather an anxious

air, " I think Jane finds the climate of Bath a little relaxing.
She always used to say that the city did not agree with her.
She does not get out enough, perhaps. At Steventon she was
always running about the lanes. I will ask her if she will
walk up Beechen Cliff with the Misses Mapleton on Sunday."
And Jane herself said, with a forced smile, " I am sorry you
do not think I am in good looks, Uncle James. I am never
at my best in black, I think I am too sallow to wear it. Next
spring I will buy a rose-pink summer gown and astonish
you all." He burst out, " I wish you would, my dear. I
remember when you first came to live in Bath you had a
very pretty yellow muslin. I used to think it became you
very well. I don't like these brown and grey gowns you
wear, they make you look like a Quakeress, and I wish you
would not go about in these little close caps. In my young
days the girls wore pink and blue and let their curls hang
down on their shoulders." " You forget," said she, drily,
" that I was twenty-seven in December. I cannot look for
much admiration nowadays, except from my kind and
deluded uncle. I am not a young girl any more."

10

Cassandra could never remember afterwards whether it had
been she herself or her father, or perhaps even Henry who
had first suggested to Jane in the spring of 1803, " Might
you not finish that story you began about the girl who came
to Bath for a holiday?" Jane did not take fire very quickly!
she shrugged her thin shoulders and believed she had the
manuscript laid away somewhere, but did not think it would
take. Mrs. Radcliffe's novels were going out of fashion and
a parody of *Udolpho* would fall very flat. There was nothing
much else in the story and she was not in the mood for
writing, she did not feel that she could ever finish it. However, she rummaged the manuscript out and looked it
through. Cassandra sat quietly watching her and after a
time Jane stretched out her hand absently for a quill pen.
She frowned, scratched something out sharply, turned the

page, read a little further, smiled faintly and added a word or two between the lines. Presently her pen began to travel steadily, and Cassandra, who had been holding her breath, went back to the sheet she was hemming. It looked as if the plan might work.

Henry came down to stay with them about that time. He wanted his rich uncle to put some money into the new firm of Austen, Maunde & Tilson, which the old gentleman was easily persuaded to do. Jane showed the manuscript to her brother, always her kindest critic, who laughed over it consumedly. The little heroine, who was called Susan in this version, he voted a soft sweet puss, and the Thorpe family a joy ; General Tilney was the very portrait of James's father-in-law, the old governor, and the parody of Mrs. Radcliffe's novels he thought sparkling, wicked and exact. " And as for the hero," said Henry with a pretended smirk, " he is really a pretty gentleman, so well-bred and handsome and such an excellent dancer. Miss Susan was lucky indeed to catch him. He is the most delightful creature, as fine a young man as you would see in a summer's day ; he has dark eyes and hair and his name is Henry. I should not wonder if Jane intended him for me. She blushes and will not say, but I am quite sure of it. Before I became an old married man I was just such another. It will take, I am sure it will take ; finish it quickly and I will engage to find you a publisher."

Jane was encouraged by Henry's delightful enthusiasm and worked hard to finish the story. There was a cool shade upon the chapters which she now added, but the earlier part sparkled like morning sunshine. The completed novel was offered to Messrs. Crosbie of Paternoster Row. They had a branch in Bath at Cruttwell's, the stationers, who had printed the account of Mrs. Leigh Perrot's trial. They read the manuscript, were taken by the Bath setting and bought it from the inexperienced authoress for ten pounds. She was triumphant and planned a new novel, but did not begin it immediately, for in May war was again declared.

The family did not know until afterwards that Henry and Eliza had been among the English tourists who had to get away in a hurry, when Napoleon suddenly ordered all English subjects to be arrested and closed the Channel ports. Henry rolled himself in his furred travelling cloak and feigned sleep at each post-house while the horses were changed, for fear his English accent should betray them, while Eliza put her head out of the window and scolded the ostlers and grooms in her perfect French. Ten thousand English people were left behind to languish interned, but Eliza and Henry scrambled into the last vessel which sailed before the boom was secured across the mouth of Boulogne Harbour. All that Eliza brought back from Paris was a striped bandbox with a new hat inside. It was more like a dragoon's helmet than a hat, of fine yellow straw with a great *panache* of crimson feathers over the top and down the back and it framed her small face in a most piquant manner. When people admired it in London Eliza would shrug and sigh, " Yes, it is a most charming hat, is it not ? I do not know when I shall get another like it. My husband says that it is all I shall ever see of my French inheritance."

At home all officers had been recalled to their units, leave was suspended and the Volunteers and Fencibles were drilling again with all their might. Bath was full of people who had flocked there to get as far as possible from the east coast, for the invasion scare was on again with a vengeance. The Fleet had put to sea and Lord Nelson had gone to the Mediterranean, but nobody inquired about him from his shy, frowning disagreeable wife in Bath. He had left her altogether for Lady Hamilton, and the deserted woman went about as stiff as a poker, looking at no one.

That summer dear Frank got himself engaged to be married. His intended was called Mary Gibson and she lived at Ramsgate in one of the clean new stucco terraces which went step by step up the white chalk cliffs. All the ladies of Ramsgate had turned out in their best bonnets, scarves and parasols, to watch the Fencibles drilling on the wide hard sands at low tide. He had walked with Mary in the bright salt airs of summer up and down the pier, they had danced together in the Assembly Rooms and gone out to look at the moon on the water. Frank was a remarkably fine young man with a great deal of intelligence and good spirits and Mary was an extremely pretty girl (trust Frank for that), with her head screwed on the right way. They had wasted no time in getting acquainted and falling deep in love. A sailor could not afford a long courtship in time of war, so he had quickly proposed and Mary had accepted him. Certainly there was not enough money on either side for them to marry immediately, but Frank was full of confidence and rising fast in his profession. " This cursed peace," he grumbled, " has kept me on shore a year, but now that we are at war again I believe I may say that Lord Nelson has his eye upon me. I am sure I shall get a ship on a good station where there is plenty of prize money to be had, and then Mary and I can marry quite quickly."

Frank had always great faith in his own luck, and certainly it served him well when he fell in love with Mary Gibson. Visits were exchanged between the two families and everyone approved of his choice. Mrs. Austen's only trouble was that now she would have two daughters-in-law, both called Mary. The old lady fretted herself about this for some time until Jane found her a remedy. " You will have to call them Mrs. J. A. and Mrs. F. A.," said she in jest. The nicknames stuck and the two young women were always so distinguished in the family. Jane and Cassandra decided between them that Frank's wife was going to be a very pleasant addition to their circle. " I should not wonder," said Jane, making a face, " whether we may not find Mrs. F. A. more to our taste in the long run than Mrs. J. A. " ; and Cassandra, who seldom spoke ill of anyone, reluctantly admitted that Mary Lloyd had changed a good deal for the worse since she married their brother James. They did not say to each other what they both knew very well, that poor Martha Lloyd, nursing her sick mother up at Ibthorp, would have a few tears to shed when she heard the news of Frank's betrothal. Martha had always had a very soft spot in her heart for handsome Frank, who was so kind and pleasant and used to bring her little presents when he came home from sea, but the truth was that he had never yet thought of Martha as anything but another sister.

That summer, 1804, the First Consul proclaimed himself Emperor by the name and style of Napoleon. He had a pavilion built for himself high up on the airy chalk downs above Boulogne and there he sat with a hundred and seventy-five thousand men encamped about him, holding reviews and councils and staring through his telescope at Dover Castle. He had two thousand small craft ready, he only wanted a favourable wind and the Channel at his command for thirty-six hours to come over, but that he could not get with the Fleet on guard. However, it was not considered advisable to make the usual family visit to Kent and Dr. Bowen recommended Lyme Regis. The little watering place had a soft and tepid climate which always suited his older patients, and it was a direct and easy coach ride over the Mendips to Shepton Mallet and down by Crewkerne. His advice proved excellent, as usual. The little town, with its steep and narrow streets, had a sunburnt foreign air which pleased them all and Henry and Eliza, who joined them there, voted it extremely romantic.

They were lodged in a queer ramshackle house, weatherboarded against the south-west gales, with low ceilings, small windows and a twisted staircase. The rooms were not of the cleanest, but much may be endured at holiday time, and they were all happy there. The cottage clung to the side of the hill, so that you could walk out of the first floor into the lane behind ; but the parlour in front had a whole storey under it and commanded a charming view. Sitting in the circular bay window you could look one way right over to the Cobb and the other way to the long lovely line of the cliffs, rising and falling like one wave after another and fading into the eastward haze. Just below this window was a terraced garden, filled with marigolds and sunflowers ; beneath it lay the jetty, the Customs House and a white fisherman's cottage perched on the corner of the sea wall, which seemed to lift it and its garden out of the waves. This cottage hung like a swallow's nest above the beach. Jane delighted in it, wished that she might live there and promised Henry that some day she would put it into a book.

Altogether Lyme seemed the best place in the world in which to pass a few idle and enchanted weeks. While the old couple sat together in the mild autumn sun, the younger ones strolled out to the end of the Cobb to watch the flowing tide and the children jumping each other down from the rough steps called Granny's Teeth. They bathed and stayed in a little too long, they made idle purchases in Broad Street of fine striped writing-paper, of parasols, shells and fossils, they performed the proper excursions to eat clotted cream and fruit at Pinney and Charmouth. Henry hired a curricle from *The Three Cups* and drove them in turn up and down the steep hills and through the shady lanes ; they visited one of Mr. Austen's old pupils, Mr. Buller, now vicar of Colyton. Jane had last seen him at the dance at Ashe Parsonage nine years earlier when she had said farewell to Tom Lefroy.

On Tuesday and Thursday evenings they could visit the Assembly Rooms at the bottom of Broad Street, where there was a pretty ballroom with windows looking out upon the harbour. The painted garlands on its walls were faded by the sun, its mirrors and the lustres of its three tinkling chandeliers were always a little misted by the damp which crept in from the sea. The three violins and the 'cello were often a trifle out of tune from the same cause, but the visitors were not at all particular. Henry, always a ready performer, stood up with Eliza, Jane was invited to dance by a bold odd-looking Irish stranger, Mrs. Austen enjoyed her evenings in the cardroom ; old Mr. Austen even came down once and sat contentedly looking on at the cotillions until Henry's manservant came at nine o'clock with a lantern to fetch him home. In the pauses of the dance they became aware of the waves dashing on the shingle and the seagulls crying and complaining, going home they smelt the night air coming in over the rocks and seaweed and saw the harbour lights, red, white and yellow, making long corkscrews down into the water. Jane squeezed Cassandra's arm and said with a laugh, " How very odd this is ! I had far rather dance here then in the Upper or Lower Rooms at Bath ! "

12

Lyme was the best, the last of the family holidays ! there never was another like it. When their time was up the Henry Austens proceeded to the fashionable resort of Weymouth, where the old mad King with his Queen and the five ageing Princesses always spent the summer, and Cassandra went to Ibthorp, to help poor Martha nurse her mother. The little Welsh widow was now lying bedridden, scarcely able to eat anything or even to turn herself. She was past knowledge or remembrance of anyone and could not live many months longer. The others returned to Bath but not to Sydney Place, for the lease had run out and Number 4 was now a lodging-house. They had taken rooms in Green Park Gardens, thinking that in the summer it would be pleasant there walking under the willows beside the muddy Avon ; but in November it was certainly damp and foggy. It did not suit Mrs. Austen's rheumatism, and Mrs. Leigh Perrot, when she came to visit them, sniffed the air and pronounced it mouldy. " Did I not warn you, Sister, when you first came to Bath against taking a house in this dreary street ? Before Christmas you will have the river in your cellars."

In Green Park Gardens Mr. Austen failed rapidly. He could only totter along slowly, very much bent and leaning on a stick and needed a sedan chair to visit the Pump Room or the Paragon. In December he caught a bad cold, had one of his feverish attacks and took to his bed. His daughters spent much time sitting with him by turns, but very often he could not bear talking at all. He required only gentleness and silence and lay for long hours looking at the ceiling, gradually releasing his hold on life.

December was a black month when everything seemed in disorder at home and abroad. The papers were full of descriptions of how Napoleon had been crowned Emperor in Paris, with every magnificence imaginable of purple velvet, golden bees, gilt laurel wreaths, uniforms and satin gowns ; the Pope himself had been present and the Dictator seemed firmly established on this throne. Jane was writing a novel which she would afterwards call *The Watsons*. It began engagingly enough as another of her Cinderella stories, with a fresh and spirited young heroine obliged to step down from riches to poverty. There was a ball in the opening chapters, much like the Basingstoke Assemblies of her own youth, where pretty Emma was slighted by the fashionable company and annoyed by a young coxcomb, but succeeded in catching the eye of a supercilious lordling. She had tried the same situation before in *First Impressions*, but now she gave it another wry-mouthed twist. As she sat in her father's sick-room working on her book its colour changed and darkened. It became a dirge of helpless rage and compassion for Cassandra and Martha, for herself and for all neglected overlooked women who had missed their market, who had begun to despair of ever getting a husband, home and children. The elder sisters in her novel were like hen sparrows shaking and trailing their wings ; always desperately seeking to catch the careless eye of any man who came near them, they were bitterly like real life. Cassandra did not laugh at them, indeed she could scarcely bear to read about them, they cut too near the bone.

Jane never finished *The Watsons*. In that dark December of 1804 she had sad news which touched her particularly. Dear Madam Lefroy, out riding in the lane between Deane and Steventon, was thrown by her horse and picked up dead. Jane wept long for the kind and charming woman. It made a sad Christmas for all of them, and the New Year had scarcely come in when Mr. Austen closed his long and happy life. He had been taken with one of his old attacks, of which there had been several since Lyme, an oppression in the head, trembling and fever and sudden weakness ; but after Dr. Bowen had bled him he recovered a little though not so rapidly as he usually did. Towards the evening, however, he seemed stronger. He passed a tolerable night and on the Sunday insisted on coming down to the morning meal with his family. He walked about the house a little, leaning upon his stick, and Dr. Bowen felt sure of his doing perfectly well, but as the day advanced all these comfortable appearances gradually changed. Mrs. Austen took fright and sent again at 10 o'clock at night for the doctor, who pronounced his patient's situation most alarming. The old gentleman seemed not to suffer at all, but gradually became insensible. He knew neither his wife nor his daughters and was quite unconscious of his own danger. Dr. Bowen came again early in the morning, bringing with him a Dr. Gibbs, a consulting physician from Gay Street, but it was then absolutely a lost case. Dr. Gibbs told them gravely that nothing but a miracle could save the sick man and before midnight he drew his last quiet breath. It had been a death almost as free from suffering as his family could have wished.

VI

Bath—Southampton

1805-1809

I

AFTER he was dead they had to endure the darkened rooms, condoling visits, letters, and intruding business affairs, everything which could distract them from the contented smile on the gentle and pious face of the dead man. Uncle and Aunt Leigh Perrot came round immediately and their aunt, who was always at her best in time of trouble, sat with the widow, who was bearing her loss with admirable courage. Their uncle sent off an express immediately to Edward at Godmersham and another to Steventon. Jane wrote to Henry in Brompton, to Charles in Bermuda and a couple of letters to Frank, whose new ship, the *Leopard*, was somewhere in the Channel ; she missed him at the signal station at Dungeness, but caught him at Portsmouth with the sad news. Cassandra interviewed a little apple-faced undertaker's man, much like a Shakespearean clown, who turned his hat humbly about in his hands and whispered questions about oak and elm, about brass and silver handles, about bearers, plumed horses, black gloves and mourning bands. A sympathetic dressmaker from Milsom Street followed him with widow's bonnets, veils and weeds, and the Rector of St. Swithin's, Walcot, came to condole with Mrs. Austen. There had been some talk of the Reverend George Austen being buried at Steventon, which had been his only living throughout his ministry ; but his widow, with her usual good sense, declared that such an extravagance would displease her. " I had rather my poor George might be buried in Walcot," she told the Rector, wiping away one of her rare tears. " We were married there, you know, and it was only at the New Year that we heard you preach together." The arrangements for the funeral were settled

almost before Henry descended, pale and distressed, in all
the elegance of his London mourning, from the coach in the
White Horse Yard and James arrived from Steventon. These
two brothers alone followed their father's body to his grave
in the steep sunny little churchyard below the high side of
St. Swithin's, a haunt of dogs, nursemaids with children and
old gentlemen like himself.

After the funeral James would have taken his mother back
to Steventon, but she did not feel equal to the change. She
preferred to remain in the house where her husband had
died for a little longer. It was already clear that she and
her daughters would have to leave it at Lady Day, and the
girls had hoped for a move from Bath, but their mother
wanted to remain in the city. There were a great many
family discussions, for when the lawyer had made up his
accounts it proved that there was very little money for the
three of them. Mrs. Austen had a small portion under her
marriage settlement, Jane had nothing at all of her own, but
Cassandra had the tiny income from Tom Fowle's legacy.
" And a very good thing too," pronounced their aunt, " for
it is not to be expected that either of the girls will marry
now. It is a thousand pities that Jane did not take Mr.
Bigg-Wither. I hear he is just married to a Miss Ann Frith.
I daresay Jane regrets him, but it is too late. Well, Sister,
I do not know how you will contrive. You will have to be
very careful, for my good man tells me you will only have a
hundred and ten pounds a year among you." The rich old
woman was very ready to advise them in such matters as
rent and lodging, but she did not make any offer of help.

The boys, however, were not going to let their mother
and sisters want. Edward wrote at once, a very proper
letter. He intended to allow them a hundred a year.
Elizabeth and he had a family of eight children by this
time and would gladly have taken Cassandra to live with
them at Godmersham, but one proud silent glance of entreaty
from Jane settled the matter ; it was not possible for the two
sisters to live apart. Henry, looking startled and worried,
could only offer fifty pounds a year, but promised more later
if his firm prospered. Frank, out of his scanty flag-captain's

pay, immediately promised the same, but later, while the lawyers were still talking, came great news. He had got command of a new eighty-gun ship of the line, a real beauty. She was French built, a Nile prize, she had been the *Benjamin Franklin* (though God alone knew how the Frogs had mispronounced that), and had been refitted and renamed for the bright Nile star, the *Canopus*. Frank wrote from Spithead that he would now have five hundred a year and meant to set aside a hundred of this for his mother. The old lady shed tears over his generous offer. " Nobody ever had such good children as mine," she sobbed, " but I will do no such thing. The poor boy will need every penny for himself when he marries." She was with difficulty persuaded to take half.

James, her eldest son and hoping to be his aunt's heir, might well have done more than the fifty pounds which he finally offered. Now that his father was dead he would enter upon an income of a thousand a year from the two livings of Deane and Steventon, though to be sure he had to pay his curate eighty pounds of that, but Mrs. J. A. would not let him be more generous. She bore her second child that year, a little girl as it proved, christened for her side of the family Caroline Mary Craven, and she was greedy for every penny she could get for her own children. " My dear James, your mother and sisters will have a good four hundred and fifty pounds a year between them, when all is said and done. They may all three live very comfortably together in lodgings in Bath in the winter and spend their summers visiting among the family. They will keep no carriage, no horses, no servant ; they will go nowhere, except to tea-parties and so forth among their friends in Bath. Their expenses will be so small that I cannot imagine how they will spend the half of their income. There is no occasion for you to ruin yourself by giving your own fortune away to them. Remember we shall have three children now to consider. Anna, to be sure, is off our minds now that her grandfather has provided for her in his will, but we shall have many expenses with the others. This allowance will come over and over every year, and though your mother may not last very long your sisters are both younger than you are and may easily outlive you. A time may well come when it would be very inconvenient indeed to pay out fifty pounds yearly for Jane and Cassandra. You really are much too generous." "Aye, I believe I may be," admitted James, " but on these occasions one would rather do too much than too little. I am the eldest son and should not let myself be outdone by my brothers." But Mrs. J. A. went on scolding away at him until she wore him down. In her state of health she was not to be crossed and she had no notion of letting her own children be robbed for her husband's mother and sisters.

At Lady Day the widow and her daughters moved out of Green Park Buildings. It had been an unhappy house for them and they were glad to leave it. Cassandra went to Ibthorp to help Martha nurse old Mrs. Lloyd, who was then on her deathbed; while Jane and her mother went into a furnished lodging in Gay Street, where they whiled away the spring months of their mourning quietly but not unpleasantly. They were asked about a good deal by other widows with unmarried daughters so that their own tea and sugar lasted a great while, a consideration in wartime. Acquaintances came to take the waters ; Cousins George and Mary Cooke had to be shown the sights of Bath, Mr. Buller, the rector of Colyton, came in a failing state of health to take the cure. They walked to see a Miss Lefroy look hot on horseback at the riding school, they visited Lord and Lady Leven, whose son Lord Balgonie, a junior officer in the Fleet, had been befriended by dear Charles, now in command of the *Indian* sloop off Bermuda. The Leigh Perrots showed kindness after their fashion. Uncle Leigh Perrot visited his widowed sister regularly and often took his nieces to the play or to a concert. Aunt Leigh Perrot talked of settling some of the milliner's bills for their mourning, but in the end did no more than offer a ticket for an *al fresco* breakfast in the Sydney Gardens, which Jane coolly declined ; she did not take easily to being a poor relation.

In September they went to Godmersham. Kent was still agog with invasion reports, Martello Towers had been built and a canal dug across the Romney Marsh and the coast was lined with troops ; across the hazy Straits embarkation rehearsals were going on, with barges loading and unloading. That summer Admiral Nelson had been in chase of the French Fleet, right round the Mediterranean and all the way to the West Indies ; Frank's *Canopus* had been in that operation, but now the Fleet was home again and Admiral Villeneuve had taken refuge with the Spanish Fleet in Cadiz. While the Austens were in Kent Admiral Nelson sailed from Portsmouth in the *Victory*, never to set foot again on any shore ; but across the Channel the Emperor had given up his plan of invasion, his troops had left Boulogne and were gone to seek fresh laurels beyond the Rhine. His design was to conquer Austria.

2

In October when they went back to Bath Martha Lloyd came with them. Her mother was dead, and she was to make her home in future with the Austens, a pleasant arrangement. This winter they lodged in Trim Street ; they seemed to be moving from one to another of the streets which their aunt had rejected for them when they first came to Bath. Trim Street seemed respectable enough now that they were actually in it. It was certainly dark and narrow, the sun dropped behind the roofs very early on winter afternoons and in that part of the town wherever you went you seemed to get a whiff of steam round every corner, or out of the open door of a bathhouse ; but they only needed to pass under the archway and turn along Quiet Street to reach the pleasant shop windows of Milsom Street and their Uncle could look in almost daily as he went to the Pump Room. He was actually walking through the yard of the White Hart Inn, one raw November morning, on his way to visit them, when the London coach clattered into the yard, bringing the news of Lord Nelson's final victory over the French and Spanish Fleets at Trafalgar. The whole coach was dressed in laurels for this triumph, but among the green glistening leaves were broad bands of crape for the hero's death in action. Everybody in Bath began running and shouting when they heard the sudden glorious clash and jangle of the Abbey bells, high above the rooftops ; but before the peal had been ringing ten minutes it stopped dead and a passing bell started to toll. In all the streets there were pale faces and black clothes, people pulled down their blinds as if for a personal loss and crying women asked each other, "Have you heard the news ? We have lost Lord Nelson."

In Trim Street there was much anxiety ; but the news-papers, scanned again and again, among all the details which they gave of the battle, did not print the name of H.M.S. *Canopus*. They could not understand her absence until a letter from Frank, unlucky Frank on this occasion, arrived from Mary Gibson. He wrote quite frantic, poor fellow ! for after being for so many months on the alert he and his men had missed their part in the action by the service accident of having been ashore at Tetuan taking in water and stores. They had actually been on their way to rejoin the Fleet, but the great gale which scattered the ships at the end of the battle kept them so long beating past the Rock that they did not sight Cape Trafalgar till the day after the fair. "It is heart-breaking," wrote poor Frank, " after so many months in a state of constant and unremitting *fag* to be at last cut out by a parcel of folks just come from their homes, where some of them were staying at their ease the greater part of the last war and the whole of this." Frank was in the greatest distress for the loss of the little hero, under whom he had served so long and feared too that it must affect his future. He had no interest with stiff Admiral Collingwood, who had taken command of the Fleet. He told Mary Gibson that he should not be home just yet, but he could not say that he was bound for the West Indies.

That December, 1805, the city entertained a most distinguished invalid, Mr. Pitt the Prime Minister. People flocked into Bath to see him drive out from his lodging in Laura Place to the baths ; they stood in the gutter in the winter weather, waiting for a sight of him, watching the messengers with their dispatch-boxes come posting down from London. In the Pump Room the visitors fell back and made a line for the great man when he appeared, hobbling on two sticks with his gouty foot in flannel, so pale and anguished that he looked like a death's-head. It was a terribly anxious time. Just before Trafalgar the Emperor had surrounded a great part of the Austrian army at Ulm. After that came one anxious rumour after another and over Christmas the talk was all of a great battle at Olmutz, though nobody knew which side had won it, followed by an armistice between France and Austria ; but nothing was certain.

On Christmas Day the Prime Minister took an airing in his carriage, looking much the better for his cure and on New Year's Day he was so far restored to health that he went to spend the day at Shockerwick House. This fine classical mansion had been built by a Mr. Wiltshire, a local worthy, very much respected, who had made his fortune in the carrier trade. His wagons were always on the Bath Road. He was something of an art collector and had befriended Gainsborough, when that artist was young and unknown. Wiltshire's waggons used to take his great canvasses up to London free of charge. Now the rooms at Shockerwick were adorned by some of Mr. Gainsborough's finest landscapes. Mr. Pitt was actually inspecting these admired works when a galloping messenger came after him from Laura Place. The Secretary of War, Lord Castlereagh, had come down post-haste from the capital with frightful news. Napoleon had utterly routed the combined armies of the Austrians, Russians and Prussians at the Battle of Austerlitz, a place so small that most people could not find it in the map of Europe. That map, the Prime Minister said with an anguished groan, might as well be rolled up again ; it would not be needed for ten years. The news was the death of him. A day or two later the crowd in Laura Place saw him helped into his carriage and driven away up the London Road. He was dead in three weeks and the Whig Party came into office.

That winter in Trim Street Jane was doing a little writing, picking up old stuff, playing with it half-heartedly, putting it down again, struggling to spread her wings like a moth in cobwebs, unable to fly. Her Bath novel was lying unpublished with Messrs. Crosbie and she had not the heart to go on with *The Watsons*. Instead she rummaged out *Lady Susan*, that novel in letters which she had begun long ago after Eliza's visit to Steventon. With Martha in the house, there was all the time she needed to talk over that strange sinister history of the Lloyds' grandmother, the wicked Mrs. Craven. She polished the manuscript a little, but her sharp eyes saw too many faults in it. She lost patience and scrambled it to an end, with a gibing conclusion about the loss to the revenue when its characters ceased their interminable correspondence. She said to Cassandra drearily, " I cannot write any more. My mind is quite dry, nothing grows in it here. I wish I could leave Bath for ever."

Outside the cobbler's shop where they took their shoes to be mended there was a green linnet in a cage. It ruffled up its dirty feathers, hopped restlessly about, pecked without appetite at the seed that was given to it, or moped on its perch. The country bird could not sing in Trim Street.

Towards the end of the winter came news of Frank to make their hearts beat faster. The *Canopus* had been in a victorious action under Admiral Sir John Duckworth off Santo Domingo ; strange how that West Indian island, with its roaring reefs and high wooded peaks, so often became visible on the horizon of their lives. Three good prizes had been taken and other ships driven ashore, the English Fleet remained in command in those waters and Frank came home full of glory and prize money, to marry Mary Gibson at midsummer. He visited his mother and sisters in Trim Street and was shocked to find them in such dark and stuffy quarters ; he had always vaguely thought of them as living in some large house like the Rectory. Jane in particular he thought looked very pale. He turned the matter over in his mind, went to Ramsgate about it, and came back with a

generous plan. Mary and he would rent a house in Southampton and his family should share it, then when he went
to sea again his young wife would have company instead of
living alone in lodgings. The whole family were delighted ;
only Aunt Leigh Perrot disapproved. When Frank with his
great sea voice had shouted his notion into her deaf ears
she said in her carping way, " It will never do. I knew a
family who tried it and were obliged to separate before the
end of the first quarter. I should have thought you would
avoid Southampton in any case, considering that poor Sister
Jane died there, nursing your two girls when they were
little. I have always felt that Southampton must be a most
unhealthy place."

4

By midsummer they quitted Bath, with what happy feelings
of escape for Jane and Cassandra nobody else knew. They
had planned to spend a few weeks at the Bristol Hot Wells
until Frank found a house to suit them, but something more
amusing came their way. The head of Mrs. Austen's
family, the Hon. Mary Leigh, had died that July in London
and the old woman's death brought up the vexed question
of who should inherit the estate of Stoneleigh Abbey in
Warwickshire. There were three claimants to this ancient
house under an old and complicated will. It must go
ultimately to a nephew, but meanwhile Uncle Leigh Perrot
and his cousin, the Rev. Thomas Leigh, rector of Adlestrop,
each could claim a life interest. Uncle Leigh Perrot had
no wish to undertake the great place and was glad to com-
pound his share, but Cousin Thomas was determined not
to lose his chance. He and his sister had been awaiting their
opportunity for years. They travelled straight to Stoneleigh
Abbey, took possession of it and filled up the house immediately with their own relatives, much to the vexation
of Mr. Hill, the family lawyer, and Mr. James Leigh, the
ultimate heir.

Mrs. George Austen and her girls, after a hot and hurried

August journey, found themselves eating fish, venison and all manner of good things in a large parlour hung round with family pictures. Stoneleigh was a noble house standing in its own deer park with the Avon winding through the green meadows before it. There were positively forty-five windows in its Palladian front, wrote Mrs. Austen exultingly to Mrs. J. A. and she proceeded to describe all the glories of the place to her envious daughter-in-law. There was the great hall, the picture gallery, the two drawing-rooms, rather gloomy with brown wainscot and red damask chairs. The state bed-chamber with its high crimson velvet four-poster, was an alarming apartment just fit for a heroine ; the private chapel was all draped in black for family mourning, and there the new owner read prayers each day to his household. There were twenty-six bedchambers in the new part of the house and a great many more, some very good ones, in the old part which had been the Abbey ; how romantic that sounded ! The whole place was so rambling that one could hardly find one's way about in it, and she had advised Cousin Thomas to set up direction posts at the corners of the passages.

As one good housekeeper to another she made Mary's mouth water with the provisions sent in daily from the estate, the quantity of soft fruit in the kitchen garden, the profusion of cream, butter and cheese in the dairy and the number of casks in the beer cellar. While Cousin Thomas was busy with his lawyer the ladies had walked in the cool humming shade of the August woods, they had driven to Kenilworth and Warwick, visitors had come and gone, including a particularly silly Lady Saye and Sele from Broughton Castle, who had amused Jane. The party were being waited upon by eighteen manservants, who had all been put into mourning liveries, a sad expense ! Every part of the house, she wound up triumphantly, was so clean that if you were to cut your finger you could scarcely find a cobweb to wrap it up in. The old lady lapped up all this luxury as a cat does cream ; this, she felt, was what she had been born to inherit and it was an infinite consolation to her after Trim Street.

From Stoneleigh Abbey they all went down to Kent and it was during this visit that Mrs. George Austen suddenly said to Elizabeth, " I wish Jane would not spend so much of her time shut up in the schoolroom with your Miss Sharpe."

Ann Sharpe was the governess, who had been at Godmersham for the last year in charge of the three elder girls. She had taught them to put the map of Europe together and recite the dates of the Kings of England with the principal events of their reigns, the Roman Emperors down to Severus, a great deal of the heathen mythology and all the metals, semi-metals, plants and distinguished philosophers, besides a smattering of French and Italian. They had learnt to sew and embroider, to play scales and easy pieces, to sing in tune, drop a pretty curtsey, come in and out of a room quietly and answer politely without fidgetting when older people took notice of them. Miss Ann Sharpe was a good-humoured affectionate creature, but rather gushing and plaintive ; she was not very quick or clever and her pupils were inclined to make fun of her.

She sat in the schoolroom, up three flights of stairs, with its battered furniture, its inkstained tablecloth, its framed drawings, wool-work cushions and window-transparencies, done by the girls under her guidance. All the morning they did lessons and in the afternoon she took them for a walk in the park, unless they went out driving with their mother, in which case she walked in the park by herself or was sent on an errand to the village. In the evening she sat sewing while the girls did their preparation and made a brief appearance with them in the drawing-room.

After they were in bed she had her supper brought up to her on a tray and then she wrote letters, many letters, or did her netting ; she had netted herself an entire cloak, a hideous object, in the long winter evenings. She was a humble creature and entirely content with her monotonous existence. It was quite a novelty to her to have Miss Jane Austen seek her out in the schoolroom, listen with sympathetic humour and indignation to her complaints about her former employers and betray surprise at her raptures about her present situation. " The girls are such sweet creatures and Mrs. Austen is really so uncommonly kind and thoughtful. Only fancy, she says I am to have a fire up here every evening, whether the girls are with me or not, and I have wax candles every night ; that, you know, is quite unusual." Miss Jane's lip curled as Ann Sharpe insisted, " I have never been so happy anywhere as I am here. I do not know how I shall bear it when I have to leave."

She looked a little alarmed when Miss Jane asked, "What will you do when you grow older ? " but confided her secret dream, which was to save enough money to start a private school. She was, however, quite taken aback when Miss Jane began to question her about how she herself might obtain a situation as a governess, should she ever need it. " Oh ! my dear Miss Austen, you could never do that." " No, I suppose I am not sufficiently well educated," said Miss Jane mournfully. " We were only brought up in a scrambling kind of way at home, all that I know comes from reading in my father's library ; but I think I could manage to teach quite little children their letters." " I did not mean that at all," exclaimed the shocked governess. " You are so very well-read and you play and sing so charmingly ; you could name your own terms, I feel sure, have as many rooms as you chose and mix with the family if you liked. There are advertising offices in London, you would have no difficulty at all in finding something suitable, but your family would never allow it."

" No, I suppose not," said Jane mournfully. " I own I wish to leave home, I cannot bear to be so dependent. My spirits are sometimes quite exhausted. I have no life of my own." The two women looked at each other and Ann Sharpe, with tears in her eyes exclaimed, " You do not know what the change would be ; you could not bear it. Indeed, indeed, dear Miss Austen, you would do better to go with your mother and sister to Southampton . . ."

Southampton at that date, 1806, was rather a quiet place which had seen better days. Plymouth and Bristol had long ago taken its trade with America, and Portsmouth had all the noise and bustle of the naval dockyard. The King's ships were built across the water, at Buckler's Hard on the Beaulieu River, where Adams the shipbuilder could get all the timber he needed from the New Forest oaks. Some of the first ships in the Fleet, *Illustrious, Agamemnon, Euryalus, Swiftsure,* all had been built on the stocks at Beaulieu, and the people of Southampton had taken their children down to the West Quay to watch the great black hulls with chequered yellow sides being towed across by rowboats to Portsmouth Dockyard to be fitted up. The trade with the Channel Islands, Southampton's chief stand-by, had come to an end ten years earlier when war was declared, and the once busy port had lapsed into a quiet watering place, where retired naval and military families kept up a pretence at a spa, with little dances and concerts in the Assembly Rooms near the West Quay, glasses of water from a mild chalybeate spring, sea bathing in the season and a regatta every August in the Solent.

Dear generous Frank rather fancied himself as the head of a household of women. He liked the idea of his mother, his wife and his two sisters all settling down together and made no bones about their adding Martha Lloyd to the party. It never entered his head that they might not get on! he imagined them settled down as cosily as a flock of hens while he was at sea, without a peck or squawk among them. He had picked a big old-fashioned house for them as near the water as he could get! trust Frank for that! It was in Castle Square, Below Bar, and Frank had got it cheap because that part of the town was no longer fashionable. It was a maze of alleys with queer names, Back of the Walls, The Ditches, Winkle Street, Simnel Street, Bugle Street! they smelt of mud and fish and only tradespeople lived in them. The admirals' wives and generals' widows were all moving out into newly-built pale plaster villas with bow windows, standing in their own leafy gardens on the banks of the Test, Itchen or Hamble. The house in Castle Square had pleased Frank because of its lofty rooms and its pleasant garden, bounded on one side by the old city walls. There was even a flight of steps up to the top of the ramparts. His ladies could easily climb up there and stroll to and fro between Windwhistle Tower and Catchcold Tower, holding on to their hats, with their scarves and skirts fluttering in the bright salt airs, looking down on the West Port, from which long ago Henry the Fifth had sailed before Agincourt. There the painted sailing boats swung idly at their moorings in the double tides of the Solent, there the swans and gulls floated together between the mudbanks and green trees, and low sandy spits reflected themselves in the water.

Certainly it was charming up on the Walls and in the garden. The other side of the house, however, was not so cheerful as it should have been because the middle of the square was entirely taken up with a fantastic edifice, too large for the ground it covered, a folly of Lord Lansdowne's, a sham castle on the site of the old one, in the most Gothic taste, encrusted with battlements, turrets, oriels and flamboyant plaster ornament. This absurdity took all the morning sun from the Austens' windows. Nobody, however, was so unkind as to criticise Frank's first home and they all worked hard to put it in order.

Cassandra missed the move! a pity, because she was always the practical one. Jane wrote teasingly to Godmersham that without her Frank and Mary would be certain to buy everything wrong ; knives that would not cut, glasses that would not hold water, a broken-springed sofa to sit upon and a bookcase without any shelves. Actually Mrs. F. A. had turned out to be a very sensible young woman. Frank and she were as busy as bees indoors, hanging curtains and pictures, arranging closets and shelves, while honest blundering Martha, the friend and sister under all circumstances, followed them about or knelt humbly at their feet imploring Mrs. F. A. to consider her state of health and looking up for instructions as she tacked down

the carpets and waxed the floor boards. Frank was waiting
to hear when he would get to sea again. He had been on
shore now nearly a year, long enough to marry a wife, beget
a child and set up a home ; but now he was growing restless
and when the winter gales blew about the new house he
fretted to be afloat. It took his mind off his uncertainties to
be busy. Like most sailors, he was clever with his fingers.
He put up a very pretty set of shelves for his sister's books,
he sawed, glued, and hammered, and tried in vain to stop
up the leak in the storeroom cupboard. He took a creaking
door off its hinges and eased it, he set all the rusty locks in
the house in working order, he mended the window cords
and wedged the frames so that they would not rattle in the
wind. When he was at work he used to sing all the time
long doleful sea ditties, mostly about shipwrecks. You
would have supposed that any sailor would have avoided
that subject above all others, but no, Frank loved it. As he
pottered about the house with his tools you heard him
bumbling away about a ship that sailed to her doom on a
Friday and was sunk with all hands. It was called *The
Mermaid.* " *One Friday morn when we set sail, And our ship was not
far from land, We there did espy a fair pretty maid With a comb
and a glass in her hand.*" Then came a burst of hammering
and a triumphant conclusion, " *Then three times round went
our gallant ship, Then three times round went she, Then three times
round went our gallant, gallant ship, And she sank—to the bottom
of the sea.*" Nobody could have sounded more cheerful than
Frank over this disaster, which might so easily happen to
himself some day or another. He had another long, long
melancholy one, with a recurring chorus : " *There we lay,
All that day, In the Bay of Biscay-O.*" Then the whole house
would ring to a shout for his plane, his nails, or his glue-
pot. In the evening when everything else was done he
would sit himself down in the corner of the parlour and
make fringe for the new curtains while his wife sewed baby
linen beside him and Jane read aloud in her sweet clear
voice ; nothing could have been more agreeable than these
winter evenings beside the fire.

Old Mrs. Austen was a great gardener and never so happy

as when she was planting and weeding. In Castle Square they found a pleasant sunny enclosure, sheltered from the westerly gales by the great grey and yellow stones of the city wall, tufted with wallflowers. It was said to be one of the best gardens in the town. It had a gravel walk, bordered with roses and sweetbriar, an arbour and a number of rather neglected old fruit trees. The jobbing gardener who came in to dig the sour soil over for them could tell that they were country people, from the sensible orders they gave him. The old lady told him to root up the worn-out currants and raspberries and gooseberry bushes and plant strong new ones, she talked in a very knowledgeable way about vegetables. The young lady stood looking about her. She plucked a leaf from a sweetbriar bush and stood crushing it between her palms, then put her hand to her face and stood inhaling the spicy fragrance. Suddenly she said, " Tell him to plant a syringa, mamma ; we cannot do without a syringa for the sake of Cowper's line." She stretched out her hand, like a play actress and began to recite, " *Laburnum, rich in streaming gold ; Syringa, ivory pure.*" . . . How does it all go ? I forget the rest." She started to laugh at herself and the old lady laughed too. Their two sharp merry faces were more alike than he had thought, at first. " My dear Jane," her mother said, " we have very little room to spare. We had far better plant potatoes." The gardener fell to digging again ! he had little time to listen to young ladies' follies. " But what a pair of eyes this one had," he thought to himself after the two of them had gone indoors. " As bright and quick as any robin's ; I never saw brighter in my life."

7

The Austen family were soon looked well after in the matter of friends. James wrote about them to a family called Maitland, in Albion Place ; there were several Miss Maitlands, civil and rather silly. Mrs. Maitland had been the sister of his first wife, poor Anne Mathew. Martha recollected an aunt in the Island, as all true Hampshire folk call the Isle of Wight, a widowed Mrs. Craven ; when summer came it would be pleasant to go over in the sailing ferry to Cowes and visit her. Doctor Mant, the Rector of All Saints, came with his sister to call upon these new members of his congregation and was pleased to find himself conversing with the widow of a fellow-clergyman ; he declared with a bow that he believed he had met both old and young Mr. Austen over diocesan affairs, in Winchester. But naturally in Southampton Mrs. Austen and her daughters were regarded less as a clergyman's family than as the relatives of a naval Captain. Frank did his best for them in this respect, inviting old friends with pride to his new house. The Commander of the Sea Fencibles waited upon them and a certain Admiral Bertie and his daughter called early ; there seemed nothing to like or to dislike in either. Mrs. F. A. at this stage was unequal to the exertion of going far from home and did not much care about showing herself in her present shape, so Captain Austen usually took his younger sister with him when he dressed himself up in his best uniform to return these civil visits.

A friendly soul himself, he was a little surprised that Jane so often detected patronage where he had only found affability. There was a certain Mrs. Lance, for instance, who had a fine house among the woods across the Itchen at Bitterne, a brace of musical daughters and a drawing-room ornamented by a harp and a grand piano ; all this promised something congenial, surely, for his musical sister. Frank himself quite enjoyed the outing, Mrs. Lance appeared civil and chatty and offered to introduce them to some of her Southampton acquaintances. He could not understand why Jane received this so coolly, or why she said so tartly, as they were being rowed back over the ferry, " We shall not see much more of them, I daresay. They live in a handsome style and are very rich ; now that we have given her to understand how poor we are, she will soon feel that we are not worth her trouble." Captain Austen glanced sideways under the brim of his sister's beaver bonnet and thought that her lips were set much tighter than they used to be. Her curls were all tucked away out of sight, her face looked pinched by the cold January wind in the grey sea light striking up off the water. What had changed Jane so greatly in the long years while he had been at sea? She had been such a gay and friendly creature in the old days, when the two used to dance and jump about together at the Ashford and Basingstoke Assemblies. Then he used to think her the prettiest girl in any room, but now she seemed to be turning into a sour and suspicious old maid with a sharp eye and a mouth tucked down at the corners. Counting birthdays in his head, as he sat with his hand on the hilt of his sword and his cloak wrapped about him while the old boat creaked across the river to the slip, Captain Austen thought, " God bless my soul ! she must be turned thirty. What have all the men been doing, that nobody has married our pretty Jane ? "

8

Actually the Austens became quite friendly with the Lances and the Maitlands. They used to go to musical parties for the daughters, at which young midshipmen and lieutenants joined in duets with the girls, or roared out sea-songs. In their husky voices, not long broken, hoarse with shouting orders, they would bawl out *Tom Bowling* and *All in the Downs the Fleet was moored.* One in a sweet light heart-breaking tenor would begin, " *Oh ! Susan, Susan, lovely dear, my heart shall ever true remain. Let me kiss off that falling tear, We only part to meet again* " ; and all the young ladies would sit with their heads on one side, smiling faintly ; but soon they would cry out for a dance, the rugs would be rolled back and away they would go. Miss Jane would always play for them by the hour and, " Lord! Miss Jane, how your little fingers do fly," Mrs. Lance would say as she passed the piano, " my young people should be very grateful to you, I am sure."

Frank did not get to sea until April of that year, 1807, when he was given command of H.M.S. *St. Albans,* then lying at Sheerness. He wished he might have embarked from Portsmouth. He would have liked to have taken his family on board and show them his captain's quarters, the small sleeping cabin, the great cabin next it, all the corners of his ship, his little castle, the pride of his heart. As it was he had to leave them sooner than was necessary and spend weeks at Sheerness, taking in a pressed crew, ordering stores and livestock on board, engaged with all the business of getting his ship ready for sea. His family had worked hard, mending and marking his body linen, his towels and table-cloths, all in exquisite cross-stitch, packing his new full-dress uniform, wrapping up the gold lace against salt airs, brushing and pressing old faded blue coats, still good enough for use at sea. Jane, the best needlewoman, mended the ladders in his silk stockings and packed him up a box of books. Martha hemmed him dozens of silk and cambric handker-chiefs, dropping a tear on one or two of them ; his mother knitted him thick wool stockings for seaboots, his wife a great muffler. Cassandra, the housekeeper, packed raisins and brandied-cherries, prunes, figs and little bags of spices to flavour tough fowls and salt beef with, when he had been long at sea. James sent a couple of great Steventon cheeses down by coach, Henry three boxes of cigars from his own tobacconist in Piccadilly, Edward, the magnificent, a case of wine from the Godmersham cellars. Frank's cot was sewn up, his sea chest and his boxes corded, and away he went in the April weather.

He told his womenfolk cheerfully that there would be no battles for him this time, they could count on that. With the French and Spanish fleets sunk the war had entered upon a new phase. The Emperor was trying a new trick. He had closed all the Continental ports from Dantzig round to Trieste, not only to British shipping but to any ship which had called at a British port. He was trying to drive us off the seas, where he had not a ship of his own and we in our turn had declared a counter-blockade and would seize any vessels caught trading between his French ports and those of his allies. Frank was off on convoy work and expected to do little else in this commission. As soon as the *St. Albans* was victualled he would set sail for St. Helena, at that time the usual rendezvous of the ships of the East India Company, who waited there when homeward bound to be picked up by their naval escort. His family might turn the globe and fancy the *St. Albans* running down the Channel, across the Bay of Biscay and far out in the Atlantic. Frank would be walking the deck through the long calm idle tropic days, hearing the ship's bells, listening to the wind singing in the shrouds, watching the shadow of the rigging move this way and that across the deck, thinking sometimes of home. His first child was born that summer, a daughter, named for her mother and her two aunts, Mary Jane, a sweet good-tempered baby, no trouble to anyone. Cassandra, an admirable nurse, devoted herself to Mrs. F. A. ; old Mrs. Austen, a devoted grandmother, delighted in the baby, and Martha took over the housekeeping while Jane, to relieve the household, was packed off to Kent.

That summer they had good news of the other sailor brother, the best news of all. Charles was going to marry, indeed by this time must have already married, the daughter of a certain English barrister, Mr. Palmer, who was then Attorney-General of Bermuda. Her name was Fanny and Charles must have met her at the dances on the delightful rocky island when he came ashore from the *Indian* sloop, after chasing privateers among the coral reefs and palm-fringed islands of the Caribbean. Now there were only girls left, of all the Austen family.

James and Mrs. J. A. came down that summer and paid a solemn, rather tiresome visit. Jane said it was a pity that their company did not give more pleasure. James's chat seemed all forced, his opinions on many points were too much copied from his wife and he seemed to spend his time walking about the house, banging the doors and ringing the bell for a glass of water. The household was short-handed at the time ; servants were not easy to get in Southampton and Mrs. J. A. and her mother-in-law spent much time abusing them. Mrs. Austen lamented the stout country girls of Steventon, who were not afraid of work and did whatever they were told quite cheerfully for ten pounds a year. " In Southampton, my dear, I can find nothing but young ladies delicately arrayed in white gowns, with their heads cropped short in the latest fashion. They all tell me they are anxious for places, but I cannot see that any of them would do for us. What we need here is a strong maid of all work who will scrub and clean and can be trusted with a little plain cooking. The girl I saw yesterday told me that she had left her last place because her mistress would not suffer her to drink tea twice a day with tea at ten shillings a pound ; and would not permit of her wearing feathers in her hat on Sundays. This she thought was most unkind." And Mrs. J. A. in reply would cast up her hands and exclaim that, town or country, the race of servants was becoming extinct.

9

That summer, 1807, was the time when the Emperor, after over-running Prussia the previous autumn and defeating the Prussians at Jena and at Auerstadt and marching into Berlin, first crossed the borders of Russia. He defeated the Tsar's armies in a quick spring campaign. The two Emperors met together on a raft, laden with decorated pavilions and moored in the sluggish current of the Niemen river, near a town called Tilsit, on the borders of Poland and Lithuania. They made peace together and the provinces and kingdoms of Eastern Europe were cut up into new shapes. Napoleon's three brothers, Joseph, Louis and Jerome became the Kings of Naples, Holland and Westphalia, and people remembered, or perhaps invented, an Italian prophecy that a swarm of bees would come out of Corsica and eat up all the honey in Europe. The Tsar got a slice of Prussia for his pains and was told to declare war upon England. It was the old story once again, collecting allies against Napoleon was like trying to make a bundle of rotten sticks: they bent and broke and ran into your hand. You would have thought the Emperor would have been content with what he had got by this Treaty of Tilsit, but there was still one kingdom at his back which he had not yet conquered; Spain he must have and Spain he attacked as soon as the winter snows had melted on the Pyrenees.

In May, 1808, he turned out the Royal family, and his elder brother Joseph, then serving his apprenticeship to king-craft in Naples, was fetched over and installed in the cold grey palace, with its long rows of windows, facing the mountains in the dusty outskirts of Madrid; but he did not stay there long, for the whole city and country rose in rebellion against him.

Jane went to stay that month with Henry and Eliza in London. To go to them was like moving into another world. Henry was already making money and intended to grow very rich. They lived in a pleasant small brown brick house in a terrace, St. Michael's Place, among the market gardens of Brompton. Eliza was exactly the same as ever, thin as a rake, with enormous eyes, sweet and lively and delighted to welcome her dear Jane. Henry and she seemed ideally happy, they adored each other and teased and skirmished all day long. Henry rode into town every morning to his office in the Albany; he said that he did not intend to become a fat greasy banker and that the exercise would help him to keep his handsome figure. Eliza kept house with French thrift, Madame Bigeon did everything in the little house and in the evenings they entertained a little circle of neighbours. Brompton was then a great place for French *emigrés*, and Eliza was kindness itself to these exiles, thin pale foreigners in threadbare coats and patched shoes, who stayed their hunger eagerly on Madame Bigeon's good ragouts and casseroles. Warm-hearted Eliza sighed, "I cannot turn them away, they are so poor. They are always trying to sell me some trifle or other and I fancy do not eat all day when they expect to dine with us." The refugees in their turn would invite the Austens to pathetic little parties, where a slender provision of omelettes and salads, very thin cakes, coffee and *eau sucrèe* accompanied endless games of trictrac; and ladies and gentlemen in shabby silken finery, heavily rouged and powdered, who nowadays were language teachers and dancing masters, modistes and laundresses, but had once been courtiers at Versailles, took snuff together and talked endlessly of their lost estates, their dead friends and their hopes of returning to France. They none of them seemed to think that it could be done while Napoleon lived.

By midsummer an English expeditionary force had been sent out to lend a hand to the Spanish patriots. One-half of it went to Portugal under the command of the tall hawk-nosed Sir Arthur Wellesley ; Eliza, who still read the Indian news, had heard of him as the winner of a battle at a place called Assaye. The other half went to Corunna, on the north-west corner of Spain, and its leader was Sir John Moore with his new corps of riflemen, all picked skirmishers, the Light Brigade, who thought themselves the first corps in the service. When Jane went down to Godmersham she found that conversation in Kent drawing-rooms was about equally divided between the shocking local scandal of Mrs. Poulett's elopement with Lord Sackville and Sir John's chance of beating the French.

James and his wife arrived with Jane, bringing young Edward and little three-year-old Caroline. Elizabeth was as sweet as ever, but she looked pale. She was expecting another child, her eleventh, in the autumn, poor animal ! but she would not admit that she felt less well than usual and she let the children plague her all day long. Young Fanny, her eldest daughter, was now sixteen ; she had grown tall and showed promise of being very pretty. She was playing hostess to help her mother. She met the visitors at the door and escorted Aunt Mary, the married lady, very politely to her bedroom ; then flew to Aunt Jane in the Yellow Room and sat on the bed, laughing and chattering, while Aunt Jane changed her travelling dress. She had always adored this aunt, ever since the Bath visit and liked to think of herself as Jane's own special niece.

Mary might as well have brought her stepdaughter, Anna, there would have been plenty of room and the long-legged boyish creature just fifteen years old would have enjoyed herself running about the stables after her boy-cousins ; but the truth was that stepmother and stepdaughter did not agree very well and Mary, who was always glad to be rid

of Anna, had packed her off to Southampton, where the girl
was a great favourite with both her grandmother and her
Aunts. Mary was a troublesome visitor, always nervous and
cross, she fussed dreadfully over her pigeon pair. James
walked about the estate with Edward and discussed farming ;
on Sunday he took duty for Mr. Whitfield and preached a
fine sermon, comparing the Emperor Napoleon to the Beast
of the Apocalypse. In the evenings he read poetry aloud to
the assembled family. His choice was Sir Walter Scott's new
poem, *Marmion*. His sister Jane screwed up her face rather
dubiously over this romantic work. She believed she had
rather outgrown her youthful taste for ivied towers, gallant
knights and fair ladies, and as for nuns walled up in dungeons,
they had gone out with *Udolpho* ; but Fanny thought it all
sweetly pretty. The little boys ran about the house shouting
" *Charge, Chester, charge ; On, Stanley, on,*" and thrusting
at each other till they fell down screaming with laughter.
One only hoped they were not imitating kind Uncle James.
Louisa called her puppy Douglas, Fanny changed her pony's
name to Young Lochinvar. Little Caroline, a shy, plain,
cossetted mother's darling, found her handsome headstrong
cousins a little too much for her, but her brother Edward
stood up to them very well. Henry and William showed him
the model ship in the passage and let him feed their rabbits
and he played happily with the little girls, Lizzie, Marianna
and Louisa, while his Uncle Edward talked nonsense to him
most delightfully, though some of it was a little above his
head. Altogether the Steventon party seemed to enjoy their
visit.

Cassandra wrote faithfully, trading the small beer of
Southampton twice a week in her letters for Jane's French
wine of Godmersham. Anna had cut her hair short behind
like a boy and had a sad cropped head ; it was to be hoped
that her curls would grow again before she wanted to go
to dances. She had been measuring herself against the
parlour door and particularly wanted to hear whether she
or Cousin Fanny were the taller. She had been over for the
day to the Island with Aunt Cassy, Aunt Martha and Aunt
Mary, Mrs. F. A. ; they had got up at four o'clock of a

June morning to catch the sailing ferry and had taken the
baby with them. Little Mary Jane, at twelve months old,
was already a true sailor's daughter ; she had slept most
of the way and had not cried once.

Frank, her father, was at home again that June ; the
St. Albans had been not only to St. Helena, but as far as
the Cape of Good Hope. Now she was lying off Sheerness
and her captain had had shore leave. He and his wife had
been to Yarmouth, later they hoped to visit Godmersham.
In the spring he expected more convoy work ; he would
probably go with the East India Company's ships all the
way to China. And could not little Edward come to Castle
Square with his parents on their way home ? His grandmother had not see him for a twelvemonth, though Steventon
was so near Southampton. James and Mary were doubtful,
but little Edward pleaded for the treat. He had never seen
the sea, he pointed out, nor a sailing ship ; and he wanted
above all things to feast his eyes on the Castle in the Square,
about which Aunt Jane had told him. Nobody understood
how to manage his mother better than he and it was all
arranged.

10

Edward remembered that visit all his life. It had been a
long tiring journey for a child, all the way from Kent and
he had been squeezed in between his elders all the way.
When they arrived it was quite late in the evening of a hot
July day and he was so sleepy that he could not keep his
eyes open. His father carried him into the house and Aunt
Martha Lloyd popped him straight away into bed. He did
not wake in the morning until Aunt Jane came to kiss him
and draw his curtains. She turned round, smiling all over
her face and beckoned him with a lifted finger to come and
look out at something very pretty, so Edward hopped out of
bed and ran barefoot across the boards.

There was a most extraordinary building outside in the
Square, a kind of toy castle with little towers and battle-

ments and heavily grated windows. It was so much too big for the place it stood in that you felt a witch must have popped it down there by night. Edward fell in love with it on sight. It looked exactly as if the King and Queen of Hearts in the cribbage pack might live there with their knaves and attendants. If the drawbridge were let down and the portcullis raised, might armed men not come marching out of it ? But Aunt Jane said that a wicked lord lived inside, who was very ill ; you never saw him come in and out, but you could see his lady any day. She went out driving, not in a pumpkin coach drawn by rats and mice, as you might have hoped, but in something almost as good. If Edward went back to his warm bed now he should see her carriage brought out later and sure enough he did. It was a dear little open phaeton swung very high like a shell, with yellow doors and red wheels. The ponies were harnessed and put to out in the open square because there was no room inside to do it. There were always six and sometimes eight of them ! each pair grew smaller and became lighter in colour as you went away from the carriage, dark brown, light brown, chestnut, bay, cream and white. If you waited long enough the lady herself would come out, in a blue satin driving cloak and a great bonnet full of flowers, with her face painted in red and white circles like a clown. She would step in and take the tasselled reins and whip in her hands, the little groom would jump up behind her, the ponies toss their manes and away they would go at a good round trot over the cobblestones, round the corner and out of sight. It was the prettiest thing for a child to see, it was something that he was going to remember all his life. When he was quite an old gentleman, Edward would write down in his memoir how he went to stay with his grandmother at Number 2, Castle Square, Southampton, in the year 'eight and was shown Lady Lansdowne's carriage and ponies by his Aunt Jane.

1809 had been the loveliest of the summers at Godmersham, but there would never be another like it. Elizabeth in those last months had been like an exquisite full-blown rose, all colour and fragrance ; nobody thought that her petals could drop at a touch. After James and his family had gone home to Steventon and Jane had taken up her place in Castle Square with her mother, Cassandra travelled into Kent to be with Elizabeth for the birth of this eleventh child, as she had done so often before. The birth was a little earlier than had been expected ; when Cassandra descended from the carriage into the marble hall at Godmersham young Fanny ran downstairs crying that she had a new brother, to be called Brook John for his two uncles. Cassandra ran up just as she was from the last stage of her journey and found pale Elizabeth in her lace cap and wrapper, lying among her rose-coloured curtains. The child's downy head was in the crook of her arm. She smiled faintly and whispered, " Dear Cassy, I am so glad that you are here. You are always so very comfortable." Sackree said that her mistress had come through the birth quite easily and Cassandra went down, well satisfied, to drink tea with Edward and his family.

All seemed as usual, but in the night Elizabeth was restless, and in the morning Sackree pursed her lips a little. She took the baby away, dancing him in her old experienced arms, calling him " My lamb," and " My precious." Luckily they had already found a wet nurse for him, a stout and rosy young woman from one of the farms. Elizabeth's lips were dry and her slender hands hotter than they should have been, but Dr. Scudamore said it was just the usual thing, a little milk-fever, ordered cooling and composing draughts, and said that if this failed we might proceed to blistering and bleeding. Elizabeth cried when he was gone and would not eat her good chicken broth and custard. She began to shiver, but not from cold, for she would not be covered up and tossed and turned continually in her bed.

She did not seem to know Edward or Cassandra when they came to look at her ; she was burning with fever and went on crying and laughing by turns and talking to herself. Edward took the boys out into the park, Fanny kept the younger children quiet, Cassandra and Sackree nursed the sick woman, plaiting her long hair for coolness, sponging her long limbs, trying to make her eat and drink. The doctor came twice a day, but he could not do her any good. The slow bright hours of daylight went by, the shadow of the candles, burning all night, moved restlessly upon the ceiling. At dawn on the third day the dying woman smiled with faint surprise and recognition on the children who were brought to her bedside ; then she closed her eyes and left them.

Afterwards everything was confusion and misery. It had all happened so quickly that they were quite stunned. Poor Edward, restless in his despair, went from one room to another in the great silent house, but could not keep away for long from the bedroom upstairs with the drawn blinds, the sable hangings, the candles and heaped flowers, where his dead wife lay with a smile on her lips. Fanny was his greatest comfort. She was with him continually, watching over him with a tenderness beyond her years and struggling with her own grief to console him. Poor old Nurse Sackree kept the crying children upstairs. The shocked servants came on tiptoe to Cassandra for orders, and she tried to remember what had been done at Bath when her father died. The Rector left his own sick wife to condole with his patron and to christen the baby ; homely rustic fellows, the coffin-maker, the grave-digger, the sexton, waited in the passage outside Edward's study. There were the same letters to write to Goodnestone, to Southampton, to London, to Steventon ; black clothes were ordered from Canterbury, messages went round to all the neighbouring great houses, the carriage must fetch Elizabeth's mother and sisters. Then came the day of the funeral, the mourning carriages, the tolling bell ; six of the tenants carried the coffin under its black and silver pall down through the lime tree avenue to the village, where the farmers and cottagers had lined the road, all standing silent in their black Sunday clothes. As they went through the Temple plantation the fallen leaves made a golden carpet for the feet of the men who carried her. Cassandra saw Edward look up at the little leafless trees ; he had planted them so that he and Elizabeth might have shade when they walked together to church on Sundays, till they were an old man and woman ; but now they were carrying her there feet first, to lay her lovely head in the dust.

12

There had not been any time to fetch the two elder boys home from Winchester, it had all happened too quickly. Their Uncle James posted over from Steventon to break the news to them. They had not even known that their mother was ill, only their sister Fanny had written to them that they had another brother. They were in Big School in the middle of the morning, Ned construing Virgil, George looking out of the window and fingering a pocketful of nuts, when the porter appeared with a message that they were to go to the Headmaster's study. Both wondered what they had done wrong now ; but when they arrived in that frightening room, with the birch rods behind the door, they knew at once that something dreadful had happened which was not to do with school. There sat Uncle James in his black parson's clothes and white neckcloth, with his pale gloomy face ; there stood Doctor Gabell, looking very awful in his academicals and his great powdered wig, straddling across the hearthrug with his back to the fire. Between them they broke it to the boys that their dear pretty mother was dead. Ned and George were more frightened than anything else, it was all so solemn and shocking. Uncle James said some pious things about duty and resignation, which passed over their heads ; Doctor Gabell told them briskly that they were to have leave for a week. They were not to go home to Kent, that was thought to be too far ; they were to divide the time between Steventon and Southampton. The grown-ups had arranged everything. Their clothes were packed ; Uncle James gave them a great dinner at the White Hart Inn, which they could scarcely choke down, poor boys ! and then they drove back with him in the post-chaise to Steventon.

It was never much fun at the Rectory and this time it was worse than ever. Aunt Mary was sharp and fretful, she kept crying and breaking off to talk about mourning. She made a great to do about taking them in to Basingstoke to buy them a black coat apiece, but she was too stingy to get them black pantaloons, though they told her that all the other fellows would think it very odd if they did not wear them. Uncle James mooned about, looking as if he wanted to talk to them but did not know what to say ; however he let them go out shooting rabbits with the bailiff, that was something. Cousins Edward and Caroline were of course too young to be company for the two Wykehamists ; Cousin Anna was their best resource. She was fifteen, a leggy girl, with her head cropped short like a boy and a tuft of curls on her forehead. She talked a great deal and very loud, banged about the house, ran up and down stairs whistling, when she was nervous she stammered a little, when she was excited she stamped her foot as she talked. She and Aunt Mary did not get on a bit ; Aunt Mary was always trying to make her behave like a little lady, but Anna would do no such thing. She was mad about dogs and horses, she took her cousins straight out to the stables when they arrived and she liked nothing so much as to go ferreting with them. Uncle James would not let her have a gun and learn to shoot, but she could do anything with a ferret. The cousins went out riding together, they went nutting in the Church Walk, in the evening they roasted chestnuts and made toffee in the old, dressing parlour upstairs, where Aunt Cass and Aunt Jane used to sit together. Anna had their little bedroom now to herself. She nodded her cropped head mysteriously and boasted that she was writing stories, as Aunt Jane used to do, but that was only girls' nonsense. The boys did not get through their days too badly, thanks to Cousin Anna ; and if they cried a little at night about their dead mother nobody else knew.

At the end of the week they went on to Southampton,

leaving Anna looking very forlorn. She would dearly have liked to go with them. Uncle James drove them down to the Flower Pot Inn at Popham Lane and put them in charge of Wise the coachman. He was an old family friend, a very civil respectful elderly man, who drove Rogers' coach every day, except Sundays, from Basingstoke to Southampton in the morning and back again with fresh horses at night. The boys sat on the box with him and he beguiled the journey with talk of famous runs with the Vine Hunt and recollections of their father's youth. " I mind Master Edward well, when he was no taller than young master here ; he went very well to hounds, so he did, though not so well as your good uncle, Master Henry, but Mr. Frank was far and away the boldest rider of them all, him that's now a sea captain." And he told them all over again the crusted old family story about Uncle Frank's red pony Squirrel. The coach went right past Chawton House, and Wise, with a flourish of his whip, indicated its grey gables and Tudor chimney stacks concealed among golden October trees behind a pinnacled church. There were cattle feeding in a park, and a little white temple, just like the ones at home. " A pity for the neighbourhood that your good father don't come and live in it," said Wise ; " but I lay he has a finer one, down in Kent."

The stupid boys had contrived to set out without their greatcoats and they were perished with cold long before they rattled under the Bar at Southampton and drew up in the courtyard of the inn. There was tall Aunt Jane in a black mourning pelisse and bonnet, standing on the steps with Martha Lloyd beside her. They were hugged and kissed and swept off to Number 2, Castle Square, where they each got a glass of cherry brandy to warm them, and after it when they could feel their fingers again, hot tea, poached eggs and buttered toast to carry them on till dinner. Southampton, they quickly decided, was a great improvement on Steventon. Their grandmother fussed over them a little more than suited their dignity ; calling them poor boys and saying that George, the lively one, was the image of his Uncle Henry ; and Aunt Cassy, their favourite aunt, was at

Godmersham, where they both wished to be ; but Martha Lloyd spoilt them in every way with cakes and tarts and made all their favourite puddings for them. She would always give you as much butter, Barbadoes sugar and black Jamaica treacle as you wanted, with almonds to make hardbake over the fire, and Uncle Frank's wife, whom they scarcely knew, turned out to be very jolly. They both liked her immensely, but of course she was too busy with little Mary Jane to come out much with them, so it was Aunt Jane who chiefly devoted herself to their entertainment.

With her to look after them Southampton seemed a splendid place to live in. To be sure they could not help thinking a good deal about their mother. It made them both cry to get the first loving letter from their father and when they went to church on Sunday, to All Saints, Miss Lloyd's favourite parson, Doctor Mant, preached a sermon which might have been written for them, from the text, "*All that are in danger, necessity and tribulation.*" Ned in particular was very much affected by this. But still they cheered up afterwards, when Aunt Jane took them off for a walk on the West Quay. George was very happy, flying about from one side to the other and skipping on board a dirty collier, all in his Sunday best. Aunt Mary, up at Steventon, would have hauled him over the coals for his carelessness ; but Aunt Jane was much too sensible to make a fuss about a little thing like that. She quite understood their point about getting proper mourning when Ned explained it to her, insisting eagerly that they wanted to have what all the other boys had. She answered in her dry smiling way, " Yes, it is always best to pass in the crowd if you can," and Ned glanced at her with quick suspicion. He thought for a moment that his aunt was laughing at him, but then she smiled at him very sweetly, screwing up her bright brown eyes and said, " Your father would not wish you to be unhappy for want of what is usual." And she took them to a Southampton tailor and ordered them a pair of black pantaloons apiece ; so that was all right.

She took them for a walk every day on the walls ; once

they actually went on the water. Although it was the very
end of October it was warm and still. She hired a boat and
let them row her all the way up from Itchen ferry to
Northamland and coming back they looked into a seventy-
four that was moored off the shipyard for some repair or
other. She was famously knowledgeable about ships ; she
could answer any question you chose to put to her, saying
in her pleasant way that she had picked all that up from
Uncle Frank and Uncle Charles. She knew the names of
the stars too ; she had learnt them all from these same
brothers when she was a little girl. They went star-gazing
in the garden at night and learnt to pick out Orion and the
Plough and Cassiopeia's Chair. When it was too wet and
cold to go out she knew all sorts of indoor games. She was
famous at bilbocatch ; anybody could learn to catch the
ball in the cup with a little practice, but Aunt Jane with her
clever fingers could catch it on the point as often as she
chose. Once she did it a hundred times before, flushed and
laughing, she tossed the toy back to George. She played
spillikins better than any of them ; with her delicate fingers
she could hook out one ivory spill after another and never
shake the pile. She knew hundreds of charades and riddles,
she had a whole book full of them which she and Aunt Cass
had collected when they were girls. She taught George to
make the most lovely little paper ships ; afterwards they
sailed the whole fleet in a tub of water and bombarded and
sank them with the conkers the boys had brought from
Steventon. And in the evenings they had the most famous
games of brag and speculation, the old woman of seventy,
the three spinsters in their thirties, the young married woman
and the two schoolboys, all laughing and talking together
round the table, rattling their counters and dealing their
cards. It was almost as good as being at home. Ned and
George did not say much about it to each other at the time,
they were too young and careless for that, but they knew
well enough who had made the difference between Steventon
and Southampton. Years afterwards, when she was dead
and buried, one tall brother would suddenly say to the other,
" Do you remember how good Aunt Jane was to us both,

that autumn in Castle Square, when our mother had just died ? ''

13

They never went to Southampton again, for within a year of Elizabeth's death Grandmamma Austen and the aunts had left the place for good. Uncle Frank had not gone to China after all, instead he had been employed all through the January gales helping to evacuate the shattered remnants of Sir John Moore's army. That heroic commander had fought a skilful retreat before the Emperor himself in mid-winter. His men had stumbled ashore at Portsmouth like so many walking ghosts on their frost-bitten feet, more dead than alive ; great numbers had fallen down and died in the snow, among the terrible Galician mountains, and Sir John Moore himself had been killed in action.

Uncle Frank had been at home a good deal that winter. Now he was at sea again, but Aunt Mary, Mrs. F. A., was going to have another baby, and when he came back he would want his house to himself ; it really was not big enough to hold so many people. Their own father could not bear to live at Godmersham now that their mother was dead, he was too lonely and wretched. He had given notice to his Chawton tenants, the Middletons, and the Great House was going to be done up. The Godmersham family were going to pay a long visit to Chawton each summer and Grand-mother Austen and the aunts were to have a house in the village. It was a charming plan which pleased everybody.

Their Southampton friends were very much concerned at losing the Austens. Many people were acquainted with Chawton and spoke of it as a very pretty village ; some even professed to know the house they were to live in, but nobody fixed on the right one. Dr. Mant declared that he would miss them from his congregation and looked very particularly at Miss Martha Lloyd as he said it. There was quite a round of little farewell parties at which they were the centre of attention.

At Southampton, in that spring of 1809 there was an exiled Frenchman, a lieutenant in the naval service, who could speak a little English and sadly lacked entertainment. He went walking on the ramparts one fine sunny morning in March, arm in arm with an acquaintance he had in the English navy, a Jersey man, a certain Captain d'Auvergne. They fell in with a party ; a naval man with a wife on his arm, a couple of younger women, and an old lady who was probably their mother. Introductions were made and the Frenchman attached himself immediately and skilfully to the younger of the two ladies. She was a tall elegant woman and she wore a black velvet pelisse and a black bonnet tied with wide ribbons under her chin. She carried this mourning garb with all the elegance of a Frenchwoman. He surveyed her with open admiration. She was not in the first bloom of her youth, but the wind from the dancing water had brought a fine colour into her cheeks ; she had very regular and pretty features and a pair of large swimming brown eyes which he admired immensely. He had come to the conclusion that there were a great many plain long-toothed women in Southampton, a place which he disliked, and they all wore their clothes badly. When he took his walks abroad it depressed him exceedingly, for if you saw one pretty face it was sure to be followed by twenty or thirty frights. As he surveyed this lady his own black eyes brightened. He executed a fine flourish of his cocked hat, twirled his moustache and fell into step beside her. He had no doubt of her pleasure at this attention. He had observed that whenever he walked anywhere with Captain d'Auvergne, each woman they met was sure to steal a look at him.

He swaggered beside this Miss Austen, making a remark upon the weather, which he understood to be the custom of the country and following it up by a compliment to the colour which the wind and sun had bestowed upon her. He was enchanted when his companion replied with a few words in his native tongue which, though halting, were exquisitely pronounced. He poured out a flood of grateful compliment ; but she had to smile, put out her pretty hand and confess that while she could read French well, or had done so when she was a girl, she did not nowadays speak it very easily. His English was even more scanty than her French and he had little more opportunity for the language of the eyes. The two sea-officers, Captain d'Auvergne and Captain Austen, had finished their exchange of professional civilities and the little party disappeared by unlocking a wicket gate and descending a flight of steps into a garden below the wall. He wished he might have followed them.

He questioned his friend eagerly, but did not get much enlightenment. Captain d'Auvergne only knew them as the mother, wife and unmarried sisters of Captain Frank Austen, in command of H.M.S. *St. Albans*. They all lived together in Castle Square and the captain came to visit them whenever he was home from sea. The mother was a widow, he believed the father had been a clergyman. " And why are two such charming women unmarried ? " the French lieutenant wished to know. Captain d'Auvergne only stiffened, looked down his nose in the English way, reddened and believed that there was not much money in the case. " Ah ! she has no *dot*, that explains everything," sighed the Frenchman. " A pity : . . . a great pity," He would have put her immediately out of his mind and was surprised to discover how persistently she lingered there.

He hoped to see her again, but in this he was not immediately successful. Captain d'Auvergne was inclined to believe that she had gone away. There was a rich brother, who had an estate somewhere in Kent ; both Miss Cassandra and Miss Jane often went to visit him. It was for this gentleman's wife that the family were in mourning. This was more promising and the Frenchman continued to look out for Mademoiselle Jeanne. He was delighted when at the last of the Assemblies she walked into the room with a party of naval officers and their ladies. She was again a black swan among her fellows, wearing a mourning gown, most becoming to her clear pallor, a black lace cap with a twist of velvet about it and a tall curling feather. Her gown was cut higher than most and it had long tight sleeves ; a pity, thought he, for her skin was like milk. Most of the young women in the room had adopted the very deep

décolletage which was then the mode ; indeed he had never
seen so many ugly bony shoulders in his life. He walked to
and fro until he saw his dark lady sitting by the wall, then
strutted up to her, bowed deeply and asked her to stand
up with him for the next two dances.

She seemed surprised, smiled and told him gently that
she never danced nowadays. Fifteen years ago, she confided
demurely, her sister and she had danced in this very room
when they were only just launched into society, but that
was all over. He must find some younger partner ; she
would introduce him to one of the Misses Lance. She was
quite happy drinking tea, or watching the young folk
jumping about together. " Ladies of my age, I assure you,
monsieur," said she gently, " in England, are never asked to
dance." And she gave him a look so demurely bright and
mocking that it did his business completely. He could no
longer take any interest in the young romping hoydens of
the Assembly. He spent the rest of the dull evening gaping
at Miss Jane Austen from corners, following her about,
wishing that he might once have felt her light weight on
his arm as they promenaded between the sets, or might
have swung her round in a few turns at the conclusion of the
dance. He would have staked his life that she was a better
performer than any he saw before him. There were dozens
of young ladies sitting down without partners, but none of
them pleased him. He would dance with that lady, he
swore, or never dance again in this foreign country. But
she never reappeared to entrance and perplex him at any
Assembly in the Southampton Rooms.

Captain d'Auvergne went off to sea and there was nobody
else who knew anything about her. Greatly daring, he
called at last at the house by the Walls into which she had
once disappeared, only to find it empty. A caretaker said
that the family had gone to live in the country. He never
saw her again and she for her part forgot him very quickly.
He had been so little at home in the English language, she
told Cassandra, that there had been no chance of their
becoming better acquainted. His black eyes had pleased
her, but she feared they had been the best of him.

VII

Chawton

1809-1813

I

THAT summer, 1809, at Chawton, the whole village was agog, because the squire was having one of the houses on the estate done up for his widowed mother and sisters. It was a pleasant roomy place, of dark red brick, much the colour of those crimson velvety wallflowers which county folk call Bloody Warriors. It stood at the corner by the clear cool horse-pond, where the Winchester and Gosport roads divided ; it was close to the church and was large enough to be sometimes mistaken by strangers for the parsonage. It had in fact once been an inn, for which it was well suited. Collyer's coach with its six horses ran by the door still, shaking the house in the silence of the night with the rattle and roar of its passing and would always set down and take up there ; but of late years Mr. Austen's steward had lived in it. Now he would have to find other quarters. It was called Chawton Cottage. It had a pleasant dining-parlour and drawing-room on either side of a fair-sized entrance hall, and there were six small single bed-chambers upstairs, so that the old lady could have her children and grandchildren to stay with her when she chose.

Mr. Austen was making some little alterations to the cottage such as ladies fancied. The estate carpenter had been sent down with a couple of masons. They were blocking up the large front drawing-room window and turning it into a bookcase, because the ladies did not like being stared in upon, and a new side window was to be opened upon the garden. The cottage did stand right upon the road, to be sure ; there was nothing but a strip of green turf and some white railings to keep the cows out when they went down to the pond to drink. Most people would have thought it a cheerful window to sit in and watch the coaches and carriages rattling by to Winchester and Portsmouth. Chawton was a much more lively place than it used to be. The gentry, however, always did like to be private. The ladies were having a high wooden fence put up round the garden and planting a hornbeam hedge inside it ; when that had grown up thick and green they would be quite to themselves. The gardener had been down already from the Great House and had a look round. He was having the vegetable beds dug over and had sown a few rows of peas and beans and carrots, later on he would put in some winter greens for them.

When they left Southampton they were going into Kent, to pay Mr. Edward a visit. They would not arrive in Chawton before July ; time enough then for them to give their orders about what they wanted to plant in the autumn. They would find the garden well stocked ; there were plenty of gooseberries and currants for tarts and wine and a good strawberry bed. The old lady, he had heard tell, was a great gardener and likely to make alterations. She had already written about planting these new-fangled peonies. There was to be a shrubbery made later on, he believed, and a gravel walk carried right round the enclosure, so that the young ladies might be able to walk out in showery weather. Two or three little enclosures had been thrown together at some time to make the garden ; it was a pleasant irregular mixture of gravel and hedgerow, orchard and long grass for mowing. There were some fruit trees established in it already, they would have Orleans plums, greengages and an apricot, all in good bearing. Behind the cottage were outhouses and a range of stabling, more than the ladies could really need, if they did not mean to keep their carriage. He thought they might be very comfortable at Chawton Cottage.

The Middletons knew little about the Austen family, the business of letting the Great House had mostly been done through the agent ; but Mrs. Harry Digweed, the farmer's new wife, put herself forward immediately as an authority, for her husband and his brother Hugh had been their tenants at Steventon Great House, when old Parson Austen was alive. " Dear me, yes ; I remember him well and a sweet kind old gentleman he was. He's been dead these four years, he was taken with an apoplexy at Bath. The family went there to live, let me see, it must be eight years back, when young Mr. James took on the living at Steventon. Always his mother's favourite, he was, you'll see he'll be riding over to see her every week. She's a fine proud high-nosed lady of the old school, a cut above most parsons' wives, a notable housekeeper, very active, always ' doing about ' ; but they're as poor as church mice. The Rector and she had a long family, six sons and two daughters. There's Mr. James the parson, and Mr. Edward, our squire, and Mr. Henry, he's in the banking business up in London. Then there were two that went to sea, Mr. Frank and Mr. Charles, both captains by this time, I believe, and one that was simple, poor lad ! George was his name, he was never quite right in his head ; he had fits ; I believe, from being injured at birth. He was kept away from the others and lived with his fostermother up at Deane village ; for all I know he dwells there yet. The two young ladies that are coming here are Miss Cassandra and Miss Jane. I remember them well, when they lived at Steventon, though of course," said Mrs. Digweed, drawing up her chin, " I was much younger than they were. They must be well into their thirties by this time ; a wonder they never married. They were thought uncommonly handsome in their day. Miss Cassy was quite a beauty. She was engaged to a young clergyman called Fowle, but he went abroad and died of a fever, and she would never look at any man afterwards. My husband's nephew, Hugh Digweed's boy James, had a kindness for her at one time, I believe, but it came to nothing. I suppose the Austen family did not think him good enough for her, for all he was in the Church like her father and her brothers. Poor James had to console himself with Miss Sukey Lyford, the doctor's daughter from Basingstoke. Miss Cassy had better have taken him than stayed at home and dried up into an old maid. You'll like Miss Cassy, she's a good sweet creature as ever I saw."

About the other sister, Miss Jane, she was less enthusiastic, pursing her lips and declaring that she for her part had never found that young lady as pleasant as her sister. "She has a way of looking at you as if she thought that what you were saying was foolish and tiresome. She is clever and reads great books ; indeed, they said she wrote one herself when she was quite a girl, and her father sent it to a London publisher ; but it was never printed ; why should it be ? I daresay she will find us all very stupid in Chawton. They hold their heads very high, do the Austens, for all they are only Squire's poor relations, and think themselves better than their neighbours ; we shall probably not see very much of them."

Mrs. Harry Digweed was always on her dignity and often saw patronage where none was meant. She had been a daughter of Squire Terry of Dummer, but that family were poor and had come down in the world. Squire Terry had matched his daughter beneath her when, the year before, he had let her marry the elder of the Digweed brothers, for the Digweeds were only farmers and tenants at that, but she had been one of several plain dull sisters and nobody else had offered for her. Mrs. Harry Digweed, for all her criticisms, was most anxious to claim acquaintance with the Austens. She did not know that Miss Jane, that very week, was writing to her elder sister in her most satirical vein, " I hear that Mrs. Harry Digweed looks forward with great satisfaction to our being neighbours. I would have her enjoy the idea to the utmost, for I suspect there will not be much in the reality. With equal pleasure *we* anticipate an intimacy with her husband's bailiff and his wife, who live close by and are said to be a remarkably good sort of people."

2

Midsummer came and the furniture arrived. Passers by, lingering under the window, reported a good deal of old-fashioned heavy stuff, with a number of cases which might contain china and books and most interesting of all, a pianoforte, tenderly wrapped in sacking. One or both of the young ladies must be musical. A post-chaise brought an old lady in widow's weeds and three younger women ; this puzzled the whole village until Mrs. Digweed recollected a certain Miss Martha Lloyd, a poor relation, who now made her home with the Austens. Her elder sister had married the Reverend James Austen, the Rector of Steventon.

The Middletons sent a hamper of game and fruit, pressed the new arrivals cordially to a meal in the Great House, begged them to stroll in the park and desired to know when they would choose to be waited upon. The Rector, Mr. Papillon, and his sister made an early call upon his new parishioners, blissfully unconscious that he was the subject of a family joke. Old Mrs. Knight, down at Canterbury, had particularly inquired whether the parson at Chawton was a bachelor, of a suitable age for Jane, who had written back blithely that she would certainly do her best to marry Mr. Papillon, whether they liked each other or not ! Village neighbours, the Prowtings, the Benns, the Bennetts, paid their calls early ; presently came carriages from farther afield, old friends anxious to welcome the Austens back to Hampshire. Mr. Lefroy, the Rector of Ashe, had died that year, but his son, the Reverend John Lefroy, had succeeded to the living. Lefroys, Harwoods, Terrys, Bigg-Withers, all came to talk over old times. Catherine had married a year earlier, a quiet elderly widower, the Reverend Herbert Hill, many years her senior, who after thirty years as Chaplain to the British colony at Oporto had retired to become Rector of Streatham. Alethea and Elizabeth Heathcote both reported him a pleasant scholarly man, but the Austen girls were depressed by the news and called their old friend *poor Catherine*. The sight of Lady Heathcote's great chariot at the door finally set the seal upon Mrs. Austen and her daughters ; it was evident that they knew the best families of gentility in the county.

Mrs. Austen proved to be a lively jolly old woman, though a little given to talking about her infirmities ; she seemed most active for her age and had been seen in the garden in a round green smock, positively digging up her own potatoes. She was a great needlewoman, too, knitted gloves and stockings for her sons and made satin slippers for her granddaughters. Her chief occupation at present was a patchwork quilt, on which she expected to be engaged for the next year or so. It was a most ambitious piece of work, with a central vase of flowers, surrounded by hexagons and lozenges of silk, satin and velvet and bordered with landscape squares from a piece of *toile de Jouy*, contributed by her French daughter-in-law. It was much admired in Chawton, where all the ladies were collecting and exchanging pieces of patchwork and basting them on to scraps of old letters. It made a pleasant occupation for the winter evenings, while they sat talking together of the war news, of the disastrous expedition to Walcheren, Napoleon's defeat of the Austrian Emperor at Wagram and Lord Wellington's victory at Talavera ; the first reverse for Napoleon on land for many a long year, but, of course, one swallow did not make a summer.

The young ladies seemed quieter than their jolly old mother. They went about a great deal together and were observed walking in the lanes more than was usual at that date, or going in to Alton to do the family shopping. Miss Cassandra did some parish work, Miss Jane helped with the lending library ; she was heard playing and singing in the mornings and had a very sweet voice, but did not perform often at parties. She left that, she said, to younger women. She did not talk much and was often overlooked in company. She and Miss Cassandra did not appear to differ greatly from other quiet cultivated gentlewomen of their age, but were considered, on the whole, a pleasant addition to the somewhat limited society of Chawton.

3

Their most constant visitor was naturally the Reverend James Austen. He was very faithful about visiting his mother and no week passed during that first year, 1810, after they came to Chawton, that he did not ride over through the winding lanes to see her.

It was observed that he was always very well mounted, for a parson. Sometimes the carriage came instead and brought his wife, a sour-faced, black-eyed little woman, in a great plumed bonnet, plain and very much marked with the smallpox. Then there was a handsome stepdaughter, Miss Anna, with a cropped head, a round sunburnt face and chestnut curls ; an unripe green apple of a girl, with some promise of beauty. She had inherited the rich Austen hair, the clear Austen skin, the wide open dark-brown eyes which had made her Aunt Jane so much admired in her young days; but at this stage of her life Anna had not yet begun to think much about her looks. She was rising seventeen and had already been to a ball at Manydown in white shoes and it was dull for her among the empty fields at Steventon. She liked nothing so well as to be allowed to ride over to Chawton with her father. She had half a dozen particular friends there, with whom to sit in arbours and exchange confidences; the Middleton girls at the Great House always made her welcome, and little Harriet White, daughter of the Rector of Selborne, and niece of the great naturalist, was also very intimate. All these young creatures ran in and out of each other's houses, chattering together like starlings, their heads were as full of nonsense as their summer bonnets of laces, ribbons and roses. Then old Miss Prowting, who lived almost next door to the Austens, took a fancy to young Anna and taught her to make feather trimmings ; but the house that she always liked best to visit was Chawton Cottage. She would fling herself off the old grey pony and rush upstairs, stumbling over the skirt of her habit, sure of her welcome, calling out for Aunt Cassy and Aunt Jane.

Her father was very glad to bring her whenever he could,

for at home her stepmother was always nagging at the girl, lecturing her about holding up her head and keeping her shoulders back, sighing that she ought to wear a backboard or she would grow quite crooked, telling her not to be putting herself forward, for nobody wanted to hear her talk. James would sometimes invite his tall daughter into his study, for she had inherited his love of learning, but even there her stepmother would follow her, complaining that Anna gave her no help in the house and would ruin her eyes, as her Aunt Jane had done, by poking and straining over books. It was no wonder that Anna begged to be taken over to Steventon. There everybody petted her, she read aloud to her grandmother, helped Martha Lloyd and Aunt Cassy to make cowslip wine and learnt to trim a bonnet from Aunt Jane. She blushed with pleasure when old Mrs. Austen said, " That child is growing exactly like what Jane was at her age." Then Mrs. J. A. would toss her head and say, " I hope she will not waste half her time scribbling romances, as Jane used to do. I told her the other day that if she had no work to do I could give her plenty. There are all her father's new shirts to be finished and a dozen sheets to hem, besides the garments waiting in the poor-box. I am sure I almost broke my back cutting them out, but I cannot get Anna to put a stitch into them. To be sure she does not work very neatly, even after all the trouble I have taken to teach her! her button-holes are disgraceful, but her sewing is good enough for the poor. She is a very obstinate ungrateful girl, she plagues the life out of me. I can do nothing with her. She is as hot as pepper, the very image of her grandfather the old Governor. She should have been a boy." Mary would have liked Anna to be a quiet pretty biddable child like her own Caroline, but there was little hope of that. Anna went whistling and singing about the house, always country tunes, *Come, Lasses and Lads*, and *No, John, no* ; one day she had a new one. " *My mother bought a likely hen Upon St. Martin's Day ; She clucks and clucks, and clucks and clucks, But still she will not lay.*" " That is not at all a pretty song for a young lady," said her stepmother primly ; but Anna only tossed her head, declaring, " Aunt Jane taught it to me. She says she used to dance to it." And out she ran into the orchard, singing as shrill as a blackbird, " *Hey ho ! the morning dew, Hey, ho ! the roses and the rue. Come, follow, follow me, young man, For I'll not follow you.*" Decidedly there was something of her aunt in her.

Cassandra gave Anna some drawing lessons and she did one or two pencil sketches of the parsonage and the church at Steventon, not at all bad for her age ; then she tried a portrait of Aunt Jane, but soon gave it up in disgust. " I cannot do her eyes," the girl complained, flinging down her pencil. " I can get the shape and the colour, but not the right look ; I have made them too staring." Cassandra did a sketch herself at the same time, which was afterwards framed and preserved in the family ; Jane sitting sideways in a chair, in one of her characteristic poses, with her arms folded, looking full at you. It was in pencil, with the lips and the brown eyes delicately tinted and the hair escaping under the frill of her little round cap, but Cassandra was displeased with it ; she thought it made Jane look tired and critical. The eyes were not perfect, either, in her drawing, they were severe and unsmiling. It seemed that nobody could really do justice to Jane's eyes.

Little Caroline was always creeping up to Aunt Jane and following her about, wherever she went in the house and out of it. Mrs. J. A., who was always inclined to harry her children, kept telling Caroline that she must not be so troublesome to her aunt. Then Caroline would hang her head, her lips would tremble and a single large tear would stand in each dark eye ; but Aunt Jane always said, " She is no trouble to me, Mary." Then she would pick up the timid little creature, run out of the house with her into the garden, away from all the grown-ups, and play with her under the trees or string her a daisy chain. Her first charm to very young children was the sweetness and softness of her manner ; she seemed to love them and they loved her in return.

Caroline, however, was not yet old enough to be delighted as her brother was by Aunt Jane's cleverness ; that would come later. To young Edward, at eleven, Aunt Jane was the most amusing person in the world. With her playful talk she could light up everything for him. She told him endless stories, she made up ludicrous and fantastic imaginary adventures, which were supposed to have happened to their village neighbours, Mr. Papillon and Mrs. Digweed or old Miss Prowting ; these she would relate with a serious face and a delicious twinkle in her eye, while young Edward threw himself about in his chair and laughed till his sides ached. She taught him half a dozen new card games, she was never too busy to play spillikins with him or the letter game ; they began a collection of riddles and charades together. When he was tired of running about she would sing and play to him, or read aloud. She had a most lovely speaking voice ; once she took up a volume of Miss Burney's *Evelina* and read a few pages about Mr. Smith and the Brangtons and the little boy thought it was as good as a play. When her eyes were tired with writing and reading she would always end with a game of bilbocatch. Edward, at eleven, rather plumed himself on having outgrown this childish sport, but Aunt Jane at thirty-five loved it still. He liked to watch her slender hand and wrist holding the ivory cup and ball, her absorbed face and girlish air as she watched the rise and fall of the pretty plaything. Hers was the first face that ever Edward thought beautiful ; not that he ever used the word to himself, he was too young and simple for that, but there were moments when he could not take his eyes off Aunt Jane. They had a secret together. Nobody else in the world except Aunt Cass and Edward knew that Aunt Jane was writing a book.

Edward had caught her at it, one fine summer morning when everybody else was out in the garden and he came plunging in to look for her. She was sitting at her writing-desk, with a most absorbed face, scribbling away, with one of her brown curls falling out of her cap and she never looked up till he flung his sturdy arms round her neck from behind and started kissing her for a surprise. She turned round, pushed him away and exclaimed, " Edward, get down this minute, do not plague me." Actually her voice sounded quite cross. Edward was dumbfounded ; she had never spoken so to him before. He stood staring at her, eyes and mouth wide open, crimson with distress. She passed her hand across her forehead and then smiled in a shaken sort of way. " You startled me," she said. " I never heard you coming. I don't know how it happened. Generally I hear the hinges of the door creak and I have time to put my work away." She looked quite dazed and bewildered, so Edward offered helpfully, " Aunt Cass was telling Jenny to oil the door yesterday ! I saw them doing it." He understood perfectly now why she had spoken as she did ; he said sagely, " It always makes me cross when I am interrupted, doing anything special." His aunt smiled then, put her arm around him, said she was sorry she had been cross and kissed him very warmly. " You must tell Aunt Cass never to oil the door hinges," said he, quite satisfied, and she assured him that she would do so. " It is an excellent idea," said she ; and then she told him, as a very great secret, that she was writing a story. He wanted to know how this was done, because he had made up his mind to write one himself this summer, only he did not know how to begin. He leant against her and she explained it all quite beautifully. " You must employ the material that lies closest to your hand ; you must contrive your story curiously out of the simplest everyday matters, as a small bird builds its nest from the mosses and twigs of the tree it lives in. That is the best way to write a book."

4

That year, 1810, the news at home and abroad went from bad to worse. The Duke of Wellington had lost the three great fortresses on the Spanish border, Almeida, Ciudad Rodrigo and Badajos, and had withdrawn his troops right back to the lines of Torres Vedras. On these impregnable heights, straddling the neck of the peninsula where the city of Lisbon stood, he had the sea at his back ; while he awaited the French attack which never came he could build up his supplies and train his ill-disciplined army, but it would be many months before he would be strong enough to break out of his bridgehead. In Paris, in March, the Emperor had divorced his ageing, childless Creole wife and married an Austrian archduchess, Marie Louise. This blonde and stupid schoolgirl had been handed over to him by the peace treaty which her father had been obliged to sign after his defeat at Wagram ; the wits called her a virgin sacrifice to the Corsican Monster. Up in London in the autumn the old blind king went out of his mind again, this time they said it was from grief at the death of his youngest, dearest daughter, the Princess Amelia. If he did not recover quickly, his son would have to be made Prince Regent and that would please nobody. The Princes were greatly disliked ; there had been a shocking professional scandal, a year earlier, about the Duke of York's mistress and the sale of Army commissions, this year there was a still more frightful tale about the Duke of Cumberland, who was supposed to have murdered his valet, but the Prince of Wales was hated more than either. He could not drive through the Parks without being hissed and pelted by the crowd. The times were very hard ; one bad harvest followed another, the price of every necessity was rising and taxes were going up year by year.

But down at Chawton Jane was in her own golden world, where everything seemed bright and new. The manuscript on which she was working was another of her old ones. Before she left Southampton she had tried in vain to get back the Bath story from Messrs. Crosby, writing under an assumed name, pretending innocently to be a married lady, Mrs. Ashton Dennis, thinking that so they might pay more attention to her ; but they would neither publish it nor part with it. She fell back upon another which she had not thought about for a very long time. It had been written at Steventon when she was twenty-two and she had then called it *Eleanor and Marianne* ; like *Lady Susan*, it had been in the form of a batch of letters exchanged between the various characters. That device had grown old-fashioned and no longer pleased her. She turned it about and re-trimmed it as she used to do with her gowns and hats. It was about a widow, Mrs. Dashwood, and her two daughters, living in a cottage much like Chawton. Eleanor, the elder girl, was serious, intelligent and self-controlled, she was intended for a portrait of Cassandra ; Marianne the younger was headstrong, bewitching and absurdly romantic, a greensick girl who had set her foolish heart upon a false lover. Jane had been something like that once upon a time, but she had grown wiser, now she drew a mocking picture of her old self.

This re-dressed manuscript had a stick of a hero, a handsome heartless villain, and a plot as neat as the works of a watch ; it did not quite come alive. The elder sister in particular was a starched and critical piece of single blessedness, too cold and sensible to please Cassandra, who hoped gently that she did not appear like that to her neighbours. Here and there, like plums in a half-cooked pudding, were admirable minor characters, a silly young wife, always laughing, a rude and silent husband to match her, a pack of spoilt children with a doting mother, and a pair of scheming underbred sisters. The best character in it was Mrs. Jennings, a fat jolly common warm-hearted woman, full of jokes and small kindnesses. She was an admirable piece of nature. The best scene was one of high comedy put in at the very beginning, a discussion between husband and wife after the death of their father, about how little of their inheritance they need feel obliged to hand over to their stepmother and her daughters. This was uncommonly near the bone for Mrs. J. A. and Cassandra was a little nervous as to how she might take it, but she never guessed that she had sat for her portrait in Mrs. John Dashwood. The book was called *Sense and Sensibility* and when it was finished Jane took the manuscript up to London so that Henry might find her a better publisher than the last one.

It was April, 1811, when she went to stay with Henry and Eliza. They had gone up in the world and had got a fine new house in Sloane Street, Number sixty-four. Henry's partner, once the handsome Captain Tilson, lived next door to them with a plump and fashionable wife. Only the west side of the street was built up as yet. From Eliza's front windows you looked across the Five Fields, where cattle were grazing ; in the distance you saw the backs of the houses in Grosvenor Place, the tops of the trees in Hyde Park and the coaches and carriages going up and down to the turnpike at Hyde Park Corner. The back windows overlooked leafy gardens, with new white stucco houses glistening behind budding trees, all that pleasant suburb known as Hans Town.

The new house was one of a terrace, tall and narrow like most London houses, and Eliza had picked it because she wanted to entertain on a grander scale than she had been able to compass in Brompton. It had an admirable suite on the first floor ; a wide front parlour, with three windows, an octagon room at the back overlooking the garden and a broad anteroom like a passage between the two, where she could receive her guests as they mounted the staircase. She had furnished these rooms completely in the new Empire taste. Her tables were like classical altars and tripods, her narrow hard couches were supported by caryatides, brooding swans and thin lions, her cabinets were inlaid with brass key pattern, her chairs of pinewood and cherrywood had lyre-shaped backs, her pictures hung by tasselled cords. The whole was reflected backwards and forwards between opposed pairs of mirrors in a diminishing perspective of elegance. Great draperies of yellow satin, powdered with gilt stars, were slung across the windows, draped from the beaks of brass eagles, perched on the cornice. One might have supposed oneself in Paris. The floors were waxed and polished and bare except for a few white sheepskin rugs ; a faint scent of cedar wood and pot-pourri hung in the air, mixed with the indefatigable appetising garlic-and-coffee smell of Madame Bigeon's cooking. That invincible woman was hard at work in the kitchen, with her daughter Manon to help her. The two of them still carried the whole weight of the household on their sturdy peasant shoulders. " They are making white soup already," said Eliza, smiling and shrugging. " We have eighty people invited to a musical party on Tuesday."

Cousin Eliza had begun to look older at last and had, if possible, grown a little thinner ; her eyes looked enormous in her pale face. Henry was still exceedingly handsome, though with prosperity he had put on a little weight. He still rode to the office every morning across the Five Fields and down Piccadilly ; he cut a very buckish figure on a well-bred chestnut, in his blue coat with the gilt buttons, his tight leathers, polished Hessians and spotless white gloves. The firm of Austen, Maunde & Tilson were doing very well out of the war. Eliza and he provided plenty of entertainment for Jane. Cassandra, staying that spring at a changed and quiet Godmersham, got one gay letter after another describing their doings. They had been to the play, though they had been so unlucky as to miss Mrs. Siddons. Henry had strolled with them in Hyde Park on Sunday at three, the fashionable hour when you saw all the first-rates walking and riding and might get a glimpse of Princess Charlotte, the Regent's fair stout daughter, driving up from St. James's to visit her vulgar German mother at Kensington Palace. Eliza and Jane had walked across the Five Fields into London to do their Bond Street shopping. At Grafton House, the great drapers, perfumed coxcombs had served them with bugle trimming, silk stockings and darning cotton ; Eliza had found pink perfumed wax wall lights for the party. Mr. Egerton, Jane's new publisher, had a bundle of proofs ready for her ; she corrected them each morning, sitting in Eliza's sunny eastward-facing drawing-room. Henry had queried the incomes in the first chapter, but it was probably too late to alter that. Mr. Egerton thought well of the book, but would not publish at his own risk, however if it did not sell Jane had set aside a sum to repay him his losses.

The party was, of course, a great success. Madame Bigeon had excelled herself with soups and sauces, hot lobster, oyster patties and cold chicken in aspic ; there had been coffee and ices and little heart-shaped French cakes soaked in rum. Eliza wore a highwaisted gown of delicate yellow, with cameo jewellery and a scarf of gilt tissue wound twice round her slender arms ; her hair was dressed in countless artful silver-grey curls, like a French poodle. Henry had found a merchant in the City who could provide him with smuggled French champagne. The musicians were Wiepart, the fashionable teacher of the harp, and ballads were sung by a short Miss Davis, all in blue, who had a very fine voice and was bringing up for the public line. Three singers performed glees, *Strike the Harp* and *Poor Insect*, with a buzzing chorus. The music was so good that the amateurs refused to perform. There were eighty guests to stand about Eliza's pretty rooms, in the mild light of the pink wax candles ; to applaud the music, to gossip and enjoy the refreshments. They talked of the Emperor's new-born son, the King of Rome and of our prospects in the Peninsula. Lord Wellington, that month, had begun his long awaited spring offensive. After what had seemed endless months of waiting, he had at last burst out of his bridgehead at Torres Vedras like a spring torrent from the hills, as if he meant to drive Marshal Massena's winter-starved regiments back across the Spanish border right out of Portugal. The guns at the Tower and in the Park had already fired salutes for his early successes. " At last," said Mr. Tilson, " we have a general who is not afraid of the Emperor. The men believe in his Lordship ; the sight of that long nose of his is worth ten thousand reinforcements to them in a battle. He has been very cautious so far, he knew we could never put another army in the field if he lost this one ; but now he has begun to move we shall see such fighting as was never seen before. It's my belief," said Mr. Tilson, growing flushed and cheerful on his partner's good French wine, " if his Lordship can only keep on as he has begun, that this Peninsula campaign may prove a running sore that will wear Boney down." And they all drank success to the troops.

Jane herself had spent the evening in the central saloon; it was the coolest and there she could watch the people coming and going. She had been, she reported demurely, surrounded all the evening by gentlemen, as she used to be in her young days. Henry's guests had soon discovered a dry but piquant flavour about the quiet lady from the country, Mr. Austen's sister, who sat on the Recamier sofa, under the lighted chandelier, in a lavender silk gown. They had hung over her, held her bouquet, paid her compliments, brought her fruit, wine and ices ; but the one who had pleased her best had been a jolly roaring naval captain who brought her news of her brother Charles. He was on his way home, with his wife and two children aboard, in command of the *Cleopatra* ; by this time, swore Captain Simpson, he must be in the chops of the Channel. Delightful news, if true ! but the gallant captain had evidently been enjoying Henry's champagne as well as it deserved, so perhaps too much faith had better not be put in his predictions. Cassandra might look for and cut out the notice of Eliza's party in the *Morning Post*.

6

Another evening had greatly pleased Jane, a visit to Eliza's friends, the D'Entraigues. The husband, a noble of the old *régime*, had formerly been French attaché to the Russian Embassy in London. He was a little withered old man, waxen-pale, who shrugged his shoulders in speaking, took a great deal of snuff and made a very elegant bow. He showed Jane an admirable collection of miniatures. His wife was a handsome talkative woman, who before her marriage had been on the stage in Paris ; and there was a son, the young Count Julien, tall, dark-eyed and fiercely moustached, who had a great admiration for the Emperor's military genius. He would have liked to serve under so great a general, but that, of course, for him was impossible. These exiles thought the Emperor now secure on his throne. The birth of his son, the King of Rome, must have established him finally among the royalties ; that blond child of a Hapsburg mother could call himself cousin to every reigning house in Europe. So said Madame, but Henry smilingly assured her that the little Corsican had not bettered himself by his Austrian marriage. " To the Hapsburgs he is only a *bourgeois* intruder, they will thrust him out again and disown him if ever they get the opportunity. His empire is as hollow as one of these excellent meringues."

The son believed that once the Emperor were defeated his generals might turn against him, but so far he had given them nothing but victories. " There is one thing which might be the end of him," said Count Julien, " if he were to invade Russia. They say he plans to do it, but I cannot think he would be so mad." " He hates the Czar," Madame offered eagerly, " ever since they refused to let him marry either of the Russian princesses " ; but Henry, speaking as a business man, believed it was less a matter of the Czar's sister than of the Baltic blockade. " The Emperor must find fresh blood for his armies somewhere," Count Julien persisted and Henry, nodding, quoted a Chinese proverb, " He who rides a tiger cannot dismount."

After that Eliza and Count Julien spent an hour together at the pianoforte, trying over French music, but though the Count begged her many times to delight them with a song, Eliza only shook her head and sighed that her singing days were over. " *Nous n'irons plus aux bois ; Les lauriers sont coupés*," hummed Eliza, in her tiny thread of a voice. " That is the only song for me nowadays " ; and she laid her hand on her thin chest and gave a little hollow cough, while Henry glanced at her anxiously and hoped she had not caught another of her colds. It was most unfortunate, he explained to Madame, the horses had been restive, coming by Hyde Park Gate. A fresh load of gravel had been put down, which had made the going hard for them and one of the poor brutes, with a sore shoulder, had jibbed at the hill. " Nothing would do but that my wife must get out," grumbled Henry, " and there she was for ten minutes standing about in the cold in her thin shawl ; the worst thing in the world for her." Madame D'Entraigues was

infinitely distressed, offered *tisane* and hot gruel and begged
that Eliza would stay the night with them ; but she would
not be fussed over and insisted on going home. She did,
however, develop a bad cold on her chest which spoilt the
latter part of Jane's visit.

One other pleasant circumstance occurred that April ;
Jane was invited down to Streatham Parsonage to visit her
old friend Catherine, Mr. Bigg-Wither's daughter, now Mrs.
Hill. She found Catherine perfectly ready to be friends
again, the past was all forgiven and forgotten. She had a
son already, named Herbert after his father, and had turned
into the complete parson's wife, happily occupied in running
her household and the parish. The society of Streatham she
confessed was somewhat mixed, the balls in particular were
attended by some very vulgar people, but the private parties
in the leafy suburb were more select. The Reverend Herbert
Hill was by no means so dull as Jane had expected. He had
literary tastes, could talk in a most interesting way about his
long sojourn in Portugal, was writing a history of that
country and turned out to be the uncle of the poet Robert
Southey, who afterwards became Poet Laureate. Mr. Hill
told his visitor a great deal about his nephew's house at
Keswick in the Lake District, which he shared with the
Coleridge family and about a neighbour of theirs, an odd
fellow called Wordsworth, who might one day astonish the
world with his poems, Robert said, though as yet he had
published little. And Catherine talked of old days, kissed
Jane warmly at parting and bade her promise to come again
and bring Cassandra with her.

7

Jane went home to Chawton in May, and Henry and his
partner came down at the same time on business about a
branch of the bank to be opened in Alton in the name of
Austen, Gray and Vincent. Mr. Tilson was taken over to
the Great House, did a little water-colour sketch of the
south-west aspect, and pronounced it a very pretty property,

only he considered that it was a pity so much good timber should not be turned into money.

That summer there was very heavy fighting in Portugal, as Mr. Tilson had predicted. The French were defeated at Fuentes d'Onoro, the Fountain of Honour, in a very close-run action ; the hawk-nosed English commander admitted himself that if Boney had been there instead of Marshal Massena he did not think he could have done it. Later came the bloody field of Albuera, a combat claimed by both sides ; Marshal Soult, stamping and weeping in his French fashion, had protested that the English were beaten, but did not know it. Both sides suffered great losses, but Lord Wellington did not capture any of the fortresses he needed.

From Chawton, however, Jane merely wrote to her absent sister of fruit and blossom, peonies and syringa, plums and greengages, strawberries, thunderstorms and currant wine. Niece Anna was getting plenty of the miscellaneous un-disciplined sort of happiness which suited her best. There had been an evening party at the Great House, with syllabubs, tea, coffee, singing and dancing and everything that could be imagined agreeable, kept up till past eleven o'clock. On the King's birthday Harriet White had invited her dearest friend to a review on Selborne Common, with volunteers and felicities of all kinds. Anna had worn a patent-leather shako stuck sideways on her chestnut curls and a frogged pelisse ; in this military style she had quite cut out all the other girls in their flowered and veiled bonnets. The King was expected to die shortly and Anna had already bought some Royal mourning ; like all young girls she fancied herself in black and she hoped to impress her chief admirer, poor blundering Stephen Terry of Dummer. Rising from her pianoforte, Aunt Jane struck out a pretty musical phrase about her niece. " She is quite an Anna with variations, but she cannot have reached her last, for that is always the most flourishing and showy. She is about at her third or fourth, which are generally simple and pretty."

Her stepmother lectured and scolded the ardent young creature, complaining, " Anna is a spoilt obstinate girl. She will never mind what I say, her head is always running upon young men." Cassandra said gently, " We all think Anna very clever and warmhearted," and Jane put in with a laugh, " You must not find too much fault with Anna, Mary, for my mother says she is exactly what I was at her age." Martha Lloyd agreed with this very heartily. " She has just your bright eye and your good colour, when she has on her yellow gown and has curled out her hair she reminds me completely of you. Oh ! do you remember the dances at Basingstoke at the beginning of the war, how we all longed to dance with one of the officers and were wild to go to Brighton Camp. I am ashamed to remember how silly I was about Mr. W., as we used to call him. Now I have quite forgotten what he looked like."

Cassandra smiled at honest Martha, Jane said thoughtfully, " In spite of being so much older I am sure I am happier now than I was then." Cassandra sighed, " We never thought the war would last so long. Here we are in the year 'eleven and the war has been going on ever since we grew up ; why, we have been fighting the French, except for a very few months, ever since before Anna was born. Do you remember, Jane, that time she came to stay with us at Steventon, as a very little girl, while Mary and James were getting married ? She found that story you were writing, *First Impressions*. How upset and angry you were when she began to chatter about it downstairs ! " and after Mrs. J. A. had gone, when the sisters were alone together, she asked again, " What has become of it now, Jane ? I always liked it best of all your stories, I could not imagine why Cadell, the publisher, would not consider it. I wish you would get it out and finish it. It was much better than *Sense and Sensibility*."

Jane coloured slightly and said she believed she had it laid by somewhere or other. She did not like to talk about her writing, she was very shy about it. Nobody but her own immediate family knew that *Sense and Sensibility* was to come out in the autumn.

That was the summer, 1811, when Charles came home from the West Indies, sunburnt and gay as ever and in excellent health and spirits. He was almost a stranger to his family, who had not set eyes on him for seven years. He had changed from a gay lighthearted boy to a sweet serious responsible man. His wife Fanny came home with him and a very pleasing little brown-skinned woman she proved to be, gentle and amiable and devoted to Charles. They had two pretty little girls already, Cassy, named for the Austen side of the family, and baby Harriet, named for her Palmer aunt. It was delightful to have them back at home. They paid visits all round the family, and in the autumn Charles had one of his usual pieces of good fortune ; he was made flag captain of the *Namur*, the guard ship at the Nore under his old faithful friend and patron, Sir Thomas Williams. There he could have his wife and children to live on board with him. It was the custom of the time, Captain Fremantle had actually had his young wife aboard the old *Seahorse* during the action off Teneriffe, where he and Lord Nelson were each wounded in the arm. Anxious relatives prophesied danger to the tropic-born children in the winter gales of the Thames estuary, but actually there was no such thing. They grew and thrived, and the family were as snug and happy in their cabins as mice in a wedding cake. The fighting continued in the Peninsula, the papers were full of rioting and machine breaking in the weaving towns of Lancashire and Yorkshire, the Regent became more unpopular than ever, and in October, Mr. Egerton, the publisher, put out his autumn list, which began with Miss Maria Edgeworth's new volume, *Tales of Fashionable Life* and ended with an anonymous publication *Sense and Sensibility, by a lady*. It was in three volumes and the price was fifteen shillings. The secret of its authorship had been so well kept that young Anna, picking out novels in the circulating library in Alton with Aunt Jane, looked at the title page of the first volume and threw it down again, " That must be rubbish," she roundly declared, " with such a stupid title."

It did well, far better than its silent writer had dared to hope. People talked about it, savoured its dry sweetness, like the taste of a quince, passed the title from lip to lip. There was no great stir, but month after month it went on selling quietly all through the following year. In the end it was to astonish her by earning a hundred and fifty pounds. This modest sum, which seemed to her delightfully large, was the first money that she had ever earned in her life.

All that next year, 1812, she was hard at work down at Chawton, turning *First Impressions* inside out, cutting and shaping it, piecing it together again like one of her mother's bright patchwork quilts, putting hundreds of fine exquisite stitches into it, turning it finally into a new novel, *Pride and Prejudice*. It was a book for Cassandra and herself.

All their Steventon youth was in it, the sparkle of morning dew, which had long since dried, the sweetness of budding roses which had never come to flower. It was strange delight to Cassandra to make the journey back again into those lost years, when neither of them doubted that their stories would have a happy ending. The mild and gentle Jane Bennett was herself, though more lovely and loving than she believed she had ever appeared. The lively Elizabeth was Jane's own youthful self, but more fortunate. Mr. Darcy was the hero that every schoolgirl first falls in love with, but he had been drawn with an indulgent recollection of that first Irish lover of Jane's, Tom Lefroy, long since married and settled down into a dry, hardworking, successful lawyer in Dublin. There was a wicked caricature in Mr. Collins of all the stupid, self-indulgent, tiresome Hampshire parsons, over whose fatuous compliments and dreary platitudes the sisters had stifled their yawns in the old days. Lady Catherine de Bourgh, the rich and bullying old woman, had some hints of Aunt Leigh Perrot and of those country dowagers who used to dominate the Basingstoke Assemblies. It was a novel like a country dance, with a whole crowd of pleasant light-hearted young people in it, all setting to partners, exchanging hands and smiles, laughing, teasing, chasing each other round the room, to a gay running tune which ended up where it began.

It was written in 1812, a year of new hopes, when the wind of victory had risen and was beginning to blow across the barren hills and plains of the Peninsula. On a black frost-clear January night Wellington's young wild skylarking troops had bolted the French out of Ciudad Rodrigo, the city of the Cid, which had so long barred their way northwards; in April they cracked another nut, storming and sacking the great fortress of Badajos, which overhung the fever-stricken marshes of the Guadiana, the highway out of southern Portugal. By July they were out on the sunburnt plains of Leon, and had won a fine victory at Salamanca. They marched in triumph into Madrid and actually got far enough north to besiege Burgos before the first snows obliged them to withdraw to winter quarters in Portugal; and that summer the Emperor began his fatal march into Russia.

All went well for him at the beginning. His armies marched for weeks across the plains of Lithuania, giving the world another of his geography lessons; people were obliged to unroll new maps, to learn the unknown unpronounceable names of his victories, Smolensk, Mojaisk, Borodino. He rode in triumph into Moscow itself. Beyond that distant city what rivers and mountains would he cross? what cities conquer? There seemed nothing but blank spaces before him, all the way to China. Then came news of that strange event, the burning of Moscow and after it a mysterious retreat, with names which this time were not victories, but defeats; Malojaroslavetz, Vitebsk, Krasnoi, and thousands of men drowned beneath the ice as they recrossed the Beresina. When the snow came the Man of Destiny left his armies to freeze and perish and drove home like a madman in his travelling carriage, right across Europe, back to Paris. He had his throne to save this time; his Russian adventure would prove the end of him.

9

As for Jane, 1812 was the year in which she revised and completed *Pride and Prejudice*, the summer in which Edward and his children came to spend a whole five months at Chawton Great House, the autumn when Eliza fell sick of her last illness, and James's son went up to Winchester for the first time. Edward had given over Godmersham to the painters and decorators, it was to be completely renovated. Old Mrs. Knight was failing, not expected to last out the year. His daughter Fanny was growing up, soon there would have to be entertaining for her, it was time to change the Kentish house from what it had been in Elizabeth's time. He came, in May, to survey his Chawton inheritance and brought his whole family with him.

Nothing could have been more agreeable. Fanny had sprung up into an enchanting creature like a budding rose, unfolding and putting out one fresh petal after another. She adored her Aunt Jane and was for ever running over to the cottage to call upon her. They had many delicious mornings and interesting talks together, duly noted down by Fanny in her diary. Aunt Jane delighted in the young creature, who had a mind as well as a heart. She was admitted that summer into the circle who were allowed to hear what Aunt Jane was writing. They used to shut themselves up in the Porch Room at the Great House. Marianne and the younger children, a little vexed, used to linger on the polished oak staircase, hear the gales of laughter inside the closed carved door and think it hard to be shut out from what sounded so delightful ; Aunt Jane, Aunt Cassy and Sister Fanny reading aloud out of *Pride and Prejudice*. The chief excitement of the summer was to discuss Edward's plans for his inheritance. He surveyed it gravely, walked all round and about the grounds and the park, considered that it might be much improved ; indeed, it must be if he was to spend his summers there in the future. The house itself was heavy, dark and old-fashioned compared with his Kentish house, but there was little that you could do to

alter it. Flintwalled, Elizabethan, it lay on rising ground
at the bottom of the village behind the church. There were
three stone gables and a tall storeyed porch on the entrance
front, facing west ; the southern aspect was of Stuart brick-
work, but had been stuccoed over about a hundred years
earlier. Within was a range of dim low rooms, wainscoted
in oak and pine, with carved stone chimney-pieces and
heavy beams. Most of the latticed windows seemed to face
north or west and the rooms all opened out of each other
in a highly inconvenient fashion. The house was over-
furnished with a good deal of solid mahogany, rich damask,
gilding and carving. There were family portraits in every
room, there was a famous tapestry, called the Lewknor
Carpet, woven in 1564, a family heirloom, with many coats
of arms in it and a naked man and woman, glimmering out
of a briery thicket of red and white roses. The children
called them Adam and Eve. Chawton Great House, in
short, was as different as possible from the cool classic spaces
of Godmersham. Edward may have liked it all the better
for that. It did not remind him of his lost Elizabeth, who
had never set foot across its threshold. He allowed his
daughter to choose some new carpets and curtains, had some
dark oak panelling painted white to please her taste, ordered
some minor improvements himself of a practical kind, such
as widening the pantry door, and then turned his attention
to the grounds.

Here he found much that might be done to improve
matters. The garden was formal and quite out of date ; it
was adorned by clipped yews, box hedges and hornbeam
arbours, which smelt hot and dry on summer afternoons,
and it boasted a file of broken-nosed lead statues, which he
removed. The park was little better than a collection of
rough meadows, with a few beech trees standing here and
there like green towers, survivors of the great gale of 1810,
which had brought down much good timber all over
Hampshire. His daughters, of course, were wild for something more fashionable. They urged their indulgent parent
to employ an improver at five guineas a day, Mr. Repton
himself, if available, for landscape gardening was the latest

fashion. They pined for sweeping lawns, a sheet of water and groups of specimen trees dotted here and there, to replace the pleached colonnade of lime trees which led up to the west front from the village. " We must at all costs clump the avenue," exclaimed Fanny. " Then if we were to turn the whole house about, make a new entrance on the east, do away with the old garden altogether and lay out a new parterre behind the house, we should have a very different effect ! Do you not think so ? " But Edward thought no such thing. " Very different indeed, my child," said he, calmly, " but I believe we must be content with rather less ornament and beauty. I fancy the old place may be made comfortable and given the air of a gentleman's mansion, without taking so much trouble, and I certainly cannot make water run uphill to fill a lake for your water-parties. We will lay out a new pleasure garden, by all means. The present one is too close to good Mr. Papillon's boundary, we can leave that for our vegetables. We may very well choose the back of the house for our new garden ; indeed I had thought of that already myself. There it will have the best aspect in the world, which is sloping towards the south-east, out of the wind and getting the morning sun. The ground appears to me precisely formed for it. We will enclose it in a double row of young beeches ; when they are grown they will give you a pleasant shady walk, such as you have at Godmersham. Then if we take in enough of the parkland for a new lawn on the south side and make a plantation to shut out the church and the village, I think we shall do very well. But you must not ask me to interfere with a single one of those limes in the avenue. No, no ; that would never do. I confess I cannot bear to cut down a well-grown tree."

Fanny frowned and pouted prettily, but he shook his head at her. She smiled back, shook her curls, planted a kiss on his bald pate and ran out, swinging her great straw bonnet by its yellow strings. She had planned to go walking in the bright midsummer weather, through the park, with Aunt Jane.

They went up to the little temple beyond the house,

under the beech trees and sat on the steps ; from that point you got the prettiest prospect of the house. There she listened with delight while Aunt Jane read aloud to her the latest chapter of *Pride and Prejudice*, the one in which the heroine and her aunt and uncle went walking in the groves of Pemberley and met its entranced owner by the stream. " Oh ! I hope they will make it up together," cried Fanny, clasping her hands. " I believe it will be a match after all. Dear Aunt Jane, is it not time to tell me whether Elizabeth will forgive Mr. Darcy ? "

But Aunt Jane only gave her a wicked sidelong glance. " I daresay she will take him in the last chapter," teased Aunt Jane, " now that she has seen for herself what a fine estate he has. Would you not do the same in her place, would not your little heart soften towards him ? " " I could never forgive him," declared Fanny, solemnly, " not after the way he behaved at the dance. His estate would have nothing to do with it, nothing whatever." But Aunt Jane, shaking her head and smiling demurely, would only murmur, " Do but consider, my dear Fanny, how handsome he was and how tall and how all the young ladies in Meryton would have given their eye teeth to get him. And his park wall was ten miles round."

10

Before they went away it was decided that Aunt Jane too should plant a tree. Edward's gardener brought down a young oak sapling from the Great House and Fanny chose the place for it in the shrubbery ; she held the stem while Aunt Jane trampled down the mould about the roots with her small slippers. This green child of hers would still be living more than a hundred years after she was under ground. Then Edward and his family went home to Kent while Jane settled down to a quiet winter at her new book. This time it was to be a tale of life in a country house, exactly like Godmersham, which for the purposes of fiction she christened *Mansfield Park*.

In January *Pride and Prejudice*, her own darling child, saw the light and at Chawton Cottage they had all the fun of reading it aloud to their friend and neighbour, Miss Benn, without telling her who had written it. Excellent reviews and praise from all quarters made February a happy month for Jane ; otherwise she was hard at work all that spring upon her new novel.

Sense and Sensibility and *Pride and Prejudice* had been two versions of the same theme, written for herself and Cassandra about their youth at Steventon Parsonage ; but *Mansfield Park* was a book for her brothers. All five of them had given their sister something that she needed, though perhaps she herself did not know it. James in his younger days had sat for the sober worried scrupulous hero, bewitched against his will by a woman who could not bring herself to take a parson for a husband. Henry played opposite to him as a light-hearted, careless, charming scapegrace, hardly to be called a villain. Edward was there in his habit as he lived, the sober awe-inspiring kindly parent, with no notion that the young and frivolous might be a little afraid of him ; and his Kentish home was there too. At Godmersham, in the old nursery, his children had a dolls' house with a pillared portico and real glass in all the windows. When Fanny or Marianne or little Louisa swung open the front you saw the whole Lilliputian establishment at once, upstairs and downstairs and in my lady's chamber, as the nursery rhyme went.

Mansfield Park was a book like that dolls' house. When you opened it you had the whole life of an English country mansion displayed for you, down to the last detail. The master was in his library, dozing over *The Times*. All about him were his book-lined shelves, his collections of shells and medals, cameos and engravings ; presently he would cast up his estate accounts or have his bailiff in to discuss market prices and the rotation of his crops. In the drawing-room his wife was doing her fancy work, fondling her pug on the sofa, or entertaining a circle of elegant neighbours. Upstairs the young ladies were trying on new dresses or having their hair curled out for a ball. The young gentlemen were coming in with their dogs from shooting, or knocking the balls about in the billiard-room. The governess in the schoolroom was hearing the younger children repeat their lessons. In the dining-room the butler and the footman were laying the table ; in the kitchen the cook and the kitchen-maids were dressing a green goose and an apricot tart for dinner ; in the dairy the housekeeper was scolding the dairymaid about a cream cheese, over the stable archway the clock was striking an evening hour and up in the white room in the east wing a little visiting cousin was crying herself to sleep. Outside this core were concentric circles of growth. In the stables the grooms were rubbing down the horses, in the garden the gardeners were picking roses or wall fruit, in the cottage the coachman was just putting on his wig before bringing the carriage round to the front door. Beyond the haha you came to the wilderness, the park with its coverts and plantations, the bright curve of the river, the dependent village with its church and rectory, in the occupation of some younger son. Then came the leafy lanes and turnpike roads, the market town, the hunt kennels, the assize court, the ring of neighbouring estates, the whole ordered life of the English countryside as Jane had known it for almost forty years.

Yes, *Mansfield Park* was a book for Edward or James to read in his library, smiling and beating his hand upon his knee ; for Henry to slip into the drawer of his desk at the bank and dip into when he wanted a breath of the country air ; for Frank and Charles to take to sea with them. She had put everything that she knew and loved best of those two into a sailor brother for her hero, a young fellow with Frank's steady professional competence and quiet courage, with all Charles's ardour and gaiety. She even wrote to Frank, when half-way through the book in the summer of 1813, to beg for the loan of the names of his ships, *Elephant, Endymion, Cleopatra,* and to tell her how to berth a ship at Spithead, for she prided herself on making no mistakes in naval matters.

Frank was in the Baltic in command of a seventy-four. She was a new ship to him, but it was not the first time that the old *Elephant* had shown her black and yellow colouring as she wallowed through the Great Belt, for she was a famous ship. Legend clung about her, for though she was only a seventy-four, she had been under Captain Foley's command during the action off Copenhagen twelve years before, and Admiral Nelson had shifted his flag into her from the *St. George* because of her shallow draft, when he decided to attack the Danish fleet from the rear, all among the flats and shoals of the harbour. It was on the old *Elephant's* quarter-deck that the little hero had stumped up and down, flapping his fin and saying, " Warm work, but it can't last," to his Captain of Marines, when the splinters flew from the mainmast beside him, boasting that he would not be elsewhere for thousands. It was there that he had put his telescope to his blind eye and refused to see Admiral Hyde Parker's signal of recall. Frank Austen had all that to remember when he walked the deck himself, in the ghostly quiet of the long white midsummer nights, half-way between Denmark and Sweden.

He and Charles she knew would find something of their own past youth in William Price. For Henry she had put in all the fun they used to have, years ago, with their private theatricals in the barn at Steventon, when he was only a stage-struck boy, just going up to Oxford, and Cousin Eliza and he used to play hero and heroine. All his youth and his wife's was in *Mansfield Park* ; there his sister had pinned down, dissected and spread out for admiration the lovely butterfly which once had been Eliza, the feathery dust and great peacock's eyes of her wings.

II

Those peacock wings would never flutter again, for Henry's wife was dead. He had long known that she must die of the same disease which had killed her mother before her. The fragile creature had endured pain and weakness with unlooked-for courage, walking towards her death as gracefully as she might have gone to the guillotine. At the end of that long winter she had given up her struggle for life.

By April in that year, 1813, the blinds were down and the door-knocker tied up with crape at the fine house in Sloane Street, where she had meant to give her parties. Jane, his favourite sister, was the one who went up to help Henry move out of it ; he had said with a shudder that he could not bear to stay there a month longer. His was not a mind for affliction, she told Frank, when she wrote to him, he had adored Eliza and for that very reason was passionate to forget her as quickly as he could. The Sloane Street house was too big for a widower, and he was going to live in Henrietta Street, Covent Garden, over the bank.

He was wild to go there immediately, but that was impossible, the workmen had too much to do. Jane wrote to Cassandra at Steventon that she had been down there with him, but all was dust and confusion, though it had been amusing to be present at the opening of a new account. She had enjoyed watching Henry giving his performance as a banker, spreading his elbows on his great desk, smiling agreeably, dipping his quill pen in a silver inkstand and offering it to his client. Neither he nor she were in the mood for theatres, but he had taken her, by way of quiet entertainment, to a couple of picture galleries. She had amused herself by picking out faces which might serve as portraits of the two sisters in *Pride and Prejudice* ; but though she had found a Jane Bennett in white with green ribbons, there had not been one delightful enough for Mrs. Darcy.

Once or twice they exchanged visits with the good Tilsons next door, otherwise Henry was too busy to do much for her. She was spending her days going through the house of mourning, laying away Eliza's pretty delicate clothes, her little scented kid gloves and slippers, her Indian shawls and French scarves ; the endless pretty trifles with which she had always adorned herself, her feathers and flowers, necklaces and rings, her letters, fashion books, boxes of face powder, flasks of perfume, pots of rouge and cream. Henry wanted everything huddled out of sight as quickly as possible. He had already arranged to sell the harp across which she used to sweep those delicate arms of hers, the pianoforte on which she used to tinkle out her little French songs. The harp stood covered now, the pianoforte closed, in the octagon room at the back of the house where the party had been. It was very quiet in there now, Jane did not sit in it ; she preferred to work away at *Mansfield Park* in the sunny front parlour, when she was not going through Eliza's orderly drawers and cupboards, or sit talking downstairs to the two French servants. " *Ah ! mademoiselle,*" Madame Bigeon would cry, " *quelle perte, quelle tristesse ; Madame était toujours si gai, si amaible, elle faisait si bien la maison. Pauvre Monsieur Henri, que ferait-il seul ?* " And wiping her eyes the daughter, Manon, would lament, " *Ma pauvre dame, comme elle a souffert, toujours sans se plaindre. Monsieur ignorait tout.*"

They were full of stories of Eliza's kindness and protestations of their devotion to Henry. The two faithful creatures would go to Covent Garden with him, or to the end of the world, not so much for his own sake as for the sake of his dead wife.

Jane wrote to Cassandra that the quiet of the house of mourning did her good, she would not ask for any companion, unless it were her sister. Sometimes she drove about London in solitary elegance in Henry's barouche, a slender, upright figure in her thin black mourning gown, glancing about her from between the wings of her great bonnet at the pale town houses, the green trees in Hyde Park, the clean bright streets striped with sun and shadow, putting everything away in her mind.

VIII

Chawton

1813-1814

I

THAT summer, 1813, the Emperor was fighting his last
desperate campaign against the Allies in Saxony;
Wellington's army won the battle of Vittoria and that
autumn he began to force the passes of the Pyrenees. That
summer in London they were all dancing the waltz, and
Lady Heathcote, up from Hampshire for the season, gave
a ball at which Lady Caroline Lamb made a shocking scene
for love of Lord Bryon. That summer old Mr. Leigh died
and Stoneleigh passed to a distant cousin; a pity that Aunt
and Uncle Leigh Perrot would never come in for it. They
would have done so had it not been for that fatal com-
promise. Henry went to Scotland and took his nephew Ned
with him. Ned, to be sure, thought more of grouse and
patridges than of lakes and mountains, but his uncle liked
the lad's cheerful company and wanted to go somewhere he
would not be reminded of his dead wife. Edward brought
the rest of the family to Chawton for the summer months
and in July they had all the fun and excitement of a general
election, " Chute and Heathcote for ever " was in all
mouths. But for the Austen family it was the summer when
young Anna got herself engaged to poor blundering Michael
Terry from Dummer, against the wishes and advice of her
parents. James could not think this dull stupid young
parson, Mrs. Digweed's nephew, a fit match for his elder
and favourite daughter, while Mrs. J. A. lamented her stepdaughter's ingratitude all round the family. " She took
nobody's advice, she did not even tell her father or me before
she accepted him. I must say she has been very secretive
and tiresome about the whole matter, but that is Anna's

nature. She will go her own way, she will not listen to her elders, she is wilful and perverse like all young people nowadays. I'm sure when I was her age I did not try to manage my own affairs as she has." Cassandra could only look back with a smile at Mary's determined pursuit of James.

2

Anna, it is true, would listen to nobody's advice. She was in what her Aunt Jane would have called one of her later variations and a very showy and flourishing one it was, but when she had thought about it a little she changed her giddy mind, broke off her engagement to young Mr. Terry and began to sit about under trees with a very different admirer. He was Ben Lefroy, second son of their dear dead friend, Madam Lefroy. He lived at Ashe with his brother, the present rector, and he was going to take Orders himself. He was a tall dark sober fellow, serious-minded and very religious. Anna and he were quite opposites, he hated company and she was very fond of it, he had rather a queer temper and she was young and giddy. She fluttered about the young man like a butterfly in a high wind, but on the whole drew nearer to him as the summer went by. It was a much more serious affair than the last one. The family rather approved; did not think Anna likely to do better and wished her to settle. By the time that September came in, the month for family visits, the match was almost made up by the two young people, only Ben, poor fellow, with his difficult scrupulous temperament, had declined a curacy which he might have secured, because he could not make up his mind whether he ought to take Orders so young.

3

Uncle Henry, that September, 1813, moved into Number Ten, Henrietta Street, and Aunt Jane came up to help him do it. Edward brought three of his daughters up for shopping and the dentist, and they made a family party of it. Fanny stayed with her uncle and Marianne and Lizzie were with their father in a hotel round the corner. Nothing could have been more delightful, and Fanny had plenty to put down in her diary. A great deal had been done while Uncle Henry was in Scotland, his new apartment already looked like Sloane Street moved into Covent Garden. He had the two upper floors over the bank. There was a white panelled parlour over the busy street, where they sat and took their meals and a smaller room behind which could be used if he wanted to give any parties, only, poor man! he would scarcely have the heart for much entertaining now that Aunt Eliza was dead. Her great canopied French bed stood in the spare room now and Aunt Jane slept in it and Fanny had the little dressing-room next door, so that they would be able to chatter and call through to each other whenever they pleased. Madame Bigeon and her daughter were obliged to live round the corner, but they came in every day to do the work. Madame Bigeon went shopping every morning early in Covent Garden and came in with her old shiny black oilcloth market-bag stuffed with chickens and veget-ables, lobsters, bunches of herbs and country butter. There was nothing the old woman enjoyed more than going round the stalls, cheapening the produce and throwing up her hands in horror at the city prices. She dressed one of her comfortable French dinners for them the first night, fish, soup, *bouilli*, partridges and the apple tart which she had learnt to make to please her English master. She was delighted to have visitors to cook for and complained that when he was alone Henry was too fond of dining off roast beef and bread and cheese at his club. She promised the young ladies to make all manner of delights for them ; there should be *éclairs*, *Madeleines* and *babas au rhum* whenever they chose to ask for them.

Covent Garden was not a part of London where young ladies were much seen. The streets round it were full of taverns and coffee houses, bath houses and less reputable establishments. The arcades round the Market had always been a haunt of night strollers, and Long Acre was well known for its quack doctors and gambling dens. Edward strictly commanded his daughters not to think of going out unescorted. At night strayed revellers fought and sang under Uncle Henry's windows, coaches rattled by, going to and from the two great theatres, and between three and four in the morning the country carts began to rumble over the cobblestones, bringing in the Kent and Essex produce to the Market ; but the little girls thought it most amusing to stay there, right in the heart of London, only a stone's throw from the Strand and Drury Lane. It was a glorious change from Godmersham.

Dear Uncle Henry was as gay as ever, he did not seem much like a recent widower. He had taken a stage box for them all, for the very first evening, for three musical extravaganzas at the Lyceum. The entertainment was picked to amuse the little girls, who screamed with delight at the sight of Don Juan, dragged down to hell by a spangled devil in red velvet, with a glare of Bengal lights, a clash of cymbals and a roll of drums. Fanny was a little superior about this pantomime, as became a young lady of twenty-one ; but Uncle Henry promised her that she should choose the next play, and she voted for Mr. Garrick's *Clandestine Marriage* at Covent Garden. During the pantomime Uncle Henry and Aunt Jane sat at the back of the box and talked together about her books. *Pride and Prejudice* was a fashionable novel of the year among the discerning, the first edition of *Sense and Sensibility* was sold out and a second was printing ; altogether, Henry told his sister proudly, she had now written herself into two hundred and fifty pounds. She frowned nervously and looked down, while Fanny listened awe-struck and could not understand why her aunt was always so shy about her dear delightful books. She seemed quite vexed that night, because Uncle Henry had sent a copy of *Pride and Prejudice* to Mr. Warren Hastings and had been boasting to all his fine friends up in Scotland that his sister had written it. Fanny thought that she herself would have wanted everybody to know what she had done.

However, Uncle Henry could always talk his sister out of

being cross with him, soon he had Aunt Jane smiling and admitting that the secret was now only the shadow of a secret. When her third book came out perhaps she might as well tell everybody whose it was. " I must resign myself to being a Monster," said she in her absurd way, and Uncle Henry threw back his handsome head and laughed so loudly that everybody in the pit looked up at them.

It was delicious, thought Fanny, to see and hear them together. Uncle Henry was exactly what a brother ought to be ; he loved Aunt Jane, confided in her and talked to her by the hour. They had always been the two clever ones of the family, they liked nothing so well as to get away together. Fanny only wished that her two undergraduate brothers were half as devoted. Since Ned and George went up to Oxford they had grown very rough and rude. They seemed to think of nothing but sport, they would not mind her and only laughed when she scolded them about their selfish inconsiderate ways. How delightful it would have been to have a brother like Uncle Henry ! dark, witty, handsome, devoted, like the hero in Lord Byron's beautiful poem, the *Giaour*. Fanny would have liked to make this comparison aloud, with the proper grown-up air of critical appreciation, only she could not for the life of her be sure how you pronounced the word. It would never do to make her elders laugh by getting it wrong ; so she turned again to the stage.

4

Kind Edward gave his daughter and his sister five pounds each to go shopping with and that was truly delightful, for nobody had better taste than Aunt Jane. Layton & Shears, the drapers, was most conveniently situated at Number 11, on the opposite side of the street from Uncle Henry's bank ; he told his nieces with a twinkle in his bright brown eye that this had been one of his reasons for going to live there. Bedford House was a famous place for English and Irish poplins. Fanny and Aunt Jane selected lengths of rose colour and dark slate ; while in Leicester Square they purchased ribbons and laces, silk stockings, a beautiful square veil for Fanny and some blonde net for a trousseau gown for Cousin Anna, who would probably get married quite soon. How charming that was ! though Fanny privately thought it a little dull of her to choose a young parson. There were so many clergymen already in the Austen family. They cheapened gowns and bonnets and studied the fashions earnestly, as became two ladies up from the country. White, it seemed, was going out, except for very young ladies ; the colours that year were floral, rose and violet, primrose and pea-green. Bonnets were larger than ever and very much trimmed with plumes, flowers and flying veils. Tied under the chin with a great bow they framed Fanny's little heart-shaped face endearingly ; but she was wild for a cap. Aunt Jane had just ordered one from Miss Hare, the milliner in Cranborne Alley, of white satin and lace for evening parties, with a little white flower perking out of the left ear. Aunt Jane said it was a pity for girls to take to caps too soon, she had done it herself and sometimes regretted it, but Fanny would not take advice. She chose one in a hurry, of white sarcenet and lace, with a great deal of piping and a full gathered crown, then hated it when she got it home and wailed, " It is a dreadful cap. Do you not think it very unbecoming to me ? Oh ! I am sure you do. It makes me look like an old woman. I wish I had bought the promenade hat instead, the one that you told me did suit me, with the bunch of Provence roses and white lilac in front and the puffs of silver gauze round the crown. I really liked it the better of the two, but the milliner would have it that nothing but caps were worn for carriage wear in the morning, and I thought it would be just the thing for Canterbury Races. Now I have wasted my money and got a cap which does not even go with my new gown."

Then her gown itself did not please her as well as she had expected. Fashions were growing much more elaborate and the graceful classical simplicity which had been the mode in Aunt Jane's youth was now quite out of date. Fanny's new gown was cut straight across the shoulders and

very low ; but it was filled up with a tucked lawn chemisette
and finished off round her little throat with a stiffly starched
lace tucker which tickled her chin. The waist was still right
up under her arms, but below the waist the skirt stuck out,
hiding her slender shape altogether ; and the hem was
stiffened with half a dozen rows of pinked and scalloped
flounces, so that the skirt swung about her ankles like a bell.
Fortunately for her she had very good ankles. Aunt Jane
assured her sweetly that it was a charming gown, but could
not help sighing, as older people will, " These new styles
are not very becoming or very easy to wear ; I think the
fashions were prettier when I was young."

Little Fanny was all in a flutter, wringing her hands and
crying, " Oh ! what shall I do. I have laid out the whole
of my five pounds and all to no purpose. I cannot like my
gown or my cap either." Aunt Jane would not take her
trouble seriously; she would only say in her dry, smiling
way, " It is one of the sweet taxes of youth, to choose in a
hurry and make bad bargains. You will wait longer another
time." But when she saw that Fanny was really upset she
was quite charming about it ; saying over and over again
what a sweet frock the new one was and telling Fanny, " You
do not know how lucky you are to have so many pretty
things. When Aunt Cassandra and I were your age we had
to wear out our caps and gowns till all our friends were tired
of them. We had very little money to spend and most of it
went on gloves and stockings. We made our own gowns
and caps ; I always trimmed my own hats and made myself
a headdress for any special ball. Once I borrowed a black
lace frill off one of Cassy's hats to make myself a black
turban, once I used a Mameluke cap that your Uncle Frank
brought home to your Aunt Mary from Egypt. We used to
refresh our gowns with new flounces and dye and turn them
and when they were quite worn out we would cut them up
to make spencers and petticoats. I always envied the rich
girls who had a new gown for each assembly. No, my dear
Fanny, I shall not pity you ; I think you are very well off."
Fanny dried her tears, hugged her aunt and said affectionately, " I am sure nobody ever cared about your old gown ;

whatever you had on, you must always have been the prettiest girl at the ball."

When the gowns and caps were bought, they all went to the dentist and that was not so agreeable. Mr. Spence, of Bond Street, was the King's own dentist and very much the fashion. He charged very high fees. He took out two of poor Marianne's teeth and filled Lizzie's ; he even wanted to put gold in some of Fanny's pretty teeth, but as she had never had the toothache in her life she would not let him meddle with them. The whole family went to Wedgwood's china shop together to buy a dinner service for Chawton Great House. Fanny wanted something classical embossed with urns and garlands, nymphs and goddesses upon a sea-coloured ground ; but her father could not fancy eating his roast mutton off a pottery plate, so for all his daughter's pouting he ordered a plain white service, such as you saw in every gentleman's dining-room in Kent, with a purple and gold edge and the family crest in the middle. They all enjoyed themselves exceedingly and Fanny thought the visit all too short; she could have stayed in London forever. However, they must be at home by the middle of September, for her little sisters had been promised that they should go to their grandmother, old Lady Bridges, for Goodnestone Fair before the dowager went to take her annual cure at Bath, and that was a treat which so kind a sister as Fanny could not let them miss. However, she had one comfort for leaving Henrietta Street ; dear Aunt Jane was coming to Godmersham with them. She had not been there for four years, not since just before Fanny's mother died.

5

This time it proved an especially delightful and memorable visit, for it was the time when Aunt Jane was writing the last chapters of *Mansfield Park*. You would never have guessed what the dear woman was up to, thought Fanny, gleefully hugging the family secret and watching her aunt's performance. Aunt Jane behaved just as usual. She sat demurely at table or in the drawing-room, listening politely to the conversation and occasionally dropping a quiet comment of her own. She supported Fanny, who at twenty-one was still a little shy about playing her mother's part in society, while visits of ceremony were received and returned all round the neighbourhood ; from the Knatchbulls of Provender, the Knatchbulls of Merstham Hatch, the Tokes at Godinton, from Aunt Harriet Moore and her cross parson husband, from Aunt Sophia Deedes and her large family at Sandling, from Lady Fagg and her five dreadfully plain daughters at Mystole, from the Wildmans at Chilham Castle and the Finch-Hattons at Eastwell. Nobody took much notice of Fanny's aunt, that quiet Miss Austen from Hampshire, a poor relation who displayed very elegant manners, but had not much to say for herself. They had no idea how shrewdly she was summing them all up ; or how dryly amusing she could be about them afterwards, when they had all driven away in their fine carriages, with the high-stepping horses and the powdered coachman and footman on the box.

Aunt Jane was a delightfully easy guest to entertain, the smallest events pleased and amused her. She enjoyed a big party at Chilham Castle, with Fanny and the Wildman girls making music afterwards ; but she was equally pleased to attend a family party with the Tildens at Milstead vicarage and look at books of engravings on the sofa by the fire. She was always ready to saunter round the estate with Papa and the bailiff, making sensible remarks about crops and cattle and admiring the growth of Bentigh and the Temple plantations, saying how much the saplings had shot up in Winnigates and Seaton Wood in the last four years. She praised Fanny's improvements about the mansion, particularly the bright and pretty new Chintz Room, which was the pride of Fanny's heart ; with equal affection she exclaimed over the gold paper and Persian silk which the little girls brought back from Goodnestone Fair. She approved the sermons of Mr. Shearer, the new rector, and discussed the evangelical movement with him gravely ; she listened attentively to the complaints of Mrs. Clewes, the new governess who had replaced her friend Miss Sharpe. Mrs. Clewes it appeared, suffered from just the same sort of headache as Grandmamma Austen ; both of these elderly ladies had a constant sensation of a peck loaf on top of the head, especially in hot weather, which was most uncomfortable and alarming.

Fanny provided such small entertainments as she could. The family drove into Canterbury, to walk about the cobbled streets and poke into the small shops. Grandmamma Knight had died since Aunt Jane's last visit and been buried with her husband under the monument in the south aisle of Godmersham Church, the marble sarcophagus with the broken pillar above and a fine inscription about her virtues. So that there was no visit to be paid to White Friars ; but Papa took Aunt Jane round the County jail, which he had to visit as a magistrate and afterwards they went to tea with old Mrs. Milles, who was ninety years of age, but very cheerful and contented and her dreadful chattering daughter Molly. Fanny distinctly saw Aunt Jane's eye rest thoughtfully upon this tiresome old maid, as she undertook to give them, in three words, the whole history of the reconciliation between Dr. Scudamore and his wife. Then she talked on about it for half an hour, as she always did, using such odd expressions and being so foolishly minute about the whole matter, that you could hardly keep your countenance. Fanny was convinced that Aunt Jane would pop Miss Milles into a book one of these days, along with the new doctor's wife, a large ungenteel woman with self-satisfied and would-be elegant manners, who had really been quite rudely neglectful of Aunt Jane when she came to pay her call at Godmersham. Aunt Jane had surveyed her, too, with exactly the considering air of a cook who sees a bone which would do for the stock-pot.

She studied the visitors in the same way, as they came and went. It was a pity that there was nobody very suitable for her in the spare rooms that autumn. The house was filled with young gentlemen who had been invited for the shooting, or to escort Fanny at the county balls. Her father invited Wadham Knatchbull, who was supposed to admire

Fanny very much ; he was one of the Provender cousins, a younger son, to be sure, with nothing particular to like or dislike in him. Fanny knew that her father would be pleased if she could make up a match with Wadham ; but Aunt Jane agreed with her that he was really rather too dull. Then there was young James Wildman, a near neighbour, from Chilham Castle ; he was musical and always listened most attentively when Fanny played or sang. The Wildmans were very rich and James was the eldest son and the catch of the neighbourhood. George Finch-Hatton came, who was supposed to be the handsomest young man in Kent ; he was crossed in love too, pining for Lady Charlotte Graham, which made him all the more interesting to the young ladies. Fanny was quite surprised to find how little her aunt seemed to think of handsome melancholy George. She liked him little better than that dreadful Mr. Robert Maskall, who ate such a lot of butter and talked so much and so conceitedly and had such a vulgarly shaped mouth.

Fanny's own secret choice, in so far as she yet had one, was John Plumtre, an old friend from Fredwell, near Goodnestone ; she had known him since she was quite a little girl. John was handsome and very amiable, with quiet gentlemanlike manners, but he was dreadfully shy. Invited to partner Fanny at a ball, he spent most of his time out with her brothers, Ned and George, who were never happy unless they were shooting partridges or riding to hounds. He hardly dared to open his mouth when he was in the drawing-room with the ladies, though Aunt Jane did draw him into a discussion of Lord Byron's poetry, of which he disapproved. He earnestly recommended instead, the Poet Laureate's new life of Lord Nelson, which he thought would improve Fanny's mind. Aunt Jane said tartly, " I am tired of lives of Lord Nelson, seeing as how I never read any " ; but then smiled, relented and promised to read it herself if there were any mention in it of Uncle Frank. John Plumtre looked be-wildered, he never saw that you were making fun of him. Fanny murmured later to her aunt that John was a brilliant scholar and had done very well up at Cambridge ; but Aunt Jane shook her head and said firmly, " My dear, he is

sensible rather than brilliant." Then she sighed and added,
" There is nobody brilliant nowadays." It did not appear
that she cared very much for young men. However, you
could always count on her to play the piano very agreeably,
if anyone wanted to dance. There were not often enough
of them for a country dance ; but they used to practise the
schottische, the new dance which had come into fashion
since Sir Walter Scott's poetry sent everybody travelling
northwards to the Trossachs and Edinburgh. The Prince
Regent himself, the boys said, with guffaws, had sprained
his ankle trying to teach Princess Charlotte to dance the
schottische at Carlton House ; Prinny was too fat nowadays
for such capers. At Godmersham, however, the young
people pranced, spun and shouted ; then greatly daring,
practised the new waltz. Fanny might not dance it at balls,
only at home with her brothers.

Uncle Charles and Aunt Fanny came to stay with their
three little girls, a pleasant change for them after the tossing
discomfort of the guardship at the Nore, where little Cassy
was always sick when there was any sea. Aunt Jane devoted
herself entirely to them during their visit. Altogether Fanny
was quite ashamed that the dear woman had so little time
to herself while she was staying at Godmersham. It was a
wonder that she managed to write at all. She was like a
wren working at its nest, you had to watch very sharply
before you could catch the busy creature coming and going.
Only sometimes in the long quiet evenings, when Papa was
dozing over the newspaper account of the Emperor's last
desperate Leipzig campaign against the Allies, when the boys
were safely in the billiard-room and the girls were at their
fancy work, did Aunt Jane sometimes jump up, run to the
writing-table, scribble something down and then come back
and sit down again as if nothing had happened. And after
the visitors had all left and the boys were back at college,
while Papa was out with his bailiff, and Fanny was busy
with the housekeeper, then Aunt Jane could shut herself up
every morning in the library. There she had five tables,
eight-and-twenty chairs and two fires, one at each end of
the library, all to herself! there nobody would disturb her

at the writing-table from breakfast time until tea-time except Johncock the butler, coming in solemnly at midday with a tray of cold meat and a glass of claret. There she could be quite alone, as if she were on a desert island ; there, at last, she could finish *Mansfield Park*.

6

Fanny had the book read aloud to her, chapter by chapter, for want of Aunt Cassandra, who had always been the best critic ; not for worlds would she have told Aunt Jane that she could not like the heroine, her namesake Fanny Price. There was something dreadfully creep-mouse about her, she had all the qualities which Fanny Knight's own brothers, Ned and George, most despised in a girl. Mollycoddle, they would have called her, jeeringly ; prig, spoil-sport, lazy-bones, cry-baby, cowardly-custard, tell-tale-tit. And when she grew up she was not much better. How could she waste so much time pining after Edmund Bertram ? who was as hopelessly shy, modest and unenterprising as John Plumtre himself, though of course very good. How could she be so *missish* as to refuse an offer of marriage from that dear delightful Henry Crawford ? He and his sister Mary were the characters who best pleased Fanny Knight. She felt certain that when he was young her Uncle Henry had been exactly like that ; amusing, witty, desperately fascinating, only of course not so idle and wicked ; but then Lord Byron, nowadays, had made wicked heroes all the fashion. And had Aunt Eliza been as bewitching as Mary Crawford in her youth ? Aunt Mary, Mrs. J. A., had never had a good word for her ; she always pursed up her mouth when Aunt Eliza was mentioned and said, "I am afraid your Uncle Henry married a very worldly woman." Fanny believed there was a family story about dull Uncle James having wanted to marry Aunt Eliza, once upon a time ; but naturally she had preferred Uncle Henry (any girl would), and poor Uncle James had been forced to console himself with Aunt Mary, who was much the less amiable woman of the two. Fanny had not known Aunt Eliza very well and she ventured to ask Aunt Jane what the dead woman had been like. Aunt Jane said with a light sigh, " She was one of the most fascinating creatures I ever met ; yes, she was a little like Mary Crawford, but Eliza was never unkind or treacherous. She had the warmest heart in the world. She never intended to make trouble for anyone ; only she did make mischief in the old days wherever she went, because she was so much more delightful than anybody else."

" I wish," sighed Fanny, " that you had made it all end differently. The last part does not please me at all. Of course, it was very wrong of Henry Crawford to run off with that hateful Maria Rushworth, and I cannot think what possessed him to do it ; but if Fanny had only been kinder to him in the first place it would never have happened. You say so yourself. I wish Mary might have got Edmund and I wish Fanny might have made up a match with Henry. I am sure he would have made her a very good husband in the end." But Aunt Jane, shaking her head and looking quite stern all of a sudden, said, " Never make that mistake, my dear. Never marry a man you cannot trust, just because he has charming manners and knows how to make love prettily. You will be very wretched if you do." She seemed quite startled, went back to the point again and again ; said she had never meant to make the bad people pleasanter than the good ones. It was almost as if, thought Fanny innocently, Aunt Jane had once been very much hurt by some charming clever thoughtless person and had revenged herself by being hard on all such people in her book.

7

The second edition of *Sense and Sensibility* came out just before she left Godmersham and did very well. Aunt Mary wrote from Cheltenham in her usual tactless grudging style that people there were speaking quite well of it ; she had even met one lady who felt that she ought to buy it. Aunt Mary always wrote like that, but Aunt Jane only laughed and said,

" I wish the poor woman may. I cannot help hoping that many will find themselves obliged to buy it. I shall not mind imagining it a disagreeable duty to them, so long as they do it."

She went home for Christmas, stopping a day or two with Uncle Henry on her way, began a new novel with the New Year and then laid it aside, came up again in March, 1814, to Henrietta Street to meet Fanny and her father and to see Mr. Egerton the publisher. Henry had been at Chawton to see his mother and to fetch Jane away. Brother and sister drove up to London in the bright March weather, and in the post-chaise she read him the earlier chapters of *Mansfield Park*. The ostler at the posting house in Farnham, where they changed horses, saw them sitting in the carriage while the horses were taken out and fresh ones put to ; they were so gay that he would have taken them for a new-married couple, except that they were as like as two peas, so that even his old blind eyes could not mistake them for anything but brother and sister. The gentleman was very tall, held up his head like a king and threw out his orders as if he had been a general, he had the straight back that came from drilling and the swaggering gait of a good horseman ; he had been in the army, for sure ! The lady sat beside him in a dark-green pelisse and a little close bonnet, sipping a glass of cherry brandy which the gentleman had ordered out for her. She looked all about her at the horses being led into the stable, the groom carrying buckets across the muddy yard and the pigeons cooing on the tiles. Her eyes were as bright and sharp as a needle ; there was one who missed nothing ! Fresh horses were put to, the postilion came out in his bright yellow livery, swung himself upon the near horse and cracked his whip and away they rattled up the London road.

Henry had *Mansfield Park* to listen to all the way and approved it as much as even its author could have wished. He said it was very different to the other two novels ; but did not appear to consider it at all inferior. With his long legs stretched across the chaise, his arms folded and his hat pulled down over his eyes, he sat smiling lazily at his sister while in her beautiful voice she read him one scene after another. He took kindly to Lady Bertram and Mrs. Norris, admired Henry Crawford for a clever pleasant creature, liked Fanny and seemed to foresee how it would all be. They had married off Mrs. Rushworth before they dined and slept at Cobham, were off by half-past eight next morning, baited and refreshed at Kingston and were in Henrietta Street before two in the afternoon. Mr. Barlow, the cashier, came out smiling from the door of the bank to tell brother and sister that peace was generally expected.

It was a glorious moment to be in the Capital, for it was the moment of victory. Ever since the New Year the Emperor's armies had been falling back before the Allies on all the frontiers of France. Lord Wellington was over the Pyrenees, driving northwards, he had beaten Marshal Soult in three great final battles in the south, at Orthez, at Tarbes and at Toulouse. On the last day of March the Allied armies marched into Paris and on the fifth of April the Emperor abdicated and was banished to a small island in the Mediterranean, called Elba, which most people had to look out on their maps. When Fanny Knight and her father came up from Bath to Henrietta Street London was full of shouting cheering crowds and at night all the streets were illuminated. Little Fanny hardly knew whether to laugh or to cry, it was so strange to know that at last the war was over. It had been going on, with one short intermission, ever since she was three weeks old ; she could hardly imagine what it would be like to live in a country at peace.

They were all very gay in Henrietta Street that spring. Aunt Jane was correcting the proofs of *Mansfield Park*, which were sent up from Mr. Egerton's printing and publishing establishment, the Military Library in Whitehall, but she was not too busy for shopping and all the other amusements provided by Uncle Henry. Aunt Jane and he had chosen a Shakespeare play for Fanny to see, one which should not be too exciting for the romantic little creature ! it was *The Merchant of Venice*, with Edmund Kean giving an exquisite performance of Shylock. Aunt Jane had only her old lilac sarcenet gown to wear, but Fanny and she did it up together,

putting plaits of black ribbon round the hem and the neck
of the gown and drawing it up into gathered roses here and
there. When it was finished you would have thought that
she had bought it new for the occasion ; only she would
insist on wearing long sleeves, which was a great pity, for
she had such pretty arms. It was delightful to go to a
Shakespeare play with Aunt Jane and Uncle Henry ; he
knew all the great speeches and could recite with the utmost
expression. Of course he and Aunt Jane used to read and
act plays together in their youth, just like the people in
Mansfield Park. He gave Fanny a copy of Lord Bryon's
beautiful new poem, *The Corsair*, a most romantic thing, all
about a Greek pirate Conrad, and his bride Medora.
Conrad, a most dashing villain, sacked and burnt a Turkish
palace, rescued a lovely Circassian slave, was saved by her
in turn from death in a Turkish prison, rejected her love
and returned to find his Medora dead of grief. It was all
very sad and very, very beautiful. Fanny could not understand why Aunt Jane was so cool about it. They saw another
play which was supposed to be in part by Lord Byron, who
at that time had some interest in the management of Drury
Lane Theatre. He was at the height of his fame, a ballroom
bard, with every fashionable woman in London pining for
him. His name would draw the public anywhere ; but this
was only an Eastern pantomime, called *Nourjehad*, a fine
glittering spectacle which bored Papa mightily whether
Lord Byron had had any hand in it or not. However, John
Plumtre appeared in their box, made himself very polite all
round, walked back with them through the moonlit streets
to Uncle Harry's, was asked in and drank soup with them.
He said that they must positively see *The Farmer's Wife*, a
musical thing in three acts, in which Miss Stephens sang
some delicious ballads ; she was no actress, but she had an
enchanting voice. He took a box for the whole party the
very next night and made himself most attentive, certainly
he had waked up a good deal since the autumn. Uncle
Henry teased Fanny about him and made her blush.

Presently there were other callers, swarming about Fanny
like bees about a honeypot. Wadham Knatchbull, who had

rather been expected, only sent polite excuses ; but George
Finch-Hatton and James Wildman called upon them and
were met again next morning strolling in Hyde Park, under
the budding chestnut trees, looking at the riders. Handsome
George was out of the market now ; Lady Charlotte Graham
had accepted him and he was to be married to her that
summer, but that only made him a more cheerful companion.
Everybody seemed to be enjoying themselves that victory
month in London ; it was all *high honeysuckle*, as the fashionable phrase then was for any state of general excitement and
gaiety ; even John Plumtre was almost lively and certainly
most devoted. As to Fanny, she was quite in a flutter about
him. Sitting on the end of Aunt Jane's bed at midnight
after the theatre, in a flowered chintz dressing-gown with her
knees drawn up to her chin, she would cry, " Is he in love
with me ? do you think he is in love with me ? I am sure
he will make an offer for me one of these days and then
what shall I say to him ? What shall I do ? what would
you advise me to do ? Pray, Aunt Jane, tell me what I
ought to do."

Aunt Jane, sitting up in the great curtained French bed,
looking so mischievous and pretty in her muslin nightcap,
was delightfully sympathetic but rather guarded at first,
saying, " I shall not give you any advice, my dear Fanny.
I will have nothing to do with it. You must be guided by
your own feelings," and when Fanny wailed, " But I do not
know what they are," said in her sly way, " Well, he has not
asked you yet, and I daresay he will never have the courage
to do so." " I am sure he is quite in love with me," Fanny
declared, " but he is so dreadfully shy." " Modesty is
certainly his chief fault," agreed Aunt Jane. " If he were
less modest he would be more agreeable to you, I daresay,
he would speak louder and look more impudent ; but is it
not a fine character in which modesty is the only defect ? "
" The boys laugh at him," said Fanny, looking down.
" They say he is too straitlaced ; they make fun of him
for being so . . . so *evangelical*." " Ned and George are very
agreeable idle fellows," said Aunt Jane tartly, " but John
is such a scholar as could put them both to shame. They

have plenty of wit and like to use it on other people ; but John Plumtre has wisdom and that will come out better than wit in the long run. No, no, my dear ; you must not let your brothers laugh you out of your liking for this young gentleman, if you have one. I am by no means sure that we ought not all to be more of the evangelical way of thinking ; at any rate, those who can be so, must be happiest and safest. John Plumtre is a serious fellow with strict principles and good habits, but he is uncommonly amiable and if he were much with you I have no doubt that he would become more lively. A gay and merry wife is just what he needs to brisk him up."

Fanny smiled and hugged her knees, considering this while her aunt went on, " Well, my dear Fanny, I must tell you for your comfort that both your uncle and I think the young gentleman shows decided marks of attachment for you. We like him extremely and we do not see why he should not make you a very good husband. He is the eldest son of a man of fortune, the brother of your particular friend and belongs to your own county ; all that, you know, is very important. It would be a pretty establishment for you and you would not be far from home. But if you are not sure of your feelings you should certainly refuse him. There is nothing so dreadful as marrying without real affection. Marriage is not a state to be entered into with half a heart." Fanny looked down, twisted her fingers together, blushed prettily and said in a small voice, " Oh ! marriage is a very serious thing, to be sure, and I know I ought to make up my mind quite completely, one way or the other, before I encourage poor John any further. I daresay if he asks me I had better say ' No ' for the present, but he does seem to love me truly and I could not bear it if another girl got him." Aunt Jane began to laugh very much, kissed her, told her to go to bed and not plague herself about John Plumtre any longer. " You have time enough before you, he is not the only agreeable young man in Kent who may attach you. There are as good fish in the sea as ever came out of it ! all the old women will tell you that is a true proverb. You are a little in love with him, certainly, enough to be going on with, but not nearly so much as you think. If I were you I would wait awhile and see if you do not meet somebody whom you like better. After all you are only just twenty-one." Fanny shook her head doubtfully ! she feared that twenty-one was a great age.

8

After Fanny and her father had gone down into Kent, Aunt Jane paid a short visit to Streatham and came back with a budget of news for her brother Henry. Catherine Hill had two children by this time, and though her quiet husband and she had been very happy in Streatham they talked of leaving it soon. Old Mr. Bigg-Wither had died in the previous autumn and Harris and his wife had come into Manydown. Family changes were in the air. If Mr. Hill chose he might have the family living of Worting, down at the bottom of the park, where Elizabeth Heathcote and her husband had lived when they were first married. " And since Alethea is not likely to marry now, she has decided to live with Elizabeth and her little boy at Winchester, they have taken a house in the Close. I shall miss both of them ! we have seen them often at Chawton, but it will be very pleasant to drive in sometimes to Winchester and visit them." " But I thought," objected Henry with his quizzical air, " that Elizabeth was expected to marry John Harwood. He was her old love and he has stayed single all these years for her sake ; is the poor fellow not to have his reward now that his father is dead too and he has come in for Deane House ? " " No, it is no such thing," sighed Jane. " Now that the lawyers have gone into old Mr. Harwood's affairs they find that he has squandered everything. A new tenant will have to be found for Deane House, and poor John Harwood will be forced to support his mother and those two plain sisters as best he may out of his stipend at Ewhurst. He cannot possibly think of marriage, though Catherine says she believes Elizabeth would have had him if there had been money enough. However, it is quite out of the question.

I am very sorry for John, to be so disappointed after all these years. Do you remember how often they used to dance together at the Basingstoke Assemblies and how we all laughed at them for being *particular*, as we called it then ? "

" Oh ! love," said Henry, with one of his lively grimaces, " love is no laughing matter. Well, this is a sad ending to a long story ; it is a good thing you do not bring your novels to such bad ends, or they would never sell as they do. *Mansfield Park* is to come out next week and Egerton says that it is very well subscribed. What will you write next, my dear Jane ? Why do you not let me go to that rogue Crosby and buy back the tale you sold him, years ago, about the girl who went to look for a husband in Bath. It would take, I am sure it would take." Jane said that she thought the public no longer wanted parodies of Mrs. Radcliffe's romantic novels. " She is quite unknown nowadays ; when people wish to read something romantic and horrid they have Lord Byron." Henry would not admit this. " Look what a success *Cherubina* had last winter ; people talked of nothing else." This was an absurd and very witty parody of the Gothic school. Jane herself had laughed with Henry at the adventures of the ridiculous heroine when she first came up to Henrietta Street ; but she remained obstinate. " He has skimmed the cream off that jug," said she, shaking her head. " There is none left for me. Besides, I am not interested in the Bath book any more, I have another on the way already. I began it in January before I came up to stay with you. I am going to take a heroine whom no one will much like but myself. Her name is Emma and she is a matchmaker ; I think, my dear Henry, that her adventures will amuse you."

She was not in London when *Mansfield Park* was published ; she had gone down into Surrey to pay a family visit to the Cooks ; old Mr. Cook, Mrs. Austen's cousin and Jane's godfather, had for many years been the Rector of Great Bookham. He was a dear old gentleman who voted *Mansfield Park* the most sensible book he had ever read and was proud to take its writer round to see all his parishioners. They thought themselves quite a literary society down in Great

Bookham, for had not the elders among them all known Fanny Burney herself, the great Madame D'Arblay, she that married the *emigré* and waited upon old Queen Charlotte and wrote *Evelina*. The D'Arblays had gone back to France, since peace was declared, for the General wished to revisit his family estates ; but Miss Austen could at least be shown their cottage, Camilla Lacy. Madame D'Arblay had paid for its building out of the royalties of her novel, *Camilla*. Mr. Cook's goddaughter pleased the neighbourhood by showing herself word-perfect in Madame D'Arblay's romances ; she knew all about the adventures of *Cecilia* in Mr. Dubster's summerhouse and demurely confessed that she had taken the title of her own *Pride and Prejudice* from the last page of that admired work. She was taken all about the pretty neighbourhood and brought back some material for her new novel ; a picnic to Box Hill, a strawberry party in the vicarage garden, some aspects of a very typical English village and a couple of useful names, Randalls and Knightley, found on a visit to Leatherhead. That was a good thing, for she was abominably lazy about names, or else timid about seeming to borrow the names of strangers. She had used the plain English Christian names of the Austens over and over, Elizabeth, Edward, Jane, Frank, Henry, Fanny ; it was high time, her brother told her laughing, that she found some new ones.

9

So back she went to Chawton and all that summer of 1814 was working on her new novel, *Emma*. This time it was a book for her nieces, for young Fanny down at Godmersham, all in a flutter about her admirers and for bold brown Anna, over at Steventon, getting ready for her autumn wedding. 1814 was the summer when young Anna made such great friends with her Aunt Jane, and declared that she felt as if the original seventeen years between them had been reduced to seven, or none at all. She paid a long visit to Chawton in June, for she was glad to escape from her stepmother, who could not keep from nagging and teasing her about her engagement and was rude to Ben whenever he came to the house. It was much pleasanter over at Chawton, where her grandmother petted and made much of her and the aunts delighted in her lively talk. Anna was a great reader and it was her chief amusement to get one absurd novel after another out of the little circulating library in Alton High Street and read them aloud to her aunts, with peals of laughter as they sat stitching away at their charity needle-work. All enjoyed the fun, though Aunt Cassandra would sometimes wipe the tears from her eyes and beg Anna not to make her laugh so much. There was one particularly absurd novel in eight volumes, by a Mrs. Hunter, containing one story within another ; it had a heroine who was always in floods of tears. Aunt Jane and Anna laughed till they cried over this absurdity, they even concocted a letter to the authoress, derisively begging for more of its heroine's ridiculous adventures. Anna hid this letter away among her papers and found it again years afterwards, when all that merriment was done. She put it by among her dearest treasures, in the same bundle as the letters which Aunt Jane had written to her, that summer of 1814, about her own novel.

For Anna, who had scribbled all through her teens as her Aunt Jane used to do, was writing a story herself to while away the time until her wedding and she consulted Aunt Jane about it continually. She would come flying in with a bundle of manuscript, crying out, " Do but listen to this ; do tell me where I have gone wrong ? How can I contrive to make my hero a more spirited sort of fellow ? He is such a dull dog." And she would plump herself down on her own particular stool and chatter away by the hour, while Aunt Jane patiently put the last chapter of *Emma* under the blotting-paper and turned with a smile to listen. Even after she had gone home to Steventon she would send over great packages of her novel for Aunt Jane to correct. It was immature lively sprawling stuff ! the story dodged hither and thither like a wild March hare ; she would make a sketch of some character in one chapter and drop it in the next, as her bubbling fancy suggested. She had so many notions in her head that she could scarcely get them all down on paper. *Enthusiasm*, the thing was appropriately called at first ; later, to Aunt Jane's regret, the title was changed to *Which is the Heroine ?*

Aunt Cassandra thought it was rather too rambling ; she did not like desultory novels and feared that Anna's would be altogether too much so. Old Mrs. Austen laughed a great deal over it ; they read it aloud to her as she sat working on a pair of satin dancing-sandals for Anna's trousseau and the old lady thought it quite as good as anything of Jane's. She took it all very seriously, would send urgent messages because one of the minor characters had not returned a visit of civility with sufficient promptness and was much distressed that the heroine's mother had allowed her to wander romantically in rainy weather. " An anxious mother would not suffer it," Mrs. Austen complained. " I never liked it when Jane used to take those long walks in the dirt."

Dear Ben approved, because his love had written it ; but even he complained that there was not enough incident in the story. He did a little grudge the time that Anna spent on her scribbling, said she would never do anything worth printing and told her that once they were married she would have no more time for it. But Anna toiled on with her story and Aunt Jane was her chief comfort. Her letters were kind, charming, exactly like herself, full of dry quiet morsels of advice, about manners and etiquette, titles and introductions, about the geography of Devonshire, where the heroine lived, about the proper conduct of a widow settling in a strange neighbourhood. She praised Anna's choice of names, but uttered warnings about the use of outworn expressions, about the stilted air of conversations carried on in the third person, about using what she fastidiously called the *common novel style*. She wished everything to be simple, natural and lifelike. She would not allow Anna to pack her characters off to Ireland, a country of whose manners she could know nothing and advised her firmly to stick to Bath. She set down for her niece, with unconscious humility, what had always been her own guiding rule, never to write of anything which she did not know and love ! and concluded, " You are now collecting your people delightfully, getting them exactly into such a spot as is the delight of my life. Three or four families in a village is the very thing to work on."

10

Anna Austen was married to Benjamin Lefroy on the eighth of November, 1814, in her father's church at Steventon. There had been some question of putting the wedding off, for in September Charles Austen's poor little wife had died in childbirth on board the *Namur* and her baby with her. He was heartbroken, for the seven years of marriage with his Fanny had been exceedingly happy and all the family mourned her sincerely ; but in the end Ben and Anna got their way and were married on the appointed date, though the bride's stepmother seized upon the pretext of family mourning to make it a very simple affair. To the two brides-maids, however, it was a fairy tale. Caroline Austen was nine and Ben's niece, Anna Lefroy, only six ; they did not realise the gloom which James's disapproval and his wife's parsimony had cast over the occasion.

The bride wore a dress of fine white muslin and over it, against the November cold, a shawl of white silk shot with primrose. There were embossed flowers upon it and it had a long knotted fringe ! Uncle Frank had brought it home for her from China. On her head she had a small cap to match, of delicate yellow trimmed with lace ; the colour was infinitely becoming to her bright brown hair, her hazel eyes and sunny clear look. She was just of age and the prettiest girl in the neighbourhood. Her widely open dark eyes shone with delight as she kissed the two small brides-maids. They wore white frocks and had white ribbons on their straw bonnets, which were new for the occasion.

It was an early wedding, as was the fashion in those times. Between nine and ten in the morning the bride, Mrs. James Austen, Mrs. Lefroy and the bridesmaids, stepped carefully into the carriage in their simple finery and were driven slowly up the lane to the lonely old church. The gentlemen had walked on ahead, solemnly stalking like four black crows, all parsons ; the bride's father, the bridegroom and his two brothers. It was a dull and cloudy day, with rather a searching wind, there seemed to be nobody about in the empty fields. Within the church it was cold and gloomy, and the grey light of the November morning made its way through the narrow windows. There was no stove to give warmth, there were no flowers to give colour or brightness, even the little bridesmaids thought this part of the business rather solemn and frightening. They shivered in their thin muslins as they stood on the damp carpet of the aisle, one clutching Anna's posy, the other her glove, and listened to the mumble of words above their new bonnets. Mr. Lefroy read the service and James gave his daughter away. Cousin Ben muttered his part so low that you could hardly hear what he said, but the bride spoke up so clearly and beautifully that you could tell she meant every word she was saying ; she was not afraid of anything or anybody, she meant to be happy.

There was a great deal of kissing all round as soon as she was fairly married, and then everybody drove back to the Rectory. Mrs. James Austen had managed to avoid asking any guests outside the family, on the plea of mourning, but to the little girls the simple wedding breakfast was a great festivity. They were both extremely hungry and thought it a feast to have ham and tongue, eggs and hot rolls, with the addition of frothed chocolate ; they drank great mugs of this celestial beverage and fixed their rapt eyes upon the wedding cake which towered in the middle of the table. Aunt Anna cut it, with Cousin Ben holding her hand to steady the knife and there were speeches and more kisses. They each got a damp black slice of cake to nibble and make last as long as possible ; and they had a sip of sweet red wine out of the side of Cousin Ben's glass to drink the bride's health, that was very exciting.

All too soon it was over. The bride and bridegroom had to start away early, because they were going to drive all the way to their new home at Hendon and must be across Bagshot Heath before dark, for fear of highwaymen.

When the party was over the Lefroys went back to Ashe Rectory, and Caroline and her mother drove down to Chawton Great House, to stay with Uncle Frank and his family, who had got the loan of it for the winter. They went to see Grandmother Austen and the aunts the very next day and told them all about Anna's beautiful wedding. It was the first that Caroline had ever attended ! nodding her head very solemnly up and down she assured Aunt Jane that she would remember it all her life.

II

1814 was the autumn when young Edward first went to Winchester. Mrs. J. A. had made a fuss about letting her dear only son leave home. She had maintained that he was too young for Winchester, which she persisted in regarding as a rough rude place ; but James for once had held to his own opinion. To be sure, he had at first intended to send the boy to Eton ; but as the two of them were actually riding up to Deane Gate to catch the London coach, the reverend gentleman's horse shied with him into the bright and thorny blackberry hedge, where his small-clothes were so badly torn by a stout bramble that he could not with decency ride any farther. So he had to take Edward home again and there, as it were by the finger of Providence, lay a letter from a friend telling him such things against Eton that James changed his mind and decided to send his son to the older foundation. So when they rode out again it was in the opposite direction, to the Flower Pot Inn at Popham Lane, where they took the coach to Winchester and Edward was entered as a commoner.

His cousins, Ned and George Austen, had been there before him, Henry and William were there still. Their surname had just been changed to Knight, since their grandmother died and Edward came into his full inheritance. Ned and George had gone up to Oxford, but Henry and William had not left school yet, but were too old to do more than nod to their young cousin. There were young Heathcotes and Knatchbulls too ; Edward would find plenty of friends. " And we shall be able to drive down and see him if ever he is ill or unhappy," said his anxious mother. He was not yet twelve years old and small for his áge ; she was dreadfully afraid that the bigger boys would bully him. All November and December she talked of little else ; but when the boy came home at Christmas, at the end of Short Half, as the boys called it, though he had grown taller and thinner and much more untidy than when he went away, he seemed perfectly cheerful and none the worse for his experiences. Winchester was a *famous* school, he assured his grandmother and his aunts earnestly when he rode over with his father to visit them. At first he was inclined to praise everything, rather too loudly, saying he had far rather be in Commoners than in College, where the seventy scholars lived in medieval squalor and discomfort according to the rule of William of Wykeham. " Of course we don't see them," related Edward, " except in School or when we go Up Hills and even then they don't speak to us ; but the fellows say they wash under a pump in the yard, eat off wooden trenchers and have boiled beef four times a week. Doctor Gabell gives us much better dinners than they ever see, only it's a very long time between meals. I'm always hungry there. We get up at half-past five for chapel and do four hours *books* before breakfast and then we only get bread and beer. You can have as much as you like, but it isn't very good beer, it's too thick and new. Some of us put it into bottles," said he, leaning back against Aunt Cassy's arm and biting off a hunk of her good gingerbread. " We mix a spoonful of brown sugar with it, or a handful of raisins, and then we keep it under our beds for a day or two, till it begins to work and runs over the bottles. It tastes much better that way. We call it Bumble. I'll make some for you, Granny, if you like ; it's very good."

His grandmother commiserated with him over having to learn such great quantities of Greek and Latin verse off by heart. Ned and George, said the old lady, had always told her they were forced to work very hard at Winchester ; but young Edward was scornful about that. He had the Austen love of learning. " Ned was all right, I daresay," said he in a lordly way, " but Cousin George is nothing better than an idle dunce. He keeps a bandbox full of old *vulguses* to help him with his tasks and says he means to forget all his Greek and Latin as soon as he gets home." " Ah ! he is like his father," said Mrs. Austen fondly. " Dear Edward never had any love for his books. He has a most active mind, a clear head and a sound judgment; he is a man of business and so is your Uncle Henry. That your own dear father never was, but he has taste and learning and you must try to grow up as like him as you can." And Edward kicking his feet about a little, nevertheless said politely that he would do his best.

With Aunt Jane he was less guarded. She never fussed about anything and Edward did not need to stop and explain things to her. He found that she knew quite a lot of *notions* ! Ned and Georgy, she owned with a laugh, had taught her that Winchester language. She understood what was meant by a *remedy*, and *dispers* and *bevers*, the difference between going *Up Hills* and *Under Hills*, between a *toy* and a *scob*, between *bibling* and *tunding* and how to play marbles and *alley alley*. She understood how hateful it could be to have to fag for the older boys, how you had to light fires and polish boots, to empty and clean basins, to make beds and sweep floors, to button stiff gaiters with cold shaking fingers and then be knocked over backwards for not doing it fast enough. " Yes," said Edward, looking down, " when I first went there, I did hate it very much." He admitted that fagging on turf could be dreadfully cold too in the winter, standing and shivering on the edge of the football ground waiting to send the ball in again without a chance to show how fast you yourself could run. " We aren't allowed inside Meads, we only have a nasty small court called Commoner's Court, to play in." And it was bitter of a winter's morning, going *Up Hills* two by two on Tuesdays and Thursdays, whatever the weather. " The big fellows drop out before we ever get to St. Catherine's Hill. They go

out of bounds and buy themselves breakfast at Twyford or
St. Cross and sneak in again on the way home ; but we
little fellows have to stay inside Trench and shiver from
seven to nine without any breakfast. We call that Misery
Corner," said Edward, who was a cheerful enduring child
and did not complain about his lot. She told him, to hearten
him, that Uncle Frank and Uncle Charles had had a much
worse time when they went to the Naval Academy at
Gosport, but it had made men of them and Edward must
be a brave boy, like his uncles. " Yes, I know," said
Edward, swallowing stoutly. " I really do not mind it."
He vowed that he was looking forward to going back again
for *Long Half*. " Then we shall have a badger hunt *Up
Hills*," said Edward, " and in the summer, in Cloister Time,
we shall all go bathing in First Pot in the evenings and I
daresay I shall not be licked so often because I shall not
be a new fellow any more."

And Aunt Jane, in her pretty voice, said that Yes, it
would all be quite different then. Winchester was a
beautiful place ; she had always wanted to go to Winchester
in the summer. Perhaps some day she would come and
stay there and they might walk together in the meads, by
the river.

12

Fanny Knight, down in Kent in that autumn of 1814, was
dreadfully jealous of Cousin Anna, happily and safely
married to the man of her choice. Sulky silent Ben Lefroy,
who could not even make up his mind whether he wanted
to take Orders or not, would never have suited Fanny
herself, but by this time she was quite in two minds about
whether John Plumtre suited her either. There was no
change in his feelings and he had shown himself as devoted
as ever throughout that summer ; he was just the same as
he had always been, but the longer she looked at him the
less she liked him. Her ideal at present was something
fashionably Byronic, a pale handsome mysterious being with

one virtue and a thousand crimes. Poor John was not at all like that ; there was nothing of the *Corsair* in him, he could never play *Conrad* to her *Medora*, he was altogether too good, too sober, too much like that dreadful stick of a hero, Edmund Bertram, in Aunt Jane's *Mansfield Park*. Fanny tried to conceal the change in her feelings towards him, but John felt it and drew off. When they went to the Canterbury Assembly together he behaved very badly and only danced once with her, then stood about in corners and scowled jealously while she ran down the dance with other partners. At the races he was in one of his sulky fits, refused to admire her new bonnet, said some very rude things which quite vexed her and then stalked off and left her to sit alone in the carriage until her brothers and their friends came back to amuse her. She was really quite disgusted with John.

Then she and her father went to stay at Fredville and it was not at all as she remembered it. Old Mr. Plumtre, it seemed, was much distressed for money nowadays. Everything was shabby and old-fashioned, she was not put to sleep in the best spare room, but in a little back room, and had to sleep on sheets which had been turned side to middle. At Godmersham only the servants had such sheets. Then Mrs. Plumtre was a sour disagreeable woman who seemed to disapprove of Fanny's elegance, and there was a set of horse-faced sisters, bony and plain. John avoided her ; and her father, when they were home again, called her into the study and told her with a grave face that Mr. Plumtre had had losses. He could not promise the young couple such an establishment as would have been expected ; in fact he would prefer his son not to marry at all for the next three or four years. This was really dreadful ! Fanny's eyes filled with tears and her lip trembled. She felt that she was deep enough in love with poor John to run off with him the very next day, if he had only the spirit to suggest it ; but it made her shiver all over to think of waiting for three or four years. By that time, she was sure, she would not care about him any longer. Papa was kind, but not very helpful ; he wanted her to please herself, but she could see that he did not like the match. It was one of the times when she missed her mother more than words could say ; that kind and tender creature would have explained her own heart to her as anybody else could. She knew that she had encouraged John quite shamefully, everyone would blame her if she turned round and threw him over now. She cried herself to sleep, in her fourposter bed with the pink rose-sprigged curtains, to think how unhappy she was.

In the morning she had the splendid notion of writing for advice to Aunt Jane. Papa most luckily was going down to Chawton that week to collect his rents, give the tenants their yearly dinner, hear all about Cousin Anna's wedding and see his third and fourth sons, Henry and William, who now were commoners of Winchester in their turn. Fanny wrote sheet after sheet of her distress and perplexity in her pleasant little scrawl, packed it all inside a roll of music and enjoined Papa strictly not to let anybody set eyes on it except Aunt Jane. The fluttering little creature did not want Aunt Cassandra's cool eye to rest upon her letter, or Grandmamma Austen's loud laugh to ring out over her indecisions ; at Chawton they were only too apt to share out news. However, Aunt Jane would always keep a secret if you asked her to, and Fanny must write something else that would do to be read aloud or told.

Aunt Jane wrote her the sweetest letter in return. Fanny read and re-read the whole of it, sitting up in her bedroom when the others had gone to bed, curled up on the rug by the fire with the curtains drawn against the November night. Papa, it seemed, had hunted about most conscientiously till he found Aunt Jane alone in the dining-parlour before he handed over the packet and Aunt Jane had read the letter up in her own bedroom safe from penetrating eyes, while Aunt Cassy was dining at the Great House. Aunt Jane's letters were exactly like herself, affectionate, amused, very sensible, quite decided. You could almost see her brown eyes sparkle and hear her soft clear voice mocking you as you read ; she seemed to be talking to you as fast as she could all through the letter. She was as full of curiosity and concern as if she had been a girl of Fanny's own age, she talked the matter backwards and forwards just as they had done in Henrietta Street. " I was a good deal surprised at first. I had no suspicion of any change in your feelings ; but I have no scruple in saying that you cannot be in love. My dear Fanny, I am ready to laugh at the idea, but it is no laughing matter. From the time of our being together in London, I really thought you very much in love, but you certainly are not, there is no concealing it. What strange creatures we are ! It seems your being sure of him, as you say yourself, had made you indifferent."

She pitied poor dear John Plumtre very much and argued his case for him as charmingly as any aunt of his own could ever have done, recounting his many good qualities and making light of his dull sober ways, just as she had done in London. Then she broke off midway to exclaim, " My dear Fanny, I am writing what cannot be the smallest use to you. I am feeling differently every minute and shall not be able to suggest a single thing which could assist your mind. I could lament in one sentence and laugh the next ! Poor dear Mr. J. P. Oh ! dear Fanny ! Your mistake has been one that thousands of women fall into. He was the first young man who had attached himself to you. That was the charm and most powerful it is."

She admitted that Fanny had encouraged her unfortunate admirer to such a point as to make him feel almost secure of her and well-nigh argued herself and Fanny into taking pity on him. " There are such beings in the world," she lamented, " perhaps one in a thousand, as the creature you and I would think perfection . . . ; but such a person may not come your way, or if he does, he may not be the eldest son of a man of fortune, the brother of your particular friend, and belonging to your own county."

Fanny sighed, rumpled her curls, stretched out her bare feet to the fire and wondered not for the first time about that first lover of Aunt Jane's whose shadow fell across the pages of *Pride and Prejudice*. Grandmamma Austen with nods and winks had told her, when Anna got engaged to Ben Lefroy, that once upon a time another wedding had been confidently expected between an Austen daughter and a

Lefroy nephew, but nothing had come of it. Fanny, greatly daring, had asked Aunt Cassy whether Mr. Tom Lefroy (for that had been his name) had not sat for his portrait as Mr. Darcy ; had he been very proud and haughty, had he broken Aunt Jane's heart when she was young ? But Aunt Cassy, shaking her head, had replied firmly, " No such thing, my dear ; he paid your aunt a good deal of attention, but it was only a boy and girl affair. There was a little disappointment and disgust, I fancy, but he certainly did not break her heart. She has too much pride for that."

She spoke so firmly that you had to believe her, and when Fanny asked wilfully, " Was there never anybody else ? " put on her stiffest look, said, " You should not ask prying questions, my dear," got up and walked out of the room. Fanny was determined in her mind that once upon a time, somewhere or other, Aunt Jane had known and lost a man who was worthy of her, or she could never have written and spoken so sweetly as she did about constancy and kindness. For at the end of the letter, after she had set out all the worldly arguments in John Plumtre's favour, the dear woman veered right round like a weathercock and said exactly what Fanny wanted her to say, entreating the girl not to commit herself further and not to think of accepting John unless she really liked him. " Anything is to be preferred or endured," wrote Aunt Jane most seriously out of the sum of her experience, " rather than marrying without affection."

That really did settle the matter for Fanny, though she rubbed her forehead when she thought of the difficulties involved in breaking off her understanding with John. On this point Aunt Jane was her own brisk self. " Things are now in such a state that you must resolve upon one or the other, either to allow him to go on as he has done, or whenever you are together behaving with a coldness which may convince him that he has been deceiving himself. I have no doubt of his suffering a good deal for a time, a great deal when he feels that he must give you up ; but it is no creed of mine," she concluded in her own tart fashion, " that such disappointments kill anybody."

Fanny sent another scrawling reply and got an even more

decided answer. " Your affection gives me the highest pleasure, but indeed you must not let anything depend upon my opinion. You frighten me out of my wits! your own feelings and none but your own should determine such an important point." However, she did stick to her opinion that John Plumtre would not do. " I dare not say, Determine to accept him, the risk is too great for you. You will think me perverse perhaps! in my last letter I was urging everything in his favour, now I am inclining the other way, but I cannot help it. I am at present more impressed with the possible evil that may arise to you from engaging yourself to him in word or mind than with anything else. When I consider how few young men you have yet seen much of— how capable (yes, I do still think you very capable) of being really in love—and how full of temptation the next six or seven years of your life will probably be (it is the very period of life for the strongest attachments to be formed) I cannot wish you with your present very cool feelings to devote yourself in honour to him. It is very true that you may never attach another man, his equal altogether, but if that other man has the power of attaching you more, he would be in your eyes the most perfect. . . ." And she concluded, " The unpleasantness of appearing fickle is certainly great—but if you think you want punishment for past illusions there it is—nothing can compare with the misery of being bound without love—bound to one and preferring another. *That* is a punishment you do not deserve." Yes, Aunt Jane understood everything. She was perfectly right, the only thing to do was to give up John Plumtre, and that, before Christmas time, Fanny resolutely did.

13

Aunt Jane's second letter was dated from London. With Anna's wedding safely over Henry had invited his sister up to see his new house. Since Eliza's death his old restlessness had come out in him again very strongly. He had lost

patience that summer with the heat, noise and smell of the
streets round Covent Garden, had got rid of his apartment
over the bank and gone back to the freshness of Hans Town.
The Tilsons, who themselves had lately moved out of Sloane
Street because of the increasing traffic, had found him a
dear little cream-coloured house, very elegant and dandified,
in a newly-built crescent called Hans Place. He was at 23
and they were at 26, only three doors off ; they could go
out and call to each other across the gardens in between.
The curved houses were all exactly alike, of cream coloured
plaster, with flat fronts, mansard roofs, dormer windows
behind a parapet and little front gardens, each no bigger
than a pocket handkerchief, railed off from the cobbled
street. At the back they all had the advantage of overlooking the grounds of a big house. It belonged to a Lady
Charlotte Dennis and was called the Pavilion, in imitation
of the Regent's domed Indo-Chinese folly at Brighton. The
lady had urns, grottoes, statues, winding walks, even a
hermitage and a doll's house of a ruin, a sham castle muffled
in ivy, haunted by spiders and earwigs ; all this was crammed
into a space of some ten acres. When Henry sat on the small
wrought-iron balcony of his study, overlooking his back
garden, which was quite rural, he could easily fancy
himself twenty miles from London. In summer thick foliage
hid his neighbour's back windows, in winter there was a
dim foggy prospect of bare branches and a countrified smell
of dead leaves and damp earth.

Oddly enough, the house next door to him belonged to
Monsieur and Madame St. Quentin, of the Abbey School,
at Reading, where his sisters had been educated. They had
moved up to London some years back and the school was
now quite fashionable, noted for its deportment, its music
and its excellent French. Through the wall Henry could
hear their scales and five-finger exercises and the sound of
the dancing master's fiddle. When he looked down from
his balcony, in the recreation hour, he could see rosy little
girls in long muslin gowns, with sashes under their armpits,
playing battledore and shuttlecock, or blindman's-buff, or
walking about with their arms round each other's waists,

just as Jane and Cassandra used to do, no doubt, in the Abbey ruins. When his sister came up to stay with him, she was much amused by the sight of them.

Owing to the family mourning he was not able to give his sister a very gay time. Dinner visits were exchanged of course with the hospitable Tilsons, and Henry and his partner sat together over the port, talking about the proceedings of the peace conference. Over in Vienna, that December of 1814, the future of Europe had to be decided and that was no easy task. The Russians, it appeared, were determined to have Poland ; the Prussians demanded Saxony ; the ingenious Monsieur de Talleyrand was doing his best for his defeated country under its new Bourbon King ; the little nations were anxiously watching the Four Great Powers. There was a general scramble for territory and power going on behind the screen of banquets, fancy-dress *fêtes*, intrigue and gaiety, in the Hapsburg palaces. Henry repeated the Comte de Ligne's epigram, *Le Congrès danse, mais il ne marche pas*, and his partner shrugged his shoulders ; these two comfortable City bankers, who had once been young soldiers together, were not such fools as to suppose that the banishment of the Emperor Napoleon to the island of Elba was going to stop all fighting in Europe. There was a new weight dropped into the balance of power, Russia ; nobody could tell yet how far that might tip the balance. They said to each other gloomily that if the Czar turned sulky then they did not know what would happen to the Funds.

Meanwhile upstairs Miss Jane Austen and Mrs. Tilson sustained what Mrs. Tilson supposed to be the conversation proper to a woman of fashion. Dear Mrs. Tilson was a little afraid of Henry's sister, who had written those clever books. She herself talked most easily and naturally about her twelve children and housekeeping and the fashions ; but for Miss Austen's benefit she felt herself obliged to discourse in a very high style about the summer's festivities for the Allied Sovereigns. London had been in a ferment ; there had been three nights of illuminations and a sea battle in miniature had been staged upon the Serpentine, to the great delight of her children. All the ladies had run mad about the Czar of Russia ; she had seen him several times herself, tall, pale, handsome, dissipated ; they said he was going mad, as his father had done. " You know he brought his sister with him, the Duchess of Oldenburg, a little cat-faced woman, who wore a great bonnet, with such wide wings that you could hardly see her face. All the women in London copied it ! I have one myself, but I believe it does not suit my odd face. The King of Prussia was a very plain fellow, stout and grizzled, he was very little cheered. The Prince Regent is more unpopular than ever. He was positively afraid to show himself in the streets with his guests for fear he might be pelted and hooted at. His coachman has orders to drive as fast as he can ; whenever the Prince goes out, you see his carriage going like the wind through the park, with the Life Guards galloping after. The manner in which his Royal Highness is talked of by all ranks of people is quite frightful, I do assure you. They say he is in a very poor state of health, and will die of an apoplexy or run mad, like his poor old father. Lady Hertford does not manage him near so well as Lady Jersey used to do. The Princess of Wales is much more popular than she used to be. People are sorry for her because her husband has treated her so ill. When she showed herself at the Opera House, for the gala performance, she had all the applause. Nobody would look at the Czar or the King of Prussia until she had bowed and sat down. And dear little Princess Charlotte has broken her engagement to the Prince of Orange after all ! They say it is because she stands such a good chance of being Queen of England within a year or two that she cannot be allowed to go out of the country. They must find her a husband who is willing to live in England, but I do not know how any man is to court her, for her father is so furiously jealous of her that he shuts her up and reads all her letters." So good Mrs. Tilson ran on with an air of laborious elegance, growing more and more nervous and jingling the teacups as she served that stiff Miss Austen, who sat demurely answering Yes and No, with hardly a smile or a bow whatever you told her.

" She is such a country mouse, such a book worm,"
decided Mrs. Tilson, angrily, " that she takes no interest in
what goes on in London." Only towards the end of the
evening did Miss Austen come alive, turning the conversation to Henry's dead wife and saying, with quite a heartfelt
sigh, " You know it seems very strange to me to be in this
part of the world without Eliza." Then they had quite a
cosy talk about poor Mrs. Henry's last illness, how bravely
she had endured her miseries and how charming she had
been when she was young. " Madame la Comtesse and I
were such very particular friends," sighed Mrs. Tilson,
touching one corner of her eye carefully with her lace
handkerchief, so as not to cry in good earnest, " when we
were brides together, with the regiment, in Ipswich in the
year 'ninety-eight."

Miss Austen agreed with Mrs. Tilson that poor Henry
would probably be happier if he were to marry again. The
Tilsons, indeed, had a friend who would be just the right
wife for him, a Miss Burdett, a very agreeable fine woman
who had lately been to visit them ; and there was talk of
another lady up at Hendon. Henry, rather suspiciously, had
suggested that she might be asked to drink tea with his
sister while she was in town ; however, nothing came of
that. Henry, it seemed, had not yet had time enough to
forget his bright Eliza.

14

Charles's three little girls, Cassy, Harriet and Fanny, were
in London that winter at Number 22 Keppel Street,
Bloomsbury, where their maternal grandfather, Mr. Palmer,
had a large handsome house, full of heavy mahogany
furniture and West Indian curios, with a black footman in
the hall and a brace of unmarried daughters in the drawing-
room. When poor Mrs. Charles Austen died the old
nurseries on the third floor were opened up, and her little
girls came to live in them. They thought Keppel Street very
dull and dark ; there was nothing to look at out of the barred

nursery windows except plane trees and sparrows and the
roofs of the houses opposite ; it was a sad change from their
snug quarters on the guardship at the Nore. Dear Mamma
had gone away on a very long journey, and they must not
ask about her or wonder when she was coming back again,
because it made Papa cry. He did come to see them as
often as he could, but he had to be on board the *Namur*
most of the time ; and though Aunt Harriet Palmer was
very kind they were used to her by this time. It was far
more exciting to have dear Aunt Jane walk in one morning,
in her black velvet pelisse, with her face rosy from the
winter weather and Uncle Henry behind her, with his arms
full of presents.

Four-year-old Harriet, who was the most demonstrative
of the three, sat in Aunt Jane's lap throughout the visit and
little Fanny, who was only just two and could not talk
plain, lisped and babbled to her ; only Cassy, the eldest,
was shy and held a little off from the bright visitant. She
did not know what her elders were talking about when Aunt
Jane laughed at Uncle Henry over the three dark heads
and complained, " That puss Cassy does not shine in the
tender feelings. She will never be a Miss O'Neal ; more in
the Mrs. Siddons line, I fancy." Cassy pouted and hunched
her shoulders, but it was all explained by kind Uncle Henry
as some of Aunt Jane's nonsense about an Irish actress whom
they had seen the night before in a play called *The Fatal
Marriage*. Then the little girls wanted to go to the theatre
themselves. Henry promised that when they were a little
older and could keep awake all through the performance he
would take a box for them. Meanwhile, he would go with
them one of these fine days to Astley's Circus in the Westminster Bridge Road, where they would see clowns and
performing horses or if they preferred it, the beasts at the
Exeter 'Change. This and the sugared almonds which he
distributed cheered the three little motherless girls immensely ; they were very good and hardly cried at all when
he and Aunt Jane went away.

The young bride Anna got one visit from her dear Aunt
Jane at Hendon and thought herself entitled to another,

but it seemed that Uncle Henry had arranged too many
engagements in Hans Place for Aunt Jane to take the long
drive twice. The bride and bridegroom were lodging with
his brother, and Aunt Jane had to be taken all over the
house ! those sharp eyes of hers carefully inspected Anna's
own bedroom drawers and cupboards. She looked rather
tired, Anna thought. She was even a little cross and
difficult, shaking her head over the extravagance of a new
piano, telling the bride that the twenty-four guineas would
have been better spent on sheets and towels and refusing to
admire a dashing new violet cloth pelisse which had been
the bride's first London purchase. She had these fretful
critical fits more often than she used to do. Anna tossed
her bright brown curls wilfully when she was told that her
pelisse did not suit her. " I daresay I look hideous in it,"
said she, " but no matter, it is my dear Ben's favourite
colour." She promised to make everyone in Hendon read
Aunt Jane's books and confessed that she had done no more
work on *Which is the Heroine ?* " But we have a delicious
scheme, Ben and I. We find we both detest London, we
would not settle there for the universe. We have quite
decided to come back to Hampshire. We are going to rent
the half of Wyards farm from the bailiff and live there till
Ben is ordained and has got himself a living. I am sure I
could never be happy for long away from you and from dear
Chawton." Aunt Jane, quite melted, kissed her warmly and
said that it would be delightful to have her back again.
" And then, you know, we may go on writing our books
together and you will tell me how to finish *Which is the
Heroine ?* " cried Anna, but Aunt Jane, with her faint smile,
tired and mocking, would only answer, " My dear, you will
have better things to do than to write books."

Altogether it was a most successful visit for Aunt Jane,
except that her own business, the matter about which she
had come up to London, did not go off quite as she had
hoped ; for Mr. Egerton, her publisher, would not after all
risk a second edition of *Mansfield Park*. Henry and she went
down to see him at his shop, the Military Library in Whitehall, and found him very dubious. " The first edition sold

out very quickly—I grant you that—it was very well spoken
of ; but the public is always more ready to praise than to
buy," he told his authoress. She answered drily, " We cannot
wonder at that, Mr. Egerton," and rose to go. Relieved at
finding the lady so reasonable, he shook her by the hand
and said very civilly that he hoped she would let him see
her next novel when it was ready for the press. He was sure
that so industrious a writer must be well into another novel
by this time. Yes, said Miss Austen, looking down shyly,
she was at work upon another tale. She had done about
half of it. The theme was matchmaking among three or
four families in a country village ; but the heroine, she was
afraid, would not be liked so well as Elizabeth Bennett or
Fanny Price ; she was rather a managing young woman.
Mr. Egerton asked whether she had chosen her title yet,
but she had not and could only suggest that the book might
be called after its heroine, who bore the romantic and
fashionable name of *Emma*. He approved and they parted
with mutual compliments ; good Mr. Egerton could not
see very much in her books, himself. He thought that they
lacked incident, though he admitted that the connoisseurs
approved them. He was pleased enough to have Miss
Austen on his list, but he did not think her sales would
ever enrich him greatly.

IX

Chawton—Winchester

1815-1817

I

THREE or four families in a country village was the
theme of the novel which Jane finished in 1815, the
year of Waterloo. She had taken Alton, with its long red
street, its bow-windowed houses, its coaching inn, its
crowded little shops, and had popped it down somewhere
between Leatherhead and Dorking, near the Cooks. All
through that long golden summer she peopled her imaginary
village of Highbury with characters of her own. This time
it was a book for her nieces, for new-married Anna and
wilful little Fanny, who might both see themselves shadowed
in the heroine, the glowing warm-hearted Emma, self-
confident and spoilt, always meddling with other people's
business, but teachable and generous, able to confess and
profit by her own mistakes.

Over against Emma stood an enigmatic elegant young
woman, Jane Fairfax, dark and silent, wrapped in the cloak
of her own misery, an exiled being who reminded Cassandra
of her sister in her unhappy days at Bath. This mournful
creature, another of Jane's Cinderella heroines, was capable
of a passion which the warm and open-hearted Emma could
never display ; she was rewarded in the end by the capture
of the somewhat unworthy being on whom her sad and
constant fancy had long been fixed. Emma was handed
over to a delightful steady elderly hero, Mr. Knightley, a
little like Edward Knight ; and Emma's friend Harriet, a
goose of a girl, was matched with the sober farmer she
deserved.

There was a crowd of amusing minor characters ; a young
ambitious toady of a parson with a rich vulgar wife was

particularly well observed, and Jane Fairfax had a garrulous aunt, Miss Bates, cheerful, uncomplaining, dreadfully poor and tiresome, but with the kindest heart in the world. Fanny Knight knew exactly where Aunt Jane had found Miss Bates! she was old Miss Milles from Canterbury to the life. Emma had a father, Mr. Woodhouse, sweet, affectionate, absurdly preoccupied with his own ailments, who much resembled the Reverend George Austen in the years of his dotage at Bath; only Jane had got mixed for once with her ages and had made him much too old to be the father of a gay light-hearted girl, just twenty-one. He should really have been her grandfather. Cassandra knew, too, where her sister had got the notion of making Jane Fairfax a governess. It was from poor silly Ann Sharpe, who used to sit and tell her troubles to Jane in the schoolroom at Godmersham, after the children had gone to bed. Ann Sharpe had never been for a visit though there had been attempts to secure her, both at Southampton and Chawton; but she still wrote to Jane, telling her troubles. She had always been a great one for letters. Jane heard often from her that year; she was up in Yorkshire, in a very good situation. Her employer was a baronet, no less, a certain Sir William Pilkington, a widower with several delightful children. How charming it would be, Jane said mockingly to Cassandra, if Sir William would but marry Miss Sharpe. If she had been writing a novel about them, that was how she would have ended it.

Altogether *Emma* was a happy book, full of flickering summer sunshine, peaceful and contented, like a walk down a country lane; it was a story that she told in the afternoon of her life, before she knew how little time she had left for such pretty follies, before the clouds began to gather in her sky. She had worked at it steadily, all through the previous winter. In the spring it had suffered an interruption from public anxieties, for the Emperor Napoleon had escaped from Elba, his island-prison and had landed in France. His old soldiers had flocked to join him from every town and village, he had marched upon the capital and seized the throne again. For three months Europe had been turned upside

down, but by midsummer the battle of Waterloo had been
fought and won, and the bells were rung and bonfires lit in
England for the last time. The eagle was caught and caged
for ever; the Emperor was to be imprisoned in Saint
Helena for the rest of his natural life. Frank Austen reported
it as a lonely misty island, far out in mid-Atlantic, a God-
forsaken spot, from which rescue was impossible. " He will
never get off from there," Frank said. " We are finished
with him for good."

He and his wife that year had the loan of Chawton Great
House from kind Edward, for as long as they chose, but
Frank was restless and unhappy. He had been on half-pay
ever since the old *Elephant* got back from her Baltic cruise,
and now that the war was over and so many of the older
captains were being turned on shore, he began to fear that
he would never have another ship. He fidgeted about the
Great House like a bluebottle; Mrs. F. A. was at her wits'
end to devise little jobs for him to do about the place which
would not vex Edward when he came down to visit them.
She thought they would do better in a house of their own,
where Frank could put up shelves and cupboards and make
nets for his own wall fruit. She had heard of one in Alton
which might suit them.

Mrs. F. A., whom everybody nowadays called Aunt
Frank, had grown from the slender lively girl of the Ramsgate
sands into a comfortable cow-like mother of five children,
all with Austen names, Mary Jane and Cassy, Frank, Henry
and George. She was to lie in again that autumn and she
and Anna Lefroy spent the summer months sitting under
trees together, sewing baby linen and chatting cosily. Her
experienced advice was a great comfort to Anna, who was
inclined to be nervous and fidgety. Aunt Frank had
placidly shifted her nursery from one seaside lodging to
another, had born her children in Portsmouth, Southampton or Deal and often told Anna that she might think
herself lucky to have a stay-at-home husband. " Nothing
ever ailed me, my dear, so long as Frank was with me ;
but when he was at sea I was always fancying something
wrong with me. This is the first time we have had a true

home together and very happy it makes me. If it were not
for his disappointment I could wish that he might never put
to sea again."

2

Chawton Cottage, that summer, was swarming with grandchildren. Uncle Charles's three little girls, Cassy, Harriet
and Fanny, came down from Bloomsbury, Uncle Frank's
quintet ran in and out as they chose, and Edward and
Caroline rode over on their ponies from Steventon. They
were always crowding up to Aunt Jane. They were old
enough now to be amused by her cleverness and enchanted
with her sweetness. She could make anything amusing to a
child. She told the most delightful stories, chiefly of fairy-
land, and her fairies all had characters of their own. She
would continue a story for days together, a little bit at a
time, making it up as she went along and always leaving off
at the most exciting moment. When they wanted to dress
up she would give them whatever they wanted out of her
wardrobe, and she was always the most entertaining visitor
in a make-believe house they had under the lilacs. Once
she made up a conversation between Caroline, Mary Jane
and Cassy, supposing they were all grown-up ladies, on the
day after a ball. When they went home again they used to
write her letters, directed to Pondy House, which she
answered in a nonsense language, with P's at the beginnings
of all the words, full of family jokes about fleas and messages
about hares and pet dormice.

When Caroline came to stay her chief delight was to stand
beside Aunt Jane as she played the piano in the mornings.
There was a heap of music books at the Cottage, into which
Aunt Jane had copied out concertos and songs, Handel's
Water Music, the minuet from *Ariadne*, and a very amusing
piece called *The Battle of Prague*, which imitated cannon,
the rattle of musketry, galloping horses, bugle calls and even
the groans of the wounded in the bass ; all the children
thought this very exciting. There were songs and lessons

oo for young beginners and from these Aunt Jane taught Caroline to finger the notes, play scales and even attempt a tune called *The Hermit*.

In Spetember Aunt Frank, as became a sea officer's wife, bore another boy for the King's ships and in October Anna Lefroy had a little daughter who was christened Jemima. Caroline was intensely excited about the two new babies and particularly exalted at finding herself an aunt at nine years old. She wrote to Aunt Jane about it all, and Aunt Jane replied in a charming letter, which Caroline put away in her own precious shell-box from Ramsgate and meant to keep always. " I am sorry you got wet in your ride. Now that you are become an Aunt you are a person of some consequence and must excite great interest whatever you do. I have always maintained the importance of Aunts as much as possible and I am sure of your doing the same." She gave some good advice about Caroline's practising her scales regularly on Aunt Jane's own piano, while she was staying at the Cottage and learning to thump out some other tune than the *The Hermit*. She promised to read a story which the child had written, then wound up with quite a royal flourish, ' I am, my dear Sister Aunt, yours affectionately, Jane Austen."

3

It was sad that dear Aunt Jane was not at Chawton to join in the family visits to the two mothers, the comparison of the two new babies, the tracing of family resemblance in eyes and noses in which all the family were delighting ; but she was in London and in great anxiety, for Uncle Henry was very ill and the grown-ups were all shaking their heads over her letters about him. Aunt Jane had gone up to Hans Place on business, just before Jemima was born, because she had finished her story about the girl called *Emma* and Uncle Henry wanted her to change her publisher. The great Mr. Murray, who had published Lord Byron's poems and owned the *Quarterly Review*, thought highly of Miss Austen's work

and was actually willing to pay £450 for *Emma*, so anxious
was he to add her name to his list. However, he wanted to
take over the copyright of her earlier novels as well, but
Uncle Henry thought that made the offer quite a shabby
one, for Aunt Jane had made more than £450 out of
Mansfield Park and *Sense and Sensibility* before her name was
known.

So Aunt Jane went up to see Mr. Murray and in the
middle of the whole business Uncle Henry fell sick. One
day he came back early from the office, complaining of the
unseasonable heat of St. Luke's little summer and went
to bed with one of his bilious attacks. Aunt Jane hoped at
first that it was nothing serious, for Uncle Henry had
arranged all sorts of festivities for her which would be
nothing without him, but his illness proved more alarming
than had been expected. He developed some fever and his
old pain in the chest. That frightened Aunt Jane, for long
ago, when he was in the Militia, after he married Aunt
Eliza, they had been afraid of some mischief in his lungs.
So she sent round in a hurry for a young surgeon from the
corner of Sloane Street, who was known to the Tilsons.

Mr. Haden was said to be clever and was certainly very
attentive. He seemed to understand the case, thought little
of the pain in the chest, talked learnedly of a general
inflammation and bled Uncle Henry three times. The sick
man was an excellent patient and that in itself was alarming;
for he did not usually sit well under the doctors' hands. He
was altogether too docile, lay quietly in his bed, made no
complaint, and swallowed whatever medicine, tea, or barley
water was given to him.

Then two days after Jemima was born he took a sudden
turn for the worse. Everything was upside down; Uncle
Edward was fetched from Godmersham; Caroline's father
came over from Steventon, took Aunt Cassandra up with
him to London to help with the nursing, and Caroline was
left to keep her grandmother company at Chawton.

For a week nobody knew whether Henry would live or
die, but young Mr. Haden's skill and his own good hopeful
constitution pulled him through. Cassandra went back to

Chawton with James and Edward returned to Kent, but sent up his daughter Fanny to keep her Aunt Jane company throughout Uncle Henry's convalescence. Nobody could have been more welcome than she. It was a warm golden November, exquisite, unseasonable, a pleasant languid idle time for the invalid and his two nurses. He sat out on his iron balcony, or even took a turn in his small garden, though Mr. Haden frowned on the imprudence of a carriage drive. Friends came to visit him, sent messages, left books; pheasants and grapes came up by coach from Godmersham twice a week. Mr. Haden was quickly promoted from the degree of medical attendant to that of family friend, he dined with them several times and appeared much struck with Fanny and she with him. She could not of course take his admiration seriously. Though a London surgeon was a step or two higher than a country apothecary, he was still not a possible match for Miss Knight, the heiress of Godmersham Park, but she did flirt with him, just a little! she could not resist making a small hole in his heart. It was a peep over the hornbeam hedge of propriety, a downward glance from the barred window, before she turned away to fulfil her proper destiny. The young man was handsome, lively, he had good manners and pleasant conversation. The two young people talked uninterruptedly by the hour about Lord Byron's delightful poems, capping quotations from the *Corsair* and the *Bride of Abydos* and *Lara*; they argued whether Scott's *Marmion* or his *Lady of the Lake* were the better poem. Mr. Haden was musical too, that was his greatest charm for Fanny. He had a voice, though he was shy and would not raise it for their entertainment, protesting that he could not sing without a pianoforte accompaniment and would rather listen while Miss Knight played the harp.

She played and sang too, for she had a new song which suited her pure tender little voice. Mr. Meyer, her music master, had just given it to her from the latest volume of Mr. Moore's delicious *Irish Melodies*. There were three volumes already of these plaintive laments, full of early death, broken hopes and star-crossed lovers; they were the rage in all fashionable circles. " *She is far from the land where her young hero sleeps, And Lovers around her are sighing, But coldly she turns from their gaze and weeps, For her heart in his grave is lying.*" So sang Fanny, with as much plaintive expression as she could muster, bending to the harp, delighting in her new green gown, the soft candle-lit room and the rapt attention of her audience. Uncle Henry reclined upon the sofa, looking like a sick Sultan in his Indian chintz dressing-gown, beating time with one languid finger ; while Aunt Jane shaded her face from the firelight with her slender hand, and the young man beyond the candle-lit circle kept his dark fiery eyes fixed upon the performer. That song was going to have a long life. Years afterwards, when Fanny was safely married to a most eligible neighbour and had forgotten all of Mr. Haden except his eyes and his name, young ladies would still be singing it in Kentish drawing-rooms. She would pat her soft hands together and applaud gently, saying, " Very pretty, my dear ; very pretty indeed. I always think the old songs are the sweetest. I used to sing that one myself when I was a girl ; dear me, it must have been in the year of the battle of Waterloo."

4

Meanwhile the negotiations with Mr. John Murray had been hanging fire, for Jane had not wished her brother's convalescence to be harassed with them, but in the end the publisher himself very politely came to Hans Place and paid a call upon his unknown authoress. He proved to be a pleasant sensible man, who might have been called handsome if he had not accidentally lost an eye in his schooldays. He was then rising to the height of his prosperity. During the last three years he had brought out all those romantic poems which had made Lord Byron famous ; he owned and published the *Quarterly Review*, for which Robert Southey, the Laureate, had written so many articles and essays ; he had a share in the *Edinburgh Review*, had been part publisher of Scott's *Marmion* and would have been very glad to bring out *Waverley* and *Guy Mannering* if their author had not been bound to his own firm Ballantyne's. It would certainly be a feather in Jane's cap if her new novel could be published from his office at 50 Albemarle Street. He for his part had already smelt a change in the wind of public favour. Lord Byron had shocked too many people with his oddities. Though he was married and was supposed to be settled, people could not forget the many scandals about him. Walter Scott had turned from poetry to prose ; both Turkish and Gothic romance were going out, a new kind of novel was coming into fashion, which concerned itself much more with everyday life. Miss Austen seemed to do this kind of thing as well as any ! he was curious to see her.

She proved much what he had expected, a well-mannered gentlewoman, not too young, with a shrewd eye, a quiet smile and a dry way of speaking which appealed to the Scottish side of him ; fresh from the tantrums of his Lordship and the caprices of fashionable women, Mr. Murray was exceedingly pleased with Miss Austen. He paid her a great many compliments, he was so polite indeed that she declared it quite overcoming. " He is a rogue, of course," said she to Henry afterwards, " but a civil one." They came to terms without much difficulty ; it was always John Murray's boast that he did not play the Jew to his authors. The new novel was set up immediately, and all through November the printer's boy came and went ; Jane sat upstairs with Henry correcting proofs while the invalid, propped on pillows, enjoyed Mr. Murray's latest successes, Miss Helen William's narrative of her recent travels in liberated France and Walter Scott's poem on *The Field of Waterloo*. She was disappointed and vexed by some printer's delays and at one time almost despaired of getting home for Christmas ; but Mr. Murray sent many apologies, blamed the paper shortage due to the late war, promised immediate improvement and soothed and complimented her back into tolerable comfort.

The new novel was to be dedicated to the Prince Regent himself and this had come about through young Mr. Haden. The surgeon, willing to recommend himself to Miss Fanny's literary aunt, had begged leave to present a friend and admirer of her works, the Reverend James Stanier Clarke,

Librarian at Carlton House. This gentleman proved to be a great thick-headed toady, as stupid as an owl and as vain as a peacock, who had somehow proved supple enough to recommend himself to the Prince Regent ; and one November morning he conducted her through the State apartments of the Prince's town house. It stood in its own secluded garden on the north side of St. James's Park, crammed with furniture, antique vases, chandeliers, statues and a magpie collection of porcelain. Bowing and smirking, making knight's moves this way and that across the black-and-white marble squares of the entrance hall, Mr. Clarke attended Miss Austen through a preposterous range of saloons, a blue velvet closet, a green-and-crimson drawing-room, a Gothic conservatory shaped like an abbey, a dining-room whose columns had capitals like Prince of Wales's feathers, a ball-room hung with blue satin, in which the Regent had entertained the exiled King of France at an Oriental masquerade. Lingering among the busts and calf-bound volumes of the library and bowing with his hand on his heart in imitation of his master, the reverend gentleman assured Miss Austen that it would be very well received if she would dedicate her forthcoming work to his Royal Highness. " I assure you, Madam, the Regent has read and admired all your publications. There is a set of them in each of his libraries."

The flattered authoress consented and laid herself open to a succession of fulsome letters from the reverend gentleman, in which he begged her to write a novel all about himself. She was urged to delineate in some future work the habits of life and character and enthusiasm of a clergyman who should pass his time between town and country, who should go to sea as the friend of some distinguished naval character about a court, who should be fond of and entirely engaged in literature and be no man's enemy but his own. She gently disentangled her skirts from these briers, objecting that she had no qualifications for such a task, no classical education, no extensive acquaintance with English literature; but the absurd fellow blundered on. There was no snubbing him. He urged her to make all her friends send sketches to help her, offered two volumes of his own sermons, written and preached upon the Ocean, to pad out her story ; then went off at a tangent suggesting that a historical romance about the House of Coburg would be very interesting to the public.

For there was a Royal wedding in prospect ; Mrs. Tilson had already wearied Miss Austen at some length with her delight over the betrothal of the Princess Charlotte, the heir to the throne, and the handsome engaging modest Prince Leopold of Coburg. " It is a true love match," exclaimed Mrs. Tilson, clasping her hands and putting her head on one side. " They are so delightfully suited to each other ! he has adored her ever since the visit of the Allied Sovereigns. She is to be married in a worked India muslin gown, with a pattern of ears of corn, embossed in bright and dead silver tinsel, she is to wear a garland of white roses instead of a coronet, they are to live at Claremont in Surrey and the wedding is to be in May." Dear Mrs. Tilson could not have been more delighted if she had been marrying off her own daughter ; and the Reverend James Stanier Clarke was equally happy, for he had secured the post of English private secretary to Prince Leopold and was to remain at Brighton, in attendance upon the blond German bridegroom. This at least distracted his attention from Miss Austen ; she dismissed him more politely than he deserved, vowing that she could no more write a romance than an epic poem. " I could not sit seriously down " (her letter ran), " to write a serious romance under any other notice than to save my life : and if it were indispensable for me to keep it up and never relax into laughing at myself or other people, I am sure, I should be hung before I had finished the first chapter. No, I must keep to my own style and go on in my own way ; and though I may never succeed again in that, I am convinced that I should totally fail in any other."

One other invitation she refused, to a literary party at which the guest of honour was to be the famous, indeed the notorious, French authoress Madame de Stael. This lady at that time was living in the leafy suburb of Peckham and was much fêted by the fashionables, who always exalt a

foreign artist above a native one. Henry was very anxious
that his sister should accept this invitation, but Parson
Austen's daughter shrank into her shell at the thought of
being presented as one of Mr. Murray's latest discoveries, a
novelist of the *vie de province,* and set down to bandy compliments and literary criticism with a rouged, battered black-
eyed Frenchwoman, plumed, no doubt, and shrieking like
any macaw. Henry could not understand his sister's absurd
timidity. " Why must you make such a piece of work
about it ? You are a lioness now, my dear, and must learn
to take your proper place among the rest. Why should you
be afraid of Madame de Stael ? She cannot gobble you up,
or if she tries, you must sharpen your claws and fly at her,
English against French. I warrant your *Emma* will live as
long as her *Corinne.*"

That of course was only dear Henry's teasing, he was
always excessively proud of his clever sister. It was plain
that he wanted to go to the party himself. Very likely he
was looking forward to trying out his French, grown rusty
since Eliza's death, upon a lady who, if all were true that
was said of her, still had a greedy eye for a handsome man.
" I am sure I can persuade Haden to let me escort you," he
persisted, " or if he thinks the night air dangerous for me,
James Tilson shall go with you and good Mr. Murray see
you are well looked after." But his sister shrank back with
tears of honest distress and alarm in her bright eyes. " I
cannot go, Henry, indeed I cannot. I should dislike it
above all things, I wish you would not press me to do it."
She seemed quite worn out with all the nursing and hard
work which had come upon her lately ; now that he looked
at her, she was dreadfully white and staring. With a
trembling lip she implored him like a child, " Pray do not
tease me, I want to go home," and from that nothing would
budge her.

5

She returned to a wet Hampshire Christmas ! the pond was brimful and overflowing, the roads dirty, and the walls of the cottage damp. She, who had scampered through the lanes as a girl, hated wet nowadays as a cat does and missed the warmth of Henry's town house, yet she was thankful to be out of London.

Emma appeared in time for Christmas, but dated for the next year, 1816, in three volumes at a guinea, duly dedicated to the Prince Regent. One of her presentation copies went to Carlton House, another to Wyards, with a pretty note offering Anna an *Emma* for her Jemima. She was more anxious about this novel than usual and actually wrote down a list of opinions about it, a thing Cassandra had never known her do before. At Chawton her mother thought it entertaining, but neither she nor the Leigh Perrots would budge from their devotion to *Pride and Prejudice* ; Cassandra preferred the pensive beauty of *Mansfield Park*. Frank had a word for it which pleased his sister as well as any, praising " the peculiar air of nature throughout." Of her two nieces, Anna delighted in Emma and liked her better than any of the other heroines ; but down at Godmersham Fanny Knight flew out like a little angry kitten, protesting that she could not bear Emma herself. Both she and her father, however, thought the sensible well-bred country gentleman who was the hero quite delightful, as well they might, for he certainly resembled Edward, and Fanny, who adored her father, was always wishing that she could find a husband exactly like him. They forwarded a batch of other criticisms; the character of the snobbish young parson had drawn grave rebukes from two rectories, where the incumbents thought that in times like these the authoress was wrong to draw such clergymen. However, Fanny's aunt, Mrs. Cage, sent a charming message. " I am nearly killed with these precious treasures. They are unique and really more fun than I can express. I am at Highbury all day and can't help feeling I have just got into a new set of acquaintances. No one writes such good sense and so very comfortable."

From Steventon, of course, came faint praise. James and Mary, who always found fault when they could, liked *Emma* less than the other two and thought the language difficult. Most neighbours were lukewarm ; Alethea thought Miss Bates tiresome, Mrs. Elton overdone, and Harriet Smith altogether too silly ; Mrs. Guiton thought it too natural to be interesting, and Mrs. Digweed declared that if she had not known Miss Jane had written it she would hardly have got through it. To Chawton and Alton it was all too much like their own everyday lives, while over at Kintbury the Reverend Fulwar Fowle yawned over the first and last chapters one evening after dinner, then thankfully shut it up, for his wife had told him that he would not find Cousin Jane's latest novel at all to his taste.

People betrayed themselves by their reasons for liking or disliking the book. As usual they found originals for the characters among strangers quite unknown to the authoress ! there was even a Mrs. Dixon who liked it the less for finding her own name in it. Walter Scott gave the new authoress a very handsome review in the *Quarterly*, but that was only to be expected since John Murray owned the paper ; but even Mr. Jeffreys, the terrifying critic of the *Edinburgh Review*, actually confessed to having been kept up three nights reading it. Long after everybody else, dear Charles wrote from the Mediterranean that he was delighted with *Emma*, more so than even with his favourite *Pride and Prejudice*. Sitting in the stern cabin of his frigate the *Pheasant*, sailing among the Greek Islands, with the wine-dark Aegean rustling outside the open porthole and the sunshine swinging to and fro across his knees, he had read it three times in the passage.

6

Jane needed something to cheer her that Spring, 1816, for she did not seem to be able to recover from the strain of nursing Henry, and it was a year of family trouble. Poor Edward was involved in a most tiresome lawsuit, as a relative of the Knight family had laid claim to the Chawton Estates from which he drew two-thirds of his income. On top of this anxiety came something much worse : Henry's bank failed and he and Mr. Tilson lost everything. Eliza's Indian fortune was clean gone too and Uncle Leigh Perrot lost ten thousand pounds, though Jane only lost a few pounds out of her royalties, which were lying at the Alton branch ; even poor old Madame Bigeon's stocking full of guineas had vanished.

The family did not blame Henry, who had been swallowed up with many more experienced men in the economic confusion which had followed the long war. He and Mr. Tilson came up and down several times about the business of the Alton branch, and whenever she saw him his mother used to say, " You never should have gone into the City, you were too good for that. Your father and I always wanted you to be ordained and take a country living, and if you had done as we wished none of this would have happened." Jane said, " Henry would write very superior sermons," and Henry's bright eyes twinkled as he said, " Well, I suppose it is not too late to think of it. I must rout out my books and see whether I can remember my Greek. I daresay Ben and I might be ordained together."

Young Caroline did not think that Aunt Jane looked very well when she came back from nursing Uncle Henry in London. She seemed tired and silent and quite unlike herself. Sometimes she complained that her back hurt her, but she would not lie upon the sofa, because old Mrs. Austen liked to keep that for herself. The most that she would do was to stretch herself out upon two chairs ! it did not look at all comfortable, but she persisted that it was all she needed. In May she went to Cheltenham with Cassandra, a scheme of Mrs. J. A's, for the Cravens and the Fowles always maintained that the waters there were much to be preferred to Bath. Aunt Jane came home professing that she had enjoyed staying in the white town and walking under the leafy trees of the Promenade, but Caroline did not think that she looked any better, and although she was always sweet and kind she did not want to be bothered any more with the little girl's verses and stories. She had always hitherto found them amusing, but this year she began to say to Caroline, " Aunt Cassandra knows more than I do, she can tell you what ever it is that you want to know." It quite startled Caroline, for the shy clinging child had so twined herself about her Aunt that she could not bear to be put aside.

At last she troubled Aunt Jane once too often, coming running in with some little bits of her own scribbling when Aunt Jane was working at her desk. She turned round and exclaimed wearily, " Caroline, I must warn you against spending too much time on this employment. I know writing stories is a great amusement to you. I think it is a harmless one myself, though many people think otherwise ; but at your age it is bad for you to be so much taken up with your own compositions. If I were you I would cease writing till you are sixteen. I have often wished myself that I had read more and written less when I was your age." Caroline shrank back, her lip trembled and a large tear stood in each eye. She expected Aunt Jane to kiss them away as usual, but her aunt only leant her head on her two hands as if she were wearied out. Aunt Cassy was in the room sewing a tiny gown for Anna's next baby. She gave them both her grave watchful look, put her work aside, got up and led Caroline away, whispering, " Do not tease your aunt, my dear, I think she has the headache." Caroline cried a little, but then felt better and was soon romping in the Back Court. The children always played there ! when the window was open you could hear them calling each other with the old Austen names in their shrill airy voices, as other children had done at Steventon thirty and forty years earlier ; " Frank . . . Jane . . . Cassy . . . wait for me, wait for me."

From Christmas to midsummer of that year Jane was working very hard, as if she felt that she was in the afternoon of her life and had no time to rest. The book was *Persuasion,* and this time it was something for herself, she chose not to write about a girl's love any longer. Her heroine, the sad and steadfast Anne Elliott, had been parted at nineteen from the man of her choice, Captain Wentworth, and had to win him back again, eight years later, from a pair of young and vivid rivals, long after she had thought herself overlooked and forgotten. A change had come over the scene, the crude tart flavour of the earlier novels had mellowed into the ripeness of perfect fruit. Autumn sunshine suffused *Persuasion*, falling upon the deserted beaches of Lyme, the white pavements of Bath ; the forlorn and faithful Anne flowered like the last delicate rose of St. Martin's summer, which comes to bloom in a quiet corner, before the gales and rain together tear the garden to pieces. Jane flagged a little towards the end, could not get two final chapters to suit her, she wrote and rewrote, a rare thing with her ; but at last she scratched them all out and found a new version which satisfied even herself.

7

Early in July, when Cloister Time ended at Winchester, the ladies of Chawton Cottage saw from their breakfast table countless post-chaises rattle past the window ; full, said Aunt Jane, of future heroes, legislators, fools and villains, the Winchester boys all going home for the holidays with Edward, of course, among them. He was in his last year, he would be eighteen in December and at the New Year would go up to Exeter College, Oxford. He was a bright clever creature, very pretty-mannered, as became a good Wykehamist, and devoted to his aunt ; he spent a great deal of time at Chawton and drove her out when she was too tired to walk. He agreed with Caroline that she looked ill and he did not like to hear her complain so often of a pain in her back ! however, she insisted that there was nothing the matter with her. She took a great interest in a novel which he himself began during those holidays, declared that it was extremely clever and written with great ease and spirit, wrote to congratulate his mother upon it and popped in a message to Caroline, " I think it is hardly fair upon her and myself to have Edward and Sir Walter Scott both take to the novel line ! "

Edward and she had always had jokes together about their stories. He used to tease her about the people in her books and clamour to know what had become of them afterwards, and to please him and Aunt Cassandra she would make up little sequels. In this way they learnt that Miss Steele never succeeded in catching the Doctor ; that Kitty Bennett was satisfactorily married to a clergyman near Pemberly, while Mary got nothing better than one of her Uncle's clerks, that the considerable sum given by Mrs. Norris to William Price was one pound ; that Mr. Wood-house survived his daughter's marriage and kept her and Mr. Knightley from settling at Donwell for about two years ; and that the letters placed by Frank Churchill before Jane Fairfax would have spelt out the word Pardon.

After Edward went back to Winchester his aunt wrote to him several times, telling him that he and she had better try and get hold of one or two of Uncle Henry's very superior sermons, to pad out their stories and condoling with him over the loss of two and a half chapters from his manu-script. " It is well that I have not been at Steventon lately and therefore cannot be suspected of purloining them ; two strong twigs and a half towards a Nest of my own would have been something ! " It was their old joke about the bird which builds its nest of whatever twigs and mosses it finds to hand. " I do not think, however, that any theft of that sort would be really very useful to me. What should I do with your strong manly spirited sketches full of variety and glow ? How could I possibly join them on to the little bit (two inches wide) of ivory on which I work with so fine a brush, as produces little effect after much labour."

When Edward came home at Christmas he dashed over at once to see her and was quite alarmed. It seemed to him that all through that autumn she had drooped and withered. She was laid out upon her two chairs and all her fresh colour was gone, the bones of her skull had begun to show as never before through the pale smooth skin. She brightened up for him, however, said this was only one of her bad days and that when she could get out again in the spring she would soon recover. She admitted that she had not begun on any new book. *Persuasion* was laid on the shelf to mellow and ripen like an autumn apple, it still needed a few final touches. " You need not be impatient," said she, " I do not like the heroine, she is almost too good for me ; but something else has happened which will amuse you. Dear Henry has been to Mr. Crosby and bought back my story about the girl who went to Bath to get a husband. He got it for ten pounds and then he turned round and told them that the book had been written by the writer of *Mansfield Park* and *Emma*. You should have seen their faces." Edward flung back his head and roared with delight, and his aunt's brown eyes sparkled with something of their old mischief, but she did not seem really very interested in that old story. " I have changed the heroine's name to Catherine Morland," said she, " and have amused myself by touching her up a little here and there, but it is all rather like retrimming an old hat. However, later on the book may do for Mr. Murray. I think I may call it *Northanger Abbey*."

Anna's second baby, little Julia, was born in October ; Anna, poor thing ! had no time nowadays for writing. Ben was still struggling with his religious scruples, but Henry, who had worked hard at his classical studies all through the summer, went cheerfully down to Winchester in December and offered himself to the Bishop for ordination. " As for this book," said the good prelate, slyly smiling and laying his hand upon a Greek Testament on his table, " I suspect it is some time since either you or I looked into it " ; and to Henry's intense disappointment he got no chance at all to display his scholarship. The Bishop put one or two perfunctory questions to him, spoke of his father and brother with respect and affection, and Henry was ordained next day in the Cathedral without any more ado. He was made perpetual Curate of Bentley, near Alton, and settled there immediately.

He came to preach at Chawton one Sunday in February and the family had a nervous hour, but they need not have been troubled, for Henry acquitted himself with as much ease and propriety as if he had been in the pulpit all his life. The young couple from Wyards walked over to hear Uncle Henry preach. Anna looked so pretty that it was a pleasure to see her, so young, so blooming and so innocent, as if she had never had a wicked thought in her life, Aunt Jane said smiling. She wished Ben would pull himself together and follow Henry's example ! she would have liked to see the whole family comfortably settled in a snug parsonage. The rain and the dirt divided Anna and her aunt a good deal that winter, but in the spring, when the pretty weather came in, and the primroses and violets opened on the sunny banks, Cassandra should take her sister on donkey-back to Wyards.

Old Mrs. Austen wished that Charles's family were as healthy as Anna's two little girls. Up in Keppel Street Aunt Harriet Palmer, who for two years had been a second mother to her sister's children, was much worried about little Harriet. This pale, large-headed child, born in Bermuda six years earlier, had always been a listless clinging creature, who climbed up your lap and laid her head against you with a sigh. In this spring of 1817 the family physician called in a specialist, Sir Everard Holme ; and the great man, after much head-shaking and face-making, pronounced an alarming verdict, water on the brain. He did not, however, despair of the child's life. He believed a course of mercury might draw the waters off, for the patient was so young that the head was not yet hardened. The family were all much distressed and poor Charles was quite heart-broken.

That spring Jane made a start upon a new novel, but she did not get very far with what was intended to be a comedy. The scene was laid in a watering place called Sanditon, a raw mushroom housing scheme on a windy down above an old fishing village. Aunt Frank was glad to describe her youth in Ramsgate, and Henry, coming and going from Bentley, talked in the most sanguine fashion about the money which might be made by anyone who had the enterprise to develop such a resort. Between them with much laughter they invented Trafalgar House and Waterloo Crescent, smartened up the cottages with new curtains and signs of " Lodgings to Let," introduced holiday visitors with books and camp stools, a milliner's shop, a library, a brand-new hotel and a row of bathing machines beside the sparkling sea. Jane was amused by it all at first, but she had not the spirit to work out many new characters. Listlessly she paraded once more an old rich vulgar dowager, a sensible spirited young heroine, an enigmatic elegant beauty dependent upon the old lady, and a heartless young man of fashion making his plans to betray her. The best thing she did in it was the Parker family ; the sanguine enthusiast, Mr. Parker, who was developing Sanditon and his two sisters and his younger brother, who spent all the time doctoring their imaginary ailments, except when Miss Diana Parker forgot her symptoms and doses to busy herself in the affairs of her neighbours. Henry in particular delighted in the Parkers, but the book did not get on so fast as he would have liked. Jane worked upon it for barely eight weeks. It tired her back too much to sit up long and often she wrote in pencil and inked the words over afterwards. On March 18th she laid it aside altogether ; the date in the margin marked the last of her working days, as the watch of a drowned man indicates the hour of his death.

8

Down in Kent that March little Fanny Knight was all in a flutter again about her own affairs and must have counsel from Aunt Jane. She had a new admirer, this time most serious and eligible, young James Wildman of Chilham Castle. Everybody was teasing her about him, all his family were seeking it, and her particular friend, Miss Jemima Branfill, was wild to have him herself. She sent off one letter after another to Chawton, and Aunt Jane wrote back delicious teasing replies in her beautiful script, crossed like chequer work. " You are inimitable, irresistible, you are the delight of my life, you are worth your weight in gold,

or even in the new silver coinage . . . you are so odd !—
and all the time so perfectly natural—so peculiar in yourself
and yet so like everybody else. It is very, very gratifying to
me to know you so intimately. You can hardly think what
a pleasure it is to me, to have such thorough pictures of your
heart—Oh ! what a loss it will be when you are married.
You are too agreeable in your single state, too agreeable as
a niece—I shall hate you when your delicious play of mind
is all settled down into conjugal and maternal affections.
Do not imagine that I have any real objection. I have rather
taken a fancy to him than not, and I like Chilham Castle
for you, only I do not like you should marry anybody. And
yet I do wish you to marry very much, because I know you
will never be happy till you are. My dearest Fanny, I
cannot bear that you should be unhappy about him. I do
not like your being nervous and so apt to cry," wrote dear
Aunt Jane, and the words swam in tears, for Fanny felt
dreadfully sorry for herself. She really did not want to
marry James Wildman at all, rich as he was, she even
sometimes wished that she had taken poor John Plumtre,
who had quite cooled off and was now paying his addresses
to another young lady.

Quite at the end, however, Aunt Jane turned serious and
put down on paper for her favourite niece of all, the one
whose mind and heart promised to be most like her own,
the last words of advice which Fanny would ever get from
her. " Well, I shall say, as I have often said before, Do
not be in a hurry ; depend upon it, the right man will
come at last ; you will in the course of the next two or
three years meet with somebody more generally unex-
ceptionable than anyone you have yet known, who will love
you as warmly as ever *he* did, and who will so completely
attach you that you will feel that you never really loved
before."

At the end she frightened Fanny by the way that she
wrote about herself. " I certainly have not been well for
many weeks, and about a week ago I was very poorly, I
have had a good deal of fever at times and indifferent nights,
but am considerably better now, and recovering my looks

a little, which have been bad enough, black and white and every wrong colour. I must not depend upon being ever very blooming again. Sickness is a dangerous indulgence at my time of life." Fanny did not like the sound of it at all.

She continued feeble and wretched ; the time had come for her to rise up and be going. Cassandra nursed her carefully, but her bad days came more often than her good ones. She was too feeble to walk into Alton in the mild April weather. Once or twice she rode out on the donkey, with Cassandra on one side and young Edward on the other ; that she seemed to enjoy. She did get as far as Wyard, where Anna was already expecting a third child. " Poor animal," said her Aunt Jane bitterly, " she will be worn out before she is thirty." The village that spring had a crop of such gossip, Mrs. Frank Austen, Mrs. Clements and Mrs. Bennall were all increasing. " I am quite tired of so many children," fretted Jane, who would never now have a child of her own. The village women knew well enough that Miss Jane was seriously ill, when they saw her walking slowly through the garden or across the road, they shook their heads and raised their eyebrows silently ; among themselves they began to call her the poor young lady.

At the end of March, Uncle Leigh Perrot died and left a strange will which vexed everybody. All his money went to his wife, who could thus domineer over the next generation for the rest of her days ; only James came into a fat legacy and there was a clause that a thousand pounds each should go to any one of the other brothers and sisters who might outlive their tough old Aunt. Mrs. George Austen got nothing from her wealthy brother. It was a great disappointment, as they had always counted on some help from their rich Uncle. Jane took to her bed, and Cassandra was sent for in a hurry from Scarlets to come back and nurse her directly the funeral was over. From this attack the invalid seemed unable to recover and all through April she was very low and wretched, her old courage seemed to have deserted her. Mr. Curtis, the apothecary from Alton, shook his head over her, seemed unable to alleviate the pain and discharge which troubled her and finally asked for a second opinion. Mr. Lyford, the brother of their own dear old doctor, was sent for from Winchester, a stately gentleman in a powdered wig who prescribed various applications, but wished her to come to Winchester for some weeks for further treatment.

The thought of this change seemed to encourage the sick woman, at least she wrote cheerfully enough to her brother Charles and to her old friend Ann Sharpe, speaking most movingly of the anxious affection of her family and bravely talking of herself as a very genteel portable sort of invalid. Mrs. J. A. offered her carriage for the journey; she did this kind of thing well, mean as she was, and was always helpful when there was nursing to be done. Anna and Caroline walked over from Wyards to say good-bye. They found Aunt Jane upstairs sitting in an armchair in her dressing-gown, but she got up when they came in, greeted them kindly, and pointed to two seats by the fire. " There is a chair for the married lady," said she with her pale smile, " and a little stool for you, Caroline." They were only allowed to stay for a quarter of an hour, then Aunt Cassy fetched them away, it was the last time that young Caroline ever saw her dear Aunt Jane.

The morning of her departure was sadly wet. She was carried downstairs and settled among pillows in the carriage with Cassandra beside her and they drove away, round the corner by the hornbeam hedge. The sick woman's great dark eyes turned wistfully upon one familiar landmark after another as they were left behind, the pond, the signpost, the gables of the Great House, the pinnacles of the church tower; but presently the rain came down pelting hard and Cassandra pulled up the windows. Through the streaming glass the travellers had glimpses of Henry riding on the one side and young William Knight on the other. Jane grew paler and paler as the journey continued, but did not complain; she was only troubled about how wet the riders would be. It was high summer, the hedges were full of the wild parsley which country people call Queen Anne's lace, the hawthorn blossom was beginning to fall, the flat moons of the elder bushes were just coming out, there was no colour except green and white in the landscape. The great distances were all blotted out, and when they came down into the Itchen Valley, the raindrops were dimpling the full stream. Cassandra was thankful when she got her sister to Winchester.

9

Elizabeth Heathcote had found them a lodging with a Mrs. David at No. 8, College Street. It proved to be a small white house in a back lane just outside the Close. James's coachman and tall Henry between them carried the sick woman up the narrow twisting stairs, while Cassandra wondered with a sharp stab of anxiety if she would ever come down them again. However, the landlady was a kind woman and the lodging seemed clean and pleasant. They had a low wainscoted parlour upstairs, with a bow window which looked north upon the old city wall. Its knapped flintwork glistened in the rain, the lime trees of the Close looked over it and partly shut out the Cathedral. Behind the parlour were a couple of small bedrooms, one behind the other down a long passage, with a peep into the Headmaster's garden behind. After she had recovered from the fatigues of the drive, Jane was able to walk from one room to another, lie upon the sofa in the bow window and watch the boys come in and out of the collegers' entrance next door. Mr. Lyford came next day to see her and sat cross-legged playing with his gold headed cane, nodding pleasantly at her, attentively considering what she told him. "If you do not cure me, Mr. Lyford," said she in her old sprightly way, "I shall draw up a memorial and lay it before the Dean and Chapter. I am sure I shall have redress from that pious, learned, and disinterested body." The old doctor smiled at her, but did not or would not say plainly what he thought of her state. Cassandra perceived from his manner that he knew he could help her sister very little. She had her dying to do still, all else was finished.

She did not know it herself, and at first the change of

scene pleased and amused her faintly. Everybody was very kind, she had many letters, particularly from Fanny Knight. James rode down from Steventon, making an excuse of some diocesan errand. Henry posted the twenty miles from Bentley to sit with her and tell her amusing stories. He was still her favourite brother, and even on her bad days he could make her laugh. Charles Knight, just fourteen, was still at Winchester and she liked to have him visit her. The boy was a little awed at first by the sick room, and like a healthy young animal was afraid of he knew not what, but she soon had him at his ease, amusing her by his boyish nonsense and telling her about the school. Alethea was frisked off into Switzerland, but Elizabeth Heathcote came in faithfully every day, bringing books and velvet roses and the first strawberries from her garden. " Now we will have a strawberry party," the sick woman said, with one of her old happy looks.

Elizabeth and Alethea had a discreet small house in the Close, with panelled rooms and a walled garden and windows looking through the lime trees to the long roof and squat tower of the cathedral, where Cassandra went every day to pray for strength and comfort. Under her knees the cold pavement was itself composed of gravestones carved with epitaphs and the walls were all covered with monuments. The cool colonnade of pillars was like a ghostly avenue of white poplars, far overhead their bare branches intersected and the fan-vaulting flowered into heraldic devices and armorial bearings. The nave was always full of teasing echoes from people walking about in the distance, the mutter of prayers in a chapel, the voices of choristers trying over an anthem ; on Sundays the noise of the organ and the full choir roared through the petrified forest like a winter storm. While kind Elizabeth sat with Jane, Cassandra walked by herself among the red and brown alleys, went in and out of the old dark shops, climbed the steep High Street to the grey West Gate at the top. She saw the whole city in a clear and lovely light, a sharp and agonising beauty. The torrid summer sun drew out the scent of lilac and chestnut, giving place to roses in flower. There was a continual murmur of bees among the honey-blossoms on the lime trees and a smell of mowing grass in the meads. She walked down the quiet lane past Wolvesey Palace and beside the river to look at the green weeds waving in the current, sometimes she went as far as the bridge where the water came foaming out under the arches of the city mill.

The days were lovely out of doors, but in the College Street lodging their rooms were very small and it was hard to keep the air moving through them. At night they had all the doors open, but there was always a riverish unwholesome smell from the Lortburn running in its medieval conduit beneath the houses, the marsh water standing everywhere underground. Cassandra could not sleep well in those hot nights. She got up once to cool her bed and went to lean her forehead against the window pane. The full moon was too high for her to see, it had put out the lesser stars, the heavy trees stood motionless against the milk white sky. She heard Jane utter a sigh of weariness among the bed curtains, then she asked for water and drank greedily. " Oh ! my dear Cassy," said she, " if I get better I must never forget how patient you have been with me." Cassandra could not answer, she put the glass down and heard it tremble against the wood of the table. As she wiped Jane's hot forehead with a damp cloth, she heard the sick woman whisper, " It is very hot here, I wish I were in the country " ; then she cried a little, and said, " If I am going to die I wish it might be at home."

10

Now the smooth current of her life ran away swiftly. She began to suffer more often and more severely and on her bad days lay with a deep carved frown on her forehead, eyes half-closed and delicate hands clenched. A nurse came in, but Cassandra did not like her, she was a dirty and rough old crone who wagged her head and told dreadful stories of other cases she had tended, which all had ended fatally. Then James brought his wife, a considerable sacrifice for

him, for he said he was never well waited upon at home
when she was away. Jane would rather have had Martha,
but she could not be spared from looking after Mrs. Austen
at Chawton. Mary, however, proved unexpectedly helpful.
She was a skilled nurse, and when she had taken off her best
black silk and tied an apron over a clean gingham gown,
she was once again the active neat-handed Mary Lloyd of
their young days together at Steventon, her mean cross ways
were all forgotten. Jane seemed to like having her there
and once in her weak wandering voice said, " Mary, you
have always been a kind sister to me."

Her days were running out now like sand in an hour glass.
Mr. Lyford came oftener and looked graver, at the beginning
of July he said, " This can have only one end and that
soon." Mary did not think that the sick woman should be
told how short a time she had left to suffer and even
Cassandra's resolution wavered ; but James, for once the
head of the family, was unshaken. " *Lord, let me know mine
end and the number of my days,*" said James, looking blacker
and taller than usual, glaring round at them all with his
stern unhappy eyes. " She has a right to know that she
should prepare herself for death." Henry said, " She will
not be afraid, she is braver than any of us," and Cassandra
said, " I think she knows already."

Jane was not appalled, she had understood well enough
what her brothers came to tell her. She asked for the Holy
Sacrament, and next morning early the two women spread
a white cloth and lit candles. Then they knelt while
dissatisfied fretful James and light loving careless Henry,
strangely invested with a dignity and authority not their own,
refreshed their sister's spirit with the Holy Bread and Wine
and comfortable words for her journey. She rallied strangely
afterwards for a few days and even wrote one of her nonsense
letters about St. Swithin's rainy feast for her nephew in
college ; at the end she went quite suddenly. Cassandra
had gone out on that afternoon of July 17th, leaving Jane
smiling with languid pleasure over a letter from Fanny
Knight. The boys had all just gone home from school, and
the city was full of fine ladies and gentlemen come for the

races. Cassandra walked under the dripping lime trees of the Close and out into the crowded street. Under the shelter of the Pentice she went from one shop to another, buying little things which her sister needed, but when she came back wished she had never gone, for Mrs. David opened the door and said with a look of alarm that the poor young lady was not so well. Above stairs Mary looked anxious and Jane very pale, it seemed that she had had something like a fainting fit. She lay vaguely smiling, with her whole body drooping sideways, but she was conscious and welcoming. She touched her forehead, whispering, " I had something here, but it is gone now. I am better."

Cassandra laid her bonnet aside and sat down by the bed. As she sat talking quietly to Jane the Cathedral struck six. Almost immediately afterwards there was a strange alteration in the sick woman's face, the shadow of mortality seemed to fall across it as the finger moves on a sundial. She had hold of Cassandra's hand and she gripped it tightly and gasped, " Do not leave me." Mary rose up out of her chair, and Cassandra said to her, " Send for Doctor Lyford."

Then for half an hour the sick woman knew herself to be dying. She was still conscious, it seemed, but lay with a stern and terrible frown, scarcely daring to breathe, her teeth just showing beneath her retracted lip. Mary came back and fretted about, but there was nothing to be done to help her. " God grant me patience," they heard her say and once she murmured, " Pray for me ; Oh ! pray for me." Her voice was so changed and feeble that it scarcely seemed her own ; when Cassandra asked if there was anything she wanted she said between her teeth, " Nothing but death."

In half an hour's time there was a stir at the door ; it was Doctor Lyford, mounting the stairs and coming in with his quiet sickroom tread. He at least could do something to bring this hour to an end. After his drugs had taken effect the sick woman sank into a blessed stupor. Her last conscious look and smile were for Cassandra. By seven o'clock she seemed quite insensible, except for a slight movement of the head with every breath she drew, this remained to the last. She had slipped right down off her pillows, Cassandra sat beside the bed and held that dear head in her lap. She did not stir until after midnight, when Mary came to her and more by signs than words persuaded her to give up her place.

Cassandra was then so stiff in every limb that she could scarcely keep her feet. She groped her way to her own room and lay down dressed as she was upon her bed, but she did not sleep. In the dark breathless night she heard the small hours chime from the clocks in the city, the dripping of rain from the eaves. Soon after three o'clock she rose up again, smoothed her hair, bathed her face and went back to the other room. As that hour went by Jane's breathing became a little shallower, her hand a little colder, her pulse more faint ; at last Cassandra scarcely knew whether her sister lived or died, but by four o'clock all was over. What she held in her arms was no longer the head of a mortal woman ; it was that of an antique statue, heavy, cold and still, and the face was like yellow marble. Her sister had laid down the body in which she had endured so much suffering and had gone on to some other place.

Cassandra closed the dead eyes and straightened the limbs ; she went to set the window open wide and looked out. There was a country freshness at that hour in the lane behind the city wall, birds were twittering in the eaves and somewhere there was a noise of rooks cawing, as they used to do in her father's elms at Steventon. When she came back to the bed the face had changed and there was a smile of exquisite happiness upon the firm lips. While her sister was dying she had worn the mask of an old woman, graven deep in lines of suffering and endurance ; but now that she was dead she looked like a young girl.

The Old Manor,
    Broadwell.
Nov., 1946—Oct., 1948

Postscript

SOME readers may like to know what happened to the other characters in this true story.

Of the older generation, Mrs. George Austen lived to be eighty-seven, occupying the sofa at Chawton Cottage and gently murmuring that God seemed to have forgotten her, but would no doubt fetch her in his own good time. Mrs. Leigh Perrot lasted until 1836, still the terror of the family. She long outlived James, who died only two years after his sister Jane and the inheritance therefore went to young Edward, who took the name of Leigh and became the ancestor of the Austen-Leighs. He went into the Church, married a pretty neighbour, Emma Smith, and wrote the delightful memoir of his aunt on which all later lives are based. He was helped in this by the recollections of his stepsister, Anna Lefroy and his sister Caroline. Anna was left a widow early and had to bring up seven children on small means. She never had any more time for writing and one of her little girls remembered seeing her burn the manuscript of *Which is the Heroine?* shortly after the death of her Aunt Jane. Caroline is our only authority for the story of her Aunt's Devonshire love-affair and for the account of Anna's wedding.

Edward sold Godmersham in the end and the family moved to Chawton, where the Knights still live. Fanny did not marry any of the young men about whom she had consulted her aunt. She took Sir Edward Knatchbull, Wyndham's elder brother, a widower with several children. It was a long and happy marriage. Her Aunt Cassandra gave her a number of Jane's letters (after destroying all those which she considered ought not to be read by strangers). Fanny's son, who became Lord Brabourne, edited these letters for publication.

Henry remained perpetual curate of Bentley for the rest of his days. He married again, a Miss Eleanor Jackson, a relative of that Mr. Papillon, rector of Chawton, who did not marry Jane. *Northanger Abbey* and *Persuasion* were prepared for the press by Henry, who added a curiously dull short memoir of his sister, and were published in one set of volumes by John Murray a year after her death.

Cassandra lived on at Chawton until her death in 1845. A great-niece saw her at a family wedding, late in life, a tall, pale old woman, with fine dark eyes and a long nose, who still spoke of her sister Jane with an accent of living love. Her nephew Edward, in a family letter, gives a touching account of how he read the burial service over her, while an autumn storm whirled a great shower of withered beech leaves over her coffin.

Frank and Charles both lived to be Admirals. Frank never got another ship, but lived for many years at Portsdown Lodge, Portsmouth, and ended up as Governor of a West Indian island. He always liked to tell people that he believed he had been the original of Captain Harville in *Persuasion*. After the death of dear Mrs. F. A. he did at last marry the faithful Martha Lloyd. Charles also married a second time. His first wife's sister, Harriet Palmer. He spent most of his life afloat and died of fever in a gunboat on the Irrawaddy in 1852, in the second Burmese War.

Tom Lefroy did become Lord Chief Justice of Ireland. He sold the Limerick estates and moved to Carrigglas Manor, County Longford, where his descendants are living to this day. As a very old, stern and terrifying figure, he once admitted that he had been in love with Jane Austen.

Of the houses in which she lived, Steventon Rectory was pulled down in 1833 and the Southampton house and the supposed lodging at Lyme Regis have both vanished ; but Bath is much as she knew it, except for the destruction of the Upper Rooms ; and the Jane Austen Society has preserved and is reclaiming Chawton Cottage.